ENDORSEMENTS FOR THE ROSE JOURNAL

"Praise for Linda Stai! Her book is riveting! I found myself putting other things aside so that I could read "just one more chapter." And of course, that led to having to "just finish the book!" The characters jump right off the page and live in your heart and mind long after you have finished."

REBECCA CARTER
THE PATH DRAMA MINISTRY

"Characters and settings come alive as Linda vividly chronicles the journey of one young girl through womanhood, along the way finding faith and strength beyond her own. The reader is drawn into experiences so human, with hardships and tragedies so heartbreaking, yet imbued with hope and triumphs."

PATRICIA M. HOEFT, MD,
RICE MEMORIAL HOSPITAL

"With Linda's strong and convincing character development, you'll have to remind yourself that you're reading fiction. She has woven contemporary issues so delicately into her story you will not only enjoy this book yourself, but will be eager to pass it on to believers and unbelievers alike."

LONNIE WEST
LIBRARY STAFF AND FORMER CHRISTIAN BOOKSTORE EMPLOYEE

"As the pastor Linda has known since she took her first step on the bus to the country school house, I found special delight in reading her novel. As you come to the final chapters, you will find that there can be victory in suffering. Her scrupulous details all point to a purpose that shows God's leading all along."

REVEREND PALMER E. SEVIG
RETIRED AND LIVING IN WILLMAR, MINNESOTA

The Rose Journal

The Rose Journal
Linda Ruth Stai

*One woman's spiritual adventure shows
how good can come from suffering*

DOKKA PUBLISHING
Brooklyn Park, Minnesota

This is a work of fiction. The characters and dialogue are products of the author's imagination and are not to be construed as real. Resemblance to actual persons, living or dead, is entirely coincidental.

THE ROSE JOURNAL
Published by Dokka Publishing

© 2005 by Linda Ruth Stai
International Standard Book Number 0-9771530-8-8

Library of Congress Control Number: 2005933227

For information:
DOKKA PUBLISHING
7423 ABBOTT AVENUE NORTH
BROOKLYN PARK, MN 55443
dokka_publishing@yahoo.com

Visit our web site at www.rosejournal.com

1 3 5 7 9 10 8 6 4 2
Printed in the United States of America

The Rose Journal

is lovingly dedicated to

my mother, Ruth Dokkesven,
who always believed I would write a book,
and
my father, Andy Dokkesven,
who believed that I could do anything.

ACKNOWLEDGMENTS

Many special people have helped and encouraged me in the production of this book.

I am especially grateful to my husband, Gary, who convinced me that I could write fiction.

My son, Kaleb, has faithfully contributed endless hours of help with the publishing and marketing of my novel. I couldn't have undertaken this project without him. My son, Joshua, agreed to pose as the angel on the cover, and he and my daughter, Erika, have prayed and encouraged me all the way through this process.

My two dear friends in our critique group, Phyllis Hedberg and Lonnie West, helped with the major editing, along with faithful prayers and encouragement. Thanks also to Terry Musclow from Dickinson Press who gave me invaluable advice and encouragement.

Roxanne Celeste Grinstad, a dear lifelong friend, designed and painted the cover. Thanks also to Joanne Lorenzen who crocheted the angel doily on the cover.

Dr. Patricia M. Hoeft, a special friend who practices medicine in Willmar, Minnesota, advised me on the medical aspects of the story.

Heidi Huber did an excellent job helping me with the final editing process. Thanks also to Sue Germanson and Dee McIntyre who read through the manuscript and helped edit it.

Heartfelt appreciation also goes to my other friends who read part or all of the story and encouraged me through the ups and downs of writing. Their constant belief in my ability helped to give me the courage and discipline to finish. These special friends include: Ariel, Beth, Bonnie P., Bonnie R., Darlene, Deb, DeEtte, Denise, Diane, Donna, Patty, Rebecca, Rose, Sherrill, Sue, Susan, Tambra, and Vicki.

Special thanks also to my wonderful creative friend, Cheryl, who was my listening ear as I set the foundation for the story. And to Carol, a special new friend who supported and believed in me. I am deeply grateful to my sisters in Christ in my Women of the Word (WOW) Bible Study who "prayed me through."

I also want to thank a dear family friend, Rev. Palmer Sevig, who read the entire manuscript and supported my vision.

I am so very grateful to all of you.

"And we know that God causes
all things to work together for good
to those who love God,
to those
who are called
according to His purpose."

Romans 8:28

PROLOGUE
The Rescue
1959

The angel's first visit saved my life. I was four years old, barely able to remember the event. Maybe that is why it's always been hazy in my mind. Like my brain couldn't decide whether to file the memory in its real life or fantasy section.

Now I know it really happened, because I saw the same angel again yesterday.

He first appeared to me thirty-six years ago on a brilliant sunshiny morning in May. The sidewalk sparkled and the enticing fragrance of lilac bushes beckoned as I let myself out of the house early that Sunday. I was staying with my parents for a few days at my grandma's home in the little town of New Bergen, Minnesota. The year was 1959, and the community was a stereotype of the fifties. Its citizens were reasonably sane and friendly to their neighbors. A child could walk the streets alone and be safe.

I was excited. My papa had just gotten a job as a doctor in Grandma Lydia's town, and we were looking for a house of our own.

I loved to visit Grandma Lydia. She was like a queen, a circus clown, and a best friend all bunched up together. When we had tea parties, just the two of us, she always took her special china set down from the top shelf of the old pine hutch. That's where she kept the special dishes that she hardly used except at Christmas, Easter, and birthdays.

"Your grandpa gave this tea set to me the year he died and went to live with Jesus," she'd say. Then her eyes would start to crinkle and the crinkles would ripple down her face and turn into the brightest smile I could ever imagine. She'd bend down to me and whisper a secret, "I've only shared it with you, Cassandra." Then she'd send me into the kitchen to get some cookies while she poured real tea into china cups that were spattered all over with roses, in different shades of pink.

After our tea time, Grandma Lydia sometimes took her music makers out of the pine hutch. She had a silver tambourine with tiny bells that made a tinkling sound and a drum that had real Indian leather stretched across the top and bottom. There was even a wooden pipe with holes in it that her grandma gave her when she was a little girl. She let me choose my instrument. Then we marched around the living room singing Sunday School songs until we both started to giggle. We rolled on the floor and cuddled. Next she told me a story and tucked me into bed for my nap.

I looked forward to the times when I could be alone with Grandma. She was quieter when Mama and Papa were around. Everybody was quieter around Papa because he was so important. He was a doctor and made people well. Mama said he was very smart and that's why people looked up to him. But I wanted him to look down to me. To come down and play games with me. Important people had to be busy and couldn't do those things.

When I started my walk that Sunday morning, nobody else was awake. Grandma and my parents had stayed up late the night before and talked. I couldn't see what fun there was in talking so much, but grown-ups seemed to like doing it. I was thinking happy thoughts about Grandma and hoping we would do something together later that day. Maybe she would let me sit on her lap in the old rocking chair and read me a book about the Bobbsey twins.

Flossie, one of the youngest twins, was just about my age. I liked her the best.

I knew Grandma would take Mama and me to church later, so I put on the new yellow dress with the white polka dots that Grandma made for me. I wore yellow socks with lace that matched my dress, and brand new white patent leather shoes that had round toes with heart-shaped holes and buckles. I'd never had buckles before. It took me a while to hook them, but I did it all by myself.

I wanted to surprise Mama with flowers. It was Mother's Day, and I had seen some pretty purple and yellow ones in the park when we drove by there the night before. I skipped down the street toward the park. It was quiet except for the birds singing. Grandma said the birds sing God's music. I tried to sing like them but I couldn't, so I just listened. I had to cross the big railroad tracks to get to the park. I stopped and looked both ways like Mama did. The only person I saw was a lady sitting on a bench in the park. She had black, curly hair and wore a pretty pink and white dress. Maybe she was going to church, too. The lady was writing in a book and didn't see me. Then I listened carefully, like Mama told me to, and didn't hear a train. So I hopped across the tracks and ran to the cluster of purple and yellow flowers. Where I lived in Minnesota, flowers stayed covered under the snow all winter. Mama always got excited when they started popping out of the ground in the spring. Mama didn't smile very much, but I could always make her smile when I brought her a bouquet of flowers.

The prettiest flowers were next to the lady on the bench. I walked over quietly so I wouldn't disturb her. Then I knelt down and chose the biggest yellow flowers that looked like they were painted to match the sun. Bright purple ones were growing near-by. There were just three of them. I only took one so the others would have company and not be lonesome. I clutched them in my fist and stood up. Then the lady on the bench looked up and saw me. Her eyebrows shot up and her mouth opened wide. I was afraid she was going to tell me to put the flowers back. I didn't want to because then Mama wouldn't get to see them. So I turned around and started running back. I heard the lady call, "No!

Wait!" But I kept going.

A big noise like thunder rumbled far away. I stumbled onto the railroad tracks before I remembered to look both ways. I could see a train coming, but it was far away so I wasn't scared. I looked back at the lady. She was running at me so I twirled around and started to run again. But my body jerked back because my right foot wouldn't come with me. Horrified, I stared at my new shoe that was stuck under a rail. I tried to pull my foot out of the shoe but it wouldn't come. *The buckles!* I had to remember how to get the buckles open. My pretty new shoes. The flowers were in my way. I dumped the poor pretty flowers on the track.

The lady was yelling now. I couldn't make out what she said because the black monster train was roaring a noise that could drown out the whole world! It was running at me faster than the lady was. My eyes blurred so badly I couldn't see my chubby fingers fumbling with the buckle. Turning my head, I looked at the lady and screamed a scream that even I couldn't hear. My eyes seemed as big as my mouth.

The lady tripped and fell. Her hands stretched out as she went down flat on her stomach. She looked up at the sky and opened her mouth in a desperate way. Burning smoke made me cough. Terror turned my whole body to stone as dark blackness reached out to grab me and swallow me into its evil belly. Swoosh! Suddenly huge arms reached out and snatched me away. Good arms, strong but gentle. The rumbling, screeching train rushed past and set my ears tingling.

Then I felt safe, like I was riding on a fluffy, white cloud. Happier than I've ever been at a party. Even more excited than on Christmas Eve. I looked up at the tall stranger who held me in his arms. All his clothes were white. His face shone like a star. It made me think of a night light that helped me to see in a dark room and chased all the scary shadows away. He didn't speak. He just squeezed me gently like I was apt to break, set me down, and turned me toward Grandma's house.

I looked down at my feet. Both my pretty shoes were on and buckled. Then I remembered I must say "Thank you" to the stranger. But when I gazed up at where he had stood, he was gone!

Bits of purple and yellow lay squished on the track. I started to cry and run.

I wanted Mama.

"For to me,
to live is Christ,
and to die is gain."

Philippians 1:21

The Revealing
Chapter 1
1968

Lake Clarity reflected my moods and sometimes altered them. That must be why I felt at one with the beautiful lake, as though its waters flowed through my bloodstream. Its aura often changed from hour to hour as undulating waters rose and fell in empathy with the turbulent emotions of a young girl entering her teens.

It was the summer of 1968, and I was now thirteen.

That morning the surface of the water had been crystal clear, lavishly adorned with sparkling diamonds sprinkled by the sun when it ascended from its rosy bed. I strolled along the shore marveling in the tranquilizing stillness, searching for tiny shells or colorful pieces of stone for my collection. I'd started the precious collection when we moved to Lake Clarity seven years ago. My father, Dr. Robert Dupont, began his practice in the small town of New Bergen, Minnesota, where my grandmother lived. He was a general practitioner, or family doctor, as they called them in the sixties. We lived in town for two years. But when I started school, Papa became concerned that I would develop friendships with the

"common folk" who lived there. So he had a house built on an isolated stretch along Lake Clarity, ten miles away. It was the nicest
house for miles around. My mama wasn't happy about living so
far from other people. So to please her, Papa designed the house
in the style of an old Victorian manor. It was white with blue
gables and turrets and a huge wrap-around porch that faced the
lake. The town folk considered it an outlandish extravagance and
mockingly referred to it as the "Clarity Castle."

Even though I loved our house, it made me feel uncomfortable, like I was peculiar and untouchable. As an only child, I
was used to entertaining myself and had a vivid imagination. You
could even say I was used to loneliness. My mother, a kind and
gentle person, seemed to have lost her capacity to enjoy life. That
is, if she ever had it. My father inhabited a world of his own, a
frustrating, bleak world that I couldn't enter. Nor did I want to.
But I did wish at times that he would become a part of my world.
Papa kept busy with his work and his books. Nearly every night
after supper, he would disappear into his dark library for hours. He
had a huge collection of antique books, which seemed to me to be
the only thing that gave him enjoyment. Neither Mama nor I were
welcome in his domain, where his presence reigned even more
supreme than in the rest of the house. I wondered if Mama was as
hurt by the exclusion as I was. We never talked about it.
Sometimes I even felt like the house belonged just to Papa, not to
Mama and me.

The fact is, the lake became my haven, my center of sta-
bility in an environment that held my emotions captive, encasing
them within bars of tension as strong as steel. When the atmosphere inside the house grew too heavy, I'd break away and run to
my "thinking rock." The large flat boulder was partially hidden
from view in a secluded cove about half a mile from my house.

Sitting on my rock that sultry July afternoon, I watched the
waters begin to churn and foam. They mirrored the image of dense
gray clouds hovering over the surface. I knew I needed to start
home because Mama would be getting worried. But my mood was
now as thick and heavy as the clouds and my soul churned like the
waters. I had no desire to leave. My heart had been bouncing up

and down like a ping pong ball these last weeks since my mother had become sick. She had taken ill suddenly with a severe headache and fainting spells, but in a few days returned to normal. When it happened again, this time with "the shakes," Papa consulted a specialist and had tests taken. At first, the doctors were concerned. But when the initial tests returned negative, my father assured me that rest and a healthy diet would secure her recovery.

This morning, Mama had been out of bed for several hours. She strolled in her flower garden, sat for a time in the radiant sunshine and gazed at the myriad of colors. Her flowers looked like a botanical quilt embroidered with threads of pink and yellow day lilies, white daisies, and blue morning glories. She even laughed with me at the antics of two frisky squirrels.

But the phone call at noon that day changed my world. A more recent test showed positive results.My father took the call. A subtle inflection in his normally controlled voice sounded an alert. A flash of apprehension imbedded itself in my mind much as a deer tunes in to danger when hunters stalk the woods in search of prey. I tugged at Papa's arm and my eyes fastened on his face, silently pleading for an answer that would put my fears to rest. Instead, he hung up the phone, shrugged me aside, and marched into the bedroom where Mama lay asleep.

A long hour passed as an aloneness way beyond loneliness crept into my heart. In vain, I attempted to push the despair away. It was like quicksand. The harder I struggled against it, the quicker it overtook me and established a foothold in my mind.

Finally, Papa reappeared and spoke to me. He rambled off a bunch of scientific words that sounded like a foreign language. His face was hard, like the granite of my thinking rock, and etched with lines I hadn't seen before. As though cracks were beginning that would eventually open and spill out a torrent of feelings he'd never permitted anyone else to see.

I was afraid. I covered my ears with my hands and ran from the house, my tears mingling with fresh raindrops, uniting in rivulets that flowed down my cheeks. Ignoring the sudden downpour, I raced to the shelter of my cove as though I could outrun

Death himself, who aimed to quench the life of my mother. My heart pounded frantically and my breath came in broken gasps. I was unarmed and powerless against this new formidable enemy.

I reached the cove and collapsed on the surface of my rock. The rain had ceased. Knowing, however, that intense calm usually preceded a storm, my jumbled nerves weren't soothed. Rather, they were stimulated like bolts of electricity. The slamming of a car door startled me and I jumped. Turning my head, I saw my father striding towards me, his long overcoat whipping in the wind, his shoes sliding into the muddy ruts of the gravel path. Like a whirlwind, he grabbed my arm, yanked me off the rock, and pulled me, stumbling, towards the car.

"Cassandra, what are you doing out in the rain? Don't you know your mother is worried sick about you?" Not a mention of any personal concern for me, of course.

"I'm sorry, Papa," my lip trembled. Guilt mixed with regret at being forced to leave my safe harbor. Obediently, I climbed into the automobile and stole a brief glance at my father. He was quiet. His look was impenetrable. I relaxed somewhat. I was not used to seeing him lose control and displaying emotions. I was more accustomed to being shut out of his life.

The moments he invited me in were rare, but worth remembering. Whenever Papa returned home after a convention in Minneapolis or Chicago, he'd bring me a present. I'd squeal with delight as I tore open a box to discover a cashmere sweater, a new diary, or a keepsake to adorn the shelves in my bedroom. Then his eyes would linger on my face like I was a unique treasure.

One of my shelves displayed an assortment of music boxes he'd given me. I'd often stretch out on my white quilt with the dark violets and rich green leaves underneath my white lace canopy and gaze at them. I'd see miniature white cherubs dancing around a shimmering rainbow or unicorns cavorting in a grassy meadow. My favorite was a shiny ebony jewelry box that displayed a Japanese lady who would twirl to the music whenever I opened its door. It held center stage on my antique white and gold French Provincial dressing table.

Papa gave me a collection of china dolls, too, six of them,

dressed in costumes of children from other countries. Sometimes I wondered if Papa saw me as one of those china dolls, one he could take out and play with when it would strike his fancy. Then he would return me safely to the mantel when he tired of me and wanted to go back to his world.

Grandma Lydia met us at the door. Papa acknowledged her presence with a curt nod and strode briskly into my mother's room. He had done his duty and brought his wayward daughter home. Now I became Grandma's responsibility. She opened her arms wide and I ran into them. Burying my face in her sweet-smelling apron, I let the tears come. She stroked my hair and held me until they subsided. A rumble of thunder sounded in the distance as lightning illuminated the darkened room. Ordinarily, I enjoyed a summer storm. Since I was a little girl, I would curl up on our living room sofa by the big picture window to watch it. The display of flashing lights fascinated me as they danced across the dense sky, and the angry waves crashing against the shore sent chills down my spine. But that day I just wanted to be comforted. I was glad Grandma was there.

"Cassandra, you'll want to change into dry clothes." Grandma gently released my grasp.

I shook my head. "It's so hot. I'll dry fast." The coolness of my damp shirt felt good next to my clammy skin.

"Come, sit down, then." She led me to the table. "I made you lemonade and brought fresh cookies from home." Her mouth smiled, but her eyes revealed tears trying to hide behind a misty veil. Again, I shook my head. I sat down, but knew I couldn't eat anything. Not even one of Grandma's chewy raisin oatmeal cookies could tempt me today. I started to think I should try to cheer Grandma up. After all, my mother was her daughter. If my mother died, her little girl would die, too.

I took a sip of lemonade. The cool liquid tasted good and helped clear some fogginess out of my brain. "Thank you, Grandma," I managed to say. "Are you staying overnight?"

Grandma nodded. "I'll stay as long as I'm needed. Robert tells me you did a great job with meals when your mom was bedridden before, but I'd like to help now."

I shot her a grateful glance. "I think Papa's getting tired of hamburgers and hot dogs." She grinned.

The bedroom door creaked. Papa's tall frame filled the doorway. His mood matched his dark complexion and thick, dark, hair which was always perfectly groomed.

"Your mother wants to see you."

I felt like a commoner being ushered into the presence of royalty. Unlike my father, my mother's spirit emitted warmth and compassion. But I had to pass the imposing figure of my father to reach her. I suddenly realized that's how it always was. My relationship with my mother had to be filtered through the rigid control of my father.

"Cassandra," Mama reached out her hand to touch me. She said my name like nobody else did. It flowed off her tongue like music produced by the vibrant strings of a harp.

Mama read lots of romantic novels and named me after one of the heroines in a book. I liked it. It suited me. I was a romantic, too. *Cassandra of Clarity Castle.* Sometimes I imagined myself as a grand noblewoman who chose a life of solitude along the vast ocean coast. Then it didn't hurt so much to face the reality of being a teenage outcast who wasn't allowed to attend parties or go roller skating on Saturday night with the kids from town.

I bent down and put my arms around her, but was careful not to squeeze. Mama had always been thin, but now her slender frame was so delicate I was afraid I'd break her. The capable hands that dug in the soil of her garden two short months ago were now as smooth and white as a baby's skin. Although her eyes still lighted with affection when she saw me, they were now encased in an iridescent sepulcher.

I'd always been proud of the way my mama looked. Her blond hair fell around her shoulders in soft waves. She didn't bother to put it up any more. I wondered why Mama had such pretty fairy princess tresses while my own blond hair was so baby fine it stubbornly plastered its strands flat against my head. Mama tried everything to make my hair look pretty. She'd tried perms and curlers every which way, but eventually decided that a straight-cut chin length bob suited me the best. She told me it was most becoming and someday I would be happy that it felt so soft and cottony. I wanted to believe her.

In a way, she looked even more beautiful than ever. The loss of weight accentuated her high cheek bones and the pallor of the skin set off a ethereal glow. I could understand why Papa had chosen to marry her. He admired graceful and beautiful things. I curled up on the rug next to Mama's bed and tucked a pillow behind me. I was determined to stay as long as Papa permitted.

He sat down on the edge of the bed. "Cassandra," he began, "I don't know if I can expect you to understand, but your mother wants me to prepare you."

Mama flashed him a reproving look. "Cassandra is very intelligent," she reminded him.

Papa and I exchanged glances. Mama seldom rebuked her husband. She seemed resigned to living in his shadow. Maybe the illness was giving her new courage or determination.

Papa cleared his throat. "Yes, yes, I know." His eyes latched onto an imaginary spot on the green and rose flowered wallpaper and he started to recite as matter-of-factly as though he was reading out of a medical journal. "Amanda has been diagnosed with an incurable disease of the brain. There is no known treatment capable of reversing the expected progression of the illness since it is so far advanced. Her life expectancy is anywhere from a few months to a year. Or it could terminate tomorrow."

My lower lip quivered as I felt a tremor pass through my entire body. Mama's hand that rested on my shoulder tightened firmly. I was surprised at her strength. It seemed as though she was willing the last ounce of it to me. I struggled to squeeze back tears and clung to Mama's strength, determined to handle the tragedy like a grown-up. I would not buckle under the pressure like a little girl.

I tried once, twice, to push the words out. "Terminate means end, doesn't it, Daddy?" The tender word of endearment I'd used as a small child escaped before I had a chance to catch it. It had been years since I'd called him "Daddy." Maybe thinking of him that way would bring back the security I'd felt in his arms when I was a child. That was long before I grew old enough to understand those things that couldn't be known. Like when I'd fall asleep in the car and his strong arms would carry me and tuck me into bed. It was easier to be little and believe everything you were told and think your parents loved each other. If only we could switch ages for whatever situation we found ourselves in at the time. Then I could be grown-up when I wanted people to listen to my opinion and become a little girl when I didn't want to hear and understand sad things.

"Yes, Cassie." The way he said it made me almost feel the strong arms around me again. I closed my eyes quickly to hold the moment tight.

Mama's hand relaxed. "Robert, would you make me some coffee?" I think it was her way of wanting to be alone with me. Papa left the room. Mama groped for my hand. "Cassandra, I want you to know that I've always been glad you're my daughter. I'm proud of you." Her eyes searched my face and her countenance lit with one of her rare smiles. Her voice choked a bit. "You're so pretty."

"Mama, don't." I buried my head in her bed covers. I remembered times when I'd disobeyed her, insisted on having my own way. When I'd made her cry.

Her voice lifted and became musical. "Remember how you and I used to walk through the woods all the way to the thick row of pine trees?" I nodded. She stroked my hair and my cheeks. A finger ran lightly across the bridge of my nose and her palm cupped my chin. I held my breath, savoring her touch. "Then one day you burst through the brush and called to me. You were so excited. 'Mama, come here,' you said. 'I found a secret garden!'" Tears were again flowing down my face and Mama's hand was catching them.

She continued. "I squeezed in between the bushes to find you and had to catch my breath. It was so beautiful, just a small patch of grass, a circle surrounded by trees, full of wildflowers. They were all different colors and hues of blue, purple, yellow, and pink. We went to our secret place often when you were little." Her voice grew quieter. "Those were special times for me."

"Me, too, Mama." I wondered why we had stopped going there. I sighed. Maybe that was also a part of growing up.

My tears had stopped and the room was silent. The rainstorm had subsided and sunlight drifted in through lace curtains by the bay window where Mama kept her favorite plants, an assortment of violets.

"Cassandra, I need to tell you something important," she smiled. "I want you to listen carefully to what Grandma tells you after I'm gone."

I stiffened at the last part of her phrase, "after I'm gone." But Mama went on, "You've heard your father make fun of Grandma's beliefs about the Bible and her notions about going to church."

I knew what she meant. Papa forbade Mama and I from going to church with her many years ago. He wouldn't even let us have a Bible in the house. He said it was made up of fairy tales and his daughter was not going to have her head stuffed with such foolishness.

Mama reached over and opened the drawer next to her bed. Stashed behind a pile of linen handkerchiefs was a small white Bible. She lifted it tenderly. "Cassandra," she said, "Grandma brought me this a week ago. She said it was important for me to have one, no matter what Robert said." Her hands caressed the pages and she smiled again. "She's right, Cassandra. I've been reading it and now I'm not afraid to die. I've asked Jesus to forgive me and take over my life, whatever is left of it."

Her look was expectant. I was bewildered. "You mean Papa doesn't know it's here?" I whispered.

She nodded. "Cassandra, this is far more important than our secret garden. I'm going to a place called heaven when I die."

My eyes were wide now, and fastened securely on hers.

"It's a beautiful place. The last chapter of the Bible tells all about it. There will be no more tears, no sickness, no suffering. It's forever, daughter, and I want you to join me there."

I finally blinked. "But, how can I?"

"Read this, Cassandra, and talk to Grandma about it." She put the treasured volume back in the drawer and laid her head down on the pillow. "I'm so sorry, honey," her voice broke. "I wish I had believed sooner. I wish I'd been a better mother . . ."

"Hush, Mama." I threw my arms around her. She slid over and I crawled in beside her. We cuddled.

"After . . . I'm . . . gone, take the Bible to your room and hide it." Her eyelids fluttered and closed. Her strength had been expended for now.

When Papa brought the coffee, she was asleep. He sort of grunted and set the cup down anyway. Then he ordered me out of the room. "Leave her alone. She needs her rest." I didn't mind leaving. I was anxious to ask Grandma questions about the Bible. Now that Mama was going to heaven, it suddenly seemed important to me.

I found Grandma Lydia in the kitchen making a fruit salad. I peeked to make sure she had put in fresh strawberries from Mama's garden. They were my favorite summer treat.

The subject was difficult to broach, even with Grandma, and I hesitated.

"Your parents told you?" she asked.

"Yes, Grandma." It was strange. In spite of the overwhelming sadness, there was a kind of excitement inside me too. Grandma had tried to tell me about Jesus before. But Papa had dismissed it as nonsense and Mama didn't seem to care at the time. I enjoyed Grandma's Bible stories, but I didn't think about them much.

Standing there, I remembered a dream I'd had when I was younger. I'd dreamed I'd seen an angel. He had saved me when my foot was caught in a railroad track. The dream was so vivid and detailed that I thought it really happened. But my parents convinced me it couldn't be true. Now a faint tingling inside made me wonder if, just possibly, it could have happened the way I remembered it.

"Did she show you her Bible?" Grandma tilted her head toward me as she sliced a banana.

"Yes," I whispered. "I'm to have it."

"Good. Cassie, your mother has found Jesus and will be going to live with Him in heaven soon."

"I know. Mama says heaven is a beautiful place. Does the Bible say what it looks like?"

Grandma scooped whipped cream into the glass bowl and started stirring. She gazed into space for a moment like she was trying to see heaven.

"God tells us that there is a big city made out of many kinds of jewels. Gates of pearl guard the entrances and the ground is pure gold. No light is needed there because . . ."

"Silence, old woman!" Papa hurled the gruff words from the doorway. Grandma dropped her spoon. It made a loud clank on the tile floor. I hoped he hadn't stood there long enough to hear that Mama had a Bible in the house. His icy stare was all it took for me to want to scurry to my room, but Grandma didn't appear at all frightened. Papa stalked over to Grandma. He crossed his arms over his chest and stood straight and tall like the statue of the wooden Indian at the New Bergen Drug Store. He spoke calmly, but the tone of his voice sent chills down my spine.

"Lydia, I will let you remain here as long as your daughter requires care, but the minute this ordeal is over, you will leave my house and never set foot in it again. Cassandra is not to be taught any more foolishness. She will be instructed in the latest scientific theories and will base her future on facts, not on fabrications of weak, stupid people who aren't able to handle life on their own." His voice started to crescendo. He would not be interrupted or ignored. "Death is the end of life, Lydia. Do I make myself clear?"

A brief pause, then the finale, stated with a forceful tone that was on the very edge of control. He turned to look directly at me. "Do you hear me, Cassandra? THERE IS NO GOD!" He spun on his heels, walked calmly to the table, and sat down. "I am ready to eat, Lydia. Please serve dinner."

I didn't get a chance to be alone with Grandma all evening. Papa saw to that. When I went to bed, I thought about praying, but decided I'd better ask Grandma how to do it first. I didn't want to start out on the wrong foot with God!

Mama died during the night. Papa decided not to wake

me, but Grandma was there to love her into heaven. I felt kind of guilty, too, because I was curious. I'd never seen anybody die and the unemotional part of me wondered what it was like.

Papa was different after Mama died. Even though it didn't show much, I think part of him depended on her and maybe even loved her. The hollow grief in his eyes never completely left him. He kept his word to Grandma. He sent her packing that very day and quit taking me to see her.

As for me, I sort of functioned on automatic for a long time after I'd emptied myself of tears. I started reading the Bible, but got bogged down in the first book. Genesis had so many lists of names, over hundreds of generations. Maybe if I'd started in a different place, things would have been different. I dreamed about heaven one night. Then that dream faded into the dim areas of my mind, like the angel's visit.

Papa and I lived alone. I cooked and kept the house clean, and did my homework. Like all doctors, Papa was often called away at night. Those times were fearful for me at first, but I got used to them. Papa tried to be friendlier to me. Often, in the evenings, he'd let me come into his library and read to me from his vast collection of books, mostly scientific or medical. Gradually, my visions of the supernatural world faded as science became the prominent focus of my mind. Papa was training me well.

I suppose I was lonely, but since my emotions had numbed, I didn't notice it much.

It was a long time before I felt anything.

The Rejection
Chapter 2
1973

"Come here, Cassie, I want you to meet someone!" My best friend, Liz Beth, waved at me from the dock forty feet away from where I sat, preparing to strap on my water skis. It was a gorgeous afternoon in June, five years after my mother died. Summer came early that year, so the boating activity on Lake Clarity was already in full swing. I was eager to skim over the glassy surface, but instead laid aside my skis and hurried to join my friend.

"My name is not Elizabeth," she had informed me solemnly when we met on the beach two years earlier. "It's two words," she insisted, her green eyes flashing as she tossed her velvety auburn locks away from her face. "Like Mary Jane or Linda Lou. You can call me either Liz or Beth or both, but never Elizabeth." Her family built a cottage near us where they spent nearly every weekend in the summer. They were from "the cities," as we called the Minneapolis--St. Paul metropolitan area, which was about a hundred miles southeast of us.

Now Liz Beth sat on her dock, her bare feet dangling over

the edge and kicking up little splash bubbles in the water. At her side was the most handsome guy I'd ever seen up close. He had broad shoulders and a bronze tan that gleamed in the sun. His pleasant smile warmed me as his enticing eyes lingered on my face. His long, tawny, full head of hair reminded me of John Lennon, one of the Beatle's, a singing group from England that took America by storm in the late sixties.

I was glad I'd worn my new bathing suit, a sky-blue two piece, with tiny white polka dots. My own tan complemented my chin length blond hair that was bleached from the summer sun.

"This is my cousin, Loren Hamilton." Liz Beth introduced us. "He's spending three weeks with my family while his parents are in Europe." She flashed him a quick smile. "They evidently didn't trust him alone in that big house!" Loren responded with a deep chuckle.

"This is my best friend, Cassie Dupont."

"Hi, Loren," I extended my hand and he held it a bit longer than necessary.

"Hi, Cassie. Is that short for something?" His engaging scrutiny almost made me forget what it was short for.

"Cassandra," I finally blurted out. "Most people call me Cassie." I pulled myself together. "Welcome to our lake. I hope you enjoy your vacation."

"I'm sure I will . . . now." He smiled at me. I blushed.

Lake Clarity gradually became more populated since my father had our house built in 1961. We still had the only permanent residential home in the area, except for a farm a few miles away. Much to Papa's dismay, more and more city people had put up summer cottages. Only two hours away, people from "the cities" found our lake a convenient distance for weekend getaways. Some of the wealthier families from New Bergen and the nearby town of Lakeland, had also purchased lots and were building cottages. So far, Papa hadn't objected to my associations with teens on the lake. Their families enjoyed a higher social status than most of the town folk I met at school.

"When are you going to teach me how to water ski, Cassandra?" Loren flashed his brown eyes at me.

"You can watch me," I quickly responded. "I'm going up next. If you want to ride in the boat while I ski, I'll give you some tips afterwards."

For safety reasons, all the parents in the neighborhood insisted that someone must accompany the driver when another person was skiing. The extra person kept an eye on the skier to let the driver know immediately if he had fallen or was having trouble. The driver could then concentrate entirely on steering the boat.

"Sounds good." He jumped off the dock and followed me to a wide pier. It was the gathering spot for teens who had a free afternoon and wanted to ski. Whoever had a boat available drove while the others skied. The system worked out to be quite fair in the long run. Loren swam out to the speedboat with long powerful strokes and hoisted himself up and over the side. Meanwhile, I slid my feet into the rubber footholds on my skis, trying unsuccessfully to concentrate on the sport instead of the handsome face eyeing me from the boat.

Liz Beth settled herself next to me on the pier and kept up a stream of conversation. That's probably one reason why we were such good friends. She was a super talker and I was a good listener. "Isn't he great? I knew you guys would hit it off. You'll make a great looking couple. He's so tall and well built and handsome and you're so slender and beautiful. He's on his break from school. He's attending all year around so he can graduate sooner. He goes to the University of Minnesota in St. Paul. His dad wanted him at a private school, but Loren didn't have the grades for it." At my questioning look, she assured me, "Oh, he's smart. He just didn't want to waste his time studying in high school. Now he's hitting the books and doing great. He's a philosophy major."

"Philosophy?" I stared at her, impressed. "Loren must be an intellectual," I thought. It would be nice to know a guy who had a mind for sensible, knowledgeable conversation. The teenage boys I hung around with were typically full of their own ego, and talked mostly about cars and sports.

Liz read my mind. "See, I'm a good matchmaker, aren't I?" She gazed dreamily into the sky. "Give it a year and you'll be

31

engaged."

Ignoring her, I slipped my skis over the edge of the pier and reached for the rope hanging on a post. I looked to see who was driving this time. It was Rick. My forehead creased into a frown. Rick, the only driver I was wary of, was a newcomer to Lake Clarity. I'd noticed that the sixteen-year-old wasn't very conscientious about watching the skiers. Sometimes, he swerved in too close to retrieve a skier from the water after he fell. A dangerous situation could occur when the boat's motor drifted too close to a skier. Papa once showed me a photograph of a victim whose back was pulverized from propeller blades. It was a gruesome sight. I shivered a little, recalling the memory. Then I reminded myself that no accident had happened in our lake. I decided I was overly concerned. Loren seemed to be keeping a close eye on me. I watched the rope unfold as the boat steadily glided out. Just as it began to pull taut, I gave the signal.

"Hit it!" I yelled and surged forward as the boat lunged ahead, picking up speed quickly.

Invigorating spray hit my face as I balanced myself upright. It was a perfect day. The lake was as smooth as satin without a ripple except for the wake created by the speeding craft as it sliced a maiden route through the clear water. I dipped and swerved, flying over the surface and jumping over the wake. Foaming spray arched around me as I twisted right and left. It was exhilarating! I forgot about Loren and marveled in the rainbow patterns my spray was creating. As the boat curved around a bend, a sparking trail of glittering images reflected by the sun formed an enticing pathway in the water. I imagined it beckoning me to follow it all the way to the heavens.

The glossy surface tempted me to drop a ski and try to slalom. Before that day, my attempts to use only one ski had landed me upside down beneath the water, but I felt like this was a day meant for success. I glanced at Loren. His eyes were glued on me. Yes, today could be my lucky day!

We circled back near the pier. Tentatively, I shifted my weight onto my right foot and lifted the left one carefully. My balance held. Immediately, I sluffed the extra ski off my foot and tucked my free left foot behind me. Success! I actually stayed upright for about thirty seconds! Then I struck an unexpected wave caused by another vessel crossing our path. I hit it head on and somersaulted under the water. Rising slowly to the top, I ruefully wondered if Loren could be persuaded to believe the somersault was a trick maneuver, but decided he couldn't be that naïve.

My head popped up through the surface and I looked for my ski. It was several feet away, so I started to swim toward it. The speedboat was coming fast. It began to circle around me, in an effort to drag the floating rope within my reach. But it was coming too soon. I changed course and headed in the other direction. Rick also swerved suddenly. I was evidently confusing him.

"Turn off the motor!" I yelled. "Turn it off!"

"What?" Loren looked mystified. The noise of the motor drowned out my shouts.

Loren looked from Rick to me and back again.

"The motor!" I yelled again. "Turn it . . ."

I stopped as my body began to be pulled swiftly towards the motor, now an eerie looking contraption. I felt helpless. *What was the matter with Rick?* He should have noticed my distress. Desperately, I struggled against the current produced by the revolving propellers. In a few split seconds, it would be too late. Then a strong arm grasped me firmly by the shoulder. My feet dangled inches from the motor's blades. I lifted my head. Loren had me by the arm and was motioning to Rick to turn off the ignition.

Silence followed a slow, sputtering sound as the motor shook twice and stood still. I found my breath and went limp. "Here, Cassie, grab my hand and I'll pull you up." Loren's muscular arms hauled me over the side. I half climbed and half fell into his lap, then pushed myself away and slumped into the seat opposite him. Then the shivering started and my teeth chattered. Loren wrapped a towel around my shoulders and I clung to it. I didn't feel cold, just shaken up.

Rick's face appeared. "I'm sorry, Cassie," he spread out his hands in front of him as if to shake off guilt. "I'm new at this. I'll know better next time."

"Just take me home. Please."

The first thing I did at home was take a warm shower. My frazzled nerves craved the soothing spray of the water caressing my body. I was relieved that Papa was gone. He would have known something was wrong and demanded an explanation. He might have curtailed my meager social privileges further. I just wanted to put the unfortunate incident behind me as quickly as possible.

I dried myself and pulled on a white tank top and a pair of navy blue hot pants. This was my "uniform" for my job as a car hop. I worked five nights a week as a waitress for a drive-in restaurant just outside of Lakeland, a larger town about twenty-five miles from New Bergen. When Papa surprised me with a 1970 Chevy Chevelle on my eighteenth birthday this spring, he had one condition. I would have to get a job to help pay for gas and insurance. "My daughter is going to learn the value of a dollar," he had stated emphatically. That was okay with me, as long I had a car of my own. It gave me a freedom I'd never known. I'm sure Papa intended for a job to keep me occupied during the summer months when he was gone all day. Actually, the only job I could find mostly kept me busy in the evenings, and I had the afternoons free to hang around with my friends at Lake Clarity.

I blow dried my hair and coaxed it, with the help of a lot of gel, off my face. The "natural look" of the early seventies was "in" and I loved it. Because of my deep tan, the only make-up I needed was some light pink lipstick. I added a delicate pair of blue and gold pierced earrings to my attire and was ready to go to work. Studying myself carefully in the mirror, I liked what I saw. The gorgeous, model-like beauty of my mother hadn't been passed down to me. But her blue eyes and delicate features softened the square chin that I had inherited from my dad. I'd inherited his stubbornness, too. "Why can't you be more like your mother?" he'd complain when I opposed him. "She knew her place."

Well, maybe I didn't know my place, but I knew my own mind. And I intended to use it!

Satisfied with my reflection, I grabbed my navy blue, shoulder-strap purse, took my car keys off the hook by the door, and headed outside. A cool late-afternoon breeze greeted me. A red convertible sat in the driveway behind my car. Leaning against it with his arms crossed over his chest was Loren. He had changed into a green and white knit shirt and cut offs. I stared at him.

"Liz told me you had to work tonight, so I decided to drive you." He walked around his automobile, opened the passenger door with a flourish, and grinned. "Please be seated, my lady. My services are at your disposal."

Unsure of myself, I stammered, "Uh, well, I don't know if Papa. . ."

Loren nodded knowingly. "My cousin said your dad screens potential dates and hasn't approved anyone yet. Well, this isn't a date, young lady. And if you notice," he countered with a wicked grin, "You won't be able to move your car until I move mine, so if you want to get to work on time . . ."

"All right," I laughed, "You convinced me." I climbed into the vehicle. "I'll need a ride home, too, you realize."

"Affirmative." He slid into the driver's seat and backed the car out smoothly. We spent the first few minutes in silence. I considered asking him if he'd skied today. But I was still shaky from my close call and didn't really want to discuss the sport. "So, what are you going to do when you get out of here?" Loren's deep voice broke into my thoughts.

I looked at him blankly.

"When you graduate. You're a senior, aren't you?"

"Yes." I hesitated. I hadn't yet discussed my dream of becoming a doctor like my father, and wasn't sure I wanted to share it with Loren. "My plans aren't certain yet. I've applied to several colleges. I'm thinking of entering the medical field."

"That's great, Cassie. I can tell you've got a good mind. I think women should try for anything they want to do. I'm a phi-losophy major." He watched for my reaction.

"I know. Liz told me. The study of philosophy must be fascinating. I think a lot about the meaning of life, but I haven't really figured it out yet."

Loren smiled with satisfaction. "I knew you were differ-ent from the rest. Most people around here treat me like I'm sort of weird. They're into doing, not thinking. You're the first person I've met, outside of the family, who has a modern viewpoint and an open mind."

"My father taught me to question traditional styles of thought and be open to new and progressive ideas."

"Do you want to know what I believe, Cassie?" Loren's voice intensified with excitement. "I believe this is a new age. Have you heard that song, 'The Age of Aquarius?' I believe it's like that now. People are discovering a new freedom within themselves, a freedom to form relationships based on their true identities. We'll be released from the confining bondage of past myths and customs. Our souls are one, you know, yours and mine, in tune with the rhythm of the universe. Everyone doesn't realize it though. I intend to help as many as I can to find liberation and love and peace with the new ideology."

Loren was a fascinating conversationalist, and he was interested in my ideas, too. Papa, always quick to instruct, seldom considered my opinions valid. It felt good to exchange views with a man of Loren's intellect. The twenty minute drive to Lakeland went fast, and I found myself looking forward to the ride home.

Promptly at 10:30 p.m., Loren reappeared to claim me. I was tired from the hectic pace at the drive-in and content to settle myself comfortably for the ride home. Leaning back, I closed my eyes for a moment.

Loren let me rest. He fiddled with the radio dials and soon we were breezing down the road, listening to some sixties' tunes and reveling in the refreshing night air blowing in our faces. The Beatles boomed out, "I want to hold your haaaaand . . ." Loren reached over and took hold of mine. Instinctively, I tried to pull away, but he held tight. My eyes popped open and I noticed he'd taken a wrong turn.

"This isn't the way home," I protested.

Loren ignored me. "I like you, Cassie," he said, "and I think you like me. We've got a lot going for us."

"We just met, Loren," I reminded him.

"But we're well matched, aren't we?" He turned those bewitching eyes on me for a brief moment. "We're both physically attractive, intelligent, and ambitious. I've got an outgoing personality; you're sensitive and introspective. We balance each other."

He squeezed my hand. "Where's a good place to park?"

"Excuse me?" I couldn't believe my ears.

"Come on, Cassie. You're not that inexperienced, are you?" His attitude was as confident as it was playful. "I know you don't formally date, but a girl as pretty as you must have been with a lot of guys."

"No! I'm not with boys. I mean . . . not alone."

I tried harder to pull away, but he held firm. The car picked up speed and careened down the country road. I worried that he wasn't used to driving on gravel roads and took the curves far too fast. We could easily get caught in a rut and flip over sideways. Just the past week, a teenage driver in my class at school caught his tires in a gravel rut. His car flipped into the ditch, and he broke both an arm and a leg. He was still in the hospital. I'd gone to see him with a couple of friends. His face was all cut up and he still looked scared.

Suddenly, Loren slammed on the brakes and veered off to the right. The vehicle started down a side road that led, as far as I could make out, into a field. A lonely, uninhabited field. I decided we must be eight or nine miles from home. But I had no idea what direction home was or in whose field we were trespassing. I had never met anyone from a farm outside of school. If Papa thought the town folk were beneath us socially, I could imagine what he thought of farm folk!

My muscles tensed and I forced myself to reason calmly. Where I lived, rape was less of a danger than losing one's reputation. But Loren was from a big city. I didn't know what his morals were, or even if he had any! He had seemed like a nice guy. *How had I gotten myself into this mess? And how was I going to get out of it?*

We bumped along the dry, rutted trail for a few minutes. Then Loren stopped in the middle of nowhere, turned off the lights and ignition, and reached to pull me close. I briefly considered making a run for it, but knew he'd catch me and I was sure no one would hear my screams. I resolved to use my brain instead of my legs.

"Just a minute," I spoke firmly, still not sure what I intended to do. He looked startled and my heart pounded frantically. Putting a restraining hand on his chest, I plunged into conversation, hoping whatever came out of my mouth would make sense.

"You said we were both attractive. But I am not attracted to you. You're not my type. I only accepted this ride because I've had a tough day." Surprised, he loosened his grip and I leaned back. *"Wow,"* I thought to myself, *"I'm a good actress. Maybe I should try out for the class play this year."* I tried my best to appear casual and gazed out of the window, even though there was nothing to see but blackness. Then I pushed the drama a little too far. "Do you have a cigarette?" I didn't smoke, but at the time, any diversion seemed appropriate.

"Yeah, I do." His confidence obviously shaken, he fumbled in his pocket for a couple of cigarettes. He handed me one and reached out his lighter towards me. I leaned over as casually as I could, wondering what my next move should be. Closing my eyes, I breathed in deeply. The taste wasn't too bad, but the coughing fit was terrible. I pulled back, spit out the offending cigarette, and clutched my chest as I hacked and fought to catch my breath.

Loren's eyes narrowed. "You are inexperienced, aren't you?"

Hanging onto my chest, I nodded in between gasps. My eyes were burning. He slammed his fist on the dashboard, making me jump. "So Liz set me up with a naïve little school girl. I'm stuck in this hick town for three more weeks and this is the best she could do!" His smooth veneer was stripped away to reveal his raw nature. My coughing subsided. Loren glared at me. "I'll have you home in no time, Baby!" He turned on the switch and gunned the engine hard. Wheels spun, but the car didn't move. He tried it again.

"I think we're stuck. Maybe you should ease out slowly," I timidly suggested.

He ignored me and revved the motor again. It didn't budge. He opened the door, stepped outside, and kicked the tires.

"A lot of good that will do" I thought.

"I'm going for help." He growled and stalked away.

Now I was really in a panic. *What kind of help would he bring? Who else was destined to know about this awful humiliating experience?* Once again, I considered running. But I had no idea where I was or what was out there that could be worse. I was afraid of dogs, having been bitten in the leg by one when I was a child. I had no desire to risk an attack by an aggressive canine in the night.

I scrunched down in the seat and tried to melt into the cushion and become invisible. Five minutes passed. Then ten. It started to get chilly. Loren hadn't bothered to raise the top of the convertible. I wondered if I could do it. I leaned over and inspected the various dials and gadgets. The groaning sound of a tractor reached my ears. I froze, then looked up. Sure enough, a tractor was rumbling down the dirt path. In the dim light, I could barely make out the shape of the driver and a man, evidently Loren, standing behind him and hanging onto the side of the vehicle. Too late to hide now. I sat back and tried to appear nonchalant.

The tractor stopped. Loren and the driver stepped down. I still couldn't see the stranger clearly, but could tell he was also broad shouldered and tall. He walked with the surety of a young man's gait. I pretended to ignore him, but he strode right up to my side of the car. He appeared about to say something, then gave me a closer look and hesitated. I was unable to pull my eyes away from his intent gaze. His clear eyes studied mine and I felt like he saw right through me. But what I assumed he saw wasn't really there. I wasn't a cocky woman of the world. I was just a frightened kid.

His eyes didn't condemn me; they pitied me. I swallowed hard and turned away. The stranger walked back to Loren and offered reassurance. "Just help me get this chain on and I'll have you out in no time." Teardrops stung my eyes now, but I forced them back and stared vacantly into the blank night.

Why should I care what this man thinks of me anyway? I'll be out of here and home in a few minutes and never have to see his face again.

The clanking of the chain and voices dimmed as the farmer got on his tractor and Loren resumed his place at the wheel. The obstinate vehicle groaned and jerked, and finally started to roll. When the young man approached to unhook the chain, Loren flashed him a bill.

"Keep it. I don't need your money." The stranger turned and walked away.

Chapter 3

It was an unusually cool day for August. And it had been a long one. I had to work an extra shift at the drive-in because two girls called in sick. I pulled my navy cardigan sweater tightly around me, glad that I had grabbed it as I dashed out of the house that morning. The big clock above the serving window said 8:00 p.m. now, just one more hour to go. On weeknights we weren't very busy so I had time to sit and treat myself to a hot fudge sundae. I relished the smooth texture of the rich fudge on my tongue. Chocolate was definitely my favorite flavor.

"Cassie, I've got to leave. Would you please bring the tray out to number nine and save my tip?" Terri was already heading out to her boyfriend's new green Ford truck. Steady honking sounds coming from the vehicle expressed his impatience.

"Sure."

"Thanks a lot. See you tomorrow."

I waved and set my sundae down. This would just take a minute and I'd get back to my treat. Grabbing the correct tray, I walked rapidly to the dusty blue '65 Chevy. I enjoyed my job because I met interesting people and had fun with co-workers during the slow times.

The customers in the blue car looked typical, a couple of good looking guys in their late teens or early twenties. A closer look made me catch my breath and I almost dropped the tray. It was him, the farmer who had hauled Loren and me out of the field two weeks ago. No! I did not want to meet him again. I almost twirled around and headed back, but he'd already seen me. He sat on the driver's side, too, so I would have to talk to him! My insides quivered. *"Calm down, Cassie,"* I admonished myself. *"Maybe he won't recognize you. Play it cool."*

I slowed my steps and smiled at him. His appraising eyes were the clear, blue color of a mountain lake. The minute I looked into them, I knew that he knew who I was. Wow! He looked even more handsome in the daylight. His dark brown hair had just the touch of a wave and strong features hinted at a competent manner. He had to see the blush on my face and my nervous attitude.

"That'll be four sixty-eight," I attempted to place his tray on the window, but was so flustered I forgot to check to see if his window was rolled up high enough to support the tray. It wasn't. Four hamburgers liberally smeared with catsup and mustard, a mountain of fries, and the contents of two large root beers, with ice, landed on his lap.

"Yeow!" he stiffened and hit his head on the ceiling. At least, it took his attention away from me. Temporarily.

"I'm so sorry," I clapped both hands to my mouth. "I'll get a rag." Glad for an excuse to leave, I turned and dashed for the kitchen. Taunting remarks and chuckles from other vehicles followed me.

Returning with a rag, I found him and his companion gone. I wiped up the mess as best as I could, noting that his cushions would never look the same again. Not that they looked that good anyway. The car cushions were torn, and dirty fluffy stuff was poking out from the holes.

I hurried back to the kitchen, nearly colliding with him as he came out of the rest room. His burgundy shirt was sopping, but clean. His cut-offs, still heavily stained, looked soggy and uncomfortable. I was tongue-tied.

The corner of his mouth twitched. "Do you suppose we could get another meal?"

"Of course." My voice returned. I stammered, "I . . . I seem to be causing you a lot of trouble." I couldn't believe I was actually wringing my hands. I'd never done that before.

He caught my hands and held them still. "Four burgers with everything, two fries, and two large root beers. Got it?"

"Un huh." I darted back to the kitchen. When I returned with the tray, the car was still empty. I looked around and discovered both customers sitting at the picnic table talking to my manager, Seth Larson. I was horrified. If they complained to Mr. Larson, I'd have to go home tonight and tell Papa I got fired!

The farmer beckoned to me. "Bring it over here. It's safer!" All three of them laughed, even Mr. Larson.

I set the tray in front of them and turned to go.

"Cassie," Seth stopped me. "I see you made a great impression on my little brothers." Seth was a tech-ed teacher who used his free summers to run the drive-in. I didn't even know he had any brothers. There went my chances of avoiding the stranger in the future.

"This is Darren, and Luke," he motioned to each of them. "And this is Cassandra Dupont. She's one of my best waitresses. Usually." He tried, unsuccessfully, to hide a smirk.

I shook hands formally with both brothers. At least the stranger had a name now. Darren. And he hadn't let on that he'd already met me. I flashed him a grateful smile.

Seth stood up. "Come with me, Luke. I'll show you around." He glanced at me. "Luke will be managing the place next week while I'm on vacation." Luke got up and followed him. Which left me alone with Darren. I looked around. All the car stalls were empty now. No one needed my attention. Just my luck.

"Sit down, Cassandra," the blue eyes ordered. I sat.

"You can call me Cassie. Most people do."

"Well, Cassie, have you been working here long?" He was trying to be nice to me, which made everything seem worse.

"Just this summer." I played with a crumb on the table.

"You live close by?"

I nodded and took a deep breath. "Look, I don't want you to think . . . I mean that night wasn't my idea. I don't . . ." I finally blurted out, "I'm not that kind of a girl." My head was up now. I glared at him, daring him to disapprove.

He appraised me thoughtfully. "I didn't think you were."

My sanity returned. I began to feel like a normal person again.

"Cassie, how about you and I start over? Most days, I help my dad farm, but I told Luke I'd show up in between chores next week to see if I could be of any use to him around here. If I'm going to be hanging around, I'd like things to be okay with us." He paused. "I'd like to get to know you." He smiled, a friendly, relaxed smile.

I smiled back.

"When is he coming, Cassandra?" Papa reclined in his black leather armchair, his slippered feet resting on the stool. Wearing his brown and dark green paisley bathrobe and with the Lakeland Tribune in his hands, Papa was the picture of refinement and repose.

I, on the other hand, was as tense as a cat posting guard at a mouse hole. "Seven o'clock," I answered as I rushed past him on the way up to my room to put the finishing touches on my appearance.

I'd introduced other possible dates to my father. They smiled and made polite conversation, and then were hefted out the door. Not physically, of course, but with the same result as if they'd forfeited a jousting match. They had sparred with Papa and lost. Not that I cared much. They were silly and immature. I'd even laughed with Papa afterwards on occasion. But this time was different. This time I cared, very much. I wanted Papa to like Darren. I even wanted Darren to like Papa!

I'd humored Papa all afternoon. I think he was starting to suspect that this young man was important to me. That was not good. He'd no doubt tighten up the interrogation and Darren wouldn't stand a chance. I knew I could always see Darren on the sly, but I didn't want to live like that. I prided myself on my honesty. I wanted our relationship to be out in the open, with Papa's certified approval.

My hair was being difficult that night. I'd tried to curl it under, but it stubbornly insisted on curling up. I sighed. Maybe Darren's attention would instead be drawn to my new dress, a granny dress with tiny pink flowers on a cream colored background. The dress had a fitted bodice, a high waist, and a low square neckline. Ruffles edging the long skirt and sleeves completed the very feminine look. My accessories included large, glass bead pink earrings and high laced black boots. I gazed into the mirror, dismayed to see that my flushed face nearly matched the pink in my dress.

The doorbell rang. I flipped the radio off and opened my door so I could hear what was going on downstairs. I excitedly anticipated my first date. Darren planned to drive fifty miles to a restaurant that had recently opened in Lakeland. The "Swinging Spot" had a dance hall on one end, and I'd heard the food was very good.

I crossed my fingers. "Please, if there is a god, make Papa like Darren."

I heard Papa open the door. "Come in, Mr. Larson, and have a chair. Cassandra will be with us in a minute." What a lie! Papa told me to give them fifteen minutes, at least.

It was harder to hear as they went into the living room, so I hurried to perch at the top of the stairs. It was a good place to wait. I could catch snatches of their conversation and keep my eye on the clock in the hallway. *All you get is fifteen minutes, Papa!*

Intermittent phrases drifted up to me. Pleasant words, a bit of laughter. Papa was putting Darren at ease so he'd be caught off guard when the tough questions came.

"So," Papa raised his voice a notch. I listened attentively. "What are your future plans?"

Mumble, mumble. *Speak up, Darren!* I leaned forward and strained every nerve in my body trying to hear his response.

" . . . my dad farming. I'd like to go to college some day,

but I haven't decided on a major yet. It'll probably be agriculture."

"That means you'll be working in farming one way or another for the rest of your life."

"Yes, sir, I suppose so." I could imagine Papa's dark eyes leveled on Darren's face. Darren would stare right back.

I heard Papa rise and pace the floor. I sneaked a peek at the clock. Five more minutes. *Come on, Darren.* I felt like a silent cheerleader. *Go, go, go! Show him what you're made of!*

"Mr. Larson, you are aware of the fact that I am a doctor of medicine?"

"Yes, sir."

"Because of my prominent position in the community and my more than adequate salary," Papa continued, making an effort to sound humble and not quite succeeding, " I am able to give Cassandra all the advantages life can afford. She is accustomed to a certain life style and will expect it to continue when she marries."

"I beg your pardon, sir," Darren interrupted. "But I'm not sure Cassie feels that way, and in any case, I'm not here to discuss marriage. I want to date Cassie and get to know her better."

Please, Papa, take it easy.

"Let me put my cards on the table. You look like a young man who would appreciate that. Am I correct?"

Darren must have nodded because Papa continued. "I want to make something clear to you. I am a doctor. You are a farmer." I could imagine his posture straight and tall, towering over Darren.

One minute left. My heart was pounding.

Papa picked up speed and intensity. "Doctors study hard and long and acquire knowledge and skills that enable them to heal people and save lives! Man's life expectancy has doubled over the years. That's because doctors are doing their jobs and using the power of medicine to cure the human body. Medicine is a valuable profession and I am proud to be a part of it."

Now his voice softened, becoming almost gentle, but laced with a sharp chill that sent shivers through my body. "Darren, you're a nice boy, but how could you ever think that your choice of profession could even begin to compare in importance to mine?"

I held my breath.

Darren cleared his throat and spoke calmly, "Mr. Dupont, I have a lot of respect for your profession, but I also have lots of respect for mine. Medical skill is desperately needed to save lives. But you see, sir, nobody can even have a life without food to eat. You help sick people get well. I help keep everybody alive. I'm proud to be a farmer."

Zero minutes! I raced down the stairs, grabbed Darren's arm and we were out the door before Papa could hardly blink.

"For My thoughts are not your thoughts,
Neither are your ways My ways,'
declares the Lord.
For as the heavens are higher than the earth,
So are My ways higher than your ways,
And My thoughts than your thoughts."

Isaiah 55:8,9

Chapter 4

"Tell me about your family, Darren," I hugged my forest green parka close to my chest and snuggled up to Darren on the nearly thread bare cushions of his blue '65 Chevy. We drove along the country road that led to the farm where Darren lived with his parents and his younger brother, Billy. His older brothers, Seth and Luke, were married. They lived with their families within a twenty mile range from the farm. The air had suddenly turned crisp near the end of October. I knew it was merely a chilly foretaste of winter. When I shivered a little, Darren automatically reached over to turn up the heater.

"Sorry, Cassie, this old engine doesn't work like it used to." He wrapped his arm around me and grinned. I gathered the predicament didn't entirely displease him.

Darren had picked me up after school. "My parents want to meet you, and they won't be put off any longer," he had said, gauging my reaction with a questioning look, partly camouflaged by a casual smile. His parents had invited me to their farm several times since we had begun to date in September, but I had always found an excuse to refuse the invitation. Since my mother died, I'd been uncomfortable at family gatherings. Besides, I didn't want Darren's parents to think we were getting serious. After all, we were both only eighteen. I liked him a lot, but had goals I wanted to reach before even considering settling down.

Evidently, Darren was pressured enough to attempt a surprise maneuver. As an afterthought, he had added, "Are you free?"

I was. I had exhausted my supply of excuses and besides, curiosity had been building up inside of me. Darren's face always lit up when he talked about his family. I decided there must be something special about the people who had raised a son like him! His eyes fixed on the road, giving me an opportunity to study his profile. Darren's handsome features lacked the smooth appearance of a male model. Instead, they were cast from a rugged mold that revealed inner fortitude and strength of will.

I nudged him with my elbow. "Your family, Darren. Tell me about them."

"Well, the only ones left at home are my dad, mom, and Billy. I've told you my little brother is blind, haven't I?"

I nodded. "He's fifteen, right?"

"Uh huh. He was born blind. The doctors said it was a rare combination of genes. Somehow the rest of us, me and my brothers, missed it. Mom and Dad were really crushed. I was only four years old, but I remember Mom took to her bed for a long time, just getting up to take care of Billy. Dad and my older brothers did all the cooking and housework besides the farm chores. It was awfully dismal around the house."

I patted his arm.

"Then, all of a sudden, " he continued, "Mom seemed to snap out of it and got out of bed and took over her chores again."

"It must have been terribly hard for her."

"Yeah, I know. She had me take care of Billy a lot. I sort of got to thinking of myself as his protector. I still do, in a way. We're close, Billy and me."

"You didn't resent having to take care of him so much?"

Darren glanced at me. He seemed startled by the question. "No, I guess not. I kind of resented having him there at all, at first. I was pretty little myself, and needed a mother, too. Mom is a wise woman. You'll like her. She's an artist."

"A painter?"

"She doesn't sell her stuff, except at craft shows, but she paints well. She has kind of a poetic way of looking at life. She sees things differently than most people. It's hard to explain. You'll see."

I was already stroking my vivid imagination to conjure up an image of her—tall, willowy, delicate. Maybe I was mixing her up with my own mother, who had been sort of a poet, too.

"Dad, now he's . . ." Darren seemed to be searching for a word. ". . . unique. Just the opposite of Mom, one of a kind. Here we are."

Darren turned off the gravel road and veered into a long, narrow driveway. On our left lay a vast field, filled with sheaves of wheat dancing to the rhythm of the breeze. Darren said it was nearly ready for harvesting.

"Once harvesting begins, we'll be so busy I may not see you till Christmas!" Darren squeezed me to show that he was joking. I knew he half meant it, though. In a farm community like ours, it was a well-known fact that men worked nearly non-stop to gather the precious grain before the blustery winter weather interfered.

On our right, rows of ash and oak trees blocked our view of the house. But as we reached the last tree, the driveway sharply curved to the right, exposing a small pond that shimmered in the radiant late afternoon sunshine. A huge weeping willow tree spread it's limbs protectively above it and waved long tresses gently in the frigid breeze. Stately pillars of stones cemented together guarded each side of the road. Normally out of place in a farm setting, they seemed most appropriate in this quaint scene.

Darren followed my gaze and chuckled. "I helped build the pillars. Billy and I nearly broke our backs hauling those rocks from the fields. We objected strongly, but Mom was determined to have a proper welcome for our 'estate,' as she calls it."

"How strange," I thought to myself. As we drove up a small incline and rounded the edge of the trees, I gasped. Darren's home looked as if it had burst out of a storybook! At other times of the year it must have looked quite common. But today, with the vivid blue sky and the diminishing rays of the golden autumn sun, the scene was transcendent. A cluster of trees highlighted with brilliant red, yellow, and orange foliage formed a frame around the large, white house situated at the top of the hill overlooking the shimmering pond. An expansive porch supported by round white pillars ran the entire length of the front of the house. Above it, doors opened onto two private balconies, which led to rooms on the second floor. A gabled alcove protruded from what must have been the attic, and dark green shutters outlined each of the paned windows.

I realized that only the contrast of the stark white exterior among the beautiful foliage could have produced such a resplendent scene. As if that were not enough beauty, a plush flower garden adorned the front lawn of the house. Even this late in the season, purple, burgundy, and yellow mums lined the white picket fence leading to the front door.

Darren parked his car next to a flourishing tree decorated with crimson red leaves. As he emerged from the vehicle, a large, muscular brown dog came running from the rear of the house, barking noisily, and lunged at Darren. I had one foot out of the car, but quickly jumped back in and slammed the door. Darren laughed at my cowardly reaction, and promptly opened the door again.

"Brutus won't hurt you. He sounds fierce but he's pure mush inside." The vicious looking animal planted his overgrown paws on Darren's chest and eagerly lapped his face with a sloppy tongue.

"Hello, old boy!" Darren pushed the dog down and tussled him to the ground.

Gingerly, I stepped out of the car again. Maybe Brutus wouldn't hurt me, but I wasn't certain I wanted him to love me either!

Darren continued to reassure me. "Oh, he's polite to strangers. Sit, Brutus," he commanded. Surprisingly, the dog sat, though he eyed me with a hungry look. His tail waved furiously, like the propeller of an airplane.

"Let him sniff your hand and then pet him," he encouraged me, "That's the best way to make friends with a strange dog. Let him get your scent so he won't be afraid of you."

Him? Afraid of me? I thought Darren must be out of his tree, but I walked over and let Brutus sniff my hand. He licked me, too.

"See? He likes you." Darren was enraptured.

"So you've finally brought her! This is Cassandra, right?"

I looked up to see a small, sturdy woman approaching from the opposite side of the yard. She walked with a slight limp and carried a basket overflowing with carrots. Evidently there was a vegetable garden on the premises, also. Surely this chubby dark-haired woman wasn't Darren's mother, the artist? With a few long strides, Darren was at her side. He gave her a quick squeeze and transferred the basket to his strong arm.

"Cassie, come and meet my mom. Her name is Ingrid."

"Oh, I look a fright. You should have told me you were bringing her today!" She gently chided her son, but glowed with pride. Then she turned and smiled at me, a warm bubbly smile that lit up her whole face. Reaching up with sturdy, callused fingers, she instinctively patted soft curly hair that set off a round face with bright hazel eyes and naturally rosy cheeks.

"Please excuse my appearance. These are my working clothes." Ingrid wore baggy jeans that were covered with an assortment of patches around the knees, a plaid flannel shirt, and a denim jacket. She reached out to me with a gentle but surprisingly firm handshake. "Men just don't understand these things," she confided, shaking her head. "Well, come on in, Cassandra. You're just in time for a little lunch."

"Oh, don't trouble yourself . . ." I began to protest.

Darren silenced me with a whisper. "There's no point in objecting. Mom won't let you leave until you've been well fed."

We entered the side door that led to a large kitchen, via a tiny washroom that boasted a modern sink next to an old-fashioned wash stand that held an antique blue and white flowered pitcher and basin. Darren rinsed his hands quickly at the sink and wiped them on a towel hanging above. It was obvious that the pitcher and basin were just for looks. I was charmed by the kitchen. It reminded me of Ingrid's garden. The top half of its walls were painted a pale shade of sky blue. White wainscoting was on the bottom half, making it appear as though a picket fence ran all the way around the room. Darren immediately called my attention to the vines of lilacs, wisteria, and strawberries that his mother had painted on the walls above the "fence." The cupboards were also white, and billowy white curtains hung at the windows. A variety of green, leafy plants hung near the windows and a row of African violets lined the countertops. An older man and a teenage boy sat at the rectangular oak table in the center of the room.

"This is Cassie, Dad," Darren proudly introduced me. "This is my dad, Sven, and my brother, Billy. My parents are second generation Norwegians. All of their parents were born in Norway and migrated to America."

Sven rose from his chair and nodded to me. "Pleased to meet ya," his soft-spoken voice was laden with a heavy Norwegian accent. Though his father's manner was more subdued than Darren's, I sensed immediately the same spirit of independence and strength of character. He was tall and dark, like Darren, but his features were more subtle and worn. Graying hair around his temples and lines around his eyes testified of years of experience, pain and struggles. But the twinkle in his eyes belied these hardships, and the warm smile totally disregarded them.

Billy turned his head in my general direction and beamed. His face, like his mother's, radiated. I found myself wondering how he could look so happy and wishing that he could see his own smile in a mirror. Ingrid jabbered as she bustled around the kitchen, setting plates and cups on the table. She urged us to sit down, and we exchanged small talk while a platter of ham sandwiches on homemade buns and a liberal assortment of cookies and donuts appeared as if by magic.

"Do you drink coffee, Cassandra?" Ingrid hesitated with the pot in hand and looked at me.

"I'll have a little bit, please," I held out my cup.

Ingrid filled it to the brim. "There's nothing like a good, strong cup of coffee to warm up your insides on a cool day." She smiled with satisfaction as she filled all the cups with the steaming dark liquid and sat down next to me. Darren was on my other side, and Sven and Billy sat across the table. Silence fell and they all bowed their heads. I was used to praying with my grandma at mealtime but not just for a snack. Of course, this was a big snack!

Thank you, Lord," Sven's normally quiet voice boomed, as though he needed to speak louder than normal so the Lord could hear him. "fer this here food and fer bringin' this young lady here today. Put your hand on her, Lord, and bless her. Amen."

I felt somewhat embarrassed. Darren hadn't warned me that his parents were religious people. Darren, himself, didn't seem to have much time for God and church. I glanced at him. He looked a trifle apprehensive.

"Help yourself, honey," Ingrid passed me the heaping plate of sandwiches. I took one and passed it on. The sudden silence was awkward.

Darren's dad evidently decided he should do something about it. He leaned forward and stared at me. "Are ya havin' good luck with yer teeth?" He inquired, pleasantly.

I choked on my first sip of coffee and looked at Darren. His eyes bulged with dismay and he appeared to be having some difficulty keeping a laugh in check.

Completely unfazed, Ingrid leaned toward me and whispered confidentially, "Sven's just got his false teeth. He's having some trouble getting used to them and he's concerned that you won't have the same problem one day." She nibbled on a cookie.

"They're doing fine," I hesitantly responded, "so far."

He nodded and returned to his sandwich, seemingly satisfied. He was evidently a man who didn't waste words. I suddenly decided that I liked Darren's family. I liked them very much. Darren still looked uncomfortable, so I gave him a smile. He relaxed visibly.

"Where do you go to school, Cassie?" Billy chose to enter the conversation.

"At New Bergen," I smiled at him before I realized it wasn't necessary. He couldn't see my smile. "How do I talk to a blind person?" I wondered. I had never been face to face with one before, and I didn't want to say the wrong thing and embarrass him. "Do you go to school?" I asked, not sure if it was proper.

"Yep. At Lakeland, just like Darren. We ride the bus." Then he added, as if anticipating my next question, "I like school. I have friends there."

I was glad. This nice, friendly boy deserved friends.

The conversation turned, as I imagine it always did in farm homes at this time of the year, to harvesting. It appeared that Billy kept up his share of the work. Darren seemed rightly proud of his younger brother.

"Billy, here," Darren gestured with his free hand as he stuffed a bite of sandwich into his mouth and talked around it, "has driven a tractor since he was ten."

As my eyes widened in horror, Darren swallowed quickly and continued, "Dad fixed up a sort of harness with ropes to put on Billy and he can hold it to direct him which way to turn. Don't worry. We're careful."

"I like driving a tractor!" Billy exclaimed. "I can ride a bike, too."

I know my eyes bugged out on that one. I stared at Darren.

"He rides ahead of one of us and we yell directions at him. It works," Darren insisted.

While I attempted to compose myself in the midst of this unusual family, my attention was drawn to Sven's left arm, which hung limp at his side. He ate, drank, and gestured with the opposite limb, while the left one never budged.

Ingrid noticed my stare and ventured an explanation. "Sven lost the use of his arm in a tractor accident ten years ago. He was driving uphill at night during harvesting. That big tractor wheel got stuck in a rut an' the whole contraption tipped right over on top of him."

"Yep," Sven chimed in. "That's why we never farm at night any more. We can't see good enough and we're too tired to think straight." He shook his head. "Sure don't want that kind of an accident to happen to any of my boys. We gotta trust the good

Lord to help us git the crops in on time and not work ourselves frantic day and night. I'm glad I still got my arm, even if it's just hangin' there like a nuisance. I shore look better with two arms." He patted the useless arm with his good one.

"It must be hard for you to work," concern edged my voice.

"Well, my boys here are good helpers." He slapped Billy on the back. Billy grinned at the sign of appreciation. "An' I've cut back on my acreage. As fer me an' my wife, we help each other out. She's got a bad leg and . . . "

"I fell and smashed my knee on a rock when I was younger," Ingrid broke in. "It gives me trouble now and then, but I'm used to it."

"She's got two good arms; I've got two good legs," Sven's eyes lingered tenderly on his wife's face. "She ties my shoelaces, and I run her errands. It works out purty good. The Lord knew what He was doin' when He matched us up!"

It amazed me that these people could be so nonchalant about their handicaps. But there were more surprises to come.

"Want to take my car out for a spin, Billy?" Darren joked. I glared at him. What a cruel way to tease his handicapped brother! Maybe, Darren wasn't as sensitive as I thought he was.

But Billy's eyes glowed at the challenge, and he quipped, "Sure thing! As soon as I get the tractor in the pole barn." I looked from one to another. Nobody appeared concerned. I guess this kind of humor was accepted by the family. Billy was smiling. Maybe it was just another way to show Billy that he wasn't any different, really, from the rest of us. I began to find their "down home" humor appealing.

"William, please clear off the table while I take Cassandra on a tour of the house," Ingrid rose and took my arm.

"Sure thing, Mom," Billy stood up and groped for the dishes. Part of my heart flipped watching him, but I tore my eyes away. Sympathy was not what he needed. Independence and a sense of capability were more important. Sven and Darren strolled outside, on some farm errand, I supposed.

"I hope you don't mind me calling you Cassandra," Ingrid

flashed me a warm smile. "I see Darren calls you 'Cassie.' But I think Cassandra is such a lovely name, and I never did see the sense of bestowin' one name on a person and calling her somethin' else! Take William, fer instance," she led the way into the dining room. "I've always liked the name, William. It's got dignity and substance. But Billy," she shook her head, "Can't fer the life of me get folk to stop callin' him 'Billy'."

" I don't mind at all," I replied. "My mother and grand-mother usually called me Cassandra."

Ingrid nodded, as if to acknowledge the fact that there were still some sensible people left in the world.

"I had a daughter," Ingrid's eyes moistened and she paused a moment. "She died in a car accident two years ago."

I stared at her. Darren had never mentioned a sister.

"Her car was hit by a drunk driver jest a mile from her house. She was comin' home from a ladies' meeting at church. Killed instantly, they said. It's some comfort to me to know that she went to heaven fast.

"Her name was Sunniva. I named her after Saint Sunniva, a princess who lived on the coast of Europe many centuries ago. She was promised in marriage to an evil king. Sunniva wanted to escape from the evil king, so she took her faithful servants and got on a ship. She prayed that God would make the ship land wherev-er He wanted her to go. When she landed on the coast of Norway, she told the local people about Jesus and many of 'em got to be Christians. Later on, the king sent his soldiers lookin' for her and found out where she was livin'. So she ran away an' hid in a cave. But a soldier found her and killed her. That's why they made her a saint."

Ingrid pursed her lips and wiped a tear that had escaped from her eye.

I felt like crying, too, at the sight of Ingrid's grief. I was wondering how to comfort her when she started to speak again.

"I'm so glad that my own dear Sunniva came to know the Lord before she died. Now I will see her again some day."

I felt very uncomfortable. Her talk of God brought back memories and emotions I'd hidden away years earlier, memories of things my mother and grandmother told me. I didn't want to think about those things any more. Ingrid must have noticed my discomfort. She smiled again and changed the subject.

"This is my sea room." Her eyes widened with satisfaction, and I turned mine away from this fascinating woman to gaze with admiration at the exquisitely decorated room in front of me.

"I've always loved the way God decorates His world, and secretly wished," she confided, " that I could live out of doors. But I guess, in Minnesota, I wouldn't get away with that too long!" she chuckled, and the smile lines surrounding her hazel eyes widened. "I especially love the sea." Her vision clouded slightly and she gazed into the distance, as though watching scenes beyond my comprehension. "When I was a little girl, my mama and papa took my sister and me all the way to California to see my aunt and uncle who settled out there. My, but that was a long trip. One day they took us to the ocean. I can still almost feel the water sprayin' on my face when I ran out into the waves. It sort of tingled," she laughed. "My parents were surprised I was so daring. I was such a shy young thing. But the ocean was so big an' powerful an' exciting! I was drawn to it like it was a part of me." She sighed. "I know that sounds silly, comin' from an old woman, like me."

"No, no, not at all. I grew up on a lake." I had never traveled to the ocean. My father had no time or interest in taking me there. It was my turn to laugh now, self-consciously. " I suppose that sounds silly to you, comparing a lake to an ocean!"

"Cassandra," Ingrid's sober gaze met my own and she gently touched my arm. "Our own experiences are always real and important to us. Your lake is as big and exciting to you as the ocean was to me as a child. It's a very special part of your life, I can see." I found understanding in the depth of her eyes.

"Now," her arm swept over the room, " I use lots of blues and greens in my sea room. God must like those colors best. He put them everywhere. Have you ever noticed how many shades of green there are?" She drew me to the window, and stared out in fascination with a little-girl look of wonder in her eyes. "Most people see the grass and trees as just plain green, when God bothered to make so many different kinds of green that look perfect together! 'Course now the leaves are all different colors," she admitted, "but there's enough of the old ones left to see what I mean. And then there's the spruce trees, with their blue green color."

I stared also, realizing that she was right. Darren was right, too. His mother did see things that most of us missed. I made a mental note to observe the various shades and hues of green on the ride home. I turned my attention back to the room. The walls were painted a pale shade of soft foam green. White eyelet curtains trimmed in blues and greens framed the windows. Seashells seemed to be everywhere. On one wall, shells adorned a burlap wall hanging. A mirror over the massive round oak table was framed with more shells. A centerpiece of potpourri and shells sat on top of the cream-colored tablecloth embroidered with blue and green scrolls. I picked up one of the corners to examine it.

"I made it myself," a note of pride attested to the fact. "The stitching is called Hardanger Embroidery, after a place in Norway." The exquisite pattern was composed of fine needlework surrounding tiny holes that were painstakingly cut out of the fabric. With a tone of awe, I exclaimed, "It's beautiful." Admiringly, I ran my fingers over the cloth. Ingrid beamed. "Most young people now-a-days don't appreciate the crafts that have been passed down to us from the past. But I treasure that part of my heritage. I'll be glad to teach you how to do it, if you like."

"Thank you. I just may want to learn someday."

The living room impressed me even more. Ingrid called it the rose room. A dark blue rectangle carpet lavished with rose designs was centered on the hardwood floor. Antique white walls set off the long, navy velour drapes. A Queen Anne style sofa was covered with shades of white and cream-colored roses, interspersed with navy blue and pale pink pin stripes. Two rose easy chairs sat at both sides of a brick fireplace, giving the room a combined look of coziness and elegance. Pictures, vases, and oddly shaped little boxes were painted with an unusual rose design. I picked up one of the boxes, fingering it with care. A beautiful blue and rose design also covered the small miniature trunk.

"Rosemaling is a hobby of mine," this amazing little

woman announced. "It's another art from Norway. You see, here," she pointed to the picture on the box, "all the strokes have floral and scroll designs. The one you're holding is my favorite. It's a free design I made with Valdres strokes. The flowers seem to grow out of the center of the box. The one on that shelf," she pointed to a small square container, "is painted in Rogaland style. See here, it's got the same design on all four sides." She pointed to a large, round plate hanging by the fireplace. "That one is a Telemark style. It's mostly made of scrolls that look like flowers and vines."

"How did you manage to do all this when you had five children to raise and a farm to run?" I couldn't keep a tone of awe out of my voice.

"Oh, I've had lots of years to work at it. When my kids were younger, I didn't have any time for hobbies. But they're mostly grown now, and some of them have left home. I find time here and there, between the housework and the gardenin', and helpin' Sven with his chores. It's only been the last few years I've really enjoyed my hobbies. I thank the good Lord for givin' me clear eyesight and a steady hand."

The downstairs bathroom was the "orchard." It was done primarily in peach and green, with a touch of lavender and pictures of fruit, painted by Ingrid, on the walls and counter.

The last room Ingrid showed me was the family room, or the "sunset room," as she called it. Deep wood paneling lined the walls and a dark brown carpet covered the floor. Comfortable furniture and cushions were in shades of browns, reds, oranges, and yellows.

"God must like brown, too," Ingrid declared. "He sure made lots of it.

"I'd take you up to the bedrooms, Dear, but my old knee is giving me trouble today." She bent over to rub it.

"That's all right."

"The bedrooms are normal lookin'. They don't have themes." Somehow, I wondered if anything Ingrid had her hand in could be normal. I listened as she continued her description. "There are six of them with a long hallway running down the middle. Two of them have a balcony. Some day I intend to move our bedroom down to the family room so I don't have to go up and down those stairs. As it is, most days I just go upstairs to sleep and clean."

"I like your house very much, and your garden outside is beautiful, too."

"I used to have a rose garden when I was young and spry. But it got to be too much work for me and now my knee won't let me keep one up. I mostly plant perennials these days, so there's not much I have to do except weed it. Sometimes, I can get . . ."

Shouts from outside interrupted us. The words were indistinguishable, but sharp blades of fear cut through our peace.

Ingrid and I ran to the kitchen door. "Oh, Lord, have mercy!" Ingrid covered her heart with her hands. "He's gone and done it! Oh, dear Lord," she wailed with anguish. "Don't take my son, too!"

Who's done what? I peered out in time to see Darren's car careening down the hill straight toward the pond, with a frightened, but determined, Billy at the wheel!

Chapter 5

I froze, thunderstruck, as I watched Darren's blind brother steer the runaway vehicle straight toward the pond.

"Lord Jesus," Ingrid implored, clutching my arm and lifting her eyes to the heavens. "Send your holy angels to help him!"

Listening to her desperate pleas made me want to pray! But I knew God wouldn't listen to me after I'd pushed Him out of my life all these years. That is, if there was actually a god to push.

Brutus barked furiously as he dashed back and forth from the front of the careening car to the rear. Sven emerged from the barn, shouting something we couldn't make out over the roar of the motor.

Darren had nearly reached the car and, with a look of steel in his eyes and a set jaw, lunged for the handle of the driver's door. At the last minute, he slipped on the wet grass, still soggy from a rain that morning, and landed flat on his stomach. Billy jerked the wheel and steered erratically from left to right, evidently confused by noises on all sides. Darren was up now, but I knew he'd never make it to the car before it hit the icy pond.

Suddenly, a ferocious howl erupted from Brutus' mouth as he dashed directly into the path of the oncoming car. The beast heroically stood his ground, barking wildly. In a split second, Billy swerved sharply to the left, barely missing the dog, and brought the car to an abrupt stop with the right front tire imbedded in the shallow end of the pond. He was thrown against the steering wheel and slumped to the floor. Sven caught up to Darren and they reached the car at the same time. Ingrid and I were spurred into action. She clung to my arm as we tried to race down the hill, her injured leg hindering our speed.

When we reached the car, the men were leaning over Billy. His eyes were open. A mixture of unbelief and shock on his face melted into embarrassment.

"Are ya all right, son?" Sven stretched his good arm around his son's shoulders as the boy's entire frame began to tremble.

"Ya, sure, Dad," Billy's voice was feeble. "I'm okay . . . now. Brutus saved my life! He stood there, right in front of me, so I had to turn the car."

"Never thought I'd thank God for that mangy mutt," Ingrid puffed, slightly out of breath from the excitement and the dash down the lawn. She looked at Brutus, who was panting heavily, then turned to Sven. "Should we take William to the doctor?"

"Naw," Sven drawled, "I guess he just got shook up a bit. Nothin' seems to be broke." Then, a bit sterner as he stared into the boy's face. "Ya ain't gonna try that again, are ya, my boy?"

Billy shook his head slowly. "I guess I sorta figured I could do anything I wanted to do, just like everybody else, ya know?" His empty eyes pleaded for understanding.

Tears filled my own eyes as I heard Darren's choked voice respond, "Well, you did, Billy. You did drive."

Billy's face broke into a big grin. "I did, didn't I?

Ingrid showed me her flower garden while the men worked feverishly to haul the car out of the pond before darkness. She sent me home with a fresh bouquet of burgundy mums and golden asters. I was invited to supper, but suddenly remembered Papa would be home soon and would expect a meal waiting for him. In all the confusion and excitement, it had totally slipped my mind. I thanked her and asked for a rain check.

The ride home was tense. My nervous stomach anticipated the rude welcome I would likely receive when Papa returned home from a long day at work to find an empty house and a bare table.

Darren was apologetic. "I'm sorry it took us so long to get the car out, but we couldn't leave it there any longer."

"It's all right," I brushed a lock of hair away from my face as casually as I brushed aside his apologies. "It wasn't your fault."

He looked puzzled. "What's wrong, Cassie?"

When I failed to respond, he sighed. "You don't like my family. I hardly blame you, after Billy's escapade with . . ."

"No, no, Darren," I quickly silenced him. "I love your family. They're wonderful people. It's just that . . . well, my father . . ." My voice trailed off.

"What about your father?"

"He told me to make supper tonight and it's already quarter to seven."

"You mean he'll get mad at you? But you can explain . . ."

"Papa's never taken much stock in explanations," I murmured ruefully.

Darren set his mouth in a grim line. "I'll explain. And I'll help you make supper."

We continued to drive in silence. I wondered how Papa would react to our story of a blind boy driving a car into the pond. Somehow, I didn't think his opinion of Darren's family would be elevated.

"He's home," my heart thudded in my chest as we turned into the driveway and saw the lights shining through the kitchen window. Darren watched me solemnly as I hurried out of the car, ran to the doorstep, and stood in the cold darkness while I fumbled for my house key.

Methodically, he followed and stood behind me as the door suddenly flew open from inside, silhouetting Papa's forbidding frame against the interior light. His sullen spirit saturated the room, absorbing any remnants of normalcy like a sponge soaking up water. Something was sputtering on the stove and I caught the spicy odor of canned beef-vegetable soup simmering on a burner.

"I'm sorry, Papa," I tried to force my voice to sound cheerful. Instead, it came out sounding hollow and squeaky.

"It's my fault, sir." Darren spoke up behind me. "I took her to our farm to meet my folks and we had some car problems."

In my tense condition, an uninvited giggle threatened to pop out of my mouth and I tightened my lips firmly. Car problems, indeed! True enough, though!

Papa's eyebrows arched as his dark penetrating eyes darted quickly from Darren's face to mine and back again. He ignored our explanation and, taking a deep breath, straightened his back and said, "I was compelled to open a can of soup and grill a cheese sandwich for my dinner." He emphasized the word "dinner." The look of disgust he aimed at the stove turned to me when the persistent giggle escaped. "My daughter," he directed his complaint to Darren, "seems to feel that it's more important to go gallivanting about the countryside than it is to stay at home and cook a hearty meal for her hard-working father." The smell of bread burning caused him to spin on his heels and head back to the stove. He turned off the burner and scooped the sandwich onto a plate.

"Mr. Dupont," Darren cleared his throat.

Papa's sharp, cascading voice cut him off. "Because . . ." he paused for effect and ladled the steaming soup into a bowl. ". . . because Cassie failed to assume her responsibilities, she will not be permitted to see you for two weeks."

Darren's mouth opened, but I nudged him. "It's okay, Darren. Please go. Now." Fearing that Papa's punishment would only grow more severe if Darren protested, I sent him a pleading look. Darren's eyes showed only disbelief as Papa leaned both hands on the table and glared at him.

Darren stared back but evidentially decided that this was not the right moment for confrontation. He turned and lifted my chin. "You all right, Cassie?" The concern in his voice drove tears to my eyes, but I blinked them back. Unable to speak, I nodded.

"I'll call you in two weeks," he glanced at the clock above the sink. "At 6:07." His parting glare, leveled at my father, was a combination of contempt and resignation, intermingled with a heavy dose of determination. He turned and left, closing the door softly.

"Go to your room, Cassie." Papa ordered. "When I am finished eating, you may fix your own supper and clean up the kitchen. I will spend the evening in my study." It was clear that I was dismissed from his presence for the rest of the night.

Upstairs in my room, I lay on my stomach on the bed, elbows propping up my chin, and gazed out the window at my lake. The silver luster of the moon sent shimmering slivers of light onto the glassy surface below. Tiny rows of cabin lights lined the edge of the lake, reflecting above it and just as clearly, below the surface.

Conflicting thoughts of differences between Darren's family and mine, the contrast between his father and mine, flooded my mind. I'd always assumed Papa was like other kids' fathers. I'd never been allowed to spend much time at the homes of other children, so I'd had little exposure to other types of families. I also realized suddenly how little time I'd spent around men. My Uncle Edward, Papa's older brother from Chicago, came to visit occasionally, but he didn't stay long. His relationship with Papa was strained, and it seemed like his visits were more of a duty than a pleasure. I wondered often about my father's childhood. He didn't speak of it much, and neither had my mother. I sometimes wondered if Mama even knew much about her husband's former life.

Darren told me his dad was unique. I recalled how patient he had been with Billy over the car incident. He was firm, but understanding. Like he cared and didn't want to hurt Billy any more. I shuddered to imagine how my own father would have handled that situation. Here I was, grounded for two weeks because I didn't make supper. Papa wouldn't even listen to an explanation!

My thoughts rambled. Of course Billy was blind. Maybe parents were gentler with blind kids. They must feel sorry for them. I knew I would. Maybe Sven had been harder on Darren. I decided to ask Darren more about his dad when I saw him again. I rolled over, clasping my hands beneath my head, and stared at the ceiling. There was so much love in Darren's house. It reminded me of the nearly tangible love that surrounded me when I was with Grandma. Now that I had a car, I often stopped to see her on my way home from school. Our renewed relationship was a source of joy and encouragement to me.

Of course, my father loved me. He must. He just had a different way of showing it. He was gone a lot. Most nights, I just took care of myself. He was often gone on weekends, too. It was part of his job, though he never talked about what he did, and I quit asking a long time ago. He didn't see any reason to share his world with me.

My eyes were starting to burn again. It had been a long time since I'd had a good cry. Something that had happened today must have begun to thaw out my frozen emotions. I'd never before questioned my relationship with my father. It just was; that's all. I could function the way things were. Loneliness was not completely unacceptable. Emotions were snuffed out at the gate of my mind before they had a chance to take root in the fertile soil and develop into full-grown feelings that could affect my life. The tears faded away before they reached my eyelids. I went downstairs, made myself a tuna sandwich, and ate it at the kitchen table, alone. Then I took a bath and went to bed early.

The following day matched my mood perfectly, gray and dismal. The sky out of my window was full of dark, puffy clouds that looked like they were ready to break into tears. Thick waves topped with foam tossed around the few premature chunks of ice that had formed during the night. I lay curled up under my covers wishing I could stay there for the rest of my life. What a life! Every time something good happened to me, Papa seemed to find some way to sabotage it. Darren and his family were good to me. Is that why he wanted to keep me away from them? Was he jealous? Was he afraid that I would grow closer to them than to him? Probably not. I just didn't think he cared that much at all.

Since today was Saturday, I rolled over, determined to go

back to sleep. But the smell of fresh pancakes drifted up to my nose. *Papa was making pancakes?* He usually slept in on the few weekends he spent at home, and then expected me to cook a brunch for the two of us. Surprised, I hurried out of bed, grabbed my blue fuzzy robe, and started down the stairs. There he was, standing at the stove, flipping hot cakes. He was dressed in casual clothes and had his sleeves rolled up. He turned when I appeared in the door-way.

"Well, Cassie, I thought this would get you out of bed." Papa scooped a few cakes onto a plate and set it on the table. "Get the silverware and cups," he ordered. Stunned, I hastened to obey. "Do you want eggs?"

I shook my head. "No, thanks." He broke a couple for himself into the pan and they sizzled. I finished setting the table and sat down to wait for him. He poured two cups of black coffee, turned the eggs over for a minute and dished them onto his plate.

"Pass the syrup, Cass." I stared as I handed it to him. "Well, don't just sit there. Dig in."

I cleared my throat. "Thanks for fixing breakfast, Papa."

"You didn't think I could do it?"

"No, no I mean, I appreciate it."

He grunted as he stuffed a forkful into his mouth. We ate in silence. When he had finished, he leaned back in his chair, wrapped his large hand around the stoneware mug, and observed me. I felt like a bug under a microscope.

"You're growing up, Cassie."

I nodded. That obviously didn't need a reply.

"I'm concerned about your future." He sighed and contin-ued. "I know you expect to marry one day and . . ." He put up his hand to stop me as I started to interrupt. "Let me finish. I have dreams for you, daughter." Any term of endearment was unusual coming from him. I shifted in my chair and started to wish I'd stayed in bed. He went on, "Darren is a nice boy. I even like him. He has some good qualities. He's honest. He's got a strong will and determination. He appears to be a hard worker. But he is not ambitious. He will never amount to more than a farmer. He's not for you, Cassie. You are an intelligent, beautiful young woman who is capable of marrying beyond her class. You've got the potential to attract a wealthy, properly educated man."

"Well, at least I know now what the pancakes were for," I thought to myself. *"He's trying to sweeten my emotions with thicker syrup than he put on his pancakes!"* I tried to stay calm. "I like Darren. I like his family. And I'm not ready to even think about marriage yet. I just want to have a friend and have some fun."

He shook his head. "You don't realize, Cassie, that the longer you date this boy, the more likely you'll end up staying with him. I know how that goes. Next year, you'll be going away to college and he will, most likely, stay on his dad's farm. You can get a degree and amount to something. I'll send you to a school where you'll meet men from the right circles. I know some families that send their kids to Hamline and Carlton in the cities. The sooner you break it off with Darren, the better off you'll be. Now this two-week period of being separated from him will provide a good opportunity . . ."

"No. No. No." My emotional temperature rose as I stood up, and I could feel my face turning red. I hated the fact that my fair complexion caused me to blush easily, but I could no more stop it than stop rotten apples from falling from the trees. The words to convince Papa eluded me, but at least he would know that I disagreed strongly with his plans! I fought back tears that threatened to drown any rational arguments I could use. My thoughts were tangled, but I took a deep breath and dived in anyway. "I don't care about money. I'm not going to marry for wealth or position or status or anything like that. Not ever! I just want to be loved, Papa. Can't you understand?"

His voice, firm and controlled, began to rise. "You are so innocent, Cassie. You don't know what life is all about. You turn your nose up at money. Do you know why?" He was standing now and shaking his finger at me. "Because you've always had money. You take it for granted. You've had all your needs provided. Everything you've asked for, I've given you." His form loomed over me now and he stabbed his finger into his chest for emphasis. "Me, me, me! I've been your provider, Cassandra. And I've been a good one! How dare you take my money for granted?

How dare you take me for granted!"

He backed me up against the wall and raised his hand as though to strike me. I flinched as his dark eyes penetrated like knives. Papa had never struck me, but all my self-protective instincts were activated in that moment. I froze, like a frightened animal cornered by an adversary. I held my breath. Slowly, he lowered his arm. "Sorry, Cassie, I guess I got carried away." I had never before seen my father go over the edge of control and I was shaken. He stalked over to the table and poured himself another cup of coffee. "Do you want some more?" He glanced at me politely as though nothing unusual had occurred.

I sank into the nearest chair and cradled my head on the table. My arms shook as tension drained out of my body. *What was wrong with my father? Why was he acting this way? Was he afraid of losing me?* Though released from immediate danger, I still felt trapped. Helpless.

His voice was quiet. He sounded tired and suddenly, old. "You don't know what life is about." He turned his gaze to the window as if viewing a scene from the past. "I've never spoken much about my family. There just wasn't much to say. My parents came from France around the turn of the century. My brother, Edward, was born soon after. Papa was poor. He kept getting ideas about how to make it rich. One scheme after another failed. He never succeeded at any of them. Mama would take in laundry and sewing just to buy groceries when he was recovering from the demise of one of his great plans. My bother, Edward, when he was here a few months ago told me that Papa left my mother for a year to go out east and start a trading business with an acquaintance from New York. Of course, it didn't pan out and he returned, hanging his head like a whipped puppy. He was finally ready to give up his schemes and take on a steady job. He found employment at a local grocery store and stayed there the rest of his life."

Papa had never opened up to me like this before and I was anxious to discover whatever I could about my grandparents. I leaned forward to catch every word as his voice faded.

"Edward told me . . . " his voice caught briefly. He took a deep breath and forced power into his words. "Edward told me that when Papa returned home after that year away, he discovered that Mama was pregnant. There was no chance he was the father. The baby that was born six months later was me."

I gasped. "Oh, no, Papa."

"My father was a hard man. He gave in to his failure. Edward was the favored one; he was the only real son. Me, I was unwanted garbage. Papa told me over and over that I was no good and would never amount to anything. More than anything in life, I wanted to show him he was wrong. I never knew why he hated me until last summer." He glanced at me. "Remember Edward's visit?"

I nodded. I had sensed tension between them. But Edward had never been a pleasant man, so I didn't realize how traumatic the experience was for Papa.

Papa chuckled. "Edward told me the 'news' in order to prevent me from protesting Papa's will. Papa died last June."

I was stunned. The grandfather I had never known died that summer and Papa didn't even see fit to share the news with me. I knew his mother was dead when he married Mama and I had assumed my grandpa died earlier as well because my parents never talked about him.

"My father left everything to Edward. It wasn't much, but he had managed to put together a small nest egg. As another legal son, I would have a right to contest the will. But Edward took it upon himself to enlighten me as to my proper standing in the family." A low chuckle again escaped his lips. "Why would I protest? I don't need his money. I've got more cash in my back pocket than he had in his whole life!" A smirk broke over his face. "Actually, I was relieved to hear the truth. Finally, I know why Papa hated me." Again, he was lost in a distant scene.

I fumbled for words. In spite of the antagonism he had showed toward me earlier, I wanted to bring him back to me. For a few brief moments, he had let down his guard and invited me into his life. Even a bitter taste of closeness was like a bite of candy to me. I clutched at it hungrily, afraid to lose him to his private world again.

"I'm sorry, Papa. I understand." I reached out my heart to

pull him back, my eyes silently pleading. *Please, Papa, I need you.*

But his return to normalcy included the ever-present grasp for control. "I'll leave the decision up to you, Cassie, but if you refuse to take my advice, you'll be sorry. Love is a fragile commodity, one day here and the next day blown away with the wind. Money is a solid base on which to structure your future."

He got up and left the room, leaving me alone to ponder his words.

"When I am afraid,
I will put my trust in Thee."

Psalm 56:3

Chapter 6

The first snowstorm of the winter always made me long for Christmas. It was late this year. We'd had flurries on and off since October, but the Thanksgiving holiday had come and gone with no major snowfall.

Now, in the latter part of November, my world was turning into a frosty wonderland. I'd reveled in winter's special fairyland beauty since I was old enough to put my snowsuit on all by myself and drag my sled out to the big hill across the road from our house. I'd heard other people complain endlessly about the heavy snow, slippery roads, and the constant anxiety of knowing unexpected bad weather could force the cancellation of a planned event. Winter weather in Minnesota was able to override the best of men's intentions! But I didn't have to face the job of shoveling our long driveway. My father always hired someone to take care of it. And the only planned event for me was school. I certainly didn't mind having that canceled!

In fact, this was one of those days. On Sunday, the weather forecaster announced that we would have a "brief period of light snow." Two days later with fifteen more inches of snow tossed around by a twenty mile per hour wind, he finally admitted we had a blizzard on our hands. But now, at midday, the snow stopped falling and the wind died down, after littering the roadways with drifts.

Blizzards always scared me. Harsh winds, at times up to forty-five miles an hour, created snow pellets that beat against my face. Wind chill factors could even drop to minus eighty degrees, so anyone without proper covering on their face could freeze their skin in a matter of minutes. Visibility made driving extremely hazardous, often causing cars to veer off the roadways into ditches. Even walking outside could be dangerous. Old Fred Johnson, who lived a few miles from us, froze to death in the parking lot of a large grocery store in Lakeland during the last blizzard. He'd gotten out of his car and evidently couldn't see well enough to find his way to the store. Papa told me that in the olden days farmers used to tie ropes from the barns to the house so they could hold onto them when they needed to go to the barn to feed the animals. When they were unable to see either the house or the barn, they could find their way by following the ropes.

After lunch, I curled up on the window seat in our living room and gazed at the snow-encrusted lake. It seemed to stretch forever beyond the delicate patterns that Jack Frost had made on our windowpanes. The whole world seemed chiseled out of an immense chunk of ice. Plows had just finished clearing the heavy snow from the roads and hurled it along the sides, where it was packed as high as six feet in places. Every object was coated with a layer of white film. Fences and mailboxes were sculptures, precisely carved by the hand of an unknown artist. The sun's rays caused sparkling snowflakes to cling tightly to the barren limbs of trees, transforming the scene into a winter fairyland.

Papa managed to get to his office that morning after the first plow came through. He'd called to tell me he wouldn't be home until late. So I decided to ask Darren if he could come over for a while. Though I usually gave in to Papa, I had surprised both of us with my stubborn refusal to stop dating Darren. Papa finally said he didn't want to deal with the issue any more and was sure

I'd eventually "come to my senses." As the weeks passed, Papa got used to the situation, but still didn't like to have Darren around. Since Papa was working late that day, I called Darren and asked him to come over and give me a snowmobile ride. He came within half an hour and we bundled up in our snowsuits. Darren's was black with a wide orange stripe running up the sides. The green one I wore had once belonged to his mother, who had given up the sport when she turned sixty. "Why should I go to all that trouble to break my neck when I could do it just as easy fallin' down the stairs?" she'd insisted. I can still see her shaking her head with exasperation as she pressed the suit upon me. "Now, you take it and have fun, honey. I never cared much for whippin' about in the cold anyway like a jackrabbit being chased by a swarm of bees. My old bones can't take the cold any more." The corners of my mouth lifted slightly, recalling the incident.

Our snowmobile ride was invigorating, and the chilly air tired us out. We were happy to come back to a warm, cozy house and rest. Now I glanced over at Darren, who had fallen asleep on the sofa, where he'd stretched out after downing a cup of cocoa I'd made him. His thick hair was plastered against his head from wearing his ski mask. Darren had insisted we wear heavy knit caps that covered our heads, leaving only holes for our eyes and nose. I protested, but gave in when he laughingly suggested we stop in town and rob a bank. He said we might as well put our disguises to good use! I told him nothing could hide his broad shoulders and everyone would recognize his nose. It was slightly crooked from having a baseball smash into it when he was a kid. Darren had laughed, tweaked my nose, and lightly kissed the top of it. I took another sip from my mug and wrapped my hands around it in an effort to warm up. Darren stirred and opened his eyes. A slow smile lit up his face and he reached out his hand to me. I set my mug on the end table and curled up on the floor next to him, wrapping my hands around my knees and laying my head back onto his chest. Darren's fingers gently twirled my hair.

"How do you celebrate Christmas, Cassie?" His voice intoned softly.

"We don't do much for Christmas anymore," I sighed, as

distant memories cropped up in my mind. "When Mama was living, we had special celebrations. Grandma would come over on
Christmas Eve after her church service. She always invited us to
come with her, but Papa said 'no.' So we'd have a late dinner
together. Mama made juicy pineapple ham with mashed potatoes
and creamy milk gravy. And tiny green peas that I would stir into
my pool of gravy like they were swimming in a potato pond. She
made my favorite strawberry salad with heaps of whipped cream.
For dessert, we had four cookies. We each asked for our favorite.
Mine were Russian teacakes. They looked like little snow balls
covered with powdered sugar, and melted in my mouth." I paused
as memories sprang into a clear focus in my mind.

"What did you do after dinner?" Darren coaxed me.

"Then we decorated our tree. Papa wouldn't let us put it
up early. He said he didn't want to have to look at it every day.
Christmas was foolishness, according to him."

"I'm sorry, Cassie."

I tossed my hair back and smiled at him. "It's okay.
Really. Christmas was special for me, anyway. It was so much
fun when Grandma was there. We draped the strings of lights all
around the tree and hung the round glass ornaments, all different
colors, red, blue, green, silver. And when it was finished, Papa lifted me up so I could put the angel on top. She's a special angel.
First she belonged to Grandma, then Mama, and now me. Her face
is porcelain and her golden hair feels like silk. She wears a long,
flowing white dress that has gold braiding at the waist and all
around the bottom.

"Mama played Christmas carols on the grand piano and
Grandma and I sang. Papa didn't often join us, but he'd sit in the
chair with the big arms and watch Mama as she played." I gazed
at the arm of the sofa, and traced the flowered pattern with my finger. "I felt a little jealous. I wanted him to look at me, but I was
really happier when he looked at Mama." I turned my head to
catch Darren's eye. "Does that make sense to you?"

"Uh huh. What about your presents? You had presents,
didn't you?" The sudden look of concern in his eyes made me
laugh.

"Yes, we opened our gifts on Christmas morning. I got lots of presents and I played with them all day. Mama often went to bed with a headache and Papa usually found some excuse to go to the office, so Christmas Day usually belonged to Grandma and me."

"What do you do now?" His voice was still edged with concern. "Christmas is always a big deal for my family."

I shrugged my shoulders and pulled an afghan off the sofa to wrap around me. "Now it doesn't amount to much. Papa won't have a tree since Mama's gone. Grandma doesn't visit any more, but I'm allowed to go to her house on Christmas Eve. She takes me to church and we have a candlelight dinner, just the two of us. She tries to make it special, but it's just . . ." I searched for the right word, "different, you know?"

"What does your father do?"

I sighed. "He's always invited to parties with other doctors who work at the hospital in Lakeland. I don't think he enjoys them, but he says it's good for business. He usually doesn't stay late. He picks me up at Grandma's house on the way home. I get some presents when I wake up in the morning, and then it's all over."

Twilight was beginning to upstage the sun as I turned my gaze back to the picture window. Darren would need to go home soon and do chores. He'd explained to me that cows don't have much patience when it's milking time. He pulled himself up and stretched. "Cassie, I want you to spend this Christmas Eve with us. I know it's early, but Mom said to invite you and she won't take 'no' for an answer." He reached his arms around me and gave a gentle squeeze. "We'll treat you to an old-fashioned Norwegian Christmas at the Larson house with lefse and lutefisk and potato sausage and yulekake and krumkake." He licked his lips "See, my mouth is watering just thinking about it."

"Oh no, Darren. I don't think Papa would want me to celebrate with your family."

"But he won't be with you anyway! What difference would it make?"

I shook my head. "No, Darren, I can't. Grandma would

miss me."

He turned away and started to put on his snowmobile suit. "You can go to church with your grandma and I'll pick you up afterwards." He paused and caught my eye. "Or your grandma could come, too. There'll be plenty of food."

"No, Darren," my voice sounded sharp and panicky. I didn't know why. Maybe it was the thought of sharing the holiday with a real family, a big family that loved each other. Afterwards, I'd have to go back to my small family, where love was . . . I couldn't complete the sentence, even to myself.

The pleading in my eyes reflected the hurt in his. He didn't understand. And I couldn't explain.

"Okay, Cassie." His desire to make me happy couldn't dissolve the barrier that suddenly sprang up between us. He yanked the zipper on his suit and turned to go.

"Darren, I . . ." I hesitated. He turned around and looked at me with expectation.

"We're so different, Darren. Our backgrounds." I took a deep breath. "I still want to see you. I just don't belong with . . . a family."

"Sure, Cassie." His tone was blunt, but not uncaring. "I'll pick you up Friday for the show."

I nodded. He left. I pressed my forehead against the door and began to cry.

Chapter 7

That Christmas Eve was like something out of a storybook. Grandma and I walked the few blocks to her home after the candlelight service in her little white church. I imagined I was stepping back in time to simpler days when life was placid and less stressful. People didn't hurry to and fro in panic, but took each day as it came without having a need to figure out some vast, universal plan. Gentle flurries of white flakes drifted down from the pasty gray sky, adding layers of soft snow to the picturesque landscape. The Christmas atmosphere filled the twilight scene before me. Quaint store fronts exhibited displays of evergreen wreaths tied with lavish red bows. Bundles of holly and mistletoe adorned the black iron lampposts that lined our path.

Grandma was quiet as we strolled side by side. She always seemed to know when I needed to think. My thoughts rambled like a river rushing downstream. Christmas was like a big magnifying glass held up to people's hearts. It exposed all the emotions and turmoil that were raging inside. Fears were enlarged so they couldn't be buried down deep and ignored any more. Lonely people grew lonelier, forced to confront their aloneness against a background image of the hustle and bustle of happy family gatherings. *Where did I fit in?* Most of the time, I was contented, or at least thought I was. Financially, I had no worries. Papa made plenty of money and could afford to give me a good college education. After college, I would move out of the house and support myself. My father was hard to live with, but we got along most of the time. And now I had Darren.

Still, a restlessness pricked at the edge of my soul, threatening to tear away the fragile strips of confidence encasing it.

The pastor's sermon hadn't helped. He said the spirit of Christmas should go on forever. I didn't go for that "let Jesus into your heart" stuff. It was all too mystical for me. Papa may be harsh, but he was intelligent and wise to the world and its ways. But Grandma was smart, too, and she had an almost tangible sensation of peace, an emotion I seldom saw in my father. Grandma loved life and treasured her days, while my father attacked each day like it was a force to conquer. He seemed to be winning, but maybe it was too early to tell. Grandma used to tell me about Jesus, but she stopped years ago when Papa threatened to keep me away from her if she continued to try to "brainwash" me with mystical nonsense. He didn't seem to mind that I went to church with her at Christmas and Easter. I suppose he thought a little bit of religion now and then wouldn't hurt me. It was just a part of the seasonal celebration. Grandma reminded me every now and then that she was praying for me. That was okay. I reasoned that if there really was a god, it wouldn't hurt. It might even do me some good.

Our steps hastened as we turned down the sidewalk to Grandma's house. The twilight dusk was accompanied by a chilly wind. I was suddenly anxious to get indoors and warm myself by her massive brick fireplace. Grandma shivered a bit as she unlocked the door and stepped inside. "Time to get the fire going, Cassie," she said, "Then we'll have a cup of hot apple cider." The fragrant scent of cinnamon drifted in from the kitchen, where she had left a kettle simmering on the stove while we were at church. It mingled with the tantalizing aroma of roast beef in the oven and the fresh pine of the Christmas tree in her living room.

"Can I help with something, Grandma?" I breathed deeply of the delicious scents as I hung my coat in the closet.

I entered the living room to find Grandma kneeling by the fireplace, stoking a tiny flame. With her patient coaxing, it would soon burn brightly and cheer up the dark room. "No, Cassandra. Tonight, you're my special guest. The table is set. Everything is almost ready." Flames suddenly shot up. The wood began to crackle and hiss as firelight started to jump and dance among the sweet-smelling cedar logs.

The fire's glow accentuated the sheen in my grandma's silver hair, tied back in a classic french twist. She had worn it that way as long as I could remember. When I stayed overnight as a child she would let it down every evening and allow me to brush it exactly one hundred strokes with the ornate silver hairbrush Grandpa gave her on her fiftieth birthday. He gave her a whole set, a comb, brush, and mirror. She displayed it on a crocheted doily on top of her dressing table. Often I had sat in front of her dressing table, brushing my short hair and pretending I was a princess.

She glanced at me and smiled. Her smile crinkles and laugh lines shone in the firelight. "Well, I guess you could pour us some cider. I've set the tea cups by the cider pot."

I walked into the homey kitchen, made cheerful in shades of lemon yellow and green. Frilly lace curtains adorned the windows that overlooked a small yard framed by snow-laden branches. I poured the rich liquid and brought Grandma a cup. Sitting myself comfortably on the rug by the hearth, I joined her to soak in some warmth after the cold walk home.

Grandma smiled her "you are special to me smile" that I loved. "I'm glad you decided to join me tonight, Cassandra."

I reached out my hand and touched her arm. "Grandma, I can't imagine spending Christmas without you. I've always been with you."

She reached over to stoke the coals. "I thought maybe this year you'd want to spend it with Darren's family."

"Oh," I stirred my cider with a stick of cinnamon. "He invited me, but I don't belong in a big family and . . ." I looked up at her. "I would never let you spend Christmas alone, Grandma. It means so much to you."

Grandma's gaze lingered on my face. She seemed to be studying something far away. "What does Christmas mean to you, Cassandra?" She gently pried into my thoughts with a tenderness that made me want to let her inside.

I shrugged. "I guess it's . . . presents," I laughed, a bit self-consciously, "and good food, and special times with you."

Grandma pursed her lips together like she was trying to keep them shut. It didn't work. "What do you think of Jesus?"

My eyes dropped again. My father would think she was treading on dangerous ground, but her questions didn't bother me tonight. Maybe it was the joy of the season and the story we heard at church about the baby Jesus and love entering the world. Still, I knew Grandma valued honesty. I met her eyes.

"I don't want to hurt your feelings, Grandma, but I agree with Papa. Jesus is a nice fantasy for people to hold onto if they have a hard life. I suppose it gives them something to hope for. But I'm content with reality and I want to make something of my life. I don't need stories and superstitions." Grandma's eyes were teary, but her face smiled. She patted my hand. "Forgive me for intruding, Cassandra. I had to ask."

I felt like I should say something nice, but the ringing of the telephone interrupted my thoughts.

"Now who would be calling on Christmas Eve?" Grandma rose and hurried to answer it.

"Hello. Merry Christmas to you, too, Darren. Yes, she's here. Cassie . . ." She held out the phone to me.

I set my cup on the mantel and took the receiver. "Hi, Darren."

"Merry Christmas, Cassie." His voice was soft and tender.

I couldn't help but smile. "Merry Christmas, Darren."

"Cassie, um, I suppose I shouldn't have bothered you at your grandma's house, but, you see . . ."

"What is it, Darren?"

"Well," a slight pause and an intake of breath, "my mom made a present for you and I forgot to tell her you weren't coming and she's disappointed, and . . ."

"Darren, I told you . . ." He couldn't do this to me. Not tonight. I was comfortable with Grandma. This was where I belonged.

Silence on the other end.

I tried another tactic. "Dinner is almost ready. Grandma's been working all day."

"No, no, Cassie, I don't mean now. Go ahead and enjoy your dinner with your grandma. But eat light. We're having dinner at 8:30 because my aunt and her family are driving from the airport in the cities. They flew out this afternoon from Pennsylvania.

"Can I pick you up at eight? Please, Cassie?"

I sighed. Excitement vibrated from his voice like from an eager child. "Okay, Darren."

"Good. See you then. Good-bye."

"Good-bye."

*"Oh, the depth of the riches
both of the wisdom and knowledge of God!
How unsearchable are His judgments
and unfathomable His ways!"*

Romans 11:33

Chapter 8

The wind picked up speed and started to howl as Darren and I arrived at the farm. Snow flakes that landed gently in flurries a few hours earlier had turned into harsh pebbles that beat at my face. Brutus wandered briefly from his doghouse to give us a quick, moist greeting and hastily returned to his cozy shelter. Darren took my arm and we hurried up the dimly lit path to the welcoming farmhouse, which gleamed brightly with an assortment of candles and lanterns at each window. Lights from the Christmas tree shone through the big picture window in the living room.

Ingrid swung the door open and held it for us. "Merry Christmas!" Her face shone like the candles at the windows. "Come on in! My, that wind is starting to sound fierce. How are the roads?"

Darren brushed the snow off his coat and shivered. "Snow's starting to drift in. I had a little trouble at the corner by Holstads. It won't be passable in a few hours." He grinned at me. "You may be here for the night, Cassie."

"I wouldn't mind." Already I was starting to absorb the

holiday mood that seemed to emanate from the walls of this peaceful place. I wasn't concerned about staying over. In Minnesota, we were used to quick changes of plans matching quick changes of weather that the unruly climate threw at us. If I couldn't make it home, Papa probably wouldn't get there either. I had called to tell him I'd be at Darren's farm and, since he was in the middle of a party, he didn't make any objections. Maybe now, with the weather getting worse, he'd just stay over at a motel in Lakeland.

Cousins of all ages clustered around us, trying to get a glimpse of Darren's new girlfriend, I supposed. The kitchen smelled as good as Grandma's, if not better. Darren had offered to bring her along, but Grandma said she'd had a full day and would just curl up by the fire and read for a while.

Sven's giant smile appeared out of the crowd and he whisked our coats away. Someone placed a foamy mug of eggnog in my hands. We all drifted into the kitchen, where activity around the table appeared to be increasing. Ingrid began assigning names to faces that popped up everywhere.

"That's Hannah and Trine, Samuel and Sunniva's girls. Remember, Sunniva is my daughter who died two years ago. That's Samuel, with their little boys, Lars and Erik. And there, over in the corner, are Reidar, Olav and Karl." She pointed to three lanky teen-agers. "They belong to my sister, Juron. She was widowed ten years ago. She's done a good job raising her boys. They all turned out good. And this is our little Jonathan."

A boy of about four stared up at me with curiosity and questioned with mischief written all over his face, "Are you gonna marry Darren?"

Everybody laughed as my face turned red as holly berries. Two generous arms reached down and swept Jonathan away.

Ingrid continued, "You know Jonathan's father, Seth." Of course I did! He was my boss at the drive-in who introduced me, officially, to Darren. She gestured to the large man hanging on tightly to his wiggling son. "This is Seth's wife, Constance. And their darling little girl is Ingeborg Elizabeth." The child was adorable, with blue eyes and pudgy rosy cheeks. Her pale blond hair was tied with bright red ribbons that matched her velvet dress.

Seth and Connie (as everyone but Ingrid called her) nodded to me. I tried to smile at each face, but knew it would take awhile to connect them with the proper names.

"You also know Luke. This here is his wife, Deborah." As expected, Ingrid didn't refer to anyone by their nicknames. I was sure I'd learn a few as the evening wore on. I expected Deborah to be called "Debbie" by the others. "And the little dark-haired sweetheart is Katrina," Ingrid continued. "Her baby sister, Beatta, is sleeping in the bedroom.

"Out, out, all of you children," Ingrid waved her arms and shooed the kids into the living room to inspect the tree adorned with ornaments and hemmed in on all sides by presents.

After a few last minute preparations, Darren and I were ushered to the dining room table. "Here, you two sit down. Come on and find your places, everybody. We can be a little overwhelming, Cassandra, until you get used to us." Somehow, amid all the commotion, they all managed to seat themselves, as if by habit. The grown-ups were at the big dining room table, younger kids in the kitchen, and the teens at a card table in the living room.

After a booming prayer by Sven, an array of platters heaping with delicious food made their way around the table. Darren was right about the Norwegian specialties. I loved the lefse, a thin soft round bread made of mashed potatoes, flour, and butter, spread with butter and sugar or jam. The meatballs and potato sausage were tasty, and the fruit soup was wonderful. A special raisin bread, yulekake, flavored with cardamom, was a real treat. I was enjoying the meal when Sven set a bowl of slimy whitish gray fish in front of me and doused it with melted butter. "I make the lutefisk every Christmas Eve," he stated proudly. He stood back and beamed, evidently pleased to share his culinary delight with me.

I hesitated. Fish wasn't my favorite food anyway and this specimen looked particularly unappetizing.

"Dad makes the best lutefisk in these parts." Darren winked a challenge at me. Sven stood even straighter and his smile widened.

Ingrid leaned close to me and whispered, "Go ahead and taste it, Cassandra, but don't worry about finishing it. I never do.

Every year I try a bit, just to please Sven, but I'm no closer to enjoying it than when I was a new bride." Sven's face fell slightly.

I sighed with relief and dug my fork into the waiting morsel. I sensed the group around the table holding their breath to see my reaction. Unfortunately, the fish tasted as bad as it looked. Or rather, it didn't actually have a taste of its own, just a slimy texture. I swallowed quickly and turned to Sven. "I just finished dinner at my grandma's house. I'm not real hungry any more, but thank you for letting me try some." A few snickers and glances of admiration raced around the table.

Sven shook his head, picked up the dish and started to gobble up the rest of my serving. "No matter. I get more to eat this way." He winked at me.

After protesting the addition of more food, I was inclined to skip the desserts. But it was impossible. Ingrid had made a bountiful assortment of Christmas goodies. I especially enjoyed the traditional Norwegian delicacies. Krumkake, a thin, flaky crepe-like pastry in the shape of a cone, was my favorite. The light, deep fried rosette cookies sprinkled with powdered sugar were also fabulous. Those two desserts were the only ones I could squeeze into my expanding stomach. But Ingrid assured me she had made plenty of treats so we could nibble later in the evening.

"Grandma, can we start our program?" Luke's four-year-old daughter, Katrina, ran to the doorway. Her body halted but her feet kept jumping and dancing. The children had finished eating some time ago and were anxiously waiting for the festivities to begin.

"Just as soon as dishes are finished, honey." Women rose from their chairs, so I got up, too, and began helping to clear the table.

Half an hour later, we all gathered in the living room, which seemed about to burst at the seams, overflowing with bodies and the emotions of the night. I was semi-squished on the sofa, between Billy and his dad. Out of the corner of my eye, I noticed Darren and his mom whispering by the doorway. I caught a few segments of their conversation.

"Aw, Mom," Darren protested with a sheepish expression. "Not tonight."

"Darren," Ingrid's face was sober. "You must." When he still hesitated, she ordered firmly, "Now."

Darren groaned and put his hand to his head, as if in agony.

I'd never seen Darren refuse his mother before. *What could be so critical and distressing to disturb our celebration?*

Darren's voice reached me again. " . . . will she think?" His mother patted his arm and spoke into his ear. Darren seemed to come to a decision. He straightened his shoulders and approached me. "I need to run an errand," he muttered nervously. "Be back soon."

I opened my mouth to ask for more information, but Katrina hopped into my lap, her feet swinging as she twirled a dark braid around her fingers. "I get to be a lamb tonight!" She beamed at me. Darren disappeared.

A brief moment of worry clouded my mind. *What about the roads? What was so important that Ingrid would send her son out in a raging blizzard? And what did it have to do with me?*

Ingrid was announcing the program, for my benefit. "Every Christmas Eve, the grandchildren act out the Christmas story while the rest of us read some scripture verses. Would you help us out, Cassandra?"

I nodded. At least, it would keep my mind occupied so I wouldn't worry about Darren.

"Good. Would you please run upstairs and get my Bible? It's on the top of the bookcase, first room on the left, lying by my journals." I quickly climbed the stairs to find a lengthy, dimly lit hallway with six doors that opened to bedrooms and a bathroom. The quiet was such a sudden change from the commotion downstairs that I instinctively started to tip toe.

The first bedroom on the left was serene and quaint. A four-post oak bed with a massive headboard stood against a wall in the center of the room. On it was a handmade quilt of roses on a light blue background. An antique dressing table on the opposite wall stood against blue and white striped wallpaper. Rag rugs in various sizes adorned the polished hardwood floor. A comfortable chair stood by a small table in the corner.

I walked to the bookcase by the bed to get Ingrid's Bible. A pile of notebooks stacked on the edge appeared to be journals. Some were plain with loose-leaf binders, some with spiral bands, and a few had rich tapestry covers. I ran my hands over the pile. What a collection of memories and thoughts they must contain. I picked up the Bible and saw that it was lying on top of another notebook, with a red velvet marker protruding from it. *Dare I peek?* The temptation was strong. Faded sounds drifted up the stairs to the still and quiet room. Without making a conscious decision, my hand reached out and touched the book. It fell open to the last entry.

"December 24, 1973. My whole family will be together tonight. All my chicks will be in the nest. I can't wait to celebrate the gift of your precious Son to this mixed up, crazy world, Father God! How could You bear to let Jesus out of heaven? One minute, all the angels were adoring Him, like He deserved. The next instant he was crying in a rough and dirty manger bed warmed by the breath of smelly animals. You sent your only Son into this troubled world so I can send my sons to a perfect world one day. Thank you so much, dear Father God. Please keep all my children and grandchildren safe in Jesus' arms so we can all eat at the grand feast in Heaven with you.

"Oh, and Lord, Cassandra is going to be with us tonight. She doesn't know you yet and neither does Darren. He's so stubborn and independent, just like his father used to be. Maybe Cassandra will be open to Your goodness. She's so sweet. I love her already and want her to be happy. Show yourself to her, Jesus, please."

Tears stung my eyelids. I didn't understand Ingrid's god, but I knew she had a good heart, a heart that overflowed with enough love to share with a lonely young girl. My father told me only weak people needed a god or religion. I supposed he was right, but neither Grandma nor Ingrid seemed weak. And they both had a beautiful spirit.

"Cassie, you up there?" Sven's voice boomed and I was suddenly aware that I had spent way too much time in their bedroom. It must be obvious that I had been snooping! *Would Ingrid realize what I'd done?* If she knew, she would probably change her mind about me being so "sweet!" Hastily, I closed the journal and put it away, grabbed the Bible, and headed for the stairs.

A sudden thought hit me. *Why had Ingrid asked me to go get her Bible? Did she deliberately send me upstairs for her Bible, knowing it was lying on top of her journal? Did she want me to discover and read it? Read what she said about me?* My heart was thumping when I handed her the Bible. Ingrid looked deep into my eyes, then reached out and drew me close for a hug. *"She knows,"* I thought to myself, *"she knows I read her journal and she doesn't mind!"* Ingrid let me go and smiled once more. "Have a seat, Cassandra. The program's about to begin." The adults had seated themselves on the sofa and chairs around the glowing fireplace. As I joined them, thoughts of Darren pushed their way back into my mind. I began to worry. *Where had he gone? What was he doing?*

A scrawny, pig-tailed angel, wrapped in a white sheet and sprinkled liberally with silver tinsel strings from the tree, entered the room. Poised on her tiptoes, she lisped, "Hark! I bring you all glad tidings. Jethuth the thavior ith born tonight in the town of Bethlehem!"

In spite of my concerns, I thoroughly enjoyed the simple pageant. It progressed quite smoothly, except for the part where the shepherd dropped his staff on the angel's head. And we all laughed when two-year-old Beatta tried to crawl into the manger and cuddle with the doll who was playing the part of baby Jesus. In the interests of quality theatrics, Ingrid quickly hefted her granddaughter up on her lap and gave her a candy cane to suck. The adults read the narrative of the Chistmas story aloud while the children acted it out. My assigned scripture was about the wise men who were warned in a dream not to return to King Herod, but instead to go home another way.

We burst into applause as the wise men picked up their gifts, the manger and doll and left the room, with the white angel sheet that had caught on the corner of the manger trailing behind. Connie, or 'Constance,' as Ingrid called her, seated herself at the piano and began to play a lively rendition of "Joy to the World, the Lord is Come." The rest of the group soon joined her. Deep, throaty voices blended with soft, melodious and squeaky ones in familiar Christmas carols.

The peaceful scene was suddenly interrupted by the slamming of the back door.

"Ho! Ho! Ho!" A strong, masculine voice reached our ears. The spell was broken.

"Santa Claus!" Shouts of surprise and welcome filled the air as a chubby red-garbed body appeared in the doorway. A knitted red stocking cap with a white puff on the top sat on a bountiful head of glossy white hair. Almost hidden behind a long flowing beard were two familiar blue eyes. The pillows in his "belly" shook with each repeated "Ho! Ho! Ho!" and the "ruddy-looking" cheeks were actually a deep tone of red, flushed with embarrassment, no doubt.

"Darren!" The words popped out of my mouth and I clasped a hand over my lips in a delayed effort to prevent myself from spoiling the effect. My exclamation wasn't heard, however, above all the racket and clamor as excited kids stumbled over each other trying to reach the surprise visitor. If I had shouted his name, no one would have heard me! Santa carefully avoided my eyes as he waddled to the fireplace. I suppressed a giggle. *This must be the secret mission he and his mom were talking about earlier!* He must have gone to the barn to change clothes. I suppose he protested because he was afraid of what I would think. I thought he looked kind of cute and couldn't wait until I could tell him so later in the evening.

The younger children pressed against Darren, begging for goodies from his sack. Trying to appear nonchalant, the teens held back, but were studiously eyeing the heavy black bag slung over his shoulder. Beatta slid off Ingrid's lap in hopes of collecting more candy canes.

"You have to sit down if you want a treat." Santa's slight Norwegian accent gave him away. I could tell most of the kids weren't fooled, but the little one's eyes were wild with wonder.

"Why didn't you come down the chimney, Santa?"

Jonathan pointed his chubby finger at the blazing flame.

Santa leaned close to him. "It's awfully hot in there, son. Would you want all the chocolates to melt?"

"No, I guess not." Jonathan solemnly shook his head. The grown-ups made all the kids sit down and the surprise guest handed them an assortment of candy canes, chocolate Santas, packages of gum, and bags of peanuts. When the bag was empty, Santa turned it upside down and shook it. "See you all next year!" He headed for the door and yelled one last "Ho! Ho! Ho! A Merry Christmas to all and to all a good night!" Darren gave his padded belly one more hearty pat. As he did so, a pillow tumbled out and bounced on the floor.

"Santa's tummy fell out!" Jonathan yelled in anguish as Katrina's horrified shrieks filled the air. Darren quickly scooped up the wayward pillow and, with a look of alarm on his face, made a hasty exit.

Hours later, after the kids had been comforted and sent to bed, Darren and I sat alone in the living room, watching the dying embers in the fireplace and relishing it's final rays of warmth. The rest of the adults and teens either retired for the night or were finishing off the remainder of cookies and bars in the kitchen. I had called Papa, who drove home through the drifts, to tell him I'd been invited to spend the night because of stormy conditions. He hadn't protested. I don't think he relished the idea of driving through more snow to get me, or letting Darren drive me home in the inclement weather. He insisted on coming to get me first thing in the morning.

I rested my head against the sofa. The evening had been good. It had taken over two hours to open all the gifts. Each one was opened in turn so everyone could rave about the gift, and the receiver could properly express his thanks. Ingrid's gift to me was a hand made ivory dresser scarf delicately embroidered in the Hardanger geometric pattern I had so admired the first time I visited the farm. Darren gave me a pair of dangling gold earrings. I told him I had a gift for him at home that I would give him later. I hadn't taken it with me to Grandma's house since I didn't expect to see him that night. My gift was a black pair of leather gloves that I was sure he would like. The ones he wore were starting to get holes in them.

Darren stretched and rested his arm around my shoulders.

"So, what did you think of Santa Claus?" His mouth looked a bit grim and he gazed straight ahead.

I burst out laughing. "I thought he looked adorable."

Shifting his head slightly, his eyes sought my face.

"Really?"

"Uh huh."

"I sure felt stupid."

"I know."

"I told Mom I'd do it before I knew you were coming. She wouldn't let me back out." He shook his head. "You know Mom."

"Your mother's a dear, and you're a dear to do it for the kids." I leaned over and kissed his cheek.

Darren's face brightened. "That's good. I feel better now."

"I love your family, Darren. All of them."

"Cassie, I've been wanting to ask you something." He looked uncomfortable again. "Does all this religious stuff bother you? I mean, I know how your father feels about it, and I don't think you . . ."

"No, my Grandma's religious, too. She talks about it sometimes, but she's not pushy."

Darren winced.

"Oh, I didn't mean your parents are pushy, Darren. They're just more open about . . . everything." He nodded and replied, "I figure, if they need God, it doesn't hurt them. My mom got religious after Billy was born. I was just a little kid. My dad didn't believe in God 'til after he hurt his arm." He shrugged. "I guess they needed some faith to get them through tough times. They're happy now. It's okay for them.

"But for me, I want to run my own life. I can handle it. I don't need anybody telling me what to do. I want to live any way I choose, as long as I don't hurt anybody else."

"That's about the way I feel, too, Darren. Papa taught me to be independent and think for myself. But I don't think religion has hurt my grandma any, or your family. They're nice people." I paused and heard the next words come softly out of my mouth, "You're lucky to have them."

"Cassie," Ingrid poked her head in the door. "I'll show you up to your room now. You're sharing a bed with Hannah. I hope you don't mind."

"Of course not." I arose as Ingrid began turning out lights and tired people climbed the stairs.

Turning back to Darren, I spoke softly, "This has been a special Christmas."

He glowed. "For me too, Cassie."

"For I hope in Thee,
O Lord;
Thou wilt answer,
O Lord my God."

Psalm 38:15

Chapter 9

The table looked festive. On the way home from school, I stopped at the grocery store to pick up a couple of steaks and saw a display of fragrant red roses. Impulsively, I purchased a bouquet to use as my centerpiece in a beautiful crystal vase. The antique vase had been given to my parents from Grandma Lydia.

I loved having fresh flowers in the middle of winter. It seemed the best way to defy the drab season's power over my life. Winter's dramatic black and white portrait was refreshing when it first appeared, but by January, I was color-starved and craved a foretaste of spring.

I dug out Mama's green lace tablecloth from the bottom drawer of our mahogany hutch and ironed it. The cloth hadn't been used since Mama died. Imported Bavarian china with a design of dainty roses entwined with delicate green leaves completed the setting.

I'd been wondering all day how to break my news to Papa when the idea of a special dinner formed in my mind. We didn't usually eat a fancy meal unless it was a holiday. Mama used to prepare one on the rare occasions when Papa agreed to have company. When she was in an energetic mood, she made a vivacious hostess. Since we seldom had company, those memories stand out in my mind like an oasis in a desert land.

I remembered Mama spending all day in the kitchen baking fancy cookies or chocolate eclairs for her dinner parties. She allowed me to help and I always got to lick the bowls. Her entrée was usually chicken cordon bleu or stuffed pork shops with rings of spiced apples she canned herself. Her popovers were my favorites. I'd open one and lather it with butter that melted quickly along with a teaspoon of honey. It was gooey and made my fingers sticky, but I loved it.

Since Mama died, Papa and I had to get used to my haphazard style of cooking, edible and satisfying, but miles away from gourmet! It was Papa's job to put food in the house, and mine to put it on the table. Neither of us expected more than that.

I stepped back to examine the table. Everything was in order. Papa would be home any minute now. Baked potatoes were wrapped in foil, and dishes of butter and sour cream were set at our places. I'd tossed a huge lettuce salad with green peppers, mushrooms, and tomatoes. Papa was a meat and potatoes man, usually famished when he arrived home after a day's work. I wondered if he still missed Mama. They'd been married nineteen years when she died.

A roaring fire burned in the large brick fireplace. The room looked welcoming and cozy. Mama's grand piano stood proud and stately in the corner. Papa had the piano shipped all the way from Chicago. He wouldn't let me take lessons. He didn't like to hear the piano played by anyone except Mama. But sometimes in the evening when Papa was away, I'd sit and play it. I played mostly by ear, but had picked up some knowledge about the keyboard in music classes at school. So I was able to teach myself simple tunes from Mama's books. Grandma told me that I had music inside of me just like Mama.

I didn't ever hope to play piano as well as Mama did. She had studied at the Juilliard Institute of Music in New York and was pursuing a concert career when she met Papa. Mama told me how they met. She said Papa was a struggling intern, barely surviving financially and nearly overwhelmed by fatigue caused by long hours and heavy studies.

A friend had given him tickets to a series of concerts held in Chicago. The first one was advertised as featuring a promising young woman, Amanda Hartell, in her first solo performance. Papa was enamored with Mama's beauty as well as her talent. Old pictures portray her as demure and delicate. She wore her hair in an array of curls piled on top of her head. Her clothes were elegant. Her father, Grandpa John Hartell, was a ship builder in Duluth. When he died from a heart attack in his forties, he left Grandma Lydia with a small fortune. Most of it went to provide the best education to help Mama develop her talents. Grandma expected Mama to have a fine career, but Papa talked her into settling down with him instead. Though poor when he married Mama, he told her that, in five years, he would buy her a grand piano. He kept his promise. Mama told me once that she had never regretted exchanging her career as a musician for that of a mother. But the far away look in her eyes made me wonder what kind of a life she would have had without my father.

Papa was a hard man. Neither of my parents talked much about his early life. I wondered if Mama even knew much about his past. Papa's father and older brother, Edward, had lived in Chicago. Edward was the only relative who ever came to see Papa. He had never married and only visited us a couple of times. Once, Papa went to Chicago to see Edward. He didn't mention whether or not he visited his father. After Mama died, I stopped asking questions.

Looking back with the understanding of maturity, I realize that Papa demanded absolute control over Mama's daily schedule, her choice of clothes, her associations. His high expectations and critical mindset worked havoc with her sensitive nature and desire for approval. Gentle Mama lacked the inner fortitude to stand up for herself. Drip by drip, Papa drained the life out of her so that my reflections portray her as a woman resigned to her fate. She had given up on life. Still, I know that she deeply loved me because, even in her depression, she forced herself out of bed each day to care for me. I wish I had known her when she was young and spirited, like the woman Grandma Lydia described to me.

My emotional make-up was so different than Mama's. Papa exercised considerable control over my activities, but I determined after Mama died never to give him my mind and emotions, like she had done. Yet, in spite of my resolve, at times I desperately longed to please him. An aching vacuum in my heart cried out every day for a parent's unconditional love. I found it impossible to relinquish the tiny speck of hope that, one day, that kind of acceptance would be mine. Papa and I clashed frequently. Yet sooner or later he had to realize I wasn't just a shadow of him, like Mama. Tonight, he'd be forced to recognize that I was becoming a person with a unique identity.

My face flushed with excitement as I lit the candles. My good news could be the catalyst to foster a stable bond between my father and me. He would have to see that I was a grown-up woman with ambitions equal to his own.

I heard a key turning in the lock. With a rapidly beating heart, I hurried to greet my father. A gust of frigid wind accompanied him when the door opened. Papa shut it quickly and removed his heavy, gray overcoat and scarf.

"I'll hang your coat up for you, Papa." I took his wraps and hung them in the closet. He rubbed his cold hands together while his eyes scanned the room.

"What's this, Cassie? Are we expecting visitors?" I detected a faint note of disapproval in his voice.

"No, Papa. See, only two places. We're celebrating tonight."

A slow smile lifted the corners of his mouth and he walked to the table. "What's the occasion?"

"First we eat. Then I'll explain. Sit down. I'll get the steaks." I hurried to the kitchen to check on them. They were perfect, juicy and medium well, just the way Papa liked them. I put one on each plate and set the cloverleaf rolls on the table.

Papa tasted a hearty chunk of meat. "Good, Cassandra. You got it just right."

His praise warmed me. I dug into my salad.

"You going out with Darren tonight?" he inquired abruptly.

"Yes, Papa. He's coming for me at eight. We're going to a show."

In time, Papa had formed a respectful tolerance of Darren and voiced no more objections to my seeing him. We'd dated nearly every weekend since fall. Papa was getting used to having him around. We finished our meal in silence.

"Is there dessert?" Papa asked.

"Just a minute." I retrieved two glass goblets of chocolate parfait from the refrigerator and poured him a cup of coffee.

Papa took a spoonful. "So, what's the surprise?"

I set down my spoon carefully and, with my elbows on the table, locked my fingers together under my chin and smiled. "You know I've applied at several colleges."

"Yes, yes," Papa waved my words aside. "What'll it be? Concordia? Hamline?" Both private colleges were located in the cities. He didn't know I had applied to one other school.

I paused briefly to let my words sink in. My eyes twinkled. "I've been accepted at the University of Minnesota and plan to major in pre-med. I'm going to be a doctor, Papa, just like you." I waited with eager anticipation. My mouth was dry, but I still expected his eyes to light up like they did when I was a little girl handing him a straight A report card. It didn't happen. Papa leaned back and pushed his chair away from the table.

A slight chuckle escaped his lips and he shook his head. "Cassie, Cassie, when will you give up these idealistic dreams of yours? It takes brains to become a doctor. And hard work, long hours, discipline. Now if you want to become a nurse . . ."

He looked up in surprise when I shoved my chair back so hard it crashed onto the floor. I stood up trembling. "I have brains, Papa. I'm at the head of my class. I intend to be valedictorian at my graduation ceremony." My body was stiff, immobile.

"Calm down, Cassandra. You're smart. But you're only graduating in a class of eighty-eight. Where would you rate in a class of five hundred? Or six hundred? Lots of misguided kids go through pre-med education, but only a few are actually accepted at medical school.

"You could be a secretary or fashion designer or . . ."

"Papa," I took a deep breath and fought to compose myself. I had to make him understand. "I want to make a difference in the world. I want to help people. I want to make people well, like you do, Papa. I want . . ."

"Do you think that's why I'm in the medical profession?" He was on his feet now and nearly bellowing. "To *help* people? You *are* naïve, Cassie! That's a real world out there. A hard, concrete world. You need money to make it work and power to get what you want. Doctors make money, lots of it, and they have prestige, status, in the community." He slammed his fist down on the table and I jumped. "It's my job to heal the sick. I do my job. I get paid. I get money. I get power."

A sudden wave of awareness crested in my brain. *Why hadn't I seen it before?* "Is that why you're not happy, Papa? Because you're only in this for yourself, for what you can get?"

"I had to look out for myself. Nobody else would!" He paced angrily back and forth. "How can a small town doctor be satisfied? I wanted to work in a big medical complex, to be a surgeon. I could have done it. I was qualified." He stopped and glared at me. "But I was passed over. The opportunities went to students from wealthy families who had influence with the system. My father was blue collar. I was passed up by men that weren't half as skilled as me. They got the best scholarships and landed the top medical positions. I had to settle for second best, general practitioner, with no chance of anything better, ever."

I was silent. He stood by the window and smoothed his hand over the back of his head. I saw his shoulders slump for the first time in my life.

He continued, softer now. I strained to hear him. "When Amanda's mother found this job for me . . ."

"Grandma got you this job?"

"Yes, Cassie. It was the only offer I received at the time. It was either that or use my medical degree to pump gas." He gave a cynical grunt. "I took it. I had to feed you and your mother. In the back of my mind, I always hoped something better would come along." He stared into space.

"Is that why you hate Grandma? You blame her for losing your chances?"

Papa turned to face me. His voice was flat, and his arms hung limp at his sides. "I'm a big fish in a small pond. But I could have been a big fish in a bigger pond." He shrugged. "I'm a loser, Cassie. A failure."

The empty look in his eyes touched my heart. This broken man was, after all, my father. I had no understanding of the hurt that had caused the dismal reality of frustration he lived with. At least, now I could understand where the bitterness came from, along with his cynical outlook on life. Yet he had faithfully pushed himself beyond his own misery all these years to provide for me, to give me a home. Yes, he was a hard man, but maybe his experiences made him that way. I was growing up. I needed to look past the crusty exterior my father showed to the world, and touch the damaged core of his heart.

I went to him and reached out my arms. "I'm here for you, Papa." A fierce light suddenly blazed in his eyes. His stature stiffened and he backed away. "I don't need your pity." He almost spat the words out. "And you don't need mine. Face it, Cassandra, face reality. It's a tough world out there. You'll never make it as a doctor. You don't have what it takes."

I yanked my coat out of the closet and ran from the house, his final words paraphrased and ringing in my ears. *"You're not good enough, Cassandra. You're not good enough."*

I don't remember driving to Darren's house. Somehow I got there, in spite of my emotional turmoil and the heavy snowfall that was piling in peaked drifts along the road.

Darren answered the door and immediately read the misery on my face. "Let's get in the car, Cassie." He grabbed a jacket, yelled a good-bye to his parents, and took my hand. We didn't go to the theater. He seemed to know I needed to talk and cry. Instead, we drove out to a small isolated inlet on the other side of Lake Clarity where he parked the car. Wind outside our cozy vehicle howled and visibility was low. The vast, ice-encased lake looked formidable and treacherous. Even the woods appeared to be a mere vapor in the dusky twilight. We left the motor on for a while to keep the heater going. Darren held me until the tears stopped flowing, then gently prided the details out of me.

I felt physically sick. I was so certain that I could please Papa in this one area of my life. I had actually expected him to be proud of me. My heart had even melted at the realization of the hurt and injustice he had suffered. And yet, Papa had thrown my love away. My last feeble hopes for genuine love and acceptance were dashed to pieces and ground underneath his heel.

We sat for a long time with Darren holding me close. The wind finally died down and darkness settled in comfortably for the long night. He brushed my cheek tenderly with his rough hand. Rough from years of honest manual labor. "Cassie, I respect you. You've had a tough life, and I respect the way you've handled everything."

I still don't fully understand my feelings that night. I guess at that moment Darren's respect seemed as cold an emotion as my father's rejection. I was so tired of cold. I wanted warmth, tenderness, affection. Emotions long buried within me suddenly burst to the surface and I blurted out, "I don't want respect. I want love." I clung to him, passion rising inside of me. I could feel Darren trembling.

"Are you sure, Cassie?" he whispered.

I kissed him fervently and he embraced me.

Chapter 10

"I didn't know I could get pregnant the first time I did it, Liz Beth." My sobbing had stopped long enough for me to place a phone call to my best friend in Minneapolis. Almost two months had passed since that fateful night when despair led me to give in to my physical desire for love and affection. I had to talk to somebody and I wasn't ready to tell Darren.

"I didn't either, Cassie." Her voice expressed amazement. "Are you sure you're pregnant?"

"Uh huh. I skipped school today and drove fifty miles to a clinic Papa doesn't work with to get tested."

"You haven't told your father?"

"Are you crazy, Liz? I can't tell him. I don't know what to do." My voice was laced with panic. "That's why I called you."

"Okay, Cassie. I'll help." A brief pause. "Have you told Darren?"

"I haven't told anybody except you."

"He'll marry you, Cassie. He loves you."

"I don't know, Liz. He's awfully independent."

"But you can't have a baby if you're not married!"

"I know. I've been thinking about that a lot. Last year there was a girl in the senior class who got pregnant. She graduated, but she looked awfully big when she walked across the stage to get her diploma.

"It must have been so embarrassing. Everybody was talking about her. She left town right after graduation. Nobody knows what happened to her."

Another slight pause. "Are you feeling sick?"

"Just in the mornings. It's good Papa leaves for work early so he's not here when I'm throwing up. I couldn't hide it from him if he was home."

"Cassie, did you know you can get rid of it if you're not too far along?"

"I know," I choked on the words. "I've heard about that."

"A girl in my class had an abortion last month. I could ask her about it and set something up for you. Darren could bring you down here for a weekend. He could stay at Kirk's house." Kirk was a friend of Darren's whose family had a cottage on the lake, too.

I nodded, oblivious to the fact that Liz Beth couldn't see my response. Switchblades of fear clashed with swords of desperation in my mind. I wondered which one would win the battle.

"I'll talk to her and you talk to Darren. Even if he wants to marry you, Cassie, this might be better. You want to go to college."

"I know. I'm already enrolled for fall quarter at the University. Papa 's not pleased, but so far I'm being stubborn."

"The abortion will be expensive."

"I've got money. You want to know what the worst thing is? Darren and I . . ." a lump caught in my throat. "Darren and I had decided not to do it any more. We both felt kind of dirty, like it was wrong. We were going to save it for marriage. With each other, or whomever. And now this happens."

"I'm sorry, Cassie. But it'll work out okay. You'll see."

"Bye Liz Beth."

"Bye Cassie. I'll call you soon."

"Thanks."

There was a downpour the next night that I went out with Darren. We'd had an unusual amount of rain lately, even for the beginning of April. It took me a couple of days to work up the nerve to tell him about my pregnancy. I'd called him after school and asked him to take me out so we could talk. Darren went to high school in Lakeland, so we usually didn't see each other during the week. Once I'd made up my mind to tell him, I wanted to get it over with. Papa objected to me going out on school nights, but he'd been called out to deliver a baby, so I was sure I'd beat him home. If not, I'd deal with him later. My talk with Darren couldn't be put off any longer.

Darren was in a carefree mood when he picked me up. He was catching raindrops on his tongue and making up silly poems about the rain. I couldn't match his mood, so I just kept silent.

We shared my umbrella as we dashed from the car into the small country café. It was a hangout for teens on weekends, decorated with movie posters and pictures of Elvis. Pop melodies blared out of the jukebox and drifted to every corner of the room. Little round tables draped with bright red and white checkered tablecloths lined the sides, surrounded by white wrought iron chairs. Each table had its own window that looked out on a woodsy area. Sometimes you could catch a glimpse of a fox or deer between the trees.

The place was quiet tonight and nearly deserted, but I asked for a corner table anyway so we would have privacy. Darren's mood began to settle. He must have finally realized I had something heavy on my mind.

A giggly sophomore waited on us. She ignored me and flirted with Darren. He was nice to her, but brisk. He ordered a hot fudge sundae and tried to talk me into having one, too. I refused. A soda was all my queasy stomach would handle. The butterflies that were flying around in there now turned into canaries that beat their wings against my stomach walls trying to get out. I hadn't thrown up yet in the evenings, and I surely didn't want to start now.

A few sips of the soda helped a little. My heart was pounding, my hands were clammy, and I just wanted to get this talk over with and go home to bed. Darren's eyes were calm now and fastened on me. "I know something's bothering you, Cassie. Tell me about it."

I didn't know how to start. I didn't want to start. I wished I hadn't come. I wanted to go home to bed and sleep. Just sleep forever. No more problems. No more worries. No more life. It was too hard.

"Cassie." He spoke softly and reached out to cover my trembling hand with his firm one. "You can tell me anything."

I opened my mouth but nothing came out. Looking down at the table, I swallowed hard and tried again. "I'm pregnant." *Too low. Too soft.*

Darren leaned towards me across the table. "What, Cassie?"

My eyes darted around the room. No one was close by. I tried again a little louder. "I'm pregnant."

Darren froze. "No, Cassie. You can't be." He wasn't angry. He just couldn't believe it.

My stomach started to settle down. At least, I'd gotten the words out. "I'm sure, Darren. I took a test Monday."

"But how could . . . I mean . . ." He released my hand, leaned back, and stared blankly into space. He looked like he was in shock. I sat and waited. He needed time to absorb the reality. Then he looked at me like I was some kind of contraption he'd never laid eyes on before. I could see thoughts racing across his eyes.

I giggled nervously, the tension inside me broken.

"Are you well, Cassie? Are you feeling okay?"

"Except in the mornings."

"Oh. Does your dad know?"

I shook my head. "Nobody but Liz Beth."

"You told her before you told me?" He was hurt, offended.

"I needed advice, Darren. She knows about . . . things." I dropped my eyes.

He sighed heavily and wiped his mouth with the back of his hand. Then he folded his hands together and looked at me again. "You want me to marry you."

Very calm. Matter-of-fact. Not at all the way I'd envisioned a proposal. *I would be reclining on a flowery sofa with my suitor on his knees before me. My beloved would clasp my hand and gaze enraptured into my eyes. I could almost hear the soft romantic music playing in the background.*

The canaries had left. Now my stomach felt empty. All of me felt empty. My mouth was dry. "I don't know, Darren."

He regained his poise. "Cassie, I care a lot about you. But I don't know if I love you. To me, marriage is for life. I want us to be sure."

I nodded. Tears were stinging my eyes. I squeezed them back.

"Did Liz suggest anything?" he asked.

"Yes," I whispered.

"Tell me what she said."

"She said some girls have an abortion. She could set me up." Part of me was trying to be practical, like Darren. The other part was dying inside.

Darren decided to reason with me. "You want to go to college, Cassie. You're looking at many more years of school."

"I know."

"Dad is pushing me to go to college, too. Seth and Luke have good jobs. I always expected to take over the farm. But now Dad is getting worried that small farms aren't going to make it in the future. So he's trying to talk me into something else. You know my dream has always been to farm. But now I don't know if it's going to work out. I don't know what I'm going to do. I can't support you. And . . . a kid."

I nodded again, unable to speak. Darren's dreams seemed to be turning into vapor, too.

"Maybe we'll get married someday, Cassie. But if we do, I don't ever want you to wonder why I married you. I'd want you to know it was for love, not because we had to get married."

"I understand, Darren." My voice was controlled.

"I'll help you all I can."

"I want to go home now."

The next day, Lake Charity was smooth in the middle and tiny ripples sought a path to the shore. Clouds blocked out the sunlight, engulfing me in deep shadows thrown from high bedrock walls beside me. I sat alone on my thinking rock, the same one I had come to the day before Mama died. I had come here often during the years, but had never had so serious a problem to think about, so crucial a decision to make.

Now for the first time in a week, I had slept well. I suppose telling Darren released part of the pressure in spite of the outcome of our conversation. I don't know if I really wanted to marry him. I certainly didn't feel ready for marriage. But his response had tasted like rejection.

A particle of hope had already pushed its way into my dreams. *I imagined a cozy cottage, by a lake, of course, with a vast field on the other side of our house for Darren to plow or sow or whatever farmers do. Rows of purple irises and yellow tulips lined a winding stone pathway to the door. Inside, the three of us, Darren, me and little Johnnie or Annie, snuggled together on the blue and white striped provincial davenport telling stories.*

I sighed. It was good Darren was practical. I might not have been. I reminded myself that I had plans to become a doctor. A family doctor. I was smart and determined. Even if Papa didn't believe in me, I believed in myself. *I would be the kind of a doctor my father wasn't. I would be involved with my patients' lives, care for them, help them any way I could.*

The deepest secret part of my heart knew there was a human life growing inside of me, but I wouldn't let my heart communicate with my brain. My brain was determined to be logical, to follow Darren's lead, to evaluate the circumstances, to reason. *Maybe I could have the baby and put it up for adoption. But then I'd have to face my father. I couldn't bear the thought. All the neighbors would talk. My friends might stay by me. They might not. Liz Beth probably would. Darren, I wasn't sure of any more. Grandma Lydia would never turn against me. But, oh, how disap-*

pointed she would be! No, adoption was out.

The sun peeked out from behind the dismal clouds, trying to send rays of hope into my dreary day. But clouds kept rolling over and over the sun and wouldn't let it loose.

Suppose I had the baby and kept it. Papa would never accept that. Single women didn't raise babies in those days. My grandma was getting too old to care for it. None of my friends were married. I had no close relatives to help me. Keeping the baby was out of the question.

What was left? It appeared the awful way out was looking more acceptable, even advantageous. Only Liz Beth and Darren would ever know. I could trust them not to tell. Darren and I could go on as before. I could have more babies when I got married. I'd graduate from high school and go on to college as planned. Three options were fighting for supremacy in my mind when I awoke that morning, adoption, raising it myself, or getting rid of it. Now it appeared I only had one option left.

It's a baby. It's a baby. My heart tried frantically to reach my brain, to make an urgent appeal for Truth. But my mind pushed the words back before they had a chance to register, to be imprinted in any section of my conscious thought process. They sank feebly into the realms of my subconscious.

The sun gave up and buried itself behind the clouds.

April 8th dawned bright and sunny, a vivid contrast to the turmoil raging in my soul. Darren was going to pick me up at 10:00 a.m. Papa gave him permission to drive me to Liz Beth's house for her birthday slumber party. Actually, her birthday was in May, but we didn't expect Papa to remember. He didn't. Darren would stay with his friend, Kirk, and take me home Sunday evening.

Papa was cheerful that morning. "Have a good time, Cassie," he called as I went out the door. "Be prudent!"

"Okay, Papa. Bye!" I choked on the words. *If only he knew where I was going and what I planned to do.* But he didn't, and I wasn't going to tell him. In a few hours, it would all be over and my life would be back to normal.

It's amazing how un-normal life can be on a perfectly normal looking day. Darren and I should have been going on a picnic,
with a wicker basket stuffed with fried chicken, potato salad, and
brownies.

It was a quiet ride. We were talked out. Small talk didn't
fit the occasion, so we mostly listened to the radio.

My appointment was for 1:00 p.m. Liz Beth had given
Darren directions to the clinic and to her house, where he would
bring me when it was over. Her parents were away for the weekend and she had no brothers or sisters, so she said I could make
myself at home and rest as much as I wanted.

I was nervous, but tried to concentrate on my future goals
and dreams. Darren appeared calm, but seemed easily distracted
and forgetful. His neck was rigid and his arms stiff when he drove.
Surprisingly, the two hour drive went fast. We located the place
and went on to a small café a few blocks away for lunch. Darren
ate burgers and fries, but I'd been told not to eat before the surgery.
Not that I had an appetite anyway. My insides felt like they were
trapped in a vise. My mind was made up, but my body was protesting.

Darren finished eating and we drove back to the small
office building. It looked old and run down. Paint was chipping
off and the door squeaked as we entered. A lady dressed in a crisp
white lab coat sat at a desk in the sparsely furnished office. I
breathed a sigh of relief. The inside looked clean and bright, a
sharp contrast to the outside of the building. The walls were painted pastel pink. *"For baby girls,"* I thought fleetingly.

She looked up as we entered. "Your name?" Her pen was
poised over a black book on her desk.

"Mary Kimble." Liz Beth had given her a phony name.

The woman checked it off and closed the book. "The payment, please." She held out her hand. I gave her an envelope filled
with cash. She quickly riffled through it and seemed satisfied. She
stood and leveled firm eyes at Darren over the tops of her glasses.
"You," she commanded, "will wait here." She motioned to a couple of wooden chairs in the corner by a square table stacked with
magazines. "Come with me, Mary." She turned and headed for a

door on the opposite side of the room.

Startled, I hesitated. I wasn't used to responding to the name of Mary. I hoped she had not noticed. But she bustled on, expecting me to follow. I glanced at Darren. He attempted a smile and gave me a half-hearted wave.

I followed the intimidating woman, whose personality seemed as crisp as her starched white coat, into a small but clean room. The smell of antiseptic was strong. An examining table was set up in the center, and a metal cabinet stood against the wall with a few instruments placed orderly on the countertop. A white gown was draped over a chair in the corner. The lady gestured to the gown. "Disrobe completely and put the gown on. I'll be in presently with some medicine to relax you." She exited briskly.

I felt somewhat relieved by her business-like manner. But something was missing. *Shouldn't there be soft background music, a bouquet of flowers, and a moment of remembrance for what might have been?* Who *might have been . . .?*

Stop it, Cassie. You've thought it out thoroughly and rationally and made the right decision. The only possible decision. My heart throbbed so hard I was sure they could hear it in the other room. I began to fumble with the buttons on my blouse. The door opened suddenly and the lady burst into the room. I looked at her in surprise.

"You're moving too slowly. Here, take this pill and hurry it up. The doctor has a tight schedule." She thrust a tiny paper cup toward me along with a glass of water. I fished the small, green capsule out of the cup, put it in my mouth, and swallowed. She yanked the glass away and left the room. "The doctor will be in shortly."

"The doctor will be in shortly." That phrase caught my attention. *"One day,"* I envisioned, *"a white-clothed nurse will make that same announcement about me. I won't be 'Mary Kimble' then. I'll be 'Doctor Cassandra Dupont."* My fingers were trembling now but I began again to work on my buttons. *Why hadn't I worn a sweatshirt? It would be so much easier to get off.* My mind was growing foggy. The medicine was already making me sleepy and giddy. I managed to get the gown on and tried to

climb up on the table. My first attempt failed. I slipped. "Whoops!" I giggled. Back to my daydream, my future as a doctor.

"Dr. Dupont, we have a difficult case that requires your attention. A baby—a premature baby—is sickly. What should we do?"

I hoisted myself onto the table. Success finally. I did it. My head was floating. *Okay. What would I do? I'd save the baby, of course.* A smug smile lifted the corners of my mouth. *Save the baby.* My heart was pricking at the door of my mind again. Now it was hammering. There was something important. I shook my head in an attempt to settle my brain cells.

Suddenly, they clicked into place. *Save babies! Save lives! That's what doctors do. They're not supposed to kill babies. I can't start my career as a doctor by killing my own baby!*

Determination propelled my body off the table. I grabbed my clothes. Mental fogginess was closing in again. My jeans . . . zippers. . .buttons, too much to think about. I slumped against the door.

Save my baby. Save my baby. My brain was now operating like a stuck record. It was all the inspiration I needed. Grasping my gown tightly around me, I ran from the room, panting from the exertion, fighting against the medication. I spotted Darren reading a magazine in the waiting room. "Darren, take me away." His head shot up. He was thunderstruck.

Miss "Cool 'n Crispy" looked flustered. "Now, now," she came at me with a soothing voice. "It's going to be . . ."

"Darren, I'm leaving, with or without you." I swayed on my feet.

He stood, but didn't move.

I yelled at him. "Don't think, Darren. Act!"

I sensed, rather than saw, someone else enter the room. The nurse twittered. "Oh, Dr. Dupont, you're early. The patient isn't ready yet."

Dr. Dupont? Was I back in my dream? A familiar imposing figure approached and stared at me.

"Papa! What are you doing here?" *How did he find out?*

Why does the nurse know him?

A light dawned on my father's face. Horror filled my eyes as the realization entered my mind. The nurse had called my father, "Dr. Dupont." *My own father was preparing to abort my baby!* Darren's mouth hung open for a moment before he sprang into action. In a split second, he was across the room, lifting me in his strong arms, and running with me to the car.

Voices yelling behind us, footsteps chasing. I was hurled like a football into the back seat. Darren leaped into the front and gunned the engine. The car shot forward with a jerk.

My mind and body slipped into neutral. I remembered no more of that fateful day.

"Wait for the Lord;
Be strong, and let your heart take courage;
Yes, wait for the Lord."

Psalm 27:14

Chapter 11

Fear churned in the pit of my stomach as I huddled on the seat next to Darren. We were on our way home to talk to my father. My mouth was as dry as cotton and the pressure inside my head made me feel faint. The effects of the medication I'd had in the clinic had not yet completely worn off. But the agony I suffered most was the knowledge that Papa would be there waiting for me. I did not want to face him again, not so soon. Darren offered to take me home with him but, as much as I dreaded the coming ordeal, I longed desperately to get it over with and get on with my life. And my baby's life. When I remembered how close I came to losing my baby forever, just thirty hours ago, my heart almost failed. It amazed me that emotions could reverse themselves so completely in such a short time. For the past weeks, all I had wanted was to get rid of this burden who was my child. I was desperate, willing to do almost anything. *To think I nearly paid my father to kill his own grandchild!*

Now the decision was made. The fear that first filled my heart was replaced with a fierce desire to protect my baby. I longed to hold my child, look into his eyes, or maybe hers, and say, "I chose to give you life." I was overwhelmed with that elusive quality called "mother love." Even my feelings for Darren had receded, at least temporarily, into the background.

I worried some about how Darren's parents would accept the news of my pregnancy, but was sure they would support my decision to keep the baby. Ingrid would be disappointed in both Darren and me, and I didn't relish the thought of facing Sven. But I knew they would accept their grandchild with love, just as they'd accepted me. Darren insisted on accompanying me when I confronted Papa, but agreed that I should be the one to tell him of my intention to raise my child.

The medication did a good job on Saturday. I slept until well after midnight. Darren drove me straight to Liz's house after we left the clinic. My friends put me to bed and watched over me the rest of the afternoon. Darren spent that night with Kirk, and Liz slept in her parent's bed so she wouldn't disturb me. In the morning, I took a shower and ate breakfast, which helped to clear my head so I was able to think rationally again. Fortunately, Liz Beth and I wore the same size, so I was able to borrow some clothes. My impulsive action of the day before left no regrets.

Darren, Liz and I discussed my options on Sunday afternoon. Liz Beth thought I'd made a mistake, but was willing to offer support and advice. She offered to check out an adoption agency for me, but I refused her help. I told her this was my baby and somehow I would find a way to take care of it. Darren supported my decision, since he had gone through the horrible experience with me at the clinic. He was mostly concerned about my father's reaction and how I would be treated at school when people found out that I was pregnant. I refused to look very far ahead at the time. I only knew that I'd come so close to losing my baby and I didn't intend to be separated from it at birth. I guess I hungered for someone who would belong completely to me. I still didn't understand love. I only knew it was there.

Twilight was wrapping its hazy arms around the sun when Darren and I left Liz Beth's house. By the time we arrived at my home, it was late. The night sky was dense and heavy like a wool blanket carelessly tossed on top of my world. Scant illumination escaped from the moon and no stars were visible in the cloudy expanse. Only the kitchen light burned inside the house. Papa was probably having a snack before he retired for the night.

Darren retrieved my suitcase from the trunk and walked silently with me along the sidewalk leading to the side entrance. My heart thumped wildly against my chest and my knees turned to rubber.

When we reached the door, Darren laid his hand on my shoulder. That simple gesture gave me courage. I took a deep breath and inserted the key into the lock. Papa looked up when we entered. He sat at the end of the kitchen table with a half-eaten donut in one hand and a cup of coffee in the other. He glared pointedly at the clock, which said 11:30 p.m.

"So you decided to come home?" he grunted. His demeanor was calm, but deceptive. I sensed in him a potential force, kind of like a dam whose stored up energy might crash through at any moment, wreaking havoc over the surrounding countryside. Darren and I stood quietly as Papa finished his donut and gulped down some coffee.

I cleared my throat, and spoke in a voice that sounded far away, "I'm sorry I'm so late, Papa."

Darren set my suitcase by the door, pulled out a chair at the other end of the table, and sat down. My body was frozen. I was unable to speak further, or even move. I feared that anything I said would pierce a hole in the dam's fragile barrier.

Papa's forehead creased into a frown as he watched Darren. "You planning on staying a while, Boy?"

"Yes, sir. Cassie and I need to talk with you."

Papa waved his hand in my direction. "Well, get him some coffee, Cassandra."

Spurred into action, I poured a cup for Darren and myself and sat down between them. We took cautious sips of the steaming liquid. My anxious brain scrambled frantically, overturning words and phrases, searching for the right ones to break the ice. None were acceptable. I began to investigate a tiny knot in the pine table with my fingertip. Only the steady ticking of the clock over the sink broke the oppressive silence.

My father's fingers drummed a rhythm on the table. He glared, first at me, then at Darren. "Well, are you going to do right by my daughter and marry her?"

"Papa," I finally found some words to throw into the ring. Not the right ones, I guess. "We haven't discussed marriage, but I've decided to keep my baby."

Papa pushed his chair back and stood up. His rigid, imposing figure towered over me. Summoning all the courage I possessed, I lifted my chin and faced him. His dark eyes flashed. I imagined steam coming out of his nostrils. Every cell in his body was poised for action. *Rage carved in stone.* My heart dropped at the thought of the dam breaking and releasing the pent-up anger.

His voice was still calm, but laden with contempt. Disbelief flooded his eyes, "You'd live under my roof and flaunt your kid in my face! After all I've done for you!"

"Mr. Dupont," Darren broke in. "I'll do whatever I have to do. We haven't had much time to think . . ."

Sparks flew from Papa's eyes. "I'll deal with you in due time, young man." All his attention was focused on me. "You, you . . . slut!"

He grabbed my arm with a steel grip and shook me. In a flash, Darren was on his feet with a fist aimed at my father. Jumping up, I struggled to free my arm and fend off Darren with the other one.

"No, Darren!" I screamed.

Papa let go.

Darren spun around. I jumped as I heard the sudden crack of his fist crashing down onto the table. His breath came in heavy gasps. His eyes were steel hard, but he said nothing.

Papa sat down. His shoulders slumped, like an old man. When he spoke, resignation mingled with fear in his voice, "Everything I've worked for has gone to waste, all the hours, all the education, my skills. I worked hard to build up a thriving practice, a name for myself in the community. Look, Cassandra. Look at this house. My money built this fine, sturdy structure. I had the foresight to know that this plot of land by a lake would be a good place for a home. Now," his arm waved an expansive area, "people are building homes all over out here, where we once lived in seclusion. I've demanded respect. I've earned power. I've gained control and recognition." Fury was building up again. His tone was etched with sarcasm. "And now my beautiful, intelligent daughter, only daughter, in one sleazy night, has leveled my empire."

Darren gripped my shoulders. "You can't talk to Cassie like that."

Papa shook his finger at him. "I have a right to talk to her any way I want." He turned back to me. I cringed involuntarily.

"You, young lady, have caused my ruin. My reputation will be destroyed."

Darren cleared his throat, but managed to speak clearly. "What was that about your reputation, sir? Does anyone know about your. . . weekend job? What would your neighbors think about that?"

Papa's eyes were like coals. He spun around and stalked to the door leading into the dining room. He turned and faced us with an icy calm. "I've made some phone calls. An acquaintance in Boston who is starting a new practice needs an assistant. It will mean a decrease in salary, at least for a time, but I have decided to accept the position. You both are aware that abortion is now legal, but there are people in this community who unfortunately hold a dim view of that . . ." he groped for words, " . . . particular medical procedure." He stood straight and tall with his hands clasped behind his back. "Since I can no longer count on my professional activities to be kept quiet," he glared pointedly at Darren. "I have decided to relocate in Boston in two weeks."

My mouth dropped open and my eyes burned. Darren tightened his grip on my shoulders as I swayed a little on my feet. *Papa was going to leave me. He didn't want me. What about my home? Where would I go? What would happen to my baby? Darren said he would do what he "had" to do. Was he willing to marry me out of love? Or just a sense of duty?*

Papa answered a few of my unspoken questions. "You may spend one more night in this house, Cassandra. Tomorrow, you will pack your things and go to live with your grandmother. I have already spoken with her and made the arrangements. She will be expecting you."

Stunned, I realized that he was washing his hands of me. In a cold, calculated manner, he was dismissing me and setting me on the doorstep, outside of his life.

He continued, "Your grandmother has always wanted you. Now she can have you. I have an appointment with a realtor tomorrow to begin the process of sale on this house."

Unshed tears formed blurry pools behind my eyelids, but I was determined to restrain them . . . for now.

Shaking myself free from Darren's hands, I mentally shook myself free from the cold fingers of panic that were grasping at me from all sides. I would stand firm. Alone, if necessary. I took a step toward my father. Our eyes met. My throat closed for a moment and I nearly choked on the words. "Take a good look at my face, Papa. It's the last time you'll ever see it." In spite of my pain and confusion, I found myself trying to memorize the ridges, the clefts, the countenance on the face of the man who had been and always would be a vital influence in my life.

His gaze wavered for just a second. Then he deliberately closed me out of his emotions.

"So be it. Good night, Cassandra. Good night, Darren." He nodded to both of us as though we had just spent a casual evening relaxing by the fire. Then he turned and walked upstairs.

The ordeal over, my whole body started to tremble. *This couldn't be happening. It wasn't real. It had to be a nightmare. Any minute now, I'd wake up.* Then Darren reached for me, gently turned me around and drew me to him.

"I'm sorry, Cassie, I'm so sorry." His hand stroked my hair. "I should have been stronger. I shouldn't have let it happen."

I knew he was not referring to the events of this evening, but to the night we spent in the car.

I pulled myself away. "It wasn't all your fault. You'd better go now."

He hesitated. "What about your dad? Are you safe?"

I stared at him. *Didn't he comprehend what had hap-*

pened?

"Darren, that man doesn't want anything more to do with me. Ever!" I formed each word slowly and definitely, as though speaking to a child. "Don't you understand? *I have no father!*"

He sighed. "I'll come by in the morning and help you."

"No."

"Why not? You'll need help packing and carrying boxes."

I made another impulsive decision. "Darren, I don't think we should see each other for a while." "Cassie," he moved close. Waves of emotions swept over me, but I put up my hands to stop him.

"I'll let you know when the baby comes. After all, it's your. . ." I choked the word out, ". . .child, too. But this is something I need to handle by myself."

"Cassie," his voice was firm. "I meant what I told your dad. I'll marry you."

"Why?" My flashing eyes dared him to speak the truth.

He avoided my gaze and fumbled with his words. "Well, it's the right thing to do, Cassie. Your baby needs a father. And I . . . I care a lot about you." His eyes met mine again.

From deep inside myself, the strength came to ask him, "Do you love me, Darren? Do you know for certain that I'm the one you want to spend the rest of your life with?"

His silence was my answer.

"I've got to grow up, Darren. I'm going to be a mother. This precious life," I patted my stomach, "is going to depend on me. I need to find myself, to figure out who I am and what kind of a future I can give my baby. I need time alone to think, without any other emotions messing me up."

He looked hurt, lost, and suddenly alone. Abandoned. The longing in his eyes, which must have been reflected in mine, tore at my heart. But I stiffened my resolve, picked up my suitcase and turned to go. "Good night, Darren." Now I was the one who was cold and distant, shutting him out of my life the same way my father had shut me out. He let himself out the door.

Way into the dim hours of the morning, I sat on the windowseat in my room, contemplating the scene before me. Saying "good-bye" to the only home I could ever remember was hard, but even harder was bidding farewell to the lake. *My lake.* I knew I could always return to my thinking rock. The land it stood on was public property. But I didn't expect to come back. It would just reopen my wounds.

The clouds had drifted past and stars were peering out of the darkness. A falling star caught my attention. "Star light, star bright. I wish I may, I wish I might . . ." The lines of the old rhyme sprang unbidden into my mind, " . . . have the wish I wish tonight."

Oh, to be a child again and believe in silly poems and fairy godmothers that could magically solve all my problems. The world had never seemed more real to me, or more cold. A door had slammed tonight on a chapter of my life. Years ago, I'd bid my farewell to the gentle influence of my beautiful mother. Tonight I'd said "good-bye" to the harsh dominance of my father. Both parents strongly shaped my personality, my character. *Who was I without them? Who was this person, Cassandra Dupont? What sort of legacy would I leave my child? Would my son or daughter see me as a tender, loving woman, or would anger take hold of my heart and twist it into the bitter, self-centered nature that I saw in my father?* Eventually, fatigue overcame me and I stretched out, fully dressed, on my canopy bed. In my own room. For the last time.

In the morning, I drove to the hardware store in New Bergen and picked up an assortment of boxes. The day was spent looking through closets and sorting out drawers. With a shaky voice, I called Grandma Lydia. We talked for a long time, and she assured me that I'd always be welcome in her home. Supper would be ready when I arrived that evening.

After I finished packing my clothes, my attention turned to the collections on my shelves, the dolls and music boxes Papa had purchased for me through the years. I longed for strength to leave them there, to mock my father when he returned home. But I ended up putting them carefully in clearly labeled containers wrapped with double strength tape. Maybe one day I'd take them out again, touch the smooth faces of my china dolls and listen to the lilting tunes of the music boxes. At least, they would be with me, a remembrance of a period of time I couldn't ever forget.

I carried the stack of boxes to my car and returned to my room. It looked bare, lifeless. I ran my hand over the silky texture of my white, purple and green bedspread, which I had decided to leave behind. It belonged to this room. With only the bedspread and furniture, my room no longer had a personality. A glance into the mirror reflected the image of a young woman girl who was also stripped of her personality. I felt like I was leaving my soul within those four familiar walls.

Mechanically, I checked the drawers to see if I'd forgotten anything. Stuffed way back in the bedside table was the Bible Mama gave me just before she died. I carefully removed it and held it to my heart, recalling the tender way she had stroked it. This book was the only gift I had received from my mother, alone. I decided to take it with me.

A ray of sun broke through the windowpane. The surface of Lake Clarity glittered in the sudden light and sparkled with a multitude of dancing diamonds. This was the way I determined to remember it.

Tucking the memory safely into my mind, I walked down the stairs and entered my father's study. How he treasured this room, lined on two sides with a vast collection of books. A fireplace dominated one end, with large, black, leather armchairs placed on each side of it. At the other end, two long, narrow windows framed the lake. A lingering scent of pipe tobacco drifted throughout the room, enabling Papa's presence to remain and permeate every corner. I loved that smell. It made me remember special times of closeness when he would read to me or allow me to freely investigate the shelves. Often, in the evenings, Papa reclined on his chair and had me sit at his feet while he read intriguing tales of adventures from the classics. In later years, I'd sit in the other chair and he would teach me about science and philosophy from the great thinkers. He told me each book allowed us to see into the mind of another person and learn from their experiences and insights. Since he valued books so highly, I wondered why he had no interest in reading the Book I now carried in my hands. *Had he no desire to look into the mind of God?*

But, then, he didn't believe this book contained the mind of God, but was full of deceitful stories meant to entice weak people into a lifestyle of foolishness. Torn between the opposing views of my mother and father, I realized my opinion regarding this book was yet to be formed.

The light was always dim in my father's study. Heavy burgundy draperies were partially drawn, shielding a portion of the sun's rays. Papa seldom opened them all the way, preferring, even in the daytime, to light a lamp when he read. Too much light seemed to make him uncomfortable. He relaxed more easily in the darkness. I knew I should leave. He never wanted me to be in this room when he was away. I'd always wondered why. Maybe he thought my attitude would not be as reverent without his presence there, too. Or maybe he feared I would harm his precious books. But that afternoon I sat down in his chair and propped my feet up on the stool. I guess, at that moment, his chair symbolized not only the father I had, but also the father I longed for.

Still clutching Mama's Bible, I relaxed and let the tension slip away. The concrete barriers I tried to build around me temporarily dissolved. Resting my head on the back of the chair, I sank deeply into the cushions and let the chair's sturdy frame support me. How I longed for a father who was strong enough to hold onto me! One who would support me and share his strength with me. One who would wrap his arms around me and comfort me like the soft, yet solid, cushions of the huge chair that lent me its warmth.

I laid the Bible on my lap. It was my only tie to my mother and very important to her. She would want me to read it. Opening it, I scanned a few pages. Several passages were underlined. I paused to read one section on a page headed "Deuteronomy." It read, "Underneath are the everlasting arms." I shut the book with a snap. My heart began to beat faster. *This was weird. Uncanny. Just what I was longing for, strong arms to hold me up. Who, or what, did the sentence refer to? God? Jesus? Or something completely different? The Holy Ghost?* I remembered

Grandma telling me about some ghost that God sent from heaven to help me. But Mama and Papa said there were no ghosts, good or bad, so I didn't pay much attention. I tried to find that passage again, but gave up. The soft glow of a sunset was beginning, and I knew it was time to leave. I didn't want to be here when Papa returned home.

I walked back through the living room to the kitchen, where I left my house key on the table. Papa wouldn't need to worry, or to hope, that I'd come back.

Chapter 12

Spring finally came and the trees were starting to bloom. Driving to school one day, I saw with fresh eyes the tiny green buds on the lilac bushes lining our driveway. I was ever mindful of the brand new life that budded inside me as well. Though often overshadowed with doubts and fears, the excitement of facing motherhood for the first time nevertheless sent sparks of thrills through my spirit. It was hard to keep my mind on my studies, and I kept to myself more than usual. Though I had just pulled out of my first trimester, I hoped to get through graduation before word got around about my pregnancy. My closest friends knew, but I had sworn them to secrecy. I hadn't begun to show yet, thought I made a point to wear loose shirts. Plans for the summer and beyond were nonexistent at this point. Grandma told me to take one thing at a time, and God would provide for me and my baby. I tried to believe her, but most of the time, I just avoided thinking about the future.

At noon, the lunchroom bustled with the usual activity. Since New Bergen High School was small, all the students shared the same lunch hour. Our cafeteria was stretched to the limit for space. Tightly jammed tables made it difficult to navigate between the chairs. It was a challenge to balance my tray, purse, and a stack of books as I funneled my way through the sea of sweaty bodies. Mr. Harris, my math teacher, usually continued to lecture after the lunch bell rang. Since my locker was at the other end of the building, I lugged my books with me to the cafeteria.

My friend, Candy, waved to me from across the room. She had managed to save me a seat at a table shared with our friends, Trisha and Louise, and three guys from my physics class. The noise hit the usual multi-decibel figure. Teachers had long since given up trying to maintain any semblance of order, and settled for general chaos, as long as no one was involved in pushing, shoving, or food fights.

"Move over, Tommy," Candy nudged him with her elbow as she and Trisha, who was on the other side of the empty chair, scooted over to make room for me.

I set my tray on the table, books and purse under my chair, and cast a glance at the serving on my plate. Some sort of hot dish with mushy, over-cooked macaroni, pale orange carrots swimming in a milkly sauce, and a crusty-looking brownie. I wrinkled my nose.

Gabe sat across from me. His ears were too big for his face and stubborn acne still covered his nose. But he was the funniest kid in our class. Or at least, he thought he was. His head was thrown back and he was engaged in popping small pieces of brownie into his mouth. "My mom would turn over in her dishpan if she could see the food we have to eat!" he exclaimed.

His buddy, Bruce, joined the discussion. "Who but our expert cooks could ruin a brownie? Vegetables, I understand. But I've never before met a brownie I didn't like!"

"Lay off," Candy commanded. "I'd like to taste the ones you'd make."

Gabe roared with laughter, grabbing his sides in an effort to keep from rolling off his chair. "I've tasted them. He made a batch last week and forgot to put the cocoa in!"

Bruce grimaced. I rolled my eyes at Candy, wondering

how she'd managed to land a spot with these losers. She shrugged her arms and answered my unasked question, "I was late, too."

Digging my fork into the mushy dish, I mentally prepared myself for an entertaining meal, hoping the guys wouldn't attempt to top the milk drinking contest they had staged a week ago. Gabe had downed ten glasses of milk before he'd found it necessary to run outside and get rid of it all. Fortunately, we were sitting near the door.

"Hey, Cass!" I looked up. Standing at my left shoulder was Brad, New Bergen's foremost football hero. Broad shoulders topped a set of muscles that seemed to be permanently flexed. The glint in his dark eyes confirmed the fact that he was well aware nearly every girl in the senior class would give her right arm to date him.

Although I was one of the few who displayed no interest in him, my heart flipped at the unexpected attention. Gabe clammed up and interested eyes turned our way. The last I'd heard, Brad had been dating the sno-daze queen. Before that, it was the homecoming queen. I had no label of royalty attached to my name. In fact, since I'd moved in with Grandma, my social life had dwindled to zilch. No more dates with Darren. The girls I hung around with at school all had "steadies" so they were busy on weekends. Candy had tried to match me up with some friends, but I wasn't interested. A "hot night" for me lately had been a bowl of popcorn and cocoa with Grandma while watching *Dr. Kildare* re-runs on TV. So what did Brad want with me?

Brad casually chewed his gum, well aware of the affect he had on those around me. He popped a bubble. "Ya busy Friday night?"

Candy's mouth formed a circle to match her eyes.

"I'm not sure yet."

I wasn't interested in dating this guy, but I could tell from the expressions around the table that they all thought I was just playing hard to get. My friends' faces wore a mixture of admiration and dismay.

Brad popped another bubble. "Got two tickets to the theater. I'll pick you up at eight."

What nerve! How dare he blatantly assume that I would-n't turn him down.

"I can't."

"Huh?"

"I have to . . ." I fumbled for an excuse, " . . . I have to wash my hair."

Astonished gasps rippled through the lunchroom. No one could believe it. *Brad turned down. Impossible!*

My face turned red from the unwanted attention. Not knowing what else to do, I took a sip of milk. My heart pounded and my stomach felt nauseous.

Brad's eyes narrowed at the rejection and his face turned grim. "That's okay," he spoke with menace, "I just wondered what it would be like to date a *pregnant* girl."

I choked on my milk, which spilt all over my lap. A horrified silence filled the room, though the beating of my heart sounded like thunder to me. *How did he find out? Who told him?* In panic, I stared at my friends. Shock and concern radiated from Candy's and Trisha's expressions, but Louise avoided my gaze. *Louise! I never should have trusted her. She had a tongue that was more active than a raging volcano, but I thought she was my friend! How many others knew?* A hasty glance around the room convinced me that, if they didn't all know before, they certainly knew now!

Oppressive silence nearly stifled my breath. The constant chattering that greeted me when I entered the cafeteria turned into a crisp chill, molding every student into an ice fixture. All eyes were glued on my face. My head throbbed and the palms of my hands grew suddenly damp. *Would no one come to my defense?*

Ignoring my shaking knees, I willed my limp body to stand. Turning to Brad, I lifted my hand. *At least, I would find satisfaction in slapping his face.* But as I started to strike, he caught my wrist in mid-flight. His cruel eyes bored into mine, his lips curled, and he threw back his head and laughed. At the same instant, two teachers led the principal into the room and gestured towards us. Gabe chose that moment to be a hero and defend my honor. He rushed toward Brad and waved an uncertain fist at his face. Brad let go of my arm, bent over double, and plowed his head into Gabe's stomach, knocking the breath out of him. Gabe landed on his back on the floor. The room exploded into noise. In the commotion, I grabbed my purse and dashed out the side door.

I ran all the way to Grandma's house, my chest heaving and my feet beating a frantic rhythm on the sidewalk. Tears stung my eyelids. *How dare Brad unleash my secret in front of the whole student body?* His gloating smirk would haunt my dreams for months!

Finally, I reached Grandma's house and burst in through the kitchen door.

Grandma stood at the sink, washing dishes. She jumped as the door banged against the wall and her hand flew to her heart. "Cassie! What on earth? Why, you're shaking, child! Come and sit down." Throwing an arm around my shoulders, she gently guided me to a chair by the table. I laid my head on my arms and sobbed. I'd cried more in the past few months than I had in all the years since Mother died.

Grandma ran her fingers through my hair. "Are you sick, Cassie?"

I shook my head. Anguished words formed in the depths of my consciousness didn't make any effort to rise to the surface.

She kept stroking my hair and tenderly began to rub my shoulder. After a few minutes, my sobs subsided. Nobody could comfort me like Grandma could, even without saying a word. She pulled up a chair and put a tissue in my hand. "Here, Cassandra, blow your nose and then tell me about it." Her voice was tender and firm at the same time.

I blew my nose vigorously. "Grandma, I'm so humiliated. I knew they'd find out, but . . . not like that! Not so soon." My voice broke.

"What happened, honey?"

The whole ugly story rushed from my mouth. With all my words running together, I don't know how she made sense out of it, but she did. Her lips tightened and her eyes glittered. I knew she was angry, but I also knew her anger was not aimed at me.

Grandma took a deep breath and held herself very still, like her emotions were fighting to come out. She had to erect a concrete barrier to keep them inside. She placed her hand on top of mine. "Cassie, my dear child," she paused for another deep breath. "I hurt so much for you."

"What am I going to do, Grandma? I can't go back and face them. Not ever." I shuddered involuntarily at the thought.

Grandma sat down next to me. "What choices do you have, Cassandra?" Her soothing voice was like a cup of cold water poured on my heated nerves.

"I could drop out of school."

"So close to graduation?"

My voice quivered and rose. "He mocked me, Grandma. He laughed when I tried to slap him. I know why he laughed, too. He laughed because I was trying to defend my honor, and I . . . don't . . . have any honor to defend!" My words slammed hard into the heavy atmosphere even as my fist slammed on the table. "Grandma, I'm a failure. I won't finish high school. I can't go to medical school. I broke up with the nicest guy I've ever met. I couldn't even slap the face of my tormentor." I was nearly hysterical now.

Grandma took my hand again, this time with both of hers. My breathing eased somewhat and I stared out the window. "My life is gone, Grandma, my whole life. I feel like it's floating around up in the sky like a balloon and I don't know where it's going to land!"

"Cassie, you've made a mistake. You have also sinned before God." Her voice was matter-of- fact, not harsh. "But God *will* forgive you if you agree that you did wrong and choose to live the way He wants you to live. He will make you His own child and take care of you. *If* you let Him."

My head was shaking vehemently. "Grandma, if there is a god, why would He want me? I'm no good for anything any more. I've thrown away my future."

"None of us is good for anything, Cassie. We've *all* sinned and deserve judgment and hell, but God . . ." Now her eyes were brimming with tears, ". . . gave His only Son to suffer and die to pay for our sins. That's what the cross in all about, Cassie. Our sins, yours and mine, were nailed to that torturous cross with Jesus. If we accept His punishment in our place, He sets us free. And then we belong to Him, and He takes care of us, forever."

"Grandma, I'm not even convinced that there is a god." The logical side of my brain had taken over now. Emotions were shoved out of the way and I'd started to reason again. "I'll go back to school tomorrow. Not today. Somehow I'll hang on 'til graduation. I want my diploma. I've earned it! Maybe later on I'll go to medical school. I don't know. With a baby . . ." my voice trailed off.

"God loves you, honey," Grandma persisted. "He longs to gather you to Himself like a hen gathers her chickens under her wings. He can take your hurts and failures and turn them into something good." "Oh, Grandma, sometimes I wish I could believe, but I'm too realistic. Papa taught me . . ."

"Cassandra, the greatest reality *is* God. He's the Father of all life, the giver of peace and joy. This world you see around you is only a shadow of reality. It all looks firm and sturdy, but one day, the Bible tells us, the earth will burn up and God will make a new heaven and earth that will last beyond time."

"It says that in the Bible?"

"Yes," Grandma reached for her Bible that lay on the shelf near the table. She always started her day by reading it while she ate breakfast and had her morning tea. She ruffled a few pages. "Listen to this, Cassandra. 'And I saw a new heaven and a new earth; for the first heaven and the first earth passed away, and there is no longer any sea. And I saw the holy city, new Jerusalem, coming down out of heaven from God, made ready as a bride adorned for her husband.' That's from Revelation, the last book in the Bible. And here's another good passage, in First Corinthians 13." She flipped a few more pages.

"For now we see in a mirror dimly, but then face to face; now I know in part, but then I shall know fully just as I also have been fully known.' You see, this world is just a shadow compared to eternal reality."

"I don't know, Grandma. I admire you and your faith."

"My faith is given to me by God."

A sudden knock at the door interrupted our discussion.

"I'll get it." I rose and went to open it. My mouth fell open. There stood Darren on the steps. His eyes were soft, but he had a determined look on his face.

I spoke sharply. "How did you find out?"

Determination turned to bewilderment. "Find out what?"

"Did you talk to somebody at school? Did Candy call you?"

He shook his head. "I don't know what you're talking about, Cassie. It's taken me nearly a week to get up enough courage to come and see you."

A pause. "Can I come in?"

"Darren, please come in!" Grandma called. "Let him in, Cassie."

I backed slowly away from the door. Just seeing him again exposed emotions I'd forced under the surface for weeks. I'd known I was in love with Darren since Christmas Eve, when he showed up in that crazy Santa Claus suit and handed out treats to his nieces and nephews. All month, I'd been dealing with the problem of my pregnancy and my unknown future, along with the trauma of trying to push Darren out of my mind and life. *How dare he think he can just walk back in here and mess me up again?* But I couldn't disobey Grandma.

"Hello, Mrs. Hartell." Darren spoke politely.

"Hello, Darren." Grandma's tone was warm.

An awkward silence persisted.

Perceptive as always, Grandma rose to her feet. "Well, I'll just let you two visit. Excuse me." She left quickly before I could ask her to stay.

Hoping Darren would leave soon, I didn't ask him to sit down. I leaned against the kitchen counter and crossed my arms. Darren calmly walked over to me and uncrossed them. I didn't protest, but my eyes dropped to the floor. He took me by the shoulders and, typical of his nature, went right to the point.

"I've been thinking, Cassie," he paused. "Look at me. Please." No begging, just a polite command. I obeyed. He was so close my insides turned to mush. "Cassie," he began again. "I've done a lot of thinking these past weeks and I've come to a decision." His eyes bored into mine, but not with the hatred and ridicule I'd seen in Brad's face a few hours earlier. Darren's blue eyes glowed with a lightness and affection that caressed my soul. Now I couldn't tear my gaze away from him.

He inhaled deeply. "Cassie, I practiced how to say this, but I forgot what I'd practiced, so I'll just say it." His voice was firm and steady. "I love you."

I tried to pull away, but he only strengthened his grip. "I love you with all my heart. I want to marry you and give you and . . . our baby . . . a home."

Unbidden, my face broke into a smile. This time I blinked back happy tears. I couldn't help myself. I'd been in love with Darren for months, and now he declared his love for me, just when I needed it the most.

I threw my arms around his neck. He held me in his strong grasp and nuzzled my ear.

"Oh, Darren," I sighed. "It'll be hard, but Grandma said things would work out for me. Only she thought I'd find God. But, oh, wonder of wonders, I got *you* instead!"

"*Trust in the Lord
with all your heart,
And do not lean on your own understanding.*"

Proverbs 3:5

PART TWO
The Renewal
Chapter 13
1977

Annette's shrieks began at precisely 5:35 a.m Monday morning. Darren had already left for his part-time job at a service station in Lakeland, a larger town twenty-five miles from New Bergen. When Darren and I married, we moved into a second story apartment rented by Gertrude Hagen, a lonely, elderly widow. Gertrude lived downstairs and was eager for company. "I tell you, I'm tired of rattatlin' around in this ol' tomb of a house," Gertrude Hagen admitted the day we moved in. "Since my Herbert up and left me . . . he died of a heart attack two years ago . . . I don't have nobody to talk to, an' I'm mighty glad you young folks are here," she laughed. "Herbert used to call me 'Motor-Mouth'." Evidently she regarded it as an endearing term. Darren and I quickly discovered that Herbert's assessment of his vocal wife had been right on target. We took to sneaking in the back door on the way up to our apartment to avoid a lengthy monologue each time we came home.

I rolled over and pressed the sides of my pillow against my ears. Maybe, this once, Annie would quiet down before my nerves snapped. I'd tried everything to make my daughter sleep later in the mornings. I'd hung a heavy blanket over her window, which unfortunately faced east. We shut her door at night, and Darren was as quiet as a rabbit when he got ready for work. However, as soon as she could make out the shape of her hand in front of her eyes, it was time to get up, and she made sure I knew it!

My husband worked at the service station from 5:30 a.m to 2:00 p.m six days a week. His afternoons were spent helping Sven and Billy on the family farm, thirteen miles away. I wouldn't see him until about 10:00 tonight, since it was harvesting season. For a while it looked like Darren's dream of becoming a farmer might come true. His older brothers had moved out of the state. Seth took a teaching job in Illinois that paid more to support his growing family. I met their two little ones, Jonnie (Jonathan according to Ingrid), and Ingeborg, on the first Christmas Eve I'd shared with Darren's family. Now they had twins, Michael and Michelle, and one more was on the way. His brother, Luke, who was in agricultural marketing, accepted a job in Iowa, and moved his family there. Both Seth and Luke knew that Darren wanted to farm, but Sven kept urging him to find a new vocation. The future of the small, family farm looked more dismal as each year passed. "It's hard times ahead for us and our neighbors, son," the old farmer had prophesied, "You'll be smart to find some other way to make your livin'. I don't have much land to give ya' anyhow. Billy and I will make the best of this here farmland as long as I'm able to work." So Darren went to classes two nights a week at the technical college in Lakeland. He was studying accounting. Some nights Ingrid fed him supper and he went directly to school from the farm, so I didn't see him until late.

The shrieks increased in volume. I thought babies were supposed to sleep a lot. Nathan did. In fact, at three years, he seemed to require more sleep than Annette did at three months! Gingerly, I pried my eyes open. If I didn't get up soon and feed her, my landlady, Gertrude, would be knocking on my door, complaining, and Nathan would think it was morning, and whine for breakfast. I grabbed my worn blue corduroy robe from the floor where I'd flung it after crawling into bed, exhausted at the end of

Annie's 2:30 am feeding. Shivering, I jammed my feet into furry slippers and staggered to the children's bedroom. A constant chill hovered in the air of our apartment. It was an old house, built in the thirties with poor insulation. I fretted continually about the changing temperature, especially in the winter. Nathan had been sickly as an infant and I worried that Annette would follow her brother's pattern. So far, she had stayed well, except for a 104 fever in her second month. Terrified, Darren and I had bundled up both kids and made a dash to the emergency room in the middle of the night. With a proper medication, she recovered in a few days.

The shrieks subsided into frantic sobs by the time I arrived at her crib. I leaned over the side and patted her tiny back. "Mommy's here," I spoke consolingly. The frantic flutters diminished to sighs. Ingrid had advised me never to pick my children up when they were fussing. "You don't want to train him to demand attention," she'd cautioned me after Nathan was born. "Pat his back or rub it until he's settled down, and then pick him up." But I noticed after my daughter was born, Ingrid didn't faithfully follow her own advice. Annette didn't have to do much more than whimper these days and Grandma Larson headed for the crib to scoop her up into loving arms. I still followed her advice. I wanted to do everything right for my kids. I wondered how my own dear Grandma Lydia had raised my mother, and what advice she would have given me. How I missed her! Grandma Lydia died from breast cancer just six months after I'd married Darren. At least, she'd gotten to see her first great-grandchild. The merciless disease overcame her quickly and her suffering was hard to bear. I'd spent most of my pregnancy caring for her. Lydia claimed to have peace and be close to God. But I couldn't see past her pain and my personal agony at losing the second woman in my life I'd grown to depend on and cherish. Darren loved my grandma, too, and said a loving God wouldn't let that happen to a good person like Lydia.

"Morning, Mommy," Nathan chirped like a baby bird, his eyes as wide open as his mouth, eagerly waiting for Mommy Bird to make a deposit of cereal.

Bone tired. I had no idea what that phrase meant before I

became a mother. My aching muscles cried out for rest, but I knew there was no putting him off. Tucking my infant under one arm, I grabbed Nathan's chubby hand and led him to our dingy, messy kitchen.

"Ouch!" I stumbled, nearly dropping Annette, when the tender center of my foot landed on the miniature fire truck belonging to Nathan's little toy village.

"Mommy no break my truck!" Nathan protested.

The house was a shambles, as usual. Before Annette was born, I faithfully picked up every night. But since she'd made her grand entrance with round-the-clock feeding demands, I'd drifted from day to night and back again in a dismal fog of exhaustion and depression. Ingrid said I had the "baby blues." Darren tried to make me give her a bottle so he could help with the feedings, but I loved nursing my baby. It was about the only joy I had left. I barely saw my husband, except when I was nearly too tired to breathe.

The warm sense of contentment that enveloped me every time I nursed Annette vanished as soon as I laid her down and turned my gaze to the disaster area in the living room. I wouldn't let Nathan play in his own room or he'd wake his sister. So toys, empty glasses, and dirty clothes that fell, exhausted, on their way to the hamper, became the focal points of our living room. This wasn't how I'd envisioned marriage. Darren was so busy that I functioned like a single mom. The tiny, crowded rooms closed in on me. I felt like I was trapped in a giant playpen with no rescuer to pick me up and set me on my feet.

I grabbed a bowl from the cupboard, set it on the table, and dumped cereal into it.

"No, Mommy!" Nathan's eyes clouded. "No puff wice. Me want Tweet Wheat."

"I don't have any Tweet Wheat left, honey. I'll get more when we go to the store."

"No, no!" Nathan's pudgy fist reached out and swept the bowl off the table, scattering cereal all over the kitchen.

Annette resumed her siren-like squeals, with eyes puckered tight and little fists waving in the air.

"I yanked Nathan's arm. "You pick those up!" I demand-ed. "Now!" My short nerves were near the disintegrating point.

"Sorry, Mommy. Won't do it again," my son shook his head in dismay. I dropped his arm and stepped back.

Crunch!

"Mommy, you step on my puff wice," he was aghast. "Mine, mine. Mine wice." He grabbed his bowl and hurriedly began to fill it from the mountain of grain on the floor.

The door began to vibrate with a pounding noise. My insides sank to the floor and rolled around with the cereal. "Come in!" I yelled. She did. Though Gertrude didn't have the privilege of raising children of her own, she was a self-appointed expert on raising other people's children. Sometimes I wondered why she didn't just kick us out, but the more I got to know her, the more I realized she needed something to complain about. We gave her plenty!

"Now, Dearie," she began in a condescending tone, "I know you don't need as much sleep as an old fogey like me, but," a pointed glare at the clock, "it isn't six o'clock yet, and I had a restless night. My rheumatism got the best of me. It's the weath-er. I can feel it in my bones. Herbert used to say, bless him, that I must'av swallowed a barometer when I was a kid! And he's right, why, it seems . . ." her voice rose in a feeble attempt to be heard above Annette's sobs.

"Mrs. Hagen, I have to feed her. She'll be quiet soon," I yelled and took a few steps toward the door, hoping she'd get the hint.

"Yes, well, I do feel it's my Christian duty to offer advice, you know, just this once. I really think that you should let your children sleep a little later in the mornings. They're getting into a bad habit of . . ."

"Yes, Mrs. Hagen, I will in the future," with a glib prom-ise, I gradually closed the door as she backed out, still babbling.

I turned around to see Nathan seated at the table with his precious bowl of cereal and poking several tiny puffs into his mouth.

"Good, Mommy. Tank you." A wide grin confirmed his

satisfaction.

I flipped the TV switch on for Nathan and stumbled back to bed with Annie. I was so tired. The dull sameness of each day flowed into the next one, like an endless watercolor mural. Crawling into bed had become the highlight of my day. Just a chance to sleep until I was rested became my life's goal.

Little Annie was sucking contentedly now. She looked like a china doll. Her head was perfectly shaped and her thick, curly eyelashes were pasted on a creamy complexion. I ran my hands over her fuzzy blond hair and cheeks soft as clouds. Ingrid insisted she was the image of me, but I couldn't see it. She was just herself, my little doll, Annie. I could hear Nathan playing with his toys in the other room and singing a little made-up tune. I loved my children so much, but how I wished I had enough energy to enjoy them more!

I left Annie in my bed after she fell asleep, and curled up beside her. Frazzled thoughts raced as though through a vacuum. Darren and I were losing touch with each other. He was so busy and worried about money, and I was too tired to spend time with him at the end of the day. Tears formed in my eyes, ran over and dripped on Annie's little head. She slept soundly.

What kind of a future were we giving our children? What kind of a world did we bring them into? A world where dreams burst into view, tantalizing and full of enticing possibilities, then slowly vanished from sight? Just like the sun rose over the horizon of youth and disappeared behind gray clouds of reality before it could develop and illumine the grinding wheel of daily life?

I had a dream once, to become a doctor. My father destroyed that one with devastating, hurtful words that drove me into Darren's arms. *"How clever of him,"* I reasoned, giving him credit for far more than he could have anticipated. His words caused me to perform actions that spoiled my dreams faster than any arguments on his part. Still, I wouldn't give up Nathan and Annie for anything.

I felt a slight nudge at my arm. With Nathan's tummy temporarily filled, he climbed into bed on the other side of me and snuggled close.

I wiped my eyes. *If only . . . if only I had something to look forward to.* Maybe I could talk Darren into letting me go back to school. Not now, of course. But when he finished his education, found a good job, and was established. Then I could go to college and get my degree. I'd work hard. *Maybe . . . a goal . . . a hope.*

I decided to talk to him that very night.

Chapter 14

My eyelids were getting heavy. The clock above the sofa told me it was nearly 11:00 p.m. Darren was later than usual. *"Wouldn't you know it,"* I thought to myself, *"when I had decided to wait up for him!"*

Nathan went to bed, protesting as usual, about three hours earlier. After the third glass of water, he finally gave in to slumber. Annette woke for her feeding at 9:45, but I fed, changed, and put her back in the crib in less than an hour.

Now I waited impatiently, curled up on the sofa in our crowded living room, tucked snugly under the pink and blue afghan Ingrid crocheted for us when we got married. It didn't match the green, orange, and brown Early American furniture that I'd inherited when Grandma Lydia died, but I didn't care. It wasn't my style, but we couldn't afford to buy anything new. At least we had something to sit on, and it was in good shape. Fatigue began to overwhelm me, so I put down the mystery I was reading and flipped on the TV to keep me awake. It didn't take long for my eyes to lose their focus. Johnny Carson was fading into a blur.

I was dozing off when the sound of a creaking door awoke me. My head jerked up to see Darren standing in the doorway. His jacket and jeans were dusty and caked with clumps of mud from his afternoon in the fields. Disheveled hair peeked out from under his cap, but his eyes lit up when he saw me.

"You stayed up for me, Cass!" The pleasure in his voice tweaked my conscience. I hadn't exactly stayed up for his sake, rather for my own. "Let me shower and change out of these grubs and I'll join you." He patted my arm, pecked me on the forehead, and disappeared down the narrow hall. Ten minutes later, he woke me again, gently lifted me up to a sitting position, and squeezed into the corner of the sofa, laying my head back onto his shoulders. He propped his feet up onto the coffee table. Bleary red eyes underlined with dark circles testified to long hours of toil in the fields. With my own eyes barely open, we made a good pair!

"How was your day, honey?" Concern etched his voice. He'd commented lately on the way I dragged myself around the house. He knew the kids and close quarters were getting to me. I'd tried unsuccessfully to hide my depression, but since Annie was born, my gloomy attitude hadn't been much to come home to. I'd been snapping at Darren. *Poor man.* He was so steady and dependable. I needed to make an effort to stay up and greet him more often when he got home.

"Isn't the harvesting almost done, Darren? You can't keep these hours up much longer. I'm surprised Sven lets you work so late. He used to be a stickler for safety when it gets dark and you're already exhausted."

Darren sighed heavily. "He still is. I just overrule him." He rubbed his eyes with the thumb and middle finger of one hand. "I don't get to the fields 'til after lunch. Mom won't let me out the door without a good meal." He managed a half-hearted grin. "You know my mother. She says, 'Tractor needs fuel to run on and so do you.'" A smile lifted the corners of his lips, and I could imagine Ingrid in a military pose with hands on her hips, tilting her head upwards to her tall, muscular son as she commanded him to sit and eat. "Someday, Cassie, I'll be making enough money to buy us a house of our own, with a back yard for the kids to play in."

Gertrude's passion, like Ingrid's, was gardening. But unlike Ingrid, she refused to let children play anywhere near her vegetable and flower gardens. Her gardens took up most of the yard anyway, so there wasn't much room left for playing. On sunny days, I took Nathan and Annie to the park two blocks away. Otherwise, Nathan had to play indoors.

"I know you're working awfully hard." I traced his profile with my fingertip and the tension visibly drained from his face. Maybe I'll be able to help you someday."

"Help me?" He settled back in the cushion and laid his head on the sofa.

"Um hmm," I stroked his forehead. "When the kids get older, I can go back to school and get my degree . . ."

Darren's eyes popped open. His startled expression riveted to my face. "Go back to school?" He didn't look perturbed, only puzzled.

"Remember my dream of becoming a doctor? I was thinking about it today and . . ."

"Cassie," This was not uttered sharply, but with a definite halt. "You can't be a doctor now. You're a mother!"

"What's that got to do with it?" Excitement fused new energy into my body for the first time in months. I popped up on the couch. "In a couple of years, Nathan will be in kindergarten and we can put Annie into pre-school. I could go to the junior college in Lakeland and then take correspondence courses from the University until I graduate from college. I know medical school is still a long way off, but . . ."

"Hush, Cassie," Darren gently laid two fingers on my lips. "I'm supporting you. I'm the husband, the bread-winner, the provider. You are the mother and the homemaker."

"Darren, that's old fashioned," I protested. "Haven't you heard of women's lib? You know, voting, bra-burning?" I teased.

Darren's mouth fused into a tight line. "My wife is not going to be a women's libber. And no baby sitter is going to raise my children." He sat up and straightened his back, arms folded across his chest.

"Darren," I sputtered, at a loss for what to say next. I was used to a reasonable husband, open to my needs and concerns. I felt like I'd hit a concrete wall. I'd prepared myself for financial objections, but had no idea he'd oppose to my desire to go back to school and get a job.

"Please think about it, Darren." I heard the whine in my voice, but I couldn't change it. *This was so unfair!* "I know its years away, but it'll give me something to look forward to. This is my dream, Darren, my life-long dream!"

Darren was up and pacing now. He halted and turned to face me.

"Your dream? What about *my* dream? To have a farm of my own someday? To plant some crops, raise cattle? It's not going to work out for me, Cassie. I need a steady income. Farming is not a good risk any more, not a small farm like I could afford. The closest I'll ever get to my dream is helping my dad for a few more years." Tension lines of discouragement creased his face, and gave it an unnaturally hard look.

"I know, honey," my voice softened. "I hurt for you, but does that mean that I have to give up my dream, too?"

He spread out his hands in a gesture that looked so helpless it touched my heart in spite of my determination to see this through. "What about Nathan and Annie? I know they weren't planned, and you were nowhere near ready for them. But they're here now and they are our responsibility, Cassie. I'm working my tail off to make a living for us!"

"But that's the point. I can *help* you make a living eventually!"

No!" A shout of command. I was shocked into silence. Darren never shouted at me. Annie started to wail.

Not now, Annie. Please be quiet! I stood up and started to go to her. Darren stood also, grabbed me by the shoulders, and turned me around. He stayed calm, but as impregnable as a moat filled with crocodiles.

"No wife of mine will go out to work. I will be able to provide for us."

"But I don't mean to say you won't. Or can't." I shook my head. I was getting flustered.

"Cassie, we're both exhausted. Our nerves are frayed. But I am thinking clearly and I will not change my mind. You have a full time job, raising our kids. You're a great mother, Cassie."

"No, I'm not a great anything," I slumped against his shoulders and he held me close. Annie's sobs had subsided. I was glad I hadn't gone in to her.

My kids were the gold in my treasure chest. But I felt like the real "me" was disappearing, fading into a dark blur of nothingness. I existed as Darren's wife and Nathan's and Annie's mother. *Who was I?* Years ago, I had tried in vain to answer that troubling question when my father exiled me from the only home I'd ever remembered. Now I began to slip further and further into a spiraling tunnel that sucked me down into a pit of pure anonymity. Demands on my time, resources, and body gave me no respite. I was losing control of my life. Now my hopes were shriveling away as well. Darren was not one to change his mind easily. I couldn't fight him. I needed his support.

"Come on, Cassie, come to bed. We both need a good night's sleep."

"That's fine for you, Darren," I was thinking, *"I can't remember what a good night's sleep is!"* But I let him put his arm around me and lead me into the bedroom.

My depression deepened after that. The light bulb of my last lamp of hope flickered out. Winter was rapidly approaching. Each evening grew darker than the one before. Monotony ruled my days. Even Annie's first tooth and her efforts at crawling failed to penetrate the wall of despair I'd built around me. I scarcely noticed as she turned into a smiling charmer who enthralled anyone who came to visit us. Not that there were many visitors those days. I didn't get out much, so I had no friends in the area. I had gradually lost touch with Liz Beth after I'd left my home on Lake Clarity. I was thankful that Ingrid and Sven stopped over nearly every week when they came into town to shop. Ingrid and I grew closer, as we shared love and concern for Nathan and Annie. Ingrid adored her grandchildren, and raved about each little progress they showed. She lifted my spirits just like Grandma

Lydia had done. Ingrid always demonstrated her faith. Sometimes, if she knew Darren was going to be gone, she'd sneak me a chuck of meat loaf or pot of soup so I wouldn't have to cook that night. Then she'd insist on scrubbing the bathtub or vacuuming the carpet. Ingrid understood that Darren wanted us to be independent, but still wanted to help me. Being such an observant and sensitive person, I'm sure she saw through my plastic exterior to the despair hidden in my soul.

The mundane round of dishes, diapers, and dirt that always needed to be attacked and conquered was a battle I knew I was losing. Annie was teething again, and woke up often during the night. I always went to comfort her. I didn't have the heart to let her cry it out when I knew she was hurting. Despair clamped its stubborn grip on my mind and wouldn't let go. It drained me of the little energy I had remaining. The resulting fatigue only increased my tendency toward negative thoughts and distorted perception. I lost patience with the kids easily and snapped at Darren, when I saw him, which wasn't often. There was always something to help with at the farm, since only an old man and a blind boy were running the place. I suspected Darren would find more jobs to take on there to avoid his grouchy wife.

My misery multiplied like the ripples in a pond that flow out from the center when a pebble is thrown into its murky waters. I was drowning in my own pond of despair and didn't see any life raft coming to rescue me.

One good thing had happened that autumn. Jim and Kathy Hanson moved in next door with their daughters, Emily, who was five years old, and Tamara, three years. I met Kathy one day on my way to the park. It was a crisp morning, but sunny. Annie was nearly smothered in layers of blankets and tucked cozily into her stroller. Nathan trotted along impatiently besides me, bundled in his brown, furry jacket with a hood that made him look like a teddy bear. Kathy was kneeling by a small garden patch next to her mailbox when we walked by. Her girls played nearby on a swing set, newly installed in their yard. She was planting tulip and daffodil bulbs. Her soft, brown hair was cropped close to her head and brown eyes sparked when she noticed us. Nathan had already spotted the swing set and was yanking at my hand. "Mommy, can I play on it? Please . . ." I shook his arm off of me and stopped to introduce myself and admire her garden. It was still adorned with purple asters and golden mums.

Kathy sat back on her heels and brushed her forehead with a dirty hand, leaving fresh dirt marks. "I can't take credit for it," she smiled. "Those are perennials the Estebauns left behind when they moved. I'm anxious to see what will come up in the spring, but I don't want to take a chance and miss seeing tulips. I love it when bright red and yellow colors pop up out of the ground as soon as the snow leaves. Winter is so black and white and spring is dull brown until the flowers come. I love colors, don't you?"

"Yes." I too, loved to see the bright colors arrive in the spring. "I don't have a garden. That is, not one of my own. We're renting the upstairs apartment next door. Gertrude, my landlady, plants everything imaginable, but I'm not fond of her garden. It takes up the whole yard so Nathan isn't allowed to play there. We're on our way to the park. Nathan, wait for Mommy!" My son had given up yanking on my arm and was propelling his legs along the sidewalk ahead of me. He was almost out of sight.

Nathan halted but his legs kept going up and down. "Hurry up, Mommy. I want to play!"

"Nathan can come over here and play," Kathy invited. "Every day if you like, when the weather's good. We have a fence and I can see the kids easily from the kitchen window. My girls would love it."

"Oh, I didn't mean to hint. I couldn't impose on you."

"Nonsense," she laughed, a twinkling, joyful laugh that sounded like it came from some private store of happiness deep inside. "It'll help me out greatly. My girls are far more contented when they have somebody else to play with. Can you come in for a few minutes now?" Nathan heard the invitation and was already heading across the yard toward the swings.

Kathy's friendship made the autumn bearable, but that winter was extra cold. Temperatures dipped and stayed below zero for weeks at a time, and snowstorms were frequent. Nathan and Annie were often sick, and so was Kathy's youngest, Tamara.

Our visits were fewer and fewer. Days and nights melted into another dismal round of dishes, diapers, and dirt. With the farm work completed for another season, Darren was home more often. He had taken a part-time afternoon job as a salesman at Maxwell's Hardware Store in New Bergen. He spent evenings studying or attending classes. He was trying to earn his degree in accounting as quickly as possible so he would qualify for a job that paid a larger salary. Hank Maxwell told him that he planned to hire him soon to take over the books. His business was growing, and he needed some help with accounting. The bitter cold and snow kept Sven and Ingrid home more those days. Their trips into town were few and far between, so I saw less of them, too. I still didn't remember what it felt like to get a decent night's sleep, now that the kids took turns sneezing, sniffing, and exchanging fevers.

Ingrid worried about her grandchildren. "I declare, this old house is a breeding ground for germs," she observed, "Those nasty drafts don't give a body a chance to warm up properly and fend off sicknesses. Why don't you give up this place and come stay with us on the farm?"

I was sorely tempted, just for the sake of regular companionship and help with the kids. But Darren was adamant. "We need to make our own home, Mother. And how do you know the kids would be any healthier on the farm? Its just something they've got to go through, to build immunities and stuff. They'll be better off when they get older."

The next blow came when I got the flu and was in bed for a week. Darren was good about helping with the cooking and laundry, in spite of his hectic schedule. He didn't seem to care about the cleaning though. Sometimes I wondered if men could even see dirt. When I was finally able to drag myself out of bed, my recovery was slow, probably due to all those interrupted nights.

I remember the day when thoughts of suicide crossed my mind. It was late afternoon. A blizzard had been raging for three days. Thirty mile-an-hour winds had dumped six feet of snow on the ground in the past three days. When the snow finally stopped falling, vicious winds continued to blow it into huge drifts that rose all the way to the rooftops. I looked out my window the day before to see our neighbors' dog running around on their roof! Some of the local farmers stretched out strong ropes between the doorknobs of their houses and barns so they could hold onto the ropes when they went to the barns to feed the cattle. That way, they were sure to find their way back to the house. But my husband considered himself indestructible and faithfully went to the hardware store every day. It was only a few blocks away, but I worried. He bundled himself up in a snowsuit, down-filled gloves, and a knit mask that covered his face except for eye and nose holes, and tramped off to work. I missed him so much and wished he would at least take a snow day off work, but he was raised with a strong work ethic. I supposed I should be grateful. It put food on the table. Nathan had finally stopped throwing up from the twenty-four-hour flu. Both kids were sleeping. I sat by the living room window, staring at the patterns of frost delicately engraved on the panes. I remember Mama telling me that a strange creature named Jack Frost painted pictures on our windows with his brush made out of an icicle. *"Mr. Frost must be a master of deceit,"* I thought. He created delicate, fragile designs depicting Old Man Winter as a docile, courteous creature. Yet, at heart, he was an angry being who reveled in unleashing his pent-up fury on an unsuspecting world. I was trapped. Life had lost its zest years ago. Day melted into day with a blur of unending chores. *What was the purpose of life, anyhow? If there was any, I had been unable to find it. Why was I even born? To spend seventy or eighty years sunk in a mire of misery? And then what? Would anything come after death?* Grandma and Ingrid insisted there was a heaven, a vague image that sounded to me like a vast amusement park in the sky. Happiness forever--no tears, no sickness. As much as I admired both women, my father's view of reality seemed more plausible.

Death was the end of existence. Period.

I wondered where my father was and how he was doing. He gave Grandma his address and telephone number when he moved to Boston, but we had only phoned him on one occasion. I called to tell him I was getting married to Darren. He was distant and cold. His attitude confirmed the fact that I was on my own, for good. I had no idea if he still lived in Boston, or had moved to another place. I never expected to see him again. Surely, I would make no effort to do so. He had written me out of his life, and that was where I planned to stay.

So why did I even try to survive in this messed up world? I was raising my kids to become capable children with good grades and pleasant manners. And for what? A lifetime of futile searching for happiness? And then death? The finality of non-existence would end it all anyway. What point was there of stretching out my days beyond any measure of contentment? I was restless. My bones still ached from the flu and lack of rest. My head was fuzzy. Thoughts rambled through my brain like pieces of a jigsaw puzzle that didn't fit together. Pieces were missing. The whole picture wouldn't come together.

I got up and walked into the kitchen. Darkness was spreading its tightly woven blanket of gloom over the horizon. I wondered what it would be like to live way up north where there was no sun for months in the winter. To work in a heavy cloud of total blackness whose icy fingers reached out to grab its victims and swallow them up in its despairing depths.

Darren didn't need me. Always occupied with work or studies, he hardly had time to look at me these days. He was a good father, though the time he extended to our children was meted out sparingly. If I died, he'd adjust quickly. A man as handsome and personable as Darren would easily find someone to marry him. Someone like Kathy, lively and full of fun, not a deadbeat like me. The kids deserved a better mother anyway, one who had enough energy to play games and frolic in the snow. For years, I thought my calling in life was to become a doctor. Now that dream was destroyed, dashed to pieces, and washed down the drain.

I sank into a chair and leaned my elbows on the table with fingers massaging my brow. My thinking wasn't completely rational. I was over-tired, stretched to the breaking point. But I wanted a way out, desperately. *Why not make the end come sooner? What point was there in struggling for years?*

I raised my head and my thinking became focused. The kids would probably sleep for hours if I didn't wake them up for supper. Chances were good that Darren would be the one to come home and find my body. It would be hard on him, but not as traumatic as if Nathan were to climb out of bed and make the discovery. The early darkness would convince Nathan it was night time if he awoke, so he would just roll over and go back to sleep. A disturbance struggled in the inner recesses of my mind. A tiny but determined segment was leading a rebellion against the reasoning I thought was sound, attempting to force a note of sanity into my muddled rationalization.

There! It was coming clearer. A question I had to answer. Again I rubbed my brow, as if to push the insistent thought into the open so I could hold it up for evaluation. *How does my dream of becoming a doctor fit with the idea of taking my own life?*

I remembered when I had almost taken the life of my child. My hallucinations in the form of Doctor Cassandra Dupont illuminated my decision process and saved Nathan from death. *So how could I take my own life?* But my mind was at war. This was different. I knew it was wrong to condemn someone else, especially my own baby, to an early grave. And I had finally acknowledged a strong instinct to preserve his life. *But shouldn't I have the power to choose when to end my own life? My life was out of my control, but couldn't death, at least, be in my own hands?*

How would I do it? Pills? I didn't have enough aspirin in the house to accomplish the job. I had no desire to wake up in the emergency ward of the local hospital with a pump in my stomach. Darren had a hunting rifle I could use, but the noise would wake the kids.

My eyes wandered around my tiny kitchen and lighted on the gas stove. I hated the thing. It was old and often needed repeated efforts to light it. I handled it with trepidation, worrying that a flame might extinguish itself one day and fill the house with gas fumes. Now it seemed to be a friend. It offered a painless way to die. As I rose from my chair, my heart suddenly began to pound out a rapid beat as the enormity of what I was about to do settled into my mind. My breathing became tight and I fleetingly wondered if I would expire from heart failure before I had a chance to turn on the gas. Suddenly, a strange, powerful sensation bordering

159

on excitement invaded my senses. I felt like a foreign body was invading my own. Rebellious pulsing again rose up inside of me, this time to protest the evil presence and try to push it out. But I hammered it down. I was convinced this was my own plan, my decision, under my control.

In a fog, I moved slowly around the kitchen, checking windows to make sure they were tightly shut, pulling the shades to keep out prying eyes. Softly, I shut the door to the hallway, after listening carefully to make sure the children were asleep. I rolled up a towel and laid it down to cover the crack under the door, so none of the dangerous fumes would escape. I had made the decision. Now I was driven by a sense of urgency to carry out my plan. The thought crossed my mind that I should go and take one more look at my children, but the dark stranger had now taken over. He wouldn't let me postpone the deed any longer.

Slowly but with determination, I approached the stove and opened the oven door. My heart rate was settling down a bit and I managed to take a deep breath. An unusual calm settled in my spirit. But the calm was made of mushy quicksand that seemed stable and resilient on the surface, yet was composed of nothingness underneath. I thought I was in charge. I was unable to acknowledge that, in this act of despair, I was turning over control to an evil persona, one who wanted to lead me to the depths in order to conquer me.

I thought I had a choice.

I had none.

The evil influence was taking over. I was merely following orders. As if in a haze, I turned the oven burner on and cautiously knelt on the floor in front of it. Slowly, I laid my head on the oven door. It felt hard and uncomfortable. The thought invaded my mind that I should get a pillow. I nearly laughed out loud. In a few more minutes, my comfort would never again be an issue. I started to feel giddy as I tried to relax on the hard surface. The pungent scent of gas repelled me, and its fumes made my eyes water. Thoughts went unbidden to my childhood days. Curiosity hadn't diminished. I wondered if my whole life would flash before my eyes as I'd heard happened at the point of death. *How did any-*

body know that? No one came back from the grave to tell us! I remembered the angel that had rescued me—or so I had thought— as a child. Suddenly, my brain snapped into focus and my thoughts became as clear as polished glass. I was certain with every fiber of my being that the angel had been real. I could no longer hide the truth. I couldn't push it under my consciousness like I had tried to do as a little girl when my father and mother convinced me it had never happened. Maybe being on the threshold of eternity enabled my senses to push aside the curtain of time and view the world of reality, which most of us deny even exists.

Simultaneously, the phone began to ring. *I wouldn't answer it. Nobody was going to pull me away from this deed.* Then I realized the continued ringing would wake Nathan and he'd come out to look for me. The moment of clarity vanished. I groggily staggered to my feet, gasping for air with every movement. I groped my way to the phone, just wanting to hush up the caller and get back to business. I picked up the receiver and held it to my ear.

"Yes?" My voice sounded muffled to me.

"Cassie, can you come over? Right now?" It was Kathy. It sounded like she had been crying and there was a note of hysteria in her voice. "I need your help!"

Adrenaline now took over to pull me out of my lethargy. Of course I'd go. Kathy was my friend. I didn't even hesitate. "Sure. I'll be right over." My voice was stronger already.

"Are your kids in bed?"

"Yes. I'll be right there."

"Thanks Cassie. You're a lifesaver." She hung up.

The stove. I moved quickly to turn off the gas. Hanging onto the edge of the table, I groped my way back and turned the dial. My head felt like it was going to explode. I needed air. I stared at the window, a mere few feet away, but my fingers and toes were beginning to tingle and my body started to sway.

No, no, I can't faint now. Kathy needs me. Slowly, Cassie, one step at a time. Two, three. Come on, you can make it. Somehow, I got all the way to the window, threw up the shade, and frantically fumbled with the latch. It stuck.

"God, help me." Unbidden, the words flew out of my

mouth. Instantly the latch snapped open and I nearly tore the hinges off raising it up. Fresh, invigorating, cold air hit me like an iceberg. I inhaled deeply, over and over, filling my lungs with the welcome, life-giving oxygen. Leaving the window wide open, I grabbed my jacket and quickly stuffed my feet into boots. I dashed down the back stairs, out the door, and across the yard to my friend's house.

Chapter 15

The howling wind challenged me to defy its veracity as I fought my way across the yard to Kathy's house. I tugged my parka hood tightly in an effort to partially cover my face as I struggled against the powerful force. I climbed onto her porch and pounded on the front door. Kathy flung it open immediately and greeted me without a word. Her wild, frantic eyes said it all. She quickly grabbed my hand and pulled me into the living room, without even giving me time to remove my boots.

Her panic-stricken face totally unprepared me for the sight that met my eyes as we entered the living room. Laughter rumbled up inside of me and threatened to escape when I beheld the cause for all this commotion. Kathy's living room was much more orderly than mine. Green and rose flowered drapes set the tones for her feminine-looking décor. A sturdy but fashionable green and white striped sofa reposed against the far wall. Two patterned armchairs of varying shades of rose and pink stood on either side of her light-colored brick fireplace. The only signs of disorganization were a few children's books scattered around, open coloring books, and crayons on the coffee table.

In one corner was displayed an old earthenware crock that Kathy had told me was handed down from her grandmother. Inside the crock was the center of our attention. Out of it peered a little head framed with curls. Tamara's tear-stained face protruded from the opening of the jar. Her tiny body was solidly wedged inside the crock, and her expression was one of complete disbelief and dis-approving resignation.

Emily danced around the room in a feverish frenzy. "We were playing hide-and-seek," she hastily explained. "I was in the bedroom looking for Tamara when she started yelling." Emily rushed up to me and yanked the hand Kathy was not holding. "We can't get her out. Help us, please." Tears bubbled out of her eyes and careened down her cheeks. Both mom and daughter looked at me like I was Superman, or Supermom, or whatever!

My head was just beginning to clear from the effects of the gas stove. I had no idea what to do.

"What have you tried?" I asked Kathy.

"I pulled and tugged at her, but she's stuck very tight," Kathy explained. "I tried calling Jim at work but his phone is out of order."

"Because of the storm, I suppose," I muttered.

"Mommy tried to dump her out. She tipped the crock over, but Tamara wouldn't even budge." Emily's eyebrows crinkled in a reproving way, as though Tamara was being obstinate.

Tamara looked like she was going to start crying again.

I had to do something. But what? I walked over and pat-ted Tamara's little head. "We'll have you out of there in no time," I brightly promised with a confidence I didn't feel.

"I'm afraid to break it for fear of hurting Tamara," Kathy told me.

Tamara started yelling again.

What could I do? How did I loosen jars? Hot water? Cold water? Poor Tamara!

Oil!

"Do you have any vegetable oil or grease?"

"Yes!" Kathy ran to the kitchen and quickly returned with

a full bottle of salad oil.

"Give it to me."

The yells stopped again, though Tamara eyed me dubiously. Kathy and Emily seemed to be holding their breath. I took the cover off the bottle and started to pour the oil all around her.

"Yuck, Mommy!" Tamara protested violently. Her limbs began to shake.

"Its okay, honey. Mommy's here."

"Let's pull her over to the hall so we don't get oil all over your carpet," I suggested. Now that I knew it wasn't a matter of life or death, I started getting practical. *After all, why ruin the carpet?*

Kathy nodded gratefully. "Good idea." She was perking up, which in turn calmed Tamara. "You're going for a ride, Tamara!" The forlorn child looked like she'd just as soon stay put, but she stayed quiet. Emily pranced in circles around us now, clapping her hands for joy, and generally got in our way, creating more confusion.

"She's not out yet," I muttered under my breath, wondering what I'd do next if this didn't work. They were all depending on me.

Together, we managed to drag the crock along with its innocent victim into the hallway. I carefully began to tip it over. Tamara balanced precariously for a tense moment, and then one slender arm slid out. A beaming smile broke out on her face.

"Hooray!" Emily shouted as she knelt down and began to tug on her sister. Tamara slipped out like a piece of raw lutefisk, and Kathy hugged her daughter tightly.

"You're both going to need a bath," I ruefully observed as Tamara dripped oil all over herself, Kathy, and the floor. "You go get in the tub. I'll run home and see if my kids are all right, and come back and help clean up this mess."

Gratitude emanated from Kathy's eyes. "Thanks, Cassie. I don't know what I'd have done without you. Thanks for being there for me."

Her final words rang in my ears all the way across the dismal yard to my house. *"Thanks for being there for me."* In the short time I was with Kathy, the wind had calmed considerably. Even in the darkness, visibility was improving. A full moon illuminated the gray-blue sky and highlighted my path to the door.

Kathy had thanked me for being there for her. My friend needed me. I shook with the sudden knowledge that I had nearly copped out on her, Darren, and my kids. *What kind of a selfish beast was I? How could I even consider putting my family through the grief and sorrow that my sudden death would have caused them? Not to mention the extra work for Darren. And what if he didn't remarry? How could my children face the future, knowing their own mother couldn't handle the challenge?* I shuddered again at the realization of how close I had come to failing my family in the worst way a woman could fail them.

Did an angel come back to rescue me, to save my life a second time? The phone call had certainly come at an opportune moment. I had a brief, humorous vision of my angel stuffing little Tamara in the crock. No, I didn't imagine angels worked that way.

Still, for an instant of vivid, stark reality, I knew that the angel that saved me as a child had been real. Now that I had returned to my world of normality, doubts began to form again. Yet I had prayed over the stuck lock and it had suddenly popped free. *Was it possible that there could be a God who watched over us and sent angels to help us?* That's what Grandma and Ingrid believed.

Darren was home when I arrived and was mystified about the open window. I wasn't ready to tell him the whole story, so I just said that I needed some fresh air and when Kathy called, I had left suddenly without closing it.

He wasn't too pleased and gave me a brief lecture concerning economy and the cost of fuel. Nevertheless, he had difficulty keeping the corners of his mouth in line when I told him of Tamara's dilemma, and offered to stay with the children so I could return and help my friend.

"She did look comical, didn't she, Cass?"

Now that the tension was gone and both girls were safely tucked in bed, Kathy and I were free to sort out our tangled emotions and find relief in laughter. We sat at Kathy's kitchen table, sipping steaming mugs of chamomile tea. Kathy said it would relax our nerves. We were both wired as tightly as strings on a piano.

"I couldn't believe it. I was afraid somebody was badly hurt, and then I saw her pathetic little head sticking out of the crock. I tried so hard to keep from giggling."

Kathy and I burst out laughing. Happy laughter. Relief.

"She looked like a butterfly trying to escape from a cocoon."

"Or a chicken hatching from an egg!"

"I'm surprised she could even crawl in there."

"She's small boned and the crock is roomy."

"She'll never do it again."

"You bet! She probably won't go anywhere near that crock 'til she's sixteen years old!"

We broke out into spasms again. I finally composed myself when my stomach started to hurt, and saw Kathy wiping tears from her eyes. Finally drained of our emotions, the chuckling turned into sighs.

"Seriously, Cassie, I don't know what I would have done if you weren't home. Can you imagine me calling the police to report my daughter was stuck in a crock?"

My sudden laughter quickly subsided, and I grew thoughtful.

"What is it, Cassie?" Kathy was always quick to sense my moods. She reached out to touch my arm. "Did I upset you too much? I'm sorry. Its just that . . ."

"No, no, Kathy, I was glad to help."

"You were worried about leaving your kids."

"No, I . . . Kathy," I swallowed hard and spit it out. "It's just that, I was . . . I mean I almost wasn't there."

"What do you mean?"

I had to tell somebody. Not Darren. At least, not yet. He wouldn't understand and would worry. Of course I didn't know how Kathy would react either. I spoke in a soft, tremulous voice, "I tried to kill myself today."

"No, Cassie." Her eyes examined me with a fierce intent. "What's going on? Is it that bad? Is Darren mean to you? Or the kids?"

"No, not at all." I shook my head and felt fresh tears sliding down my cheek. "He's wonderful to us. When he's around." Now that I had started, the words tumbled out. " He's gone nearly all the time, working hard. He says he wants to make a future for us. But I'm alone so much I feel like a single mom. The kids have been sick all winter. I've been sick. I can't keep up with the house work. I'm lonely and I feel like a failure. I gave up my dreams of being a doctor when I married Darren. I feel trapped, like my life is already over. And I feel so guilty. I love my kids, but I wasn't ready for them. I didn't choose this life. It just happened. I thought if I got away from my father, I could control my own life. But I can't control one hour of one day. I'm trapped."

I sighed with despair. "I can't expect you to understand. I'm sorry. I didn't mean to burden you. You've got a great husband. A nice house." My eyes wandered over the room. Everything matched in her kitchen, too. It was a light, sunny room that faced east. The walls were off-white. Bright touches of blue and yellow added cheerfulness even on a stormy day like today. Kathy's silence seemed to confirm my mistake at barging into her emotions like this. I decided I'd better leave before I caused her any more trouble.

But her words surprised me. "I understand, Cassie. You don't know how well I understand." My friend's eyes were liquid pools. Her lower lip trembled. I was bewildered. *Why was I causing her so much pain?*

"You see, Cassie," her gaze extended far beyond me as she stared out the window at infinity. "My first child died. He was stillborn."

I gasped. "Oh, Kathy. I'm so sorry. I didn't know."

"I don't talk about him much." Her hands trembled as she poured another cup of tea from her flowered antique teapot. "It still hurts whenever I think about him." She took a sip of tea and set the cup down. "We named him Robert James, after my husband and his father. I'd had a difficult pregnancy. I was hospitalized in the third month and nearly lost him then. In the seventh month, I got toxemia. I'd been on bed rest for three weeks when Robert decided to come early."

She smiled, a sad, bittersweet smile. "Jim and I were so excited. We'd waited five years to have our first baby. I'd almost given up when I got pregnant. In spite of all the problems, neither of us really doubted that the baby would be born safely. The doctor told us his heartbeat was strong and he expected a healthy baby. He even said it would be a boy. I think he was just guessing. Jim said he had a fifty-fifty chance of impressing new parents, so why not go for it?

"Then I went into distress on the delivery table. We got scared." She bit her lip and fresh tears clouded her eyes. She grabbed my hand with the strength of urgency. "Oh, Cassie, he was so beautiful. His features were perfect, like a doll. But he was . . . his color was dull gray. I insisted on holding him. The doctor wanted them, the nurses, to take him away, but Jim stopped them. 'It's our baby,' he said. 'Let his mother say 'good-bye'.'"

Her voice broke and she laid her head on the table. I stroked her shaking shoulder. The house was perfectly still. Outside, the howling of the storm had faded away. Kathy lifted her head. "It was so hard. All I could think of was how some people don't even want children and give birth so easily. And Jim and I wanted a baby so bad. I just wanted to die."

Now it was my turn to choke up. "I'm one of those people." I blurted the words out. I didn't know if our friendship could stand this new test, but I had to be honest with her.

Kathy sat up. "I don't blame *you*, Cassie. You may not have wanted to get pregnant, but you love your children."

"I wanted an abortion at first. I couldn't face the future. I came so close to killing my baby." The last words were spoken in a whisper.

The hurt in Kathy's eyes intensified. But it was not the hurt of rejection. Rather, I could see she felt my pain. "I'm so glad you changed your mind, Cassie. You would have regretted it later, and the pain would have been overwhelming."

I nodded. I knew what she meant. Every time I gazed at

Nathan, I thought of how close I'd come to losing him. And today, I had almost caused him to lose me! Suddenly, I was faced with a critical dilemma. I could no longer bear to live, yet neither could I escape. The trap was rapidly closing me in again.

"How did you bear it, Kathy?" My innermost soul was pleading for help. I was so tired of the constant hurt, guilt, and struggles. "How did you go on living?"

Her answer was simple, yet shocked me to the center of my being.

"I found Jesus, Cassie."

The silence that followed was a precious gift. It gave me time to digest the new information. At first, I was surprised that she had not mentioned this before. But then I remembered negative remarks I had made in her presence concerning faith or the church. And I realized why she had hesitated letting me know she was a believer. I probably would have avoided her. It would have been the end of our friendship.

Why had I been so blind? The most important women in my life all agreed that God existed. Their lives demonstrated a simple integrity and goodness that proved they were dependable and wise. On her deathbed, Mama risked the wrath of her husband to hide and read a Bible, and pass it on to me. It was the only thing she'd cared about leaving with me.

Yet all these years, I'd chosen to accept my father's view of life and eternity, when he was not much more than a cruel and heartless influence in my life. Kathy, Grandma, Ingrid, and Sven, too, all had a strength that showed in their acceptance of difficulties. They had a source of peace and contentment that I needed desperately. Darren would say Christianity was only for the weak, but so what? If I got strength from Christ, wouldn't it all be worth it? And weren't we all weak in some area of our life, anyway?

I broke the silence. "Kathy, I want . . . I mean I need . . . what you have. What do I do? I have a Bible my mother gave me when she died, but I haven't read much. I know I'm supposed to pray, but I don't know how."

"Cassie, it's so easy. You can talk to God just like He was sitting here beside you. He really is here with us, you know."

I felt uneasy. This was new to me.

"What do I say?"

"Well, first you need to understand how much God loves you."

"I think I already know that." I thought of my angel and how close I'd come to death twice, but God prevented it.

Kathy reached over to the counter behind her and picked up a Bible. It was white, just like mine, with her name engraved in gold on the front and gold-glided pages. She flipped through it like she was well acquainted with it and knew where to find what she wanted.

"Here, listen, Cass," Kathy read. "It says in John 3:16, 'For God so loved the world, that He gave His only begotten Son, that whoever believes in Him should not perish, but have eternal life.' Just think, Cassie, we both have been crying over our sons. I cried because my son died, and you cried because of what you almost did to him. But God willingly gave His only Son to die for us on a cross, as a condemned criminal, even though He had never committed a crime, or even a sin. What love!" Excitement shown in her eyes along with love, which I knew was for God, and also for me. I felt valuable and cherished for the first time in my life! I could see all of Grandma's and Mama's love reflected in her eyes. For the first time, my life made sense.

"Here's another one, Cassie, in Romans 3:23," she continued to read, "for all have sinned and fall short of the glory of God.' You see, Cassie, we all sin. Every person on the face of the earth has turned his back on God at some time in his life and wanted to do things his own way." I certainly could identify with that!

"That's what sin is all about," she continued. "Its wanting to disregard our Creator and go our own way. He's the one who made us and knows what's best for us, but we want to be the master of our own lives! Sin is what makes us want to control our future and everyone around us, for our own selfish benefit."

"That makes a lot of sense. That's just what I've been trying to do."

"So you see, Cassie, Jesus died on the cross of Calvary many years ago, to pay the punishment that you and I deserve, for turning our backs on God. Only people who are in touch with God can go to heaven. All others will go to hell for eternity. To be tormented. *Forever.* But the great thing is, God loved us so much, He couldn't bear the thought of losing us, and chose to suffer in our place."

She seemed to ponder something for a moment.

"What really means a lot to me, Cass is . . ."

I could tell from the look on her face that it meant everything to her.

"He did something that proved His love so tremendously. I mean, I hope I would be willing to die to save your life, Cassie, or another person I cared about. But I know I couldn't give up my child to die for another person! *But God did that very thing.* He sent His only Son, Jesus, to face a wicked, broken world, and give us a way out. He gave us hope, Cassie. That's what it's all about."

Hope. That's what I needed. That was exactly what I needed.

"So if I just ask God to take me, He will?"

"Ask Him to forgive you for wanting to run your own life and tell Him you are willing to do it His way. He's the king of the universe, and beyond! He loves you. You can trust Him, Cassie!"

I thought again of my father and the way he lived. Suddenly I knew that I wanted to align myself with the gracious and good ruler of this world, not the deceptive power that convinced Papa he could succeed as his own master. By making the wrong choice, Papa sentenced himself to a life of futile searching and longing for a peace he never found.

I had no desire to belong to the persona that had taken control as I willingly surrendered myself to death just hours earlier. Horror filled me and cold chills raced along my spine as the full impact of the sudden realization overwhelmed me. *It was the evil persona of Death who had taken control.* Maybe that was the one that I've heard called Satan, or the devil. He almost conquered and defeated me in my own home. I reached out for Kathy's hand. She gave me her support willingly. I bowed my head and asked God to forgive me, to accept me as His child, and take over my life. I no longer wanted to mess everything up. I was ready to yield control to the One who loved me the most and was wise enough to care for me and my family.

Things changed after that. I still didn't conquer the dishes, diapers, and dirt. But it didn't matter as much. I found genuine pleasure in watching my children grow and develop. I learned to relax. We laughed and played more. Surprisingly enough, the Bible opened itself up to me. I found it to be no longer a source of confusion, but of hope. A deep yearning grew inside me to know this God who had been a protective stranger all my life. I wanted to introduce Him to my children and my husband.

Darren noticed the change in me. He seemed relieved and grateful. But he wouldn't give God any credit for his wife's new sense of contentment. Darren's respect for me actually seemed to diminish. He assumed my new interest in God and spiritual things was a sign of weakness and wanted no part of it. He had always been proud to be his own man, and therefore found it convenient to place his wife into the category of the weak-minded, the losers, the ones who needed a crutch to face life. An invisible barrier began to grow between us. I tried to knock it down, but each year, Darren added new bricks of distrust and isolation to the wall.

I read Bible stories to Nathan and Annie, and took them to church and Sunday School. I prayed every day for Darren. My world had expanded and a new vigor, a new appreciation for life, claimed my spirit. I had found a Friend who was totally dependable. His name was Jesus.

PART THREE
The Restoration
Chapter 16
1992

"Mom," Annette buckled herself in the passenger seat of the car as I drove out of our church parking lot. "Could I sign up for driver's training next month? I'm fifteen now, you know, and Terri says our school is going to offer a six-week course after school on Tuesdays." "How does Terri know?" I had expected this issue to come up since my daughter recently celebrated her fifteenth birthday, but I had been avoiding it. Nathan had been driving for two years, without any calamities, except for knocking down our mailbox the first week and backing over Darren's toolbox that was left in the driveway. Darren said he was amazed at how well his tools survived the trauma, though the box had to be replaced. Still, Annette was my baby, and I intended to postpone the inevitable as long as I could. She was growing up too fast as it was!

"Terri's dad is teaching it, Mom. He's an English teacher, but he's been certified as a driver's instructor. Our school wants to make the class available to us. Diane says her parents are going to let her take it. Please, Mom." At my hesitation, she added with a teasing glint in her eye, "Of course, I could ask Nathan to teach me."

"No!" I bit on that one and she laughed. My teenagers got along most of the time, but I could easily foresee a sibling disagreement while speeding down the highway at sixty miles an hour. Annie didn't like taking orders from Nathan, and Nathan enjoyed giving her orders entirely too much! I shook my head. That idea was totally unacceptable.

I glanced at my blossoming beauty. Ingrid predicted Annette would be the spitting image of me one day, but, for once, she had been wrong. My daughter looked more like her dad. Her thick dark brown hair hung loosely at her shoulders and bounced with a gentle curve when she tilted her head. Shimmering reddish highlights gleamed when the sun touched her hair through the car window, hinting of an active imagination hidden beneath a calm and gentle exterior. Her tranquil eyes were dark, like Darren's. But her chin was softly curved, not like the stubborn jaw of her mother or the firm cleft that belonged to her dad. Now her eyes pleaded with a restrained hint of eagerness and anticipation.

"I'll talk to Dad about it," I promised.

"He'll say 'yes'." She confidently turned her attention to the peaceful countryside as we whisked past newly planted corn and wheat fields. Spring was barely hatching out of its cold winter shell. Tiny buds appeared on trees that graced the hillsides in between the fields. Colorful blossoms of crocuses peeked their tiny heads out from patches of snow left dotting the ground. It was a warm, sunny day. By evening, I reckoned, those leftover patches of snow would melt and disappear.

Annie and I had just left the Sunday worship service, which we attended every week. I was so thankful that Annie came with me to church. She gave her life to Jesus when she was six years old. I saw a sweet spirit take root and grow in her young life. Of course, as a normal teenage, she sometimes focused on her own needs to the exclusion of the rest of the family, but usually she was kind and sensitive to others. With her quiet, thoughtful nature, she reached out to others, and had a close circle of friends, mostly teens from church.

Nathan, on the other hand, was something of a rebel. Not to the point of causing Darren and me grief, however. He was well-behaved and had a good heart, but had also inherited a stubborn nature from both his mother and father. Nate was very independent. No religion for him. His dad didn't need God. So why should he? Sometimes I worried that he had inherited his grandfather's personality. Nathan was intense and driven, not easy-going, like Darren. Nor was Nate quick to see how his actions affected those around him.

I hadn't thought about my father for some time. When he forced me out of his life, the pain was brutal. The years proved his intent to be serious. When I moved in with Grandma Lydia, he called her and said that he had gotten a job as a general practitioner at a large medical complex in Boston. I hadn't talked to him since before my marriage to Darren. I had no idea if he was still in Boston, or even alive. In any event, he was dead to me, and to my children.

"I'm hungry, Mom." Annie's words broke through my thoughts. "Do you know what Grandma is making for dinner?"

"She said roast beef, I think. And fresh apple pie for dessert."

"Yum. Are Dad and Nate already there?"

"Yes. They went over early to help with chores." Sven didn't want his boys to work on Sundays, the Lord's Day. But Darren insisted he had to work when he was available. His accounting job kept him busy during the week, so he did most of his share of the farm work on weekends.

"There's Uncle Billy!" We had rounded the bend and headed up the driveway to the house. Darren's blind brother, Billy, nearly always waited on the porch when we were expected for a meal. As soon as Billy's sensitive ears picked up the sound of our automobile winding up the long driveway, an enormous grin broke out over his face and he waved in the direction of the car. Annie cheerfully waved back, even though she knew he couldn't see us. There was something about Billy's attitude that made people treat him as though he had sight. He accepted his condition so well. Born blind, he'd never had a glimpse of one of God's majestic purple and rose sunsets. He hadn't see the radiant silvery twinkle of sun-kissed stars cast on the sheer surface of a summer lake. He didn't know what he was missing, so he didn't miss it.

"I can hear ya good an' hug ya better," he'd said once when Annie was little, grabbing her and squeezing her to his chest and burying his face in her fragrant hair. "An' smell you the best!" Annie giggled and Billy had let her go with a pat on the head. "That's gotta be as good as seein' ya." We didn't try to convince him differently. He was happy with his sheltered life on the farm and we loved him that way.

I pulled to a stop in the driveway next to a ridge of budding lilac trees. Soon they would be fragrant with fresh purple blossoms. Brutus, the faithful farm dog, came barking and bounding at us. Age didn't seem to affect his personality. He was as energetic as ever! Annie fought him off and ran up the porch steps to give Billy a hug. I followed her.

"Hi, Tweedle Dee." Billy's pet name for her as a child had stuck, though none of the rest of us dared use it anymore! He used to call her brother "Tweedle Dum," but when Nate reached his teens, he made it clear that his nickname was to be discontinued. "You drivin' that car yet?"

"No, Uncle Billy. But I will be soon!" She jabbered about the school driving course as Sven joined us on the porch. Darren and Nate slowly made their way up from the barn, engrossed in conversation.

Ingrid's voice blared from the kitchen, "Everybody come on in and wash up. The food's gettin' cold!" We knew it wasn't. Ingrid kept the meat and potatoes on a platter in the oven until everyone was seated at the table. She hated to start a meal with cold food and generally threatened disastrous results if people didn't hurry to seat themselves. We all obediently trooped inside, washed our hands, and took our places at the round, oak table in the kitchen. The large, formal dining room table was saved for special occasions or when many people gathered to eat.

"I declare, Ingrid," Sven observed, "Ya take longer to eat than the rest of us put together. The food's gotta be cold by the time you're done eatin'. So why on earth do ya care if it starts out cold?"

Ingrid set the heavy platter of juicy roast beef and potatoes in front of her husband. She put her hands on her hips and glared at him, "Sven, your taste buds ain't as particular as mine. You could gobble up dog food and be satisfied. I savor every bite, so it's gotta be worth savorin' to start with!"

The rest of us exchanged amused glances. We were used to their comfortable bantering. None of us were surprised that Ingrid had the last word.

"Lord," Sven's deep voice boomed as he bowed his head and reached for my hand and Annie's, who sat at the other side of him. We all quickly grasped the hand of the one next to us. "Thank you once again fer this here good food You provided and fer my wife who worked hard to cook it. Help us to honor You in our hearts and bring us all together to feast at Your table in heaven. Amen."

That was his way of praying aloud for his wayward son and grandson. I wondered what it would be like to be old enough to know you will probably die before you see all your family come to know Jesus. I peeked sideways at Darren. His stony expression registered neither interest nor offense. Inwardly I sighed. Darren was getting older, too, and even more set in his ways. *Would I sit beside him at the wedding feast of the Lamb, the heavenly celebration mentioned in the Bible? Or would I sit beside an empty chair?* A pinprick of anxiety began to chip away at my heartstrings, threatening to spoil this delicious meal.

"Potatoes, 12 o'clock; peas, 3 o'clock; roast, 6; and a roll, 9 o'clock." Annie filled Billy's plate and gave him instructions where to find his food. "Do you want gravy, Uncle Billy?" she asked.

"Pile it on, Tweedle-Dee. I can't wait to dig in! Nothin' smells as good as Mom's cookin' an' it's been tantilizin' me since we've come home from church."

Her duty finished, Annie turned to Darren. "Dad, can I sign up for Driver's Ed at school? They're starting a class next Tuesday and I can . . ."

Nate interrupted her. "My little sister at the wheel of a

car?" He teased. "Warn me when you start to practice so I can tell the principal to make everybody stay out of your way."

"I'll do better than you did. Our mailbox will be safe this time and so will Dad's tools!"

Nate had the grace to look sheepish, but he still responded, "The mailbox will be safe because Dad put bricks around it. He knew you'd be the next one learning to drive!"

"That's enough, Nate," Darren broke in. "Annie's responsible. She'll do a fine job. Go ahead, honey. Sign up. What's it going to cost me?"

"I don't know yet, Dad. I'll get the details at school tomorrow and let you know." Annie beamed at her father and turned to wrinkle her nose at Nathan.

"So, Darren," Sven was saying, "Can you hep me with the north forty this week? The forecast sounds clear an' I aim to get the ground ready for plantin'." As the conversation turned to farm work, the phone rang. Ingrid excused herself and went to answer it. She was gone quite a while. When she returned, she slipped quietly into her chair, but I noticed her face was pale and her eyes a bit red, as though she had been crying.

"What's wrong, Mom?" I asked. After my Grandma Lydia died, I had started calling Ingrid "Mom." She took the place of both my mother and my grandmother.

All eyes turned towards her. Billy tilted his head inquisitively. "Oh, Cassie," she bit her trembling lip. "I done a bad thing. I'm so sorry."

The rest of us exchanged bewildered looks. We were not accustomed to Ingrid doing "bad things." But the agony on her face was evident and she looked at me with a trace of intimidation. I'd never seen Ingrid like this. She always seemed so sure of herself. *What was going on?*

She kept staring at me. Her strange expression made everyone else turn to stare at me, too. My tongue caught in my throat.

Billy spoke up. "What did you do?"

"I lied."

Nate, who had just taken a sip of milk, started to choke.

Billy reached his arm over and automatically slapped him on the back, which made it worse. Now we all turned to stare at Nathan. The choking subsided and Nate started to laugh. "Grandma," he said. "Everybody lies sometimes." My eyebrows tightened and I glared at him. Now was not the time to argue the issue, but he saw my expression.

"Well, I mean," he hesitated. "Of course, you don't, Mom." Then with fervor, "It can't be that awful, Grandma."

Ingrid was strangely silent. She almost looked like she was afraid of me.

I spoke gently. "Did you lie to me?"

She shook her head. Sven seemed unnerved at the puzzling behavior of his wife. He cocked his head and spoke slowly, as if to a child, "Sweetheart, please tell us. Who did ya lie to?"

"Cassie's father."

I gasped. Dead silence filled the room. My heart skipped a beat and my palms started to sweat. My throat constricted. The first words that came out were hoarse and broken, so I swallowed and tried again.

"That was . . . that was Papa on the phone? Just now?"

Ingrid nodded and responded as she toyed with her silverware. "He asked if you were here and I said 'no.' I guess I felt you needed some time to react."

"It's okay, Mom." I got up and put my arms around her. "I forgive you. I don't think I could have talked to him anyway."

"I'm still sorry." Her tears flowed freely.

I was in shock.

"Has he called you before?" Darren asked.

"No, never," Ingrid responded. "Cassie said after she called to tell him about her wedding, she had no communication with him at all. And the rest of us never heard from him. 'Til today."

I nodded in affirmation. Now my insides that had originally turned to mush started to boil.

"Of all the nerve." I walked to the window and gazed out at the peaceful scene, willing it to calm my agitated nerves. "To call after all these years and upset Mom like this! I'm glad you lied. I don't ever want to talk to him again. Now maybe he'll just leave me alone for good." In spite of a firm resolve, my arms started to shake. I knew I wasn't handling this the right way. I wasn't honoring God in front of my family.

Darren came up from behind, wrapped his strong, stable arms around me and held me close.

"Mom," Annie's voice was timid. "Aren't you curious about Grandpa?"

The tender way she uttered his name slammed like bricks into my soul. The familiar, tender name of "Grandpa" wasn't fit for him. His rejection of me included my children. *Didn't Annie know that?* When he coldly cut me off, my heart was cut deeply. But it had mended, or so I thought. Now it felt like it was on the verge of ripping wide open again.

"What did he say, Grandma?" Nate asked with a soft voice, but one that was also filled with curiosity. *My kids had no business getting involved in this. My father was gone. Totally. Completely. And so was their grandfather. They had a terrific grandfather in Sven. They didn't need another one.*

I wanted to shut my ears. But the little girl part of me was just as eager as my own children to hear about the one person who had such a destructive influence on my life.

Darren stroked my hair. He seemed to sense the turmoil that was going on inside of me.

"Well," Ingrid began. "He asked me if Cassie was here. I said 'no.' She gulped. "Then he asked me how I was and I said 'fine.' Then I asked how he was." She paused. "He said his practice was doin' well and he was in good shape financially." *(Yes, that would be important to my father.)* "But, Cassie, he is very sick. He's got cancer of the pancreas. I think he said, at the most, he's got six to nine months to live."

It took a moment for her words to register. It's hard to describe how I felt at that moment. All the past humiliation, fear, and pain met with great force the vestiges of loneliness, longing and desire of a young girl for her father's love. I remembered Grandma Lydia speaking about a place she had traveled to long ago in Nova Scotia. She said she saw a river meet the sea, and described how the forceful merging of the waters caused the current of the river to reverse itself and actually flow backwards. My emotions had not reversed, but the two extremes, longing and repulsion, were crashing together, creating tremendous waves of turmoil in my mind and heart.

Ingrid continued, "He wants to see you again, Cassie. He wants to come to Minnesota while he is still able to travel. He gave me his phone number and asked me to give you the message."

My thoughts swirled in the spiraling current of emotions. *"He asked me to give you the message,"* not *"he asked me to give you his love."*

I had to know. "Did he ask how I was?"

Ingrid hesitated. She would not lie again. "No."

"Come, Cassie," Darren urged. "Finish your dinner. It's getting cold." There were no jokes this time about cold food. Darren tried to draw me to the table. I shook my head. "I want to go home. I'm sorry."

Now it was Ingrid's turn to reassure me. She stood up and patted my arm. "It's okay, honey. I understand. Darren, you take her home and tuck her in fer a good nap. Nathan can finish up some chores and bring Annie home later in the truck. I'll send some apple pie with you." She bustled out into the kitchen to pack some pie for us. We were all quiet until she returned. In one hand was a plate with two pieces of pie. In the other hand was a note with a phone number written on it.

I reached out for the pie. Darren took the note. He got my coat and led me out into the chilly air that held just a hint of the promise of spring.

Chapter 17

In the end, Darren was the one who made the call. I knew I would have to face my father again, but I wasn't ready to hear his voice. Not yet. So Darren made the initial contact, arranged for Papa's flight, and drove a hundred miles to pick him up at the airport in St. Paul. Ingrid graciously offered him a room in her home and, to my amazement, he accepted the invitation. I thought he would prefer the privacy of the small hotel in Lakeland. But maybe he'd had enough privacy, or enough loneliness.

Darren drove him directly to the farm after his arrival and saw him settled in. He told me that Ingrid hovered over Papa like a mother hen, seeing to his every need and making him more than comfortable.

"Honestly, Darren," I complained to my husband. "How can she treat him like a king after all he's done to me?"

Darren cornered me with a sober, piercing gaze. Those deep, blue eyes still captivated me. "Mother is a good forgiver, Cassie. And, after all, she's taking care of your father so you don't have to."

That stung. I knew Darren thought me a coward. And probably a poor example of the Christian faith I tried so hard to model for him. Looking back, I guess I was both. Forgiveness was not a part of my thinking process at the time. I couldn't forgive the man who had controlled my world for so long and then cast me away when I failed to fit into the tight niche he had fashioned for me.

Time passed. It was two weeks since Papa arrived at the farm. Nate and Annie were stricken with curiosity, but Darren convinced them to wait until I made my move. I was in no hurry to face my father, or even to contact him. I'm sure I tested dear Ingrid's patience to the hilt. Darren held his tongue after the first admonition. I seriously regretted letting him make that phone call to Boston, but how could I refuse the request of a dying man? Especially when that man was my own father? Still, I held back. Maybe I was unconsciously hoping that being nearby would satisfy him, and there would be no need to renew the strained relationship.

I wasn't praying much in those days. I knew what God wanted me to do, and I was not willing to do it. Trying to ignore the situation didn't help much. I practically imprisoned myself in the house, venturing out only to get groceries or go to church, probably more for Annie's sake than for mine. When I was with people, I smiled and pretended everything was all right. Skillfully, I fended off attempts from well-meaning friends to broach the subject of my father, although I knew the whole town was talking about the return of the estranged doctor. Even the weather cooperated with my mood. Nearly every day that May it rained. The cloudy, dreary days so perfectly matched my emotions that it wouldn't have taken much to convince me I had power over the weather.

Nate and Annie practically tip-toed in my presence. Their strained calm reinforced the numbness of my nerves, even as their unrelenting eyes traced my every move. My limbs felt heavy, as though they were wrapped in thick layers of soaked cotton. My soul was also weighted down and my mind frozen in a state of nothingness, a barren tundra. My family didn't pressure me, but their deliberate patience shrieked at me like a roaring thunderclap. Kathy, my neighbor, was more vocal. I met her on the first day of the third week by our mailboxes. They were lined in a row by the side of street, just outside of our yard. We still lived in the big, rambling house that we had rented when the kids were babies. The house was ours now. Gertrude sold it to us five years earlier. Somehow, Darren had managed to scrape together enough money for a down payment. Our former landlady moved down the street to a small, one-bedroom home which was, in her words, "a heap easier to take care of and considerably quieter to boot!" Although she steadfastly proclaimed her relief at living away from my "unruly teenagers," she continued to act out her self-imposed role as "ever-lasting landlady'." Gertrude dropped in every few days to see how we were doing, usually after school when Nate and Annie were around. Nate liked to tease her, and Gertrude seemed to find great satisfaction in bawling him out. Even Gertrude didn't come around much these days though. I must have been putting out vibes saying, "Stay away from me or you'll be sorry!"

This particular Saturday, however, the clouds parted long enough to let the sun peek through. The whole neighborhood, with the exception of me, seemed to be taking advantage of the clear weather. People were mowing lawns and digging fresh holes in the dirt to make beds for an assortment of tender vegetables and fragrant flowers that would soon grace the landscape. Annie was practicing her parking in our driveway, with Nathan at her side. I let Nate teach her how to park, though I still hadn't been willing to let him take her out on the road. Kathy's oldest daughters, Emily and Tamara, had grown into pretty, active teenagers. As far as I knew, Tamara had gotten over her phobia of crocks! I could still clearly recall her pathetic little head sticking out of the one in her living room. Now both girls had their eyes on Nathan. He mostly ignored them, though. They were too familiar, I guess, too easily accessible. He sought out girls who gave him a challenge. Kathy and her husband, Jim, were doing well financially and had welcomed their third child just four years ago. Talitha, their perky, dark-haired delight, was busy making mud pies in her mother's undeveloped roadside flower garden. She patiently coaxed their sandy-haired terrier, Tuffy, to eat the pies she held so appealingly to his nose. Kathy sat on the curb by her side, sorting out garden seeds saved from the previous year.

"Tuffy won't eat the pies I bake for him," four year old Talitha complained to her mother with her lower lip protruding. Two big tears threatened to fall and decorate the delicate confections in her hands.

"He's probably not hungry," Kathy responded. Then she turned and spotted me trying to escape, unnoticed, into the house with my pack of mail. "Cassie!" she called. "When are you going to see your father?" My best friend was known for her bluntness. She never avoided an issue, which is why I was trying to avoid *her*. "When I'm ready," I sighed and came over to the curb to sit down next to her.

"Auntie Cassie," Talitha called me by the affectionate title, though there was no family connection. "Would you like some pie? It's werry tasty. I made it myself." Her bright hazel eyes pleaded as the gentle breeze lifted wisps of light brown curls into her face to tickle her nose. A muddy, pudgy hand brushed the curls away, leaving traces of fresh mud on her rosy cheeks.

"Thank you very much," I solemnly let her place a muddy "pie" into my palm. Holding it to my mouth, I pretended to take a bite. "Ummm, good," I said, and Talitha squealed with delight.

"I'll make some more." Her bouncy legs carried her back to the garden patch where she began to dig with renewed energy.

"And when will you be ready?" Kathy was obviously not going to drop the subject. "What are you waiting for?"

"I don't know." I dumped the mud pie unobtrusively behind me when Talitha wasn't looking and picked up a blade of new grass. Methodically, I started to separate it into tiny shreds. "Maybe a sign," I laughed feebly and turned to look at her. "He hasn't contacted me either, you know."

"He's here, Cassie," Kathy gently reminded me. "He came all the way from Boston."

I stared into space. Kathy's intrusiveness didn't bother me. I knew she really cared, and I was somewhat relieved to be forced to face the issue. I knew I couldn't put the dreaded visit off forever. We shared silence for a while, penetrated only by the regular humming of lawnmowers and the chirping of robins. Nearby, a mommy and daddy robin were bickering noisily, probably over the proper location to build their nest.

Annie gunned the car engine as she drove back and forth, back and forth, trying to fit the vehicle between the two stakes Darren had set up for her practice sessions. Darren wouldn't let them take any more chances with our mailboxes.

"Come on, Annie," Nate's impatient voice rebuked her, "Hurry it up a little. You're moving three inches at a time. At that rate, your meter will run out before you even get the car parked!"

"Well, at least, I don't knock down everything in sight!" Annie sounded on the verge of tears. She jumped out of the car. "I'll wait 'til tonight when Dad can help me," she yelled.

Nate leaped out and ran around the car to the driver's side. "I'm sorry, Annie. Here, just watch me. I'll spin it around and come in for a smooth landing. Just three moves. Pay attention now." Annie stood in the driveway, temporarily pacified, and watched.

"Tuffy, you gotta eat your breakfast," Talitha's firm voice wouldn't take "no" for an answer this time. She grabbed the dog by his ear and tried to stuff one of her concoctions into his unwilling mouth. He shook his head, whined, and broke away. As he darted quickly across the street, Nathan inched the car out of the driveway.

"You bad dog!" Talitha stepped off the curb and made a dash for her wayward pet. Nathan watched to make sure Tuffy made it safely to the other side of the road. Then he speeded up slightly, only to slam on the brakes as Talitha raced directly into the path of the oncoming car. Everything happened at once, in a slow fog. Annie screamed, her hands coming up to cover her mouth. Talitha tried to stop but instead tripped and fell. Kathy jumped up and ran to grab Talitha's arm just as the bumper smacked her daughter's rib cage, sending her flying several feet away. Her head hit the pavement with a loud crack. Tuffy turned back, and raced to his tiny mistress, howling and running in panicky circles around her. I don't remember standing up but suddenly there I was, frozen, staring first at the motionless body lying on the rock-hard pavement, curled up, as though sound asleep in a cruel crib. Instantly, Kathy's arms wrapped around her in a useless attempt to offer protection. The worst sight of all was stark terror on the face of my son. I saw Nathan, my own flesh and blood, helplessly entangled in sturdy ropes of anguish. In a split second, my heart torn between the two critical images, I cried out, "God, Oh God, where are you?"

Annie yelled, "I'll call for help!" and turned to run into the house. Nathan was out of the car, kneeling by Talitha and Kathy. Tears streamed down his face and his hands shook as they reached out to grab the child and yet held back, all in one motion, like he was desperate to help them but couldn't make himself do it.

"My baby, my baby! Talitha honey, Mommy's here," Kathy's voice broke as she tenderly stroked her daughter's forehead and caressed her bruised body.

God infused me with a sudden calm. I don't remember much of the next hour, but I know I was the strong one. I supported Kathy, Annie, and Nathan. I was the one who explained the situation to the police. Neighbors raced across their yards to stare, cry and help. The ambulance came, to carry away the broken, but still breathing, body. Annie rode with Talitha and Kathy in the ambulance to the hospital. The police car carried Nathan with his bruised mind and me with my broken heart to the small station downtown, where Darren met us. The three of us held onto each other as officers hurled questions at my son like rocks. After much time had passed, the harsh words subsided. When Jim and Kathy were contacted they declined to press charges. Kathy said she had seen the accident and knew that Nathan wasn't to blame.

The police finally let us go home. To wait, sit, and pray. After Nathan went to bed, thoroughly exhausted, Darren and I prayed together for the first time. I didn't know if Darren even believed in the God we prayed to that day, but there was nothing else for him to do. My husband let me lead him in a prayer pleading with God to comfort our son. I begged Him to heal Talitha and restore her to her family.

Later, as I snuggled under the covers in bed, trying to gather warmth to soothe my aching spirit, I realized this was the first time in weeks that I hadn't completely focused on my own problems. Now my self-imposed isolation from my father seemed a minor issue in the light of Talitha's condition and her family's grief.

As I prayed again for Talitha, I remembered a Bible story that had stuck in my mind as a small child. Grandma Lydia used to bring Mama and me to church with her sometimes. One Sunday I had listened, fascinated, as the teacher told a story of a little girl whom Jesus raised from the dead. The little girl's name was Talitha.

Would Jesus heal this little Talitha, too?

"Cast your burden upon the Lord,
and He will sustain you;
He will never allow the righteous
to be shaken."

Psalm 55:22

Chapter 18

It was a dream. I knew I was sleeping, but I couldn't awaken myself. Kathy's fearful face hovered in front of me. Tears fell from her eyes, but she brushed them away and reached out to me. *Why? What was wrong? What was she trying to tell me?* The mailbox appeared out of nowhere. Kathy touched the mailbox. "For you," she said. "A letter." *A letter, a message. For me.* My head started to clear. The cloud lifted and the dream faded away. I opened my eyes and was back in my own bedroom. I focused on the dresser by my bed. It was an antique mahogany dresser passed down to me from Grandma Lydia when she died. I'd furnished my whole house with antiques, long before they were considered collector's items as they are today. The unwelcome dream was gone. Though not completely. In the midst of hard-hitting reality, I still groped for a message.

Darren and I had finally gone to bed about 3 a.m. He went back to the hospital to pick up Annie. I wanted to go with him, but I couldn't leave Nathan. Darren told me Kathy understood. "She's an amazing woman," he observed with admiration in his voice. "She really has forgiven Nathan."

Inwardly, I bristled. *"Well, of course she's forgiven him. It wasn't his fault."* Now Darren's words came back to haunt me. *Forgiveness. The message. A message from God instead of Kathy? Yes, I know, Lord, I need to forgive my father like Kathy forgives Nathan. But it's so much easier for her, Lord. Because the accident wasn't Nathan's fault. My father* meant *to hurt me.*

But look at the results, Cassie. Talitha is hovering between life and death. Kathy has no assurance that her daughter will ever open her eyes or speak the word "Mommy" again. It would be so easy, so natural, for Kathy to focus all the energy of her pain on Nathan. And me? I'm living a good life. I've got a stable, faithful husband and two beautiful, healthy children. My father didn't take anything away from me, except himself. And that may have hurt him as much as it hurt me. Yes, face it Cassie, that may be true.

It was a new thought. Previously, my mind blocked out any possibility that my father was hurting, too. Yes, he brought it on himself. But was his pain any less because of that? Maybe it was greater because he, himself, created the estrangement. I didn't know. But my father wanted to abolish the pain. And I wanted to hang onto it. *God, please forgive me and release my grasp. Pry my fingers away from the aching portion of my heart that I've learned to clutch desperately, as though by so doing, I could protect the rest of my heart from contamination. Am I as blind, emotionally, as Darren's brother, Billy, is physically? What makes me think that I can harbor unforgiveness in my soul without hurting my whole body? Why not expel it? Cast it out? Destroy it? Remove it far away so it can't hurt me any more? Take it, Father, please, take the pain of unforgiveness out of my heart.*

My gaze wandered around the room and came to rest on the telephone. The imposing object loomed larger than life, an intimidating presence next to my bed. The scent of fresh coffee drifted from the kitchen. Darren was up and getting ready for the day. I had a few moments of solitude in which to start my own day. I reached over and picked up the phone. My hands trembled, but my heart was steady now that the decision had been made.

It rang only once. Ingrid answered.

"Hello, Mom."

"Cassie, I'm so sorry. Darren called us last night. We wanna come and be with you and Nathan. But I donno what to do . . ." she hesitated.

"May I speak to my father?" My voice cracked a little.

"Yes, of course," She sounded surprised, but relieved. "I'll get him." I knew she would be praying.

Seconds passed. My heart pounded and my hands grew clammy. I swallowed hard.

"Hello, Cassandra." His voice was noticeably weaker, but still carried that familiar tone of authority.

"Hi, Papa." My voice sounded feeble by comparison.

There was an uncomfortable pause. He broke it. "Do you want me to come in today with Sven and Ingrid? Or would you rather come here?" At least he was giving me a choice.

"I think we'll come there. But I need to stop at the hospital first. Will you please ask Ingrid to make some of her meatball dumpling soup for us?" All of a sudden, I desperately wanted comfort food.

"Sure thing. We'll see you all later." Very casual, but with a slight hint of anticipation. Another brief pause, filled with the lack of anything to say. "Good-bye."

"Good-bye. Papa." I hung up the phone slowly, buried my head in my pillow, and let my tears take over.

Darren decided to spend a few hours at work finishing up some pressing accounts at the hardware store. He said he would pick us up around noon and take us to the hospital, and then to the farm. Darren, too, seemed relieved that I finally made the contact.

I washed my face and wandered out to the kitchen for a cup of the coffee Darren had brewed earlier. Annie was still in bed, but Nathan sat at the table. His eyelids were puffy and his hair unkempt. His hands were folded around a mug of steaming coffee. He stared motionless at the wall. It was obvious he hadn't slept. I went to him and wrapped my arms around his shoulders. He tensed, but didn't pull away.

"Mom," his voice cracked.

I murmured softly, "Honey, it wasn't your fault."

"But I am the one who did it, Mom," he protested. I sat down next to him and rested my hand on his arm. His eyes were glazed. I stared into them, seeing only emptiness. My heart swelled with sympathetic pain.

"Mom, I want to know," He swallowed. "Do you think God forgives me?"

Oh, the words I had longed to hear, but not under these conditions!

"You have to ask Him for forgiveness."

He nodded. "I know. But first I have to believe in Him. And I don't know if I do."

How I wanted to reach out with my fist and strike down those confusing barriers that trapped him! I wanted desperately to see my son set free. But I knew I needed to tread gently.

"God is real, honey. I know Him personally. And the Bible is the book He wrote. It's true. All of it."

He brushed my hand away. "Dad says it's full of fables and myths, just made up stories." *"Darren, I could slug you,"* I thought to myself. I took a deep breath and sent up a quick prayer for help. "Nathan, the Bible is a supernatural book. I read some-where that it has sixty-six books and . . ." I paused, racking my brain for the rest of the information. "Here, I'll read it to you." I reached over to the counter and picked up my Bible, kept nearby so I could read it with my morning tea. I was thankful I'd jotted down the information on the back page, thinking I might need it someday.

"Okay, here it is." My fingers ran down the list. "The Bible has sixty-six books, was written by thirty-nine authors, in three languages, on three different continents, over a period of fif-teen hundred years." I looked up at him, my eyes pleading for understanding. "And yet it all fits together perfectly. The message is very clear from cover to cover. No one man or group of men could possibly have written it. God used men to put the words down, but His spirit gave them the words to write."

"You might have something there, Mom," he admitted.

"I've been thinking about life and death and why we're here. You know they teach evolution in school. But it just seems like there's got to be something else." He shrugged. " It's hard to think of myself as just some higher form of animal life. I mean, there must be more to life for people. Like a reason for it all. Like we don't just die and go back to the dirt and that's it. You know?"

"You're right, Nathan. God puts a sense of eternity in man's soul. And He puts a hole in our heart that only He can fill."

"I know about that hole in the heart."

We sat quietly for a moment.

"Mom, you said that Talitha is named after a girl in the Bible."

"Yes, she was a little girl whom Jesus raised from the dead."

"Do you think God will make her well again?"

'We can pray for her right now." I spoke eagerly, too eagerly.

"I can't pray now, Mom. I'm still thinking."

"Okay, I'll pray." I bowed my head. "Dear God, thank you that little Talitha is still alive. I ask You to heal her and make her healthy and strong again and give her back to her parents. And please comfort her mom and dad, and her sisters. In Jesus' name, Amen." To myself, I added, *"And Father, please heal the hole in my son's heart and bring him to you. Amen."*

"Blessed is a man who perseveres under trial;
for once he has been approved,
he will receive the crown of life,
which the Lord has promised
to those who love Him."

James 1:12

Chapter 19

Darren came home around noon. I quickly mixed some tuna, celery, and salad dressing for sandwiches and heated a can of cream of mushroom soup. None of us were hungry, but I knew we needed to keep our strength up for whatever the day held in store. Nathan was quiet all the way to the hospital. He sat in the back seat and stared out the window with a stony gaze. I longed to penetrate my son's thoughts, but he was not willing to share them with us. Annie, sitting next to him, kept glancing at her brother with teary eyes, but left him alone.

Darren tried to prepare us for the sight of Talitha. "She's unconscious and has a mask over her nose, 'for oxygen,' they said. Lots of tubes sticking her all over."

"Do they know yet if she's going to make it?" Annie asked in a trembling voice. I looked at Darren. My daughter voiced the question that I harbored but didn't dare say aloud.

"I don't know, honey. I guess it depends if she comes out of the coma."

"Has she responded at all?" I asked.

"Not that I know of. Kathy's been with her the whole time. She hasn't noticed anything. Jim took the girls home to get some sleep."

It was a cold, blustery day, and dark clouds threatened to send a downpour. Darren let us out at the main door to the hospital and we waited in the lobby while he parked the car. I looked around at the plain, white-washed room. Chairs sat stiffly in rows. Here and there someone had placed small bouquets of plastic flowers in a feeble attempt to make the antiseptic space homey. I shivered inside. How would I feel if I were the one sitting by the bedside of a beloved child who may never come back to me? *Poor Kathy.* Then I looked at Nathan's rigid expression and wondered if he would ever decide to come back to us. I was afraid he was building emotional walls around him to keep more pain out. People cause pain. How much simpler it must seem to keep them away. *"No, Nathan, please don't block us out of your life,"* I silently pleaded.

Darren's confident and reassuring frame appeared at the door. A gust of wind blew in with him and a few raindrops sprinkled me. Darren came over and took my arm. He sought my eyes. "Are you okay?" he asked.

"I'm all right." I took a deep breath and braced myself.

"It's Room 214." He led the way to the elevator. For a brief instant, I entertained a panicky urge to run. The outside air was fresh, brisk, and invigorating, beckoning me to freedom. Inside the hospital, it settled around to entrap and smother me, to confine my senses. The heaviness of my soul increased as the elevator carried us to the second floor. When we stepped out, Darren took my hand. Annie and Nate followed us to Talitha's room. The door was closed. We hesitated, not knowing what to do. As we exchanged glances, the door opened and a nurse stepped out. "You can go in now," she informed us. "I just finished bathing her."

I looked at Nathan. He hesitated briefly and turned back. "I'll be downstairs," he said.

Instinctively, I started after him. Darren grabbed my arm. "Leave him be, Cassie. He'll come when he's ready."

With lingering eyes, I watch my son's steady pace as he

retreated. When he turned the corner, I entered Talitha's room. In spite of Darren's attempt to prepare us, my heart fell at the sight of her. The white mask nearly covered her tiny face. I could barely see her eyes, which were closed, of course. Her skin was the pallor of a morning mist. Her little body lay unearthly still under the smooth white blanket. Just the gentle rhythm of her chest rising and falling gave evidence of life. One pudgy hand was clasped in her mother's. Kathy tore her eyes away from her daughter briefly to acknowledge our presence with a nod. Then she turned back to Talitha and forced a smile.

"You have company, Sweetie." Her cheerful words sounded out of place in the dismal atmosphere. "Auntie Cassie is here, and Darren and Annie. And . . ." she looked toward the door and whispered, "Where's Nathan?"

"In the lobby," Darren explained. "He'll come in later."

Kathy looked at him doubtfully. "Sure."

Annie started to cry softly and Darren put his arm around her. She snuggled close to him.

"Have you gotten any rest?" Darren asked Kathy.

"When Jim comes back, I might go home for a while." Yet, from the look in her eyes, I doubted she would stray more than a few feet from her daughter's bedside.

Moving with a calm I didn't feel, I walked to the other side of the bed and put my hand on Talitha's forehead. "Can she hear me?"

Kathy shook her head. "It's not likely, but the doctor said there is a possibility, so we are tying to talk normally. It might help, just to have her hear voices and know we're with her."

I studied Talitha's profile by the dim light coming in from the window. "Hi, Talitha," I said. "I hope you feel better soon." *Stupid comment, Cassie. Think!* I tried another approach. "Tuffy is waiting for you at home. He wants you to make him some more mud pies." No response. *How difficult this must be for Kathy!* She looked so tired. Her sad eyes were dry, but framed by dark circles. When she wasn't smiling, her mouth formed a straight, thin line, and her shoulders sagged against the uncomfortable, metal chair. I was sure she hadn't slept at all since the accident, and I hoped that Jim would be firm when he returned and make her rest. Meanwhile, I picked up an extra blanket that was folded on the end of the bed and stuffed it behind her back. Then I gave her a hug.

"You've got to take care of yourself, Kathy. When Talitha gets better, she'll need you to be rested and healthy. Why don't you go and lie down in the solarium while we're here and get some sleep?"

Kathy shook her head. "I might miss something. I have to be here when she wakes up." She looked right at me for the first time and I saw the torment and fatigue that strained her face. I turned to Darren for help.

"She's a mother, Cassie." He said, as though I should know better.

"Nathan!" Annie sounded surprised. I glanced up. My son had come in the room. He was standing quietly in the door-way. I wondered how long he had been watching us. Annie grabbed his arm and pulled him to the bed. "Let Talitha know you're here. Talk to her."

Nathan stood stiffly at the little girl's side. The Lord must have inspired my sweet Annie. She reached out, took Nate's hand, and slowly guided it until it rested on top of Kathy's own hand, still clutching her daughter's. I held my breath, expecting Nate to whip his hand away. But he didn't. Instead, he started to speak.

"I'm sorry, Talitha . . . I didn't mean . . . " Tears formed in his eyes. He clamped his lips tightly. With a stoic expression, he turned to Kathy and said with his eyes what he couldn't say with his mouth.

My heart pounded. I was so proud of my son. It must have been agony for him to face Kathy, but he had come. *Help him, Jesus.*

No words were needed. Kathy stood up and wrapped her arms around his shoulders. She laid her head on his chest and sobbed. Nathan held her and patted her back like she was a little child. I was stunned. Thinking back, I guess Kathy needed him to help her cry. Knowing he was suffering, too, must have given her permission to be weak. The muscles in his face began to relax. In comforting Kathy, Nathan found the comfort he needed. He spoke so softly I strained to hear. "I didn't mean to hit her, Kathy. And I will never forgive myself."

Kathy pulled back as though struck. She held his eyes with a fierce gaze. "Don't you say that!" Her voice was firm and her strength renewed. "God and I forgive you. Don't you dare hold this against yourself, or our forgiveness will be wasted!"

Nate stared at her. I was amazed. What a gift she had given my son! I knew Nathan would take her words to heart and ponder them over and over.

"Mommy." The voice was pathetic in its weakness. Kathy gasped and turned around. Talitha lay as still as ever.

"Did you hear?" Kathy sounded disbelieving.

"Yes," I answered, scarcely daring to breathe. We all nodded assent.

Kathy's eyes lit up. She knelt by the bed and reached for Talitha's hand.

"Honey, I'm here. Mommy's here." No response.

"Shall I call the nurse?" Darren asked, excitement creeping into his voice.

Kathy nodded, not taking her eyes off her daughter's face. The rest of us didn't either, until Darren returned with the nurse. She hurried to the child's side and felt her pulse.

"You'd better go now." She turned to us and sort of waved us out the door. "She shouldn't have many visitors. The doctor will be here shortly."

So we said a hasty good-bye to Kathy. I hugged her again and told her I'd keep on praying. Annie was so excited she had trouble containing herself. She jabbered all the way down in the elevator. "She's going to be okay now. I know it. She sounded just like herself. Can I call Emily and Tamara and tell them?"

"Hold on, Annie," Darren rebuked her kindly. "We don't know if this means anything yet." But we all felt lighter, like a load was lifting. Even Nathan had a smile on his face.

As we stepped out of the hospital, Darren glanced at his watch and commented. "Two-thirty. Still plenty of time to spend at the farm."

My head instantly began to pound. *Plenty of time to spend*

with my father. I wasn't sure I could handle another emotional scene that day. *Maybe we should put it off for a day or two.* I started to protest, but Darren placed two fingers on my lips. "Hush, now. You'll feel better when you've done it."

Chapter 20

Our ride to the farm was quiet. Nate, Annie and I were absorbed in our own thoughts. The wind settled down during our time in the hospital, and the sun presented itself with a flourish. Darren pointed out the progress farmers had made in the fields. Wheat and oat crops were sprouting, and the recent rain pleased him. I know he was trying to take my mind off the tense meeting that was certain to come. I tried to listen as he rambled on. I turned my head toward the window and nodded at appropriate times, but my mind had already drifted to the farm. My churning stomach made me regret my earlier request for homemade meatball soup. It was my favorite, but now I wondered if I'd ever be able to eat again!

I didn't notice that I was wringing my hands until Darren reached over and clasped his brawny one over both of mine. It made me remember the time I'd dumped food all over him when I was working as a car hop at the local drive-in, and I gave him half a smile. What a nervous woman he had married! Darren usually stayed calm no matter what was going on around him. It was a trait that irritated me at times, yet I couldn't help but admire his confidence and wish I had more of it.

But I quickly rebuked myself, *"No, Cassie, it's his self-confidence that keeps him away from God. At least, I know how needy I am! Father God, please give me your peace. Help me to genuinely forgive my father and start a new relationship with him."* I had to admit that the faith with which I prayed that prayer was pathetically small, but God knew my heart and that I desperately wanted it.

Time passed too quickly. Before I knew it, we turned into the driveway and rounded the familiar bend. The sun highlighted the upper branches of giant oak trees lining the driveway. Their shiny leaves arched above us as though to announce our coming as we approached the house. Billy faithfully awaited us on the homey porch, a big smile breaking over his face. *Poor Billy.* By refusing to come and see my father, I'd kept my kids away from Billy. too. And from Ingrid and Sven, their grandparents.

I glanced about the yard. My father must be in the house. A stranger was painting the porch railing. He wore a raggedy pair of overalls over a plaid flannel shirt that looked like it had seen better days. White paint dripped down one leg of the overalls. *Why would Sven hire someone else to do his painting?* He and his sons were fully capable, and the family took so much pride being independent. As Darren brought the car to a stop and turned off the engine, the man finished painting the end post and turned to face us.

Did my own eyes lie to me? It was my father! Dressed in humble—less than humble—work clothes and brandishing a paint brush. I had never seen him in anything but dress clothes or casual pants and a crisp white shirt. Even his pajamas were always properly covered with a burgundy smoking jacket my mother gave him when they got married. *What did Sven and Ingrid do to him? Were they making him work for his keep?*

In a semi-frozen state, we all climbed out of the car. Nate and Annie hung back. Darren came around to my side and peeled me away from the door. Slowly we approached Papa and Billy, while at the same time fending off the effusive greetings from faithful old Brutus and Rusty, the six-month old German short hair that had recently joined the clan. Ingrid had vehemently declared she would never again get a puppy of that particular breed. "Land sakes," she had exclaimed. "He acts like he's got a whole column of ants in its pants. He can't keep still a minute. We used to have a lawn. Now we've just got one big hole in the ground. I ain't never seen so much energy stuffed in one creature before!"

Between yelling "Down!" and then "Good boy!" when Rusty heeded our request and managed to touch his vibrating bottom briefly to the ground, we alternately petted the pup and inched our way to the house.

Papa stood tall and watched our progress. I felt chilled under his penetrating stare. It seemed as though he was examining me for signs of deterioration over the years. I was sure there were many.

Billy, enthusiastic as always, started down the steps to greet us. Too late, I noticed the can of white paint that Papa had set on the bottom step. Papa wasn't used to living with a blind person. Billy walked confidently all over the farm, inside and out, by using his senses of hearing and smell, and counting steps. No one ever left anything out of place for him to bump into or trip over. Now he headed down the steps straight towards a bucket of white paint.

"No, wait!" I yelled, scaring Darren half to death. He jumped and looked at me like I'd lost my mind.

Annie and Nate spotted the problem at the same time and shouted to Billy. Papa looked around, having no idea of the gravity of the situation. Billy stopped with his left foot in mid-air, hanging over the bucket, tottered briefly, and with all eyes fastened on him, lost his balance. His foot slammed into the pail, splashing geysers of white liquid into the air, all over him, my unsuspecting father, and the blue-gray porch floor! Even the dogs were showered with white speckles.

"Yeow!" Billy yelped.

He continued to topple forward and landed smack on his face. Blood gushed out of his nose. As he lifted himself up, the blood drizzled down his shirt and mingled with the white paint, forming streams of pink rivers cascading down his body like a fountain.

We all rushed to help, but nobody wanted to touch him, except Papa who also looked a sight. Sven and Ingrid, upon hearing the commotion, ran out of the house. Ingrid promptly screamed at the horrible sight and fainted. Sven caught her and carried her into the house. Aside from his nosebleed, Billy seemed unharmed and struggled to his feet. Papa felt his nose right away and pronounced it unbroken. It seemed to be a matter of stopping the nosebleed and cleaning him up.

"Get a cold cloth," Papa ordered, "and help me lay him on his back."

"Put him on the sofa," Darren suggested.

"No!" Annie yelled. "You can't take him in the house like that. He'll drip all over the carpet."

Meanwhile, Billy stood totally transfixed and bewildered. "What happened?" he kept saying. "Am I dead?"

"You're okay, Uncle Billy," Nathan answered. "You just fell in a bucket of paint, and you're all wh . . . .Ha, ha, ha . . . " The ludicrousness of the situation got to him and he started to laugh until he literally rolled on the ground, holding his sides while Brutus and Rusty tackled him, licking his face with passionate tongues.

Meanwhile, Darren ran into the house to see how his mom was doing. He returned and reported she was coming to and going to be all right. Although Ingrid was a strong woman, she had an aversion to the sight of blood. Once when Nate was younger and cut his knee in a bike mishap, Ingrid had to leave the room while I bandaged him. She told me that it brought her back to the traumatic night when Sven lost the use of his arm in a tractor accident. "I jest can't take to see the life's blood flowin' out of somebody I love, even if it's not a bad hurt," she told me apologetically at the time.

Darren looked at Billy, Papa and Nate in turn and also started to laugh. Within seconds, we all followed suit, laughing hysterically. Even Papa let out a great big howl and bent half over to hold his sides. I had never before seen my father let loose like that. Tears were pouring out of my eyes. It suddenly struck me that I had never really considered my father human.

Somehow, working together, we got the two of them washed and into clean clothes. Nate found an old tin washtub in the shed out back. He and Annie carried hot water and soap to the shed so Billy and Papa could bathe privately. Fortunately, the weather was warm enough so no one got sick. The bland dark floor of the shed turned red and white. To this day, no one has ever bothered to repaint it.

Ingrid, extremely embarrassed by her ungraceful collapse, regained her composure. Sven said the rest of the porch needed to be painted anyway. Papa and Billy would take on that task the following day.

Later that evening, after a warm and satisfying meal of homemade meatball and dumpling soup (which I ate heartily), homemade buttermilk biscuits and pecan pie, we all gathered in the living room. Sven started a rich, blazing fire in the stone fireplace. Late spring evenings in Minnesota were still cool enough to welcome a fire. Its warmth soaked all the way through me as I curled up on the sofa between Darren and Papa. I can't say that Papa and I were chummy and cozy, but the ice had definitely been broken. The afternoon's episode had been hashed over and over, with more giggles each time. Billy finally had a clear understanding of what had happened, and Papa was permanently impressed with the need to put things in their proper places as long as he resided on the farm.

Conversation eventually turned to Papa and his health issues. Darren asked how he was feeling.

"Tired, mostly."

"I tried to get him to rest more," Ingrid insisted. "But he's got a mind of his own and wanted to make himself useful. I jest happened to mention that the porch railing needed painting and Sven offered to lend him some of his old painting clothes."

"Your mother has a unique was of getting people to do things," Papa confided to Darren, with a twinkle in his eye. "She lets you think it's your idea."

"Yeah," Darren replied. "I know what you mean."

I could tell that staying with Sven and Ingrid had a definite effect on Papa. But then, I hadn't seen him for over eighteen years, and had to admit he could have changed somewhat during that time. Maybe other factors had been working on him these past years, too.

A comfortable silence ensued. Sven rose from his armchair and stoked the fire.

"Cassandra," Papa began.

"Oh, bless my heart," Ingrid interrupted and started to rise. "I've been so thoughtless. We need to give you two some time alone."

"No, no," Papa was firm. "You stay." Ingrid sat back down. "What I have to say can be heard by all of you, especially Nathan and Annette." He turned his gaze to the window seat where the teens sat petting the dogs.

Papa leaned forward slightly, placing his elbows on his knees and bringing the tips of his fingers to his chin in contemplation. "I was wrong to leave you, daughter. I can't make up for those years. I know you have been well taken care of." He acknowledged Darren with a curt nod of respect. "I have heard much in these two weeks from Sven and Ingrid about their wonderful daughter-in-law." A sheepish look passed between Ingrid and Sven. I knew their bragging was intentional, and seemed to have produced the desired results. "And a fine grandson and granddaughter. And I can see for myself that it is true."

He paused and wiped his hand across his brow. The only sounds were the reassuring tick, tick of the grandfather clock and a strong wind that had begun to howl outside.

"When I found out I was ill . . . and soon to die . . . "

"Papa," I placed my hand on his arm.

"Don't interrupt, Cassie. I need to get this out."

"When a man is faced with his own death, he thinks differently. As a doctor, I've been so accustomed to the dying that I guess I considered myself immune to grief. You get to the point where death doesn't mean much. It's just another part of life, going on and on, like the seasons. But a man's own death. That is something else. It makes you think. The past weeks and months I started to think of all I could have had in life. Of all I gave up." As his eyes swept the room, they seemed to linger the most on Nathan. I wondered what he was thinking. Then I realized what the sight of Nate must mean to him. *This was the grandson that he almost didn't have.* I recalled that traumatic day in the clinic. The day that I almost had the abortion. *What if I hadn't changed my mind at the last minute? Would my own father have killed my baby?*

Papa spoke again. "I don't hold to any of that nonsense about a life after death or the glories of heaven." Blunt as always, he chuckled a little. Out of the corner of my eye, I saw Ingrid literally bite her lip. "But I want all I can get out of this world. I want to spend time with my daughter again and get to know my grandchildren." He sighed heavily. "Now I know that sounds selfish, but I intend to show you that I . . ." here he searched for a word, " . . . that I value you. I have a considerable amount of money saved up. Even though I have good insurance, some of my savings and investments will go for medical expenses. Being a doctor doesn't relieve me of the bills. But there should be plenty left to pay for Nathan's and Annette's college educations. It might help to make up for the schooling I didn't give you, Cassie." He turned to look my husband in the eye. "You're a good man, Darren. A good provider, and a man with a good amount of pride. I don't mean to insult you in any way, but I would be honored if you would accept this gift in the manner in which it is offered."

Darren swallowed hard and nodded. "We'll accept it if Nate and Annie are determined to make a success of their education and give it all they've got."

I watched my kids. They both beamed. Annie crossed over to her grandfather immediately and hesitantly gave him a peck on the cheek. "Thank you, Grandpa." Tears brimmed her eyes.

Nate came over also and extended his hand for my father to take with a firm grasp. "Thanks, Grandpa."

My son returned to his seat, but my determined little Annie wasn't finished yet.

"Grandpa," she knelt down on the floor and, taking his hand, patted it gently. He looked at her with misty eyes. Actually, all of our eyes were a bit moist. Even Brutus and Rusty were unusually attentive, as though they sensed something of importance happening. "I love you, Grandpa, so I need to tell you that heaven is real and Jesus can take you there if you confess your sins and trust in Him."

"Annie, not now," Darren reached out to rebuke her. I turned and glared at Darren. He promptly shut his mouth.

Undaunted, Annie continued while I held my breath and prayed silently. "God sent His own son, Jesus, to die on the cross to pay for our sins. It's all true. God tells us in the book He wrote, the Bible. You haven't been here with me much on earth, Grandpa. I want you to be with me in heaven."

I admired my daughter's courage, even as I wondered if Papa would be so offended he would start yelling at her.

He didn't yell though. He just patted her hand and said calmly, "Annie, I think it's just fine that you believe in something if it helps you. But religion is not for me. I'm too old to change my ways. And," he chuckled. "I've done way too much sinning in my lifetime to quit now."

Annie seemed to admit temporary defeat, but insisted, "I'll keep praying for you, Grandpa."

"Well now," he said, "I guess that can't hurt, can it?"

The shrill of the telephone interrupted their conversation. Ingrid excused herself and went to the kitchen to answer it. She returned in a minute with a worried expression. "It's for you, Cassie. It's Kathy."

I rose quickly and went to pick up the receiver. "Hi, Kathy. How's it going?"

"She's in heaven, Cass." My friend's voice was broken, but calm.

"Oh, no. Oh, Kathy, I'm so sorry for you." No other words came to me. I sank into a chair as tears clouded my vision. Ingrid came and put her arm around my shoulders.

Kathy was having trouble, too, but she spoke first. "I've got to tell you, Cassie. You heard her say 'Mommy'?"

"Yes, I was there."

"Well, nothing else happened for a long while, so I started singing to her. I sang her favorite song, 'Jesus Loves Me'."

I nodded foolishly into the phone, unable yet to speak.

"I was on the second verse, the one about heaven, you know." She sang the simply melody, "He who died, heaven's gates to open wide. He will wash away my sins, let His little child come in."

Again Kathy spoke, her voice barely containing her excitement. "Cassie, Talitha opened her eyes, wide, and looked straight at me and smiled. Then she put her arms out, like she wanted to be carried. But not to me. She put them up in the air and then her arms fell down by her side, and she closed her eyes again and . . . and went to be with the Lord."

Now Kathy started to sob. She had to get that out, but it was all she could say.

"Cassie," Jim's deep voice came over the phone. "She can't talk any more."

"It's okay," I managed through my tears. "I'm so sorry. I'm praying for you all, Jim."

"Thanks." He hung up.

Turning, I sobbed into Ingrid's arms. I wasn't crying for Talitha, but for Kathy and Jim and the girls. And for Nathan.

"What's wrong?" Nathan demanded from the doorway.

Ingrid spoke. "Talitha is gone. She's in heaven with Jesus."

I raised my tear-stained eyes to his face. He pounded one fist into the other one. Hard. Then he turned and ran outside.

"Nathan!" I ran after him. Darren joined me this time. Nate raced to the barn, where we found him curled up in a corner on some hay bales. He was howling. I'd never in my life heard such an awful sound. It was coming out of a place deep inside, almost beyond the reach of the soul. I rushed to him and tried to wrap my arms around him. He pushed me away.

"I don't want you. I don't want your God. What kind of a God would take a little girl?" His voice rose in anguish, and his wide, tormented eyes challenged me. "What kind of a God would let me kill a child?"

Shocked and confused, I stepped back.

"He doesn't mean it," Darren spoke to comfort me. "He doesn't know what he's saying." Darren's comforting words didn't even begin to penetrate my fragmented heart.

We stayed with Nathan until his broken sobs subsided. Then he let me hold him. I rocked him back and forth, like a baby. A thick darkness fell that night. A heavy, impenetrable blackness that covered our faces and our bodies and encased my spirit until I felt like I would suffocate.

I just got my father back, only to face losing him for eternity. *Would I lose my husband and son, too?* They all thought me foolish to believe in a God of love and compassion. I almost gave up that night. The evil presence that tried to take my life years earlier when I almost killed myself had returned. He reached out to grasp me and pull me down to the pit.

But I remembered Talitha. I knew without a doubt that she was in God's presence, right at that moment. And she was smiling and happy, maybe even dancing with delight. I would be there, too, one day.

There had to be hope for my family. God was on His heavenly throne, so there had to be hope.

Chapter 21

"Annie, does this skirt still fit you?" I held the garment up to examine it by the light of the window. It was that twilight time of day when I always got the urge to catch the last flickering rays of the sun and hang onto them before dusk settled over my home and bade it good night. Now that another summer was over, the days were again starting to shrink as the sun retired earlier each night. Annie's room, created out of an attic dormer with slanted walls on three sides, didn't have much natural lighting. Her desk lamp was good for studying, and the one over her bed cast a bright glow for reading at night. But the arrangement of electrical fixtures in the room wasn't very satisfactory, and so we needed to strain to see clearly in certain areas.

Annie didn't mind, though. She used lots of white and yellow to offset the dark paneled walls that were probably there when the house was constructed. We didn't have money to spend on repairs and decorating. But the room suited my daughter. Her personality was a delightful mixture of an introspective nature and sunny cheerfulness.

We were engrossed in the process of sorting clothes she had outgrown. The castoffs were intended for Kathy's teenagers, who were more petite than Annie. "No, Mom, it's tight on the hips." She reached into her closet, yanked out a couple more blouses, and threw them on the bed. "I either give it away or go on a diet." She gave me a teasing glance, knowing perfectly well what my response would be.

"Forget the diet. You're just right." I folded the green corduroy skirt and tucked it in the grocery bag with the rest of her outgrown clothes. "All your things are in such good shape. It's nice that somebody else can get some use out of them. Not that Kathy and Jim couldn't afford to buy any, but . . ."

"That's it, Mom!" Annie's voice soared with excitement as she plopped herself down on the white chenille bedspread.

Startled, I jumped. "What is?"

"My social studies assignment. We're doing a section on community outreach and my team has to come up with a project to help poor people without hurting their pride. We've been trying to think of something fun to do."

"So what did you come up with?" I tucked the last two blouses into the bag, set it on the floor, and stretched out on my back next to Annie. It felt good to rest a while. We'd worked hard that whole Saturday, "spring cleaning" her room. The walls were freshly scrubbed, along with shiny floors, and clean closets and shelves. My back was starting to ache.

"We could do a fashion show! Most poor people don't like to have things given to them. They've got pride, you know. So Terri, Cindy, Karen and I could put on a show for the community. We could model our old clothes. The ones that still look good, of course. Emily and Tamara could help." Her face gathered animation as she talked with her eyes and vibrant hand gestures. "We could hang up posters in town. Ned would let us put them in his grocery store. And the post office has a bulletin board, and so does the hardware store." Annie sat upright and examined me with a calculating eye. "You still have a good figure, Mom. Maybe you could get some of your friends to help model with women's clothes. Grandma might even be in it. Some poor people are old," she remarked with contemplation.

"Hold on a minute. Are you sure this is the kind of thing your teacher wants you to do?"

"Mr. Jamerson said we should use our creativity. He really wants us to do something that will help. 'To make a difference,' he said."

"So you would have a fashion show and then give the clothes away? How would that help?"

"No, Mom, you don't understand." Patiently she explained, as to a feeble-minded younger sibling. "We would sell the clothes, for a good price, of course. A very good price," she emphasized. "We could use the money to buy some treats for our customers. And juice and coffee. So it would sort of be giving them away, but not really." She cocked her head at me, like a puppy, with anticipation. "Get it?"

"Where would you have this show? And how would you pay for the treats? You would have to buy them ahead of time, you know."

Annie pursed her lips. "I think Mr. Jamerson would let us use the classroom, or maybe even the auditorium. It could be a class project. Well, at least for the girls. I suppose the boys wouldn't want to." She frowned, deep in thought. "I think Ned would let us charge some treats, if we paid him right after the show.

"Are we done here? Can I go and call my friends and see what they think?"

A door slammed in the kitchen. Annie jumped off the bed. "Is Dad home already? Is it that late?"

I rolled over on my side, facing the doorway. "Go ahead and call your friends. If it's okay with your teacher, it's okay with me. I'll help you."

"Thanks, Mom." She hugged me and left the room.

"Tell Dad I'm in here," I called after her.

"Hi, Dad! Mom's in my bedroom." Her footsteps hurried down the stairs. I lay peacefully and listened to the everyday kitchen sounds of a cupboard door opening and closing and the gurgling rush of coffee poured into a cup.

Things had settled down somewhat to a state of normalcy.

Papa continued to stay with Sven, Ingrid, and Billy at the farm. They had more room than we did, and he was quite content there. I was still amazed at how well they all got along together. My father turned out to be a considerate guest, and Ingrid loved having another person to cook for who raved about her food. Since Mama died when I was a teenager, Papa hadn't been exposed to much home cooking, and thoroughly enjoyed whatever Ingrid served him, including lutefisk! She made a special out-of-season batch of the slimy, buttery stuff just for him. "I don't know how long you're goin' to be stayin' with us here, so I'm gonna give you a taste of Christmas now, in case you miss spendin' the holiday with us." Tactfully, she didn't refer to his disease, which was in remission at the time. Ingrid, Annie, and I prayed that Ingrid's good home cooking and the fresh country would somehow restore his good health, even as we feared differently in our hearts. But for the moment, Papa was in good spirits and had energy to do simple chores around the farm and enjoy his newly found family. We managed to see each other a few times each week, mostly casually, at our home or at the farm, chatting over lunch or one of Ingrid's delicious meals. During the summer months, we had often met for picnics at local beaches. Once, Darren, Nate, Annie, and I drove Papa a few hours north to the coastal city of Duluth, located on the shores of Lake Superior. We watched foreign ships enter the harbor, and spent a long weekend at a campground near the city. As long as Papa acted healthy, I tended to push worries about his future out of my mind, and go on with my daily routine. Actually, I was more concerned about Nathan, whose emotions never seemed to get beyond the accident and Talitha's death. He was back at college now, a private school near Duluth, about 150 miles north of us. My son was moody now and tended to lapse into periods of gloom and negativity, just the opposite of his usual optimistic nature.

He clammed up whenever I tried to talk to him about anything serious. Darren told me to just give him time and he'd be back to himself again, but I couldn't help but worry about him. Nathan had been so close to searching out the truth about God, but after Talitha's death, he had slammed the gates of his mind shut to any spiritual discussion.

The heavy sound of footsteps in the hall interrupted my thoughts. Darren slowly approached the bedroom, and then his frame filled the doorway. One look at his solemn face told me something was definitely wrong.

I sat up. "Darren, what's the matter?"

He walked over to a blue wooden chair next to the bed and sank into it. Shoulders sagged as he stared into the warm coffee cup cradled in his hands. The soothing, warm liquid captured his eyes as though holding the answer to an unknown, insurmountable problem.

"Dear Lord," I silently prayed. *"What else could go wrong?"* Months had gone by since the death of Kathy's little girl. We were helping Kathy and Jim adjust and trying to handle the repercussions of the tragedy in our own family. Actually, Nathan seemed to be doing well at college. His grades were good, and he handled his job responsibilities at a restaurant in Duluth without any problems. But when he came home, he still seemed to function in some sort of a fog. It was as though a deep, dark weed had taken root in his mind, clinging with a tenacity that filtered out normal everyday experiences, only permitting a distorted, negative version of reality. I missed him so much, when he was at school, even when he was home.

Darren was silent for a few moments. I waited quietly, but impatiently. One thing I had learned through the years was that my husband would speak when he was ready, and only then.

A heavy sigh finally escaped his lips. "I've lost my job, Cassie."

"Oh, no." My hand went automatically to my mouth. A shock of fear permeated my entire body. This news was totally unexpected.

"The business hasn't been going well for almost a year now, since that discount store opened up on the other end of town." He shrugged his shoulders. "Frank just has too much competition. People don't go to a hardware store any more if they can get stuff cheaper some other place." He set his cup down with shaky fingers on the small, wooden end table, wiped his brow and massaged his chin thoughtfully.

"Hank says he hates to let me go. It's been fourteen years. But I'm the most expendable."

"But you're his accountant. Surely he still needs you!" I sat rigid with anxiety.

"He said now that his kids are grown up, his wife, Mabel, has enough time to take over the book-keeping. She used to do it, remember, when he first opened up the store."

"But his business has grown since then. It's a much bigger job now!" My voice rose in a struggle to conquer disbelief and uncertainty. I got up and began to pace, aware that I was not fully in control of my emotions, and jealous of Darren's outwardly calm exterior.

"Cassie, he's made up his mind. I can't do anything about it."

"Well, then, until you find a new job," I turned to face him and forced myself to speak calmly. "I will go to work. I saw an ad at Smiley's Restaurant for another waitress."

"Don't be silly, Cass. I'll find something else."

Taking his words as an insult, I retorted quickly, "I am capable, Darren, of handling a job and my household. The kids are grown up now and . . . "

"No!" The sharp rebuke from Darren propelled him to his feet. He loomed over me, the sheer force of determination infusing him with sudden vigor. All his energy was contained within his straight, firm stance, arms held stiffly at his sides, and hands clenched into fists. Tightly clamped teeth emphasized his square jaw line.

"Oh, why do you have to be so stubborn, Husband?" I cried inwardly. *"I understand how important it is for you to be the provider, but this is a matter of survival!"* I forced my voice to stay low and even, in spite of my pounding heart. "Either I get a job . . . for now . . . or you have to go on unemployment. Hank is going to let his wife help him with the business. This would be the same thing. I would help you for a time and . . . "

"Cassandra, I don't want to hear any more of this." He strode toward the door with heavy steps. I jumped up and ran ahead of him, pausing and turning at the doorway to block it. I was fuming. My legs were shaking and tears stung my eyes. I knew I should keep a firm hold on my tongue, but for better or worse, I let it fly.

"Darren, you are so stubborn! You are a hard worker, a wonderful husband and father. But you can't do everything. You can't just make a job appear out of the blue. Accountant jobs aren't easy to find in a small town. It's going to take time to figure out what to do!"

Darren put his hand up, in the "stop" position. I ignored his gesture and continued, gathering speed and energy from feelings stored deep in my heart for many long years. This was all going to gush out whether he liked it or not.

"Since you're so proud and you don't want charity, the only choice is for me to get a job. It will just be a *temporary* job, Darren," my voice started to choke, and I was pleading now, with my eyes, my outstretched hands, by body stance. "You are so strong, so capable. Too capable. Sometimes I just long for you to need me. I want to help you. I want to be your partner. We're in this marriage together, you know." I started to squeak, barely pushing the words out, "I love you." I started to collapse, ready to fall into his waiting arms, arms that had always been there for me.

But, instead, Darren grabbed me by the shoulders and shook me. Surprised, I looked up and met his eyes. They were stern and almost cold as he rebuked me. "We're not together, Cassandra. You've made it very clear for many years that God comes first in your life. How do you expect me to handle that?

"Every Sunday morning and every Wednesday night you leave me. Not for another man. I could deal with that. I could compete. But I can't compete with *God*! Not with an 'old man in the sky' who has some weird hold on your life!" Suddenly he let go of me, with a slight push, more of a pushing of himself away from me than of pushing me away from him. He strode a few paces away and stood with his back turned, hands in his pockets and his head down. He lowered his voice until I had to strain to hear him. "I want to be your man. I want to be first with you. We're not a team. I work and you pray."

"Darren, I . . . "

"I don't mean that you don't work, too, Cassie. But you expect God to take care of you. I want you to lean on me." He turned then and pounded his thumb in the middle of his chest, over and over, as he spoke. "I am a real, flesh and blood man, Cassie. God is just a vague idea made up by some pitiful, weak people who needed a reason to go on living. He's not real, Cassie. Face the facts." He took a step toward me and held out his arms. But for the first time, I didn't run into them. I stood my ground.

"Darren, if you would only believe in God, too, we could serve Him together. He loves you. He wants . . ." Against my will, I started to cave in. Tears streamed down my face. The hurt and sudden awareness of Darren's loneliness crushed my will like a giant steamroller. I had no idea he felt that way.

"Cassandra," my husband wrapped his strong arms around me. "Make your choice. Let *me* be your man. I won't compete any more for first place in your life."

Then I felt him freeze. I looked up and saw him staring behind me. I spun around, to see Annie, white-faced and scared, looking for all the world like a forlorn, rejected, orphan.

As awful as our argument sounded to Annie, Darren and I were able to assure her that we'd tough it out and somehow get through this problem together. But the tension continued to build. Darren started to keep to himself when he wasn't at the farm or looking for a job. I cried easily. I was lonesome for Nathan, and dreading the day when Annie would also leave for college. My "nest" was starting to crumble. Our lifestyle changed. We ate a lot more beans and a lot less meat. We'd managed to scrape together enough money to pay the mortgage for September and October. But we'd never had any real savings. Plans for Christmas looked bleak.

Of course, Darren refused help from his parents or Papa. Ingrid brought me some meat and bread now and then when Darren was at work. I wasn't too proud to take it, for Annie's sake. She needed to stay healthy. Along with the loss of Darren's job went the loss of insurance. Literally, none of us could afford to get sick! Any major medical bills would put us into debt for the rest of our lives. I worried and prayed a lot. Time and experience had given me proof that God would take care of us. But I still questioned where the help would come from. *And what about our marriage problems? Would Darren get fed up and leave me?* I didn't think so, but we had both changed through the years. Darren had a lot of pride. *Could I still count on him to be there for me if he felt he had to take second place in my life?*

Darren asked me to choose between him and God. My husband's continuing distance made it clear to me that he was waiting for an answer. I knew God would continue to come first. It had to be that way. *But would my family suffer more pain for my choice?*

Darren was suffering, too. I could see it in his eyes that stared vacantly at the TV, day after day. It was strange to have him home so much of the time. I'd always wanted him around more, but not like this! I felt sad for him. This crisis was hard on me, but at least I had God at my side to give me comfort and strength. Darren only sought comfort within himself. And for the first time in his life, the inner strength seemed to be depleted.

I tried to make life happy for Annie. She wasn't used to being an "only child". Nate came home only once in September and once in October. His studies absorbed the majority of his time and focus, and his job kept him occupied most weekends. But when he was with us, his spiritual restlessness was evident, at least to me. Darren was "on edge" more often these days. But he kept himself in control. That is, until the day of Annie's fashion show.

It was the first week in November. Annie, Karen, Terri and Cindy, along with Kathy's girls and a few of her other classmates, crowded into our little living room, choosing their wardrobe selections for the program to be held at 6:30 p.m. in the school auditorium. The show idea promised to be a hit. Notices were posted all around town. Smiley and Ned, the local restaurant and grocery store owners, collaborated to provide a light supper. They provided deli sandwiches, chips, and the ever-present pickles that accompanied any kind of a "get-together" in our small town, from baby showers to funerals. Several of us moms had baked cakes for the occasion. The assortment included white cakes with chocolate frosting, chocolate cakes with white and chocolate frosting, spice cakes, white with pink or green frosting, among others. The girls decorated long tables with Barbie dolls adorned in fashionable outfits in a wide variety of poses. The dolls were lined up on a runner copied after the platform the models would walk on to display the outfits for sale. The students offered to give the proceeds from the sales to Smiley and Ned after the show, but the two elderly gentlemen had refused their offer. Smiley had smiled and said, "Tell ya what. Just put the money in Ned's hands and he can use it to put groceries in bags for 'down and outers' this Christmas." Ned nodded and quickly responded, "I've always wanted to play Santa Claus. Here's my big chance!"

So the girls continued to prepare enthusiastically for the big night. Actually, our living room looked like a clothing store at this point! Assorted fabrics were draped over every available piece of furniture, spread out on the floor, and attached to wire hangers displayed on lamp stands and door ways. Kathy and I, along with a few brave friends from church, had already chosen our apparel. Some of the girls were able to wear their mother's clothes. At Annie's invitation, Ingrid had graciously declined to join us as a model, but said she would attend the show. Clothing donations were acquired from all over town, so there was quite an assortment. The clothes we didn't have time to model would be displayed on racks borrowed from the department store next to Ned's Grocery. Complete outfits were available for both sexes, ranging from infants to adults. The whole town was talking about the show, except for Darren, who was wrapped up in his own world, oblivious to all that was going on around him. That is, until he walked in the front door that afternoon.

As the front door opened, he collided with Annie's friend, Karen, who was wearing only a slip as she tugged a tight sweater over her head. "Look out," Karen giggled.

"I'm sorry," was Darren's instinctive response.

Of course, hearing a man's voice, Karen screamed and tried to pull the sweater back off to see who it was, getting her head stuck in the process.

"Man in the room!" One of the girls yelled as pandemonium broke loose. Darren stood with his mouth open as a flurry of young women in various stages of apparel squealed and grabbed nearby items of clothing as they made a rapid exit, dashing to rooms in other parts of the house. Kathy and Emily grabbed the unfortunate model with the sweater stuck over her face, whisking her away to Annie's bedroom. *"At least Darren wouldn't recognize her at a later time,"* I thought with a smile.

Annie rushed to her father. "Why didn't you come in the back door like you always do?" she exclaimed. "We had Angie posted in the kitchen to watch for you!"

"Annie, the driveway was full of cars, so I parked out front. What is going on here?" Darren's unbelieving eyes swept the room. "Are you having a party? It's not your birthday?" Pained eyes filled with dismay turned towards Annie. She stifled a giggle.

"No, Dad. It's for our fashion show. We're having it tonight at school."

I interrupted, noticing the blank look on Darren's face. "Remember, I told you about her class project?"

The blank look continued to testify of his ignorance. I wasn't surprised. He didn't seem to take in much of what I'd told him lately.

"Oh, Dad," Annie frowned. "You have to be a better listener." I rolled my eyes, thinking back to all the times I had said those very words to her.

She explained, "My team has to do a class project on how to help poor people without hurting their pride. So I got this idea. Mom said it was a good one." She smiled at me, and then turned back to Darren.

"Instead of just giving people our old clothes, we're inviting the whole community to a fashion show. Smiley and Ned donated a supper and the customers can have a good time and pick out what they want to buy, at real cheap prices, of course."

"What's the matter, Dad?" Annie stopped and a look of hesitation replaced the excitement on her face. I'd been watching Darren's countenance go from ignorance, to indifference, and now to anger. He cleared his throat and clenched his jaw. His arms stiffened.

"Don't you get it, Annie? *We* are some of those poor people you are talking about. Maybe if you ask your friends, they will give you some of *their* clothes."

I gasped, my hand over my mouth. Annie was ready to burst into tears. Never had I heard Darren speak with such blatant sarcasm to his only daughter.

He kept on, "I want you to call this off. My daughter isn't going to be the laughing-stock of the whole town. Her father's out of a job. Her own family is just about on welfare. And she wants to help poor people!" He kicked a stool out of his way and started to leave the room.

My gentle Annie couldn't hold it back. Her dark eyes burned with indignation. With a flourish, she threw the jacket she was holding onto the floor. "Daddy, I know we're poor. We've always been poor! Even when you had a job. But I care about helping people who are poorer than us! Now you've spoiled it. You've spoiled the whole thing!" She threw herself on the sofa, on top of all the neatly arranged clothes, and sobbed.

Darren froze, as still as a mannequin. Something of the misery he had caused seemed to sink into his soul.

The only sounds were Annie's muffled sobs as she cried into a sofa pillow, and the cheerful background noises of her excited friends drifting down from the staircase.

"I'm sorry, Annie. I didn't mean . . . I wouldn't hurt you for anything." Darren hesitated as her sobs continued, now tugging at his heartstrings. He walked over and knelt by her side. Tentatively, he patted her shoulder.

"Honey, can you forgive me? I just want to take care of you," his voice cracked, "Sometimes I'm afraid I won't be able to anymore."

"Daddy!" Annie turned and flung her arms around his neck. She clung to him fiercely. "Don't say that. You're a good father. You'll get a job. I'm sorry I said what I did."

Darren tenderly put his finger on her lips to shush her, like he did to me sometimes. "It was all my fault, Annie-pet. What can

I do to make it up to you? I'll come tonight, if you want."

Her face lit up. "Would you, Daddy? But . . . there may not be any other men there."

Darren grimaced. "I can handle it."

"Mom's going to be a model, too." She announced, slowly regaining her poise and enthusiasm.

Darren looked at me. I shrugged, like it didn't matter.

"Well, then, I have to go." he said. "Annie, honey, go wash your face and get changed. I'll be glad to escort you . . ." He turned and laid a gentle, thoughtful gaze on me. " . . . and Mom."

"...for the joy of the Lord is your strength."

Nehemiah 9:10b

Chapter 22

The fashion show was a huge success. Annie's face glowed as she accepted compliments. Many women came from the "other side of the tracks," as the lower class housing area was referred to in our little town of New Bergen. Most left carrying large shopping bags stuffed with assorted clothing. Those who had donated came just for the fun of it. Some of them also made purchases and went home satisfied with their "good buys."

As it turned out, Darren wasn't the only man there. Other wives brought their husbands, so they could try on clothes. Some men dropped in out of curiosity, or for the free coffee and socializing. Teachers and school staff came to support the kids. Even the principal showed up. Several people expressed a desire for the fashion show to become an annual event, and Karen's mom said she would consider heading it up the following year.

Only a couple of minor disasters complicated the evening. Hannah, one of the younger models, spilled red punch all over the white dress she was wearing. But since the dress was priced at only $1.50, it wasn't considered a great loss. Cindy, who was wearing her mother's dress which was a bit long for her, stepped on the hem, tripped, fell off the platform, and landed safely but mortified, on the principal's lap. Mr. Beakman, a rather shy, introverted bachelor, turned beet red, and the audience laughed uproariously. Cindy never did live that down. Neither did Mr. Beakman!

Darren was attentive and charming for the first time in months. I appreciated the effort he made to encourage Annie. But his recent outburst continued to disturb me. It just wasn't like him to respond to his daughter that way. Even though he tried to make it up to her, I worried.

The day after the fashion show, he gradually sank back into his dismal world with a limited perspective. A dense fog hung over our household, wrapping its gray, smothering arms around our family. The days grew quieter and we stopped laughing. Annie spent more time alone in her room. I longed for Nathan's visits, but even when he did come home, he was pre-occupied. My family was slipping away, sliding down to the edge of a precipice and hanging over the edge of a deep, dark cliff of disaster. Desperately, I prayed and tried to hang on to my loved ones as we threatened to plummet to the dreary depths of that bottomless hole.

Christmas was a brief reprieve. With Ingrid's supervision, Annie and I baked the favorite, traditional Norwegian cookies: krumkake, a thin, rolled up delicacy similar to a crepe, but sweeter; and and rosettes, another thin sweet pastry that is deep fried and sprinkled with powdered sugar. We made Ingrid's special chocolate fudge recipe and the usual lefse and yulekake, a Christmas sweetbread with cardamom and raisins. Papa got his second taste of lutefisk, and raved about it again. Ingrid couldn't do any baking that year. She could only watch us work. Her hands were gradually twisting into the knotted shape of the arthritic elderly. Both of Darren's parents were becoming more dependent on Papa and Billy.

Nathan drove home Christmas Eve in spite of a predicted snowstorm which, fortunately, amounted to just a light sprinkling of dusty white powder. We celebrated at the farm, with the entire family gathered around an enormous, lush evergreen that Sven and

Billy chopped down in their woods, as was their annual custom. Papa helped them that year, making it easier for everybody. Since Sven had only one arm, and Billy couldn't see, the whole operation went much smoother than it had in the past.

Papa even joined in the singing of Christmas carols as we clustered around the old mahogany piano while I played the traditional tunes. His eyes even looked a bit moist as Sven read the nativity story from the gospel of Luke. I wasn't sure if it was because God was working on his hardened heart, or just the warmth of a close family, which he had never before experienced.

Maybe it was Papa's presence that opened my eyes to the changes of the past years. Sven and Ingrid's grandchildren had grown into responsible young men and women. We didn't see them often anymore. Darren's older brothers, Seth and Luke, had expected him to take over the farm, so they moved out of Minnesota many years ago. Seth accepted a teaching job in Illinois, and Luke worked with an agri-business plant that moved to Iowa. Samuel, Sunniva's husband, was remarried to a lovely woman named Margaret. His four children, along with Seth's and Luke's children, were married now. Their children made up the second generation, Sven and Ingrid's great grand-children. The little ones reminded me of the first Christmas Darren and I spent together at the farm, when he captured my heart playing Santa Claus. I realized we needed babies and toddlers again to help us all see the marvelous good news of Jesus' appearance on earth through a child's eyes of wonder. Our gathering also made me realize how much I longed to celebrate the miracle of Jesus with all my family.

Dear Ingrid, who had become like a mother to me after the death of Grandma Lydia, was starting to lose ground physically. Her body was shrinking as her backbone curved in with the dreaded progress of osteoporosis. She tired easily these days. For a woman with an independent spirit, accustomed to having an abundant supply of energy, her frustration was apparent at times. But neither her optimistic outlook on life nor her sense of humor was diminished. She had commented a couple of days earlier that she realized she was now one of those "little old ladies" everyone talks about.

It still amazed me that Papa had stayed so long at the farm. His cancer had been in remission for many months now, but we all dreaded the day when it would flare up again. He made it clear that when it happened he would return to Boston. He said he wanted to be near his doctors. More importantly, he admitted, he didn't want us to watch him die.

My prayer life was at a stand still. *"Father, please bring Darren, Nathan and Papa to you before it's too late,"* I prayed every day, as I had prayed every day for many years. It sounded so rote and mechanical. Sometimes I caught myself wondering if God even heard me any more. All three of the men in my family seemed to grow farther away from God every day. In Papa's case, the situation grew more critical. *"How much time does he have left to find God?"* I wondered daily.

An uneventful New Year passed. Nathan returned to school. We survived another hard Minnesota winter, with a record-breaking volume of snow. Annie would graduate from high school in the spring and go off to college in the fall. She and Nate would be in the same school for a couple of years, which was a comfort to me and to her, I think. She was excited. I was happy for her, but dreaded it at the same time. The thought of an even quieter house alone with Darren was nerve-racking. My husband had only found temporary jobs through the winter, barely making enough money to pay the mortgage and keep food on the table. He finally agreed to let Annie get a part-time job, understanding that she would soon be eighteen and on her own. And on the condition that the money she earned would be spent on her personal needs and saved for college. Darren wouldn't have her contributing in any way to the household budget. Of course, he still wouldn't let me help. I had long ago buried my dream of becoming a doctor. In a way it was good, since I was free to spend more time at the farm helping Ingrid with household chores. Neither Papa nor Sven was, by any stretch of the imagination, a good cook. And none of us wanted Billy near the stove! It was actually a special time of making memories, time to spend with my father and the woman who had become so important to me. Though I hesitated to admit, it, even to myself, I knew the day would soon come when I would lose them both. My father, whom it had taken so many years for me to discover, and the third woman who had held the unique role of a mother in my life.

One sunny afternoon in March, Papa, Billy, and I were sitting at the kitchen table at the farm enjoying the eternally bottomless pot of coffee. Sven had taken Ingrid to see the doctor. She was now starting to have problems with a racing pulse during the night.

A quiet companionship settled over the three of us as we nibbled on fresh donuts, each absorbed in our own thoughts. Billy, now in his early thirties, didn't appear to have aged much. There were a few more smile lines by his eyes, and his skin was tougher, as a farmer's skin tends to get from exposure to sun and the elements. He still helped Sven and Darren with as many chores as fit his capabilities. But the light in his eye was as bright as ever, and his smile always an encouragement.

"Great donuts, Cass," Billy broke the silence. "Next to Mom's, yours are the best."

I smiled. "Thanks, Billy." He was always so appreciative. "How do you do it, Billy?" Papa asked bluntly. I stared at him. Part of me still went into an "intimidation mode" when he used that particular tone of voice. After all these years, I instinctively prepared myself for an explosion.

"Do what, Dr. Dupont?" Billy answered in a calm, unhurried voice. He still couldn't bring himself to call my father "Robert," though Papa had invited him to do so on many occasions.

Noticing my discomposure, Papa deliberately formed his words as he helped himself to another spoonful of sugar and stirred it methodically into his coffee cup.

"How do you keep such a positive attitude? All these months, I've watched you. I keep expecting you to crumble. You have no eye-sight and you hardly ever leave the farm. You amaze me with all you can do, but there's still so much you cannot do.

Yet, you don't seem to get frustrated." He shook his head. "I don't understand." My heart was pounding and racing. My first thought was, *"I wonder if this is what Ingrid's heart feels like in the middle of the night."* Fear coursed through my body. Papa's outspoken ways usually resulted in hurting people, and I was too fond of Billy to let him get hurt. But Billy took it all in and didn't seem to mind Papa's intrusive question. His face was a study in patience. His unseeing stare focused just above Papa's forehead and he rubbed his chin slightly just like Darren does when he is deep in thought.

"Well, Dr. Dupont," Billy replied. "My whole life is here, on this farm. And it's a good life. I've always had people who have loved and taken care of me. And tell me what I need to know. Every day brings on a new challenge, so I don't really have a chance to get bored. Since I've grown up, I have my place, and my job to do, my work." He paused, deep in thought. "I guess that's all a man really needs in this life."

"But doesn't it bother you," Papa persisted, "that you can't see anything?"

Billy chuckled, and I noticed my heart rate slowing back to normal. I shouldn't have worried. My gentle and determined brother-in-law could handle my father better than I could. "Well, maybe it would if I was used to seeing and then my sight got taken away. But I never had it. I was born blind. So you could say, I don't know what I'm missing." It suddenly dawned on me that Billy couldn't see how intimidating my father appeared at times. Facial expressions and body language meant nothing to him. Billy continued, "I figure, when I get to heaven, it's all going to be even more beautiful to me, because heaven will be my first sight. I don't have to look at this here old world that's trapped by sin." He paused a moment, and stared into space. Then he spoke with a soft voice, tempered with a touch of awe. "I reckon' Jesus' face will be the first thing I ever see."

Billy's face glowed, as with the light of another world, like he was even now catching a brief glimpse of unthinkable pleasures awaiting him in the future. His sense of anticipation was so real that I dared not move, for fear of breaking the spell. I let my eyes drift to watch Papa's reaction. He was staring at Billy, totally transfixed. Then, suddenly, he shifted uncomfortably in his chair, as though he had been the one put on the spot instead of Billy.

"Tell me," Papa cleared his throat, leaned forward, and spoke with insistence. "You are basically in a helpless position. You have no control over your own life. You can't live alone. You have to depend on other people to . . . lead you and help you all the time. Doesn't that bother you? Doesn't it make you feel sort of . . . " Here he flung out his hands in frustration. He evidently could find no words for the level of helplessness and vulnerability he attributed to Billy.

My temper was heating up again, but I knew I needed to stay out of this conversation, and let Billy have his say.

Papa's question didn't affect Billy's expression of serenity. Although the glow was fading as he came back to the here-and-now, he spoke with determination and patience, "Let me put it this way. When I was a kid, we had horses. Dad needed them for the farm work when he was a boy. Later on, I suppose he kept them more for pets than anything else. He let me ride one named Dusty. He was a mild old horse. Gentle as a newborn calf. I could trust him with my life. Dad used to ride next to me on Blackie. He'd tell me when to turn and when to slow down, and everything went okay as long as I listened to Dad. By and by, Dusty got used to taking me the same way, on the same trail every time we went for a ride. So one day Dad let me go off alone on my horse. I was a little scared," he chuckled, "probably not as scared as Dad was though! But Dad told me, 'Don't try to steer. Just let go of the reigns and old Dusty will take you for a ride and bring you home safe.' And that's just what he did. Old Dusty and I went for lots of rides alone after that, until he broke his leg and had to be put to sleep.

"I don't ride horses any more. But Mom and Dad taught me about God and Jesus and read the Bible to me. Whenever I feel like I'm getting a little scared or hopeless, I just say to myself, 'Billy, let go of the reigns. God will take you through this life and lead you safely home. To heaven." He added firmly.

"Thank you, Lord," I mentally whispered. *"Help my*

father to see the truth and wisdom that Billy just gave us." My blind brother-in-law was free to see beyond this world, to the spiritual dimension of reality. He was helping us to see what was already so clear to him.

"Billy, I . . ." Papa began.

The door opened suddenly and Sven helped Ingrid into the warmth of the kitchen. Although disappointed at the interruption, I was nevertheless relieved to have Ingrid home again and anxious to hear what the doctor had told her. I jumped up to take her coat and hat and put them in the closet. When I returned, she was seated at the table and Sven was pouring coffee for them. "What did Dr. Johnston say?" I asked. "Well, he gave me this here medicine," Ingrid showed me a small bottle of blue and yellow tablets she had taken from her purse. "He said my heart is getting weaker, but he's sure this will help me and it's nothing I need to worry about."

"Ingrid," my father sounded firm. "I must insist that you see a specialist."

Sven set the coffeepot on the stove and pulled out the chair next to his wife. He sat down slowly, his own joints aching more than usual, I imagined. "Dr. Johnston's a good man. Whatever he says, we will do."

Ingrid nodded in agreement and reached for a donut. She looked very tired.

"He may be a good man," Papa struggled for control, "But even good men make mistakes. Sven, you need to take her to someone who has studied more about the heart."

"Well, we'll think about it," Sven said. "I know you mean well, Robert. But Dr. Johnston has been our doctor for a good many years, since Billy here was born."

Ingrid interrupted. "And anyway, it don't seem like there's any hurry. I'll try these pills and we'll see how it goes."

"Mom, maybe you should . . . " I feebly attempted to express my opinion.

"We'll think about it." Ingrid's firm tone signaled the end of that conversation. She hastily redirected it. "So, Robert, did you tell her?"

"Tell me what?" I asked, a little shaken. A premonition of disaster nudged my heart.

"I'm returning to Boston next week," Papa announced abruptly.

"No, Papa," I reacted automatically. I wasn't ready to let him go.

"My condition is worsening. The symptoms are returning and I need to get back to my doctors." I nodded numbly, seeing for the first time the pale face and obvious weight loss I had not let register in my mind. My heart fluttered with apprehension. If only we could have talked a little longer with Billy. It truly seemed like something was starting to sink into Papa's soul. It didn't seem like there was much more to be said at the time. It was getting late, time for me to go home and fix supper for Darren and Annie. So I hugged them all good-bye and left.

All the way home, I pleaded with God. Tears stung my eyes and made the road hard to see. *"Oh, Heavenly Father, please let my earthly father find you. Please, God, before it's too late."* I felt so helpless. I'd tried to talk to Papa and failed. I prayed, fervently, *"Oh, God, what else can I do? How can I help him find You?"* And God answered my prayer.

As I turned into our driveway, I knew what I had to do.

Our last Sunday meal with Papa was pleasant but strained. Sven, Ingrid, and Billy brought Papa to our house. Nathan came from school to see his grandfather for the last time. I fixed Papa's favorite meal, roast beef baked with potatoes and carrots. He said he liked the way all the flavors blended together. We had home-made apple pie for dessert. But Papa could hardly eat anything. He was so weak, I worried that he wouldn't make it back safely on the plane to Boston without anyone to take care of him. But as usual, he had made up his mind and was determined to have his own way. All I could do was pray for him. After supper, Annie and Nate gathered the dishes for washing. When the others went to relax in the living room, I asked Papa to come out in the yard with me. It was a gorgeous evening. We'd had an early spring that year, which was exceptionally welcome after the hard winter. The sun was bidding us farewell as it quietly tucked itself into the horizon, honoring us with a vivid display of pinks, purples, and oranges. Papa and I sat on the black wrought iron bench that Darren had bought for me when he worked at the hardware store. The soothing scent of lilacs, carried by a gentle breeze, drifted over to us. We shared the quiet end of a busy day, listening to robins chirping and the cheerful calls of neighborhood children at play. Somewhere in the distance, a dog barked.

"Papa, I have something for you." Slowly, I reached into my jacket pocket and took out a small white leather Bible. I tenderly caressed it, realizing this was another "good-bye" for me. "This was Mama's Bible. I want you to have it."

Papa's head jerked up and he stared at me with shock. "Your mother never had a Bible." "Yes, she did, Papa. She gave it to me the night before she died."

"But how could she?" Total bewilderment was on his face.

"Grandma gave it to her. Mama kept it in the little drawer of the table by her bed. She told me it gave her hope and asked me to keep it and read it." Papa shook his head in amazement. "Lydia, Lydia. That stubborn woman." He turned to look into my eyes. For the first time, I saw hunger there. And vulnerability. "So, Amanda found God too." It was more of a statement than a question.

"Yes, Papa."

"Hmpph! Well, I'll be. Guess I didn't have control over her after all."

"No, Papa." I held the precious book out to him, my eyes filling with tears. "I want you to take this with you. Mama would want you to have it."

"No, Child. That's the only thing . . ." his voice cracked, "the only thing you have of your mother's."

Fear began to penetrate my mind. Despair was close behind. I was a little girl again. Desperately, I pleaded, "Please, Papa, take it. I've said all I can say to you about God. And you haven't taken me seriously." Suddenly, I was giving him a command, as firm as any military officer could make. And one not to be refused. "Now you take this Bible. You read it and let God speak to you." Surprised but humbled, my father took the book. "Cassandra," he began as he wiped away a tear with his thumb that escaped and ran down his cheek. "I don't make promises any more that I can't keep. I'm an old, sick man. I think in some ways I'm a better man than I used to be. But I've spent my life 'living in sin,' as your Bible preacher would say. The bad in my life far out-weighs the good. Cassie, you know something of how I've spent my life, how I've treated you . . . and Amanda." He sighed deeply. "As a doctor, I've been proud of the many lives I've saved. But you know I've also taken them, innocent lives, lots of them." He hung his head, and I knew he was thinking of the unborn babies, of his own grandson whose life was barely spared when Darren car-ried me out of the clinic. He shook his head and sought my eyes with troubled ones of his own. "If there is a god, he can't overlook all that, Cassie."

"He didn't overlook your sins, Papa. He sent His own Son, Jesus, to pay for our sins. Jesus died a criminal's death on the cross. He paid for our sins with His own blood! Just trust Him, Papa. Just give Him your sins and trust Him."

"Hush, now." He was again the master of the situation. The wall was back up and he spoke with a slight trace of humor. "Well, then, if there is a god, and if he wants this old character, I guess He's going to get me, one way or the other, right?" Once again, I had failed to reach my father. "Well, I . . . suppose, of course He is," I mumbled, not altogether happy with the way this conversation was going.

"And, if there isn't a god, we have at least made our peace, Cassandra, you and I. So something good has come out of this life."

Blinded with tears and lugging a heavy heart, I could only nod.

He stood up. "Let's go inside, Cassie. I need to be going. And I want to see you smile again before I leave." He took me by the shoulders and gently lifted me to a standing position. "There now," he tucked his big hand under my chin. Then he stroked my cheek and gazed tenderly into my eyes. "You sure do look like your mother. You are so beautiful, my Cassandra." My knees felt weak, and I trembled all over. My body begged permission to crumble, but I denied the request. I wasn't going to spoil this moment that I had waited for my whole life.

"Cassandra, I don't think I have ever said this to you. And if I did, I don't know if I meant it. But I do mean it now. I love you, daughter." His voice was a whisper. "Please, please, smile for me."

Constrained by a trembling chill, I closed my eyes, then opened them again, taking the few moments I had to memorize his face. As I had, long ago, when he left me the first time. Then, I slowly forced the corners of my lips to turn up and let my love shine freely through my eyes. He grabbed me and clung to me with a fierceness that threatened to crush the breath right out of me. I returned his embrace and sobbed on his shoulders until the hidden hollow of my heart that held my tears was emptied.

Papa took the Bible with him. *Dare I hope that he would read it?* Darren and I drove Papa to the airport in Minneapolis the following morning. It was a quiet ride, sort of anti-climactic. When his plane was announced, I asked Papa to telephone me when he got home. His predictable answer was, "I'm not much of a conversationalist, Cassie." He was calm and back in control. The end was near, and he had said his farewells.

I hugged him quickly and he walked away. My heart pounded and I started to feel like the child I was when he left me before. But this time, he turned and smiled, and gave a little wave. Darren put his arm around me and drove me home. I was confused with an overwhelming mixture of feelings. Peace, the security that only someone who has finally found a love long denied, can understand. Yet fear and dread for my father was also present, for the suffering that was sure to come, and for his eternal future. A question hammered in my brain. *Would I ever see him again?* I knew I wouldn't in this life.

Would I have another chance to reach him?

In spite of his final words, I waited for him to call.

But Papa didn't call. His action, or rather the lack of it, only confirmed what my heart was already telling me. His visit was intended from the start to be both the renewing and the conclusion of our relationship. The chapter he was mentally composing of his life, entitled "Restoration with My Daughter," was now finished. Still in complete control, he was now composing his final chapter, "Death, the End of My Existence." I refused to accept the obvious conclusion, however. That he would continue to reject the all powerful God, and thereby commit himself to a never-ending future of torment in hell. Of course, Papa didn't see it that way. He didn't believe in heaven or hell, or even that there was a god.

My father's greatest failing was pride. That worried me a lot, because I knew that Satan was cast out of heaven because of the sin of pride. Papa assumed it was up to him to decide whether there was a god, or not. It didn't occur to him that God's existence didn't depend on his decision. God was and is, and that's that. What a shock it would be for my father when he came face to face with the Creator of the universe, the One he didn't believe existed! Terror welled up in my own heart. I knew that God longed for Papa to come to Him. I recalled a story Jesus told of the good shepherd who left ninety-nine sheep to hunt for the lost one, and wasn't satisfied until it was returned to the fold. God wanted my father safely in His flock.

I had spoken all the words I could think of to say to Papa. Now I could only wait and pray. And pray I did, not only for my father, but also for my husband and son. How thankful I was that Annie found her joy in the Lord Jesus. She was not just my daughter, but also my sister in Christ. Strange how the men in my life, each one so competent and independent, had made the choice to deny the greatest truth of all, the only constant reality. *Maybe my father was forever lost, but did that mean Darren and Nathan had to follow the same twisted, irrational path to the same devastating eternity?* At one time, I thought Darren was so different from Papa. He was, actually, in personality and character. Yet, his spiritual perception was cast out of the same mold. And I feared my son, too, would find his ways of willful disregard for the truth equally set in granite as solid as that of his predecessors.

In those heavy, dark days, I truly learned the meaning of the scripture verse that told us to "pray without ceasing." I hardly noticed the days that brought us a beautiful spring. I was so absorbed in my own thoughts. I waited in dread for the phone call that would announce the death of my father. I waited as I saw Darren driven deeper and deeper into the plummeting despair of the lost. I waited while Nathan drifted farther and farther away from me, continuing to reject the message of the gospel I had fervently tried to teach him since he was a child.

If only . . . The future of my family seemed to hinge on Darren. Nathan had patterned himself after his dad. Darren was a great father and a good role model for a young boy. I had always been grateful for my husband's influence. Now I saw clearly that Darren had been leading his son the wrong way all this time, into a life of manly independence, the opposite direction from God. Maybe if Darren could see the truth in Jesus' offer of salvation and give himself to God, Nathan would, as he had always done, follow in his father's footsteps.

The Return
Chapter 23

Summer finally arrived in a full and brilliant display. My garden flourished with the colorful highlights of my favorite perennials: bright yellow daylilies, lavender foxglove, and white daisies that were gifts from Ingrid. Ingrid's garden was a celebration of the joy she found in life. Now that she was growing physically weaker, she had to cut her activities drastically. She gave many of her plants to me, and to her close friends. I tried to help Ingrid with her garden, so she would still have some beautiful flowers in her own yard. I didn't have a green thumb like her, but carefully followed her instructions. We shared many contented hours as I worked in her yard, digging in the soil and yanking out weeds.

One hot and humid day, sweat kept running down my brow and neck as I worked. I frequently stopped to wipe my damp forehead with a soiled hand, leaving particles of dirt clinging to my face. I probably looked a sight. Ingrid kept us supplied with plenty of fresh lemonade as she directed and encouraged my efforts from her reclining lawn chair.

"Cassie, you spoil me," she insisted. "Here I sit, barely

able to fend for myself any more, an' you work so hard to give me joys I don't even need. It warms my heart an' makes my days worth livin' to get up in the morning and look out my bedroom window at the glorious show of the Lord's creation you've planted for me. Cassie, I know I'm gonna start blubbering any minute now. God has been so good to give you to me as a daughter-in-law, 'specially when He took my own daughter to heaven years ago." Here she glanced up at the heavens as though she was giving the Lord a rebuke.

Then she did start to "blubber." Concerned and touched, I set down my garden tools a bit too quickly and in the process dropped my trowel on my bare toe. In mild pain, I limped over to give my dear mother-in-law a hug. My limping made her cry harder, and we clung together for a few moments. Soon I noticed that the dirt on my forehead was melting with her tears and running down her cheeks in muddy puddles. I told her and then we both started giggling through our tears. Ingrid and I could always giggle together. We shared a special intimacy, and grew even closer during the days of her infirmities.

One particular summer day, I spent hours working on my own garden, transplanting some irises that Ingrid gave me. It was a comfortable sunny day, lacking the awful humidity that characterized Minnesota at that time of year. I was restless, and decided a walk would do me good. Annie was gone. She had a summer baby-sitting job at a house down the street. Darren had left to job hunt. His latest temporary job would end soon, and I dreaded seeing him come home discouraged and depressed again with nothing to show for his efforts. I put my gardening supplies away, stretched my back a bit, and changed from my sandals into comfortable walking shoes. I started down the street, veering from my usual route which lead along a small creek near our house. Needing a change of scenery, I headed towards the oldest part of town, across the railroad tracks where earlier settlers had chosen to make a home. As I walked, I passed Grandma Lydia's old house, the home that her husband, a ship builder, had built for them when he retired. It was a familiar place to me, full of memories, where

I had spent many happy hours as a child. It's funny how time and growth changes one's perception. The house that had once appeared so huge and rambling through a little girl's eyes now seemed compact and contained, even quaint. It looked the same, sky blue with white shutters. I had heard that a family with small children lived there now, and evidences pointed to that fact. A homemade playground with swings and a small slide now resided in the back yard. A broken toy truck lay on the step. And sprawled sideways on the sidewalk was a bright red tricycle. Stepping around the tricycle, I thought back to that Mother's Day so long ago when I dreamed an angel rescued me from an oncoming train. I smiled to myself. The dream had been vivid and real. Thinking about it still made my senses tingle with the over-powering emotions of comfort and security. I had felt completely safe when the angel swept me up in his arms and held me as the rumbling train sped by us. A deep sigh escaped my lips. What I wouldn't do now to experience that same unworldly feeling of peace as an adult.

The park was just ahead of me. Once again, I looked both ways and stepped over the tracks as I made my way to the rustic park bench where the woman had sat when I was a child. I remembered how she had stared at me when I'd picked the yellow and purple flowers for my mother. Very tired, I sat down, feeling the exhaustion that came more from the hard work of worrying than from the manual labor of gardening. The park was deserted except for a tall stranger who was approaching slowly from the other direction. He looked young, robust and healthy. *"How unusual,"* I thought, *"for a young man in our small town to stroll casually through a park at mid-day."* He wore common, every-day clothes, a tan short-sleeved shirt over clean blue jeans.

I felt no fear of him. New Bergen was practically crime-free, so the threat of danger didn't enter my mind. But I wanted to be alone. I turned my gaze away from him and returned to my absorbing, anxious thoughts. I worried about Darren, Papa, and Nathan's salvation and about Ingrid's health problems. I would miss Annie in the fall when she would leave for college. She was excited, but I was nervous and dreaded saying "good-by" to my daughter like I had to Nathan three years ago. *Oh, dear God, it seems like all of my family is drifting away from me, either by death, or by distance, both physically and emotionally.*

"May I sit here?" The casual words spoken in a deep resonant tone broke my concentration. I looked up to see the stranger watching me with a polite and gentle expression.

"Of course," I glanced away quickly. Something in his eyes caught me off guard. His look was knowing, almost like he could read my thoughts. I suddenly felt confused and guilty. *What was wrong with me?* I really was out of sorts today. I deliberately returned to my previous meditations, intending to ignore him. He took his place on the bench beside me.

"It's a beautiful day, isn't it?" He spoke with satisfaction, as though he was taking responsibility for the pleasant weather.

"Yes, isn't it?" I briefly glanced sideways at him, then gave him a second look. This man had a familiar look about him. I knew I had seen him somewhere. *Yes, I was sure now. A distant time, in my childhood. No, that couldn't be. He would be much older now, if that were the case.*

"Cassandra," he spoke with calm assurance and knowledge.

I stood up. *How did he know my name?* Chills ran through my whole body and I started to shiver in the warm sun. Unexplainable fear overtook me.

"I have to go home," I mumbled and began to walk away.

"Wait!" he called. It was definitely a command, though not uttered in a threatening way at all. I stopped in my tracks, my back toward him.

"Don't be frightened," he continued in a soothing voice. "Turn around. Look at me."

As if in a trance, I obediently turned to face him. His eyes captivated me. A translucent cloud of white light—the brightest light I had ever seen—surrounded him while at the same time passing in and out of him. In seconds, he appeared normal again.

I gasped and covered my mouth with my hands. My knees were weak and threatened to give way.

"Come here. Sit." Then he came to me, and gently but firmly took my elbow and guided me back to the bench. I sat and stared at him with wonder and recognition.

The angel! The same one who rescued me as a child. It was real. My childhood experience really had happened. An angel really had rescued me. And he was sitting at my side right now!

He smiled. "Yes, I am the same one. God has sent me to you again, Cassandra. He sent me the first time to save your life. This time He wants to give you a chance to help save your husband's soul."

I couldn't speak. Words failed me. I just stared, letting his words penetrate my spirit.

He kept on smiling and gave me time.

I finally managed to throw out a few phrases. "But how? I mean, how can I really see you? How can I know you are who you say you are? How do I know I can believe you?" Then fear struck at me, swiftly and accurately. "Am I dreaming? Like I did when I was a child?"

"No, Cassandra. I am very real. Touch me." He held out his hand.

Cautiously, I ran my fingers over the back of his hand. It felt strong and warm and fleshly. This was certainly no vision, no figment of my imagination.

He turned his hand over and let me clasp it. Then he squeezed my hand gently and let go.

"You know in your spirit, Cassandra, that I am an angel, a messenger sent by God. You don't need proof."

He was right. A calmness of mind and heart had taken possession of me. What at first had seemed unreal was now as concrete as the cement under our bench.

"God wants to give you a choice, Cassandra. Are you ready to listen?"

I nodded, eyes fastened on his face.

"Darren has almost hardened his heart completely to the message of Christ. If left to himself, he will continue to walk away from God. But there is a way to reach him. Only through suffering are some people able to see Jesus, the One who suffered for them. Your husband is so independent and set on his own course that his own physical suffering would have no spiritual effect on

247

him. But for him to see a loved one in pain could break through the resistance he has put up around himself. If someone whom he loves would sacrifice for him, Darren will be able to see Jesus in that person. At the same time, he would learn how to give himself for his loved one who suffers."

"You mean," I barely spoke above a whisper, " that you could save Darren if I do my share?"

"Cassandra, I have no power or authority of my own. I am merely a messenger sent by God. Only God has the ability to save a soul, through the blood sacrifice of His Son, Jesus Christ."

I nodded mutely, totally transfixed, as I struggled to understand what he was saying.

"The forces of evil in the world are also powerful, although they are limited and controlled by God. His ways are beyond our understanding, but they are always right and just, even as He always acts in love. God allows evil for a time in this world. He uses it to work out His purposes, for good. He is giving you a choice, Cassandra. He wants to open a door that has been closed in the past. He wants to delight you with a particle of meaning, of insight. A small glimpse into His reasoning. Paul wrote in the Holy Scriptures that Christians are permitted to 'share in the sufferings of Christ'. His gift to you will be to let you knowingly and willingly participate in the act of suffering, in order to free the Holy Spirit to work in your husband's life."

He held my eyes with a steady gaze, challenging me. "Cassandra, would you be willing to show your love to Darren and to God by sacrificing your health? By accepting of your own will, a debilitating illness with the possibility of setting your husband free?"

I sat stunned, my body rigid, my mind frantically fighting to comprehend all the implications of what God asked of me.

"Would I?" my voice broke. With a sense of urgency, I wrung my hands. They were suddenly cold and clammy. I had to know the answer to a very important question. I tried to speak again. This time my tongue worked. "Would I die from the illness?"

The angel took my hands in his. " I don't know the answer

to your question, Dear Child. But I do know that fear is the enemy. Fear is a powerful tool of Satan's. Ask God to help you make this decision without fear."

He rose to leave. "I will return in two weeks. Meet me here and give me your answer."

"Wait!" I was frantic. "I have one more question. If I do this, will I know without a doubt that Darren will be saved?"

The first evidence of sadness clouded the angel's face. He shook his head. "Only God knows the outcome. I can make no guarantees. But I promise you this: your spiritual eyes will be enlightened, and you will be given a new understanding and appreciation of the glory of God. Only those who are permitted to sacrifice their life for another can begin to catch a small glimpse of the tremendous love that Christ has for us."

"But I . . ." Even as I cried out one more time, the angel vanished. He didn't disappear in smoke or a cloud. He was suddenly gone, just like he disappeared when I was a child, as though he had never been. I remained in shock, still pondering his words. *Could I do this? Could I do what was asked of me? Oh, Dear Lord, is this the only way for Darren to be saved?*

Silence. No rapid response from heaven. No response at all in my spirit.

My eyes turned to the sky, the calm, clear blue sky that looked so peaceful. Then I looked around me. I saw people, walking about, doing their daily tasks. Life was returning to normal, already blurring the memory of the angel's visit. But his words remained, etched permanently on the tablets of my mind.

How long I sat on that bench, I don't know. Finally I stood and began to walk home. My thoughts were in turmoil. If this was true, and I knew in my heart that it was, I faced a crucial decision.

Yes, I loved Darren and wanted him to be saved. But was I willing to go to the extent the angel had suggested? Especially, if I was not guaranteed the result I wanted? Could I actually give up my health? Could I choose to suffer pain and all that would involve for my husband? Did I love him that much?

Did I love God that much?

I might become like Ingrid, or worse. And I was only thirty-nine years old! I could be helpless, homebound, totally depend-ent on others, on Darren. *Would I die young? Would I ever meet Nathan's future wife and see Annie as a radiant bride? Would I play with my grandchildren like Grandma Lydia played with me? No, no, this was asking too much. But if, just if, Darren got saved? After all, this life is not what matters in the long run. This life on earth is not going to last. Where we spend eternity is what counts.*

Where Darren spends eternity . . .

When I returned home and walked in the kitchen door, Darren and Annie were sitting at the table. Darren had his back toward me, but Annie was smiling, a big smile.

"Mom's here!" she exclaimed. "Tell her the news, Dad!"

Darren turned around with a huge grin. He leaped up and, with a swoop, gathered me in his arms, picked me up, and swung me around. Then he set me back on my feet.

Dizzily, I stared at him. *What, now?* This was too many emotions for one day!

"Cassie, guess what?"

Dumbly I stared. "What?"

"I've got a job! A good job. And we can move out of this run down house into a brand new big apartment!"

"What? Where?" The bewildered look on my face made them both laugh.

"Here, sit down." Darren pulled out a chair for me, poured a fresh cup of coffee and brought it to me while he explained.

"You know those new high rises going up on the east side of town?" I nodded, taking a sip of coffee. They were all of two stories high, but big for New Bergen. Mostly they were expected to be occupied by older people who were not able to take care of the problems incurred in owning a home. "Well," he continued, "they need a live-in manager to run the place. To be on the scene for emergencies and fixing stuff, mowing lawns, that sort of thing. I got the job!"

Annie broke in, "And there's a cool apartment for us to live in--two bedrooms, a kitchen, dining room and living room. It's got a big window that looks out on the park. Dad took me over and showed me our place. You weren't home."

"I'll take you there tonight, honey," Darren promised. "And that's not all. Hank gave me a good recommendation. So they're hiring me to do the accounting and business stuff, too. I'll be busy, Cassie, but I'll be in and out all day and making plenty of money for us."

I looked from one happy face to the other. It was so good to see Darren animated again, with a purpose for living. I had one question. "Where will Nathan stay when he comes home?"

Darren laughed. "We'll buy a hide-a-bed. We'll have money to spend, Cassie."

The next few days were full of feverish activity. The apartment building would be ready for occupancy in a couple of weeks and Darren needed to be on the grounds as soon as possible. Annie jabbered on and on about how she was going to decorate her new room. "I even get to pick out the color of paint, Mom!" she excitedly announced. She freely offered suggestions for decorating the rest of the apartment, including Darren's and my bedroom. I gave in to most of her suggestions. She had good taste, and I had other things on my mind. Since Darren was between jobs, all three of us helped pack. Nathan came home on the weekend to help move our things to the new building. Jim and Kathy gave us a hand. Sven and Billy helped as much as they could. Ingrid seemed to enjoy a supervisory role as she sat in a comfortable chair and directed our movements while we hauled furniture and boxes at a constant pace all day.

The angel's proposition was shoved to the back of my mind during that time, but never completely out of my thoughts.

By Sunday night, everything had been moved to our new home. Nathan drove back to college and Annie was out with friends. Darren fell asleep, exhausted, on the couch in front of the TV. I stood in the darkness gazing out the window at the park where the angel had appeared to me twice. I still had one week to make my decision. Logical arguments for both sides pushed and shoved for pre-eminence in my mind. As much as I wanted Darren to be saved, I remembered that the angel had told me there were no guarantees. Besides that, he didn't say for sure that Darren wouldn't have another chance if I decided against it. Just something about the Spirit being free to work in his life.

Still I know it was more likely that this plan would work, since God had devised it. I knew I needed to obey God. But this wasn't really a question of obedience. God had given me a choice. He could have just made me sick and that would have been that.

But how would I handle an illness? Maybe it was more my attitude that mattered. If I became bitter and resentful, it could drive Darren even farther from God. But if I chose it, as a sacrifice, a gift of love, then Darren could see Jesus even better.

Wow! What a thought!

On the other hand, I did have a choice. I belonged to God. I wouldn't lose my salvation if I decided not to do this. And God was certainly asking a lot of me!

Darren seemed so contented, for the first time in many months. Maybe since he had a job again, we would become closer. And then he would listen to me. Maybe I could convince him about the truth of the gospel.

Face it, Cassie. You just don't want to get sick.

That was true. I didn't want to suffer, maybe even needlessly. And there was something else. Fragments of thoughts struggling to get through, sort of like the thoughts I'd had on that fateful day when I had waited in the abortion clinic for my baby's life to be taken away. Of course. My dream. My dream to become a doctor. Well, that was out of the question now. But I had chosen to keep my baby because a good doctor always chooses life over death. *So why should I now choose sickness over health? If I chose to save my baby's life, why would it be wrong to save my own? God would understand. He gave me the gift of life. Would He really expect me to throw it away? The angel obviously didn't tell me all the facts. And certainly God was capable of saving Darren without me. That I knew for sure!*

The shrill ringing of the phone brought me out of my reverie. Darren didn't even stir. I picked up the phone. It was Ingrid.

"Cassie, your father's doctor called me."

"Oh, no," I sat down, hard, on the chair by the desk.

"He died peacefully, in his sleep, about an hour ago."

Tears overflowed my eyes and my voice shook. "Why didn't the doctor call me?" I asked.

"Dr. Barton said he tried to reach you, but he didn't have your new number. And Robert had given him mine, too. So he called me instead. I'm so sorry, Cassie."

"Thanks for calling." I couldn't speak any more and started to hang up. I just wanted to be alone and cry.

"Wait a minute, Cassie."

"Yes?"

"Dr. Barton said that Robert insisted on giving you a message. He made him write it down, word for word. The doctor said he didn't know what it means. Maybe Robert was out of his head." My heart pounded so hard and loud I thought it would wake up Darren. I could barely whisper, "What is it?"

"He said, 'Tell Cassie I let go of the reigns."

I couldn't help it. I let out a yelp of pure joy! Darren popped straight up on the sofa and looked at me like I had just dropped in from Mars. Ignoring him, I quickly explained the coded message to Ingrid, who rejoiced with me. Then I hung up the phone and spent the next half hour trying to explain to Darren why I was so happy when Papa had just died. He finally got it, and in spite of the fact that he didn't see spiritual things the way I did, he was relieved I was taking it so well. Of course, after a while I did start to cry. The loss suddenly hit me, and then Darren sat with me on the couch and held me until the tears stopped.

But nothing could take away the joy of knowing that Papa had given up the controls of his life to God. The message he had sent assured me that Billy's talk about his riding days had sunk in, deeply into my father's heart. I knew that God had answered my prayers. *Surely He would save Darren, too. And my son. Even if I didn't get sick.*

Everything would be all right.

Chapter 24

When Nathan came home the following weekend, we were settled in our new apartment. Annie and I had painted her bedroom horizon blue. Darren let her buy a new bedspread. She chose a white satiny material that was dotted with clusters of blue and yellow flowers and edged with white ruffles. Her rug was also blue, and yellow throw pillows and lamps completed the cheery theme. We painted Darren's and my bedroom a pale green. I wanted to keep the antique furniture that once belonged to Grandma Lydia. But we purchased a new quilt that had an old-fashioned rose and green tapestry pattern. It gave a calm, soothing effect to the cozy room, which was considerably smaller than our previous bedroom. New living room furniture would have to wait, but we all felt good about having our completed sanctuaries to retire in at the end of a busy day.

Now it was Saturday, the day of Nathan's twenty-first birthday. Annie and I spent the day making a cake and decorating the living room with balloons and crepe paper, in honor of the momentous occasion. I wanted the day to be a special gift to my son, who had been withdrawn ever since Talitha's death.   Maybe just as much for my own sake as his, I needed to assure him of our ongoing love and affection.   I dared to hope that this party might break down communication barriers that had unintentionally sprouted up between us like stubborn weeds needing to be dug out of the soil.

Nate's restaurant job kept him out late Friday night, so he slept in on Saturday morning and arrived at our apartment mid-afternoon.   Ingrid, Sven, and Billy came for the afternoon cele-bration.   Nathan was surprised and touched by a party given so soon after our move and his grandfather's death.   His protective, icy covering started to thaw as we shared memories and laughter of his childhood, and even memorable times with my father. Everyone expressed gratitude that Robert had been restored to us. The months we recently shared enabled him to build a valuable connection with the family.

By late afternoon, Darren's parents and brother had left. As we were cleaning up, Darren said he wanted to take Nate out for supper, just the two of them, to mark the occasion of his "entrance into manhood." I laughed at the phrase. I knew Darren was sentimental, but he didn't normally use such proper phrases. I agreed, reluctant to give up my time with Nate, but hoping that the evening together would have a positive impact on both of them. Nathan didn't have to leave until Sunday afternoon, so I would see him the next day. Annie went out with friends and planned to stay overnight at a friend's house. Katie's family would bring Annie to church in the morning.

Actually, I probably needed some time alone. The next day was the end of the two week period, when the angel would return to the park to hear my decision. I suppose I should have spent more time that night in prayer. As I look back, I wonder if it would have made a difference in the lives of my husband and son. But at the time, I felt that things were going well. Darren was happy about his new job, and Nate seemed to be returning to the family. The party had strengthened some bonds between all of us. On the whole, I looked forward to the future with renewed hope. I was prepared to refuse the "opportunity" offered by the angel. It just didn't seem necessary.

I was so tired after the hard work of moving, painting, organizing, and preparing for the party. So I curled up on the sofa with a bowl of popcorn and a glass of cold lemonade, and turned on the television. The musical, "West Side Story," was showing that night. I wanted to watch it, and knew the guys weren't too excited about it anyway. I relished the chance to rest. More tired than I had realized, I dozed off on the couch before the show ended. When I awoke, the room was dark except for the hazy light emitting from the television set and the soft glow of moonlight peaking through the sheer, frilly curtains.

Noises from the kitchen told me Darren and Nathan were home. I heard laughter and the banging of a cupboard door. I smiled to myself. They must have had a good time.

"Where did your mother put the coffee grounds?" Darren's voice sounded sleepy and his words sort of ran together. I got up and went to show him where I had stored the can.

Nate's voice in response had the same slurring quality. "You'd better find it fast, Dad. You're gonna need it."

Even in my own groggy state of sleepiness, I sensed something was wrong, out of place. My nerves sent their antenna out, groping for an explanation to satisfy the unusual messages my mind was receiving.

Suddenly alert and on my guard, I entered the kitchen.

Nathan sat at the kitchen table with a silly smirk on his face watching his dad who was half-sprawled on the counter waving a jar of instant tea in his hands.

"Do you think this will do the trick?" Darren chuckled and clumsily reached for a coffee filter. He missed and his hand banged instead into the cupboard door. Nathan threw back his head and laughed.

I grabbed Darren's arm and the jar of tea slipped out of his grasp and fell to the floor, shattering into pieces.

"Whadja do that for?" His glassy eyes searched for my face and he aimed a puckered mouth in the general direction of my own. "Hi, honey. Are ya happy Daddy's home?" He stumbled once, and I let go of his arm, instinctively backing away.

All my senses were enraged. My husband was drunk. And he'd gotten my son just as drunk. Anger permeated every pore of my skin and I soaked in humiliation and disgust like I was a human sponge. Bloated with misery, I glared at the two of them. Nate, more subdued than Darren, avoided my eyes. But Darren seemed to have totally lost his inhibitions. Furiously, I yelled at my husband, "What on earth? Where have you been?" Now visibly shaking, I turned to Nathan. "Tell me what's going on."

"Aw, Mom, don't be upset," he pleaded. "I'm twenty-one years old now. We were just celebrating. Having a good time."

I was overcome with shock. My husband hadn't drunk alcohol since the early months of our marriage. He'd told me that he used to go out with the guys before we married and got drunk, though I never saw him in that condition. After we married, he sometimes had a beer or two after work or in the evenings. But when Nathan was born, he'd gradually stopped doing it. I never bought the stuff for him and had plenty of coffee and pop on hand, so he just quit. I'd teased him through the years about his "addiction" to coffee, but inwardly I'd been happy that was his only problem. He'd been under an unusual amount of stress this year, but I never dreamed he'd resort to drinking again!

Completely forgetting the concept of my son's new found "manhood," I did the first thing that popped into my mother-oriented brain. I ordered Nate to his room.

He laughed. "I don't have a room here, Mom."

With a stiff arm and shaky finger, I pointed. "Then go to Annie's room." I commanded.

Sheepishly, he got up and staggered out of the kitchen. I turned to Darren who was leaning against the kitchen cupboard and staring at me with a smug expression. "Let the boy alone, Cass. He's not doing any harm, and it's his birthday. We're just having a little fun."

"How could you . . ." my voice broke. I took a deep breath. "How could you do this? To me?" I barely forced out a whisper through my trembling lips. "To our son?"

With a struggle, Darren heaved himself away from the counter and stumbled to a chair. He sank in and leaned into his arms. Now the table supported him instead of the counter top. *"Is he making progress?"* I thought half-hysterically to myself. *"Or is he just on his way to the floor?"*

Darren raised his head and focused on forming his words. Slowly he spoke. "He's a man now, Cassie. You can't tell him what to do any more."

I was furious, beyond sense. "You think it's a sign of manhood to get drunk? To lose control of your body? And your mind?" He just looked at me with a stupid smile on his face. I wanted to shake him, but instead I paced. I supposed it was futile to reason with a drunk, but I couldn't help myself. "Darren, I've always looked up to you and admired you for your self-control. You've been so strong, through everything. You were always there for me to lean on. Even when you were depressed and discouraged."

I stopped and stared at him. Languid, glassy eyes stared back at me. A few drops of drool ran from his mouth. "Darren, I don't know you any more." Then, mostly to myself, "Maybe I never did."

Nate's drunkenness had manifested itself in shame. Darren's drunkenness escalated to anger, with adrenaline shooting energy into his veins. Suddenly his eyes glowed with fury and he stood up, looming over me. I had a flashback of my father, standing before me in the exact posture with the same stony anger etched on his face.

"You think you know what it means to be a man?" He shook his finger in my face as his voice rose. "You don't even know what it means to be a woman! A real woman knows when to leave a man alone." He grabbed my arms, tightly. The fierceness in his gaze caught me off guard. I trembled, terrified that he would hurt me. "You and your god! You think you have all the answers. Well, Little Lady, I've got some answers of my own." He started to shake me.

"Dad, let her go." Nathan stood in the doorway, eyes glazed but fixed on his father.

Darren dropped my arms and, with rage, faced his son. He took a couple of steps toward Nate, then, with considerable effort, turned, grabbed his hat, and stormed out the door.

In the silence, my son's eyes met mine. He spoke softly. "I'm sorry, Mom." Then he turned and walked back to Annie's room, closing the door behind him.

I fled outside. Darren wasn't in sight. Not that I had any desire to face him again. Not yet. I just wanted to run. Not towards town, where there were lights, people, and traffic.   I turned to the park, my place of retreat. It was quiet and deserted at this time of night.   Ahead of me, branches waved gently in the evening breeze. Dark coolness beckoned me. Shaking all over, I half ran and half stumbled across the road and over the railroad tracks. My breath came in gasps and tears poured down my cheeks like the overflow from a busted dam. The anguish and turmoil that I had soaked up like a sponge flowed out of me. The loneliness of the park welcomed me. The black silence where I could hide.

Until . . .

Hide until when? I didn't ever want morning to come. I never wanted to return to my home. *Oh, if only this night would never end!*

"Oh, Lord," my heart cried out. *"When will the pain end? Is it just beginning?"*

Exhausted and trembling, I reached the bench where the angel had appeared. This was where I was to meet him again tomorrow. No, today. It was now the early hours of Sunday morning. Like a frightened child, I curled up tightly on the bench with my feet tucked under my body and my head buried in my arms, resting against the back of the bench. I was trying to pull into myself, making myself smaller, maybe with an unconscious desire to shrink away into nothing and not have to face life anymore. Or seclude myself safely into a protective shell. One that was hard as steel, so I couldn't be hurt anymore.

Confused thoughts tumbled through my brain, irrational, unconnected thoughts. Anger, despair, deep disappointment, and a sense of betrayal. I ordered the sun not to rise. I reasoned that if I sat there long enough, my body would petrify and I wouldn't have to return to life. The evil presence that had tried to claim my life years earlier, when I considered suicide, again began to clutch at me. Grasping claws reached out toward me with an overpowering force.

I'll turn into a stone, a solid rock with no feelings, no hope, no fear.

A rock. A rock. The simple phrase kept hammering at my mind. *The rock. Jesus is the rock. Jesus is my rock. The Bible says so. Jesus is the rock of my salvation. " I will hide myself in the Rock . . ."*

"Oh, Jesus!" In anguish, I pleaded aloud. *"Jesus, help me!"*

Instantly the tangible sense of evil departed. Jesus chased it away, out of the depths of my anguished soul. Peace returned, enveloping and sustaining me. I floated on a cloud of ecstasy. The presence of light touched me. I lifted my head to see the angel seated calmly beside me.

Gentle loving eyes sought mine, eyes of peace, serenity, and wisdom. "I've come for your decision." The words were calmly spoken. He already knew what my answer would be.

So did I. Traveling the road of natural desires and inclinations would inevitably bring Nathan to the same eternal destiny as his father. The opportunity presented by the angel to free the Holy Spirit's influence in Darren's life was my only hope. *The only hope for my husband and my son.* I nodded and whispered. "Yes, I'll do it." The angel smiled, a smile of hope and promise. I took a deep breath. "Can I tell somebody about this?" I wanted to share it with Ingrid and to have her prayers.

"No, Cassandra." A gentle rebuke. "God is trusting you with this illness, as He, in His wisdom, has chosen to trust others. Why He has decided to give you a choice is not in my knowledge. His ways are greater than our ways, beyond understanding. This is only between you and God."

"All right, I understand." I swallowed a giant lump in my throat, yet remained calm.

"One more question." Liquid pools floated in my eyes as I sought his face. "When? When will it start? And will I see you again?"

The angel laid a warm hand on my shoulder. "I do not

know, Cassandra." And then he was gone. The vision of the magnificent one faded instantly, but God graciously let me feel the presence of the angel's hand for a few moments longer. I must have sat for hours, though it seemed like minutes. I talked to God, pouring out my worries and fears. When the sun rose, His peace was with me. I stood, stretched, and returned home.

Sunshine bathed the kitchen in light as I walked through the door. The strong scent of fresh coffee penetrated my nostrils. Darren and Nathan sat by the table with cups in their hands. Nate's hair was still wet. He had evidently just gotten out of the shower and looked sober.

Darren jumped up. He rushed to me and hugged me. "I've been so worried about you. I was going to call the farm soon, but I didn't want to worry Mom and Dad."

Automatically, I stiffened at his touch and he let me go.

"I know I behaved badly last night, Cassie. I'm sorry." He shook his head. "I don't want to get like that again. Ever." He got a cup and poured coffee for me.

"Not me either, Mom." Nathan added.

I sat down, temporarily relieved, but not completely reassured. I looked from one sober face to the other and wondered if they could be trusted. Neither of them had God to depend on for help when they reached the limits of their own strength.

I smiled weakly, to let them know they were forgiven. Suddenly, my head started to pound.

"Oh," I clasped my hands to my forehead.

"What's wrong, Mom?" Nate was concerned.

"I don't feel very good. I think I'm getting sick."

Chapter 25

The pounding continued. The horrible, rhythmic pounding in my head. Like the soft mass of my brain was engaged in a futile battle to escape the confining framework of my cranium.

When the pain first started, I thought I would get used to it. But after four months, the dread and torture showed no signs of relenting. Of course, the headaches weren't constant. They left me completely for long periods at a time. But I never knew when they would strike again with a sudden, fierce slash like a steel blade of a guillotine hurled upon the neck of the waiting victim. The dread of torment returning cast a bleak shadow over even the brightest of pain-free days. Its uncertainty hovered over me, personified in my imagination as a hideous gaunt stranger stalking me. The monster searched for a weak, vulnerable leak in my armor in which to thrust his ugly fingers and deposit additional doses of pain and terror.

In those days and nights racked with spasms, the knowledge that this monster of darkness had been sent by God was unbearable. However, Jesus got me through it all. I cried out to Him when the pain was at its worst, and the presence of my

Comforter was so real I could almost feel the flesh of His scarred hand holding mine as He sat by my bedside. The worrying didn't stop though. How I wished I could allow my mind to float away on a cloud of tranquillity and banish all the effects of my illness. At times, the doubts were overwhelming. *Wasn't this disease supposed to bring Darren closer to God, not push him away?*

My husband was changing, yes. He cared for me so tenderly and gently. When the bad spells gripped me in its tormenting vise, Darren pulled me into his arms and stroked my forehead like my mother would have done. "Cassie, Cassie, my love," he'd whisper in agony. "I wish it was me instead. I'd take your suffering myself if I could." Sometimes I'd feel the trickle of his tears running down my own cheek. I'd fold my body into the loving arms surrounding me and pray for the healing of his soul. I pitied my husband who had no God to pray to for help and strength like I did.

Darren worked at home now. Besides his flexible caretaker role for the tenants, he handled his accounting responsibilities in our apartment. When Annie left for college two weeks earlier, in the middle of August, Darren decided he needed to be close at hand as much as possible to help me. He installed a computer in Annie's bedroom so he didn't have to work in the apartment office any more. Fortunately, his new job provided the minimal health insurance to cover the increasing medical care that I desperately needed.

Darren took me to doctors in Lakeland when the symptoms started. The medical community in our area was perplexed over the cause of my illness. After months of testing, they reluctantly narrowed down the diagnosis to a vague manifestation of the disease called lupus. Neither Darren nor I had heard of it before. Doctor Johnston explained that lupus is a chronic illness that shows itself in a variety of ways. Basically, my body's immune system was misdirected against my own body tissues, causing the system to attack and destroy my tissues and organs as though they were foreign invaders. He also told us that many lupus symptoms mimic other illnesses, are generally vague, and can come and go, making the disease difficult to diagnose. Eleven criteria are used for the diagnosis, and a person has to have at least four of them to be considered one of its victims. I suffered four of these symptoms in the first month.

I wasn't concerned about giving a name to my disease, since I knew where it came from and that God was in charge of its progress. Of course, I couldn't share this information with anyone, and I desperately wanted whatever help I could get to control the pain. Some of the symptoms weren't so terrible, just bothersome. The butterfly rash on my cheeks and nose showed up at the beginning, and oral ulcers were irritating, but relatively painless. One serious spell of pleurisy nearly did me in, but I recovered.

The blood clots were more worrisome. When I had a clot in my leg, I was forced to be on total bed rest to prevent it from loosening and floating in my bloodstream to my lungs or heart. I mostly feared having it lodge in my brain, where it could cause a stroke. I was prepared to handle the physical calamity, but reminded God that mental incapacity was not a part of the original agreement. At least, not in my understanding! Nevertheless, the throbbing headaches, accompanied by nausea, were the most dreaded. And I never knew what other symptoms might pop up, unexpected, at any time.

Also weighing on Darren's mind, and mine, was the uncertainty of his mother's health. Ingrid was hospitalized with congestive heart failure soon after my disease had manifested itself. She was on medication now that stabilized her to some extent, but we were all concerned for her. I knew Darren was torn at times, wanting to "be there" for both his women. And I, too, felt the frustration of not being able to be of much help to Ingrid.

In my moments and days of physical freedom, I had to catch up with my own housework. Darren, a typical male, ignored the cleaning, so I did as much of it as I could during my competent times. In an effort to reassure me, Darren said that they were managing all right at the farm. I knew better. Sven is also oblivious to dirt, and Billy can't even see it! Ingrid must have been so frustrated. She had always been an immaculate housekeeper.

And as far as cooking, Sven was no prize chef! Billy offered to try his hand at it, but neither Sven nor Ingrid would let him near the stove. Ironically, though, the one time they faced a near disaster in the kitchen, Billy saved the day. Sven was making some venison roast from meat that Darren had given him during hunting season the previous fall. It was a windy day, and the door blew wide open when Billy came into the house for lunch. The wind must have caused the gas flame under the pot to go out, and Sven hadn't noticed. He was about to light the back burner to cook some potatoes when Billy sniffed the air and muttered, "What's wrong?" Especially sensitive to smell because of his blindness, Billy was able to alert Sven to the imminent danger. After that incident, Darren told me, Sven insisted that Billy keep him company in the kitchen whenever he cooked!

Annie, bless her heart, came home from college as many weekends as she could manage. She helped me for a while, and then went to help at the farm. I treasured those special times with my daughter. I tried hard not to complain. I wanted her to have good memories of being with her mom and not to dread coming home to care for a grumpy, peevish old woman!

Nate didn't come home as often. I missed him so much. His part time job at a restaurant near the campus often required him to work on weekends. We couldn't afford to buy either of our kids a car, so they had to depend on neighboring students for rides or take a bus.

I did have a tiny flicker of hope, as far as Nathan was concerned. He faithfully kept in touch with me through letters. I saved every one of them and kept them in a box on the table by my bed. When my head was clear, I'd take them out and re-read them. Reading those letters never failed to lift my spirits. Mostly they contained brief clips of his daily life, cheery anecdotes about school, his studies, and well-liked and not-so-well-liked professors. Details of escapades with his friends always brought a smile to my face. Nathan was a responsible student and earned good grades. But reading between the lines, I sensed an undercurrent of dissatisfaction with his life, a lack of purpose and meaning, which I knew was the inevitable result of the emptiness of a sorely neglected soul. His last letter, however, gave me encouragement and put wings on my prayers. Just a glimpse of genuine soul searching was evident, enough to give me a reason to hope.

The pain was once again beginning to recede. Doused in sweat, my body exhibited the exertion of another battle with pain. I longed for a cool, reviving shower. But first, I commanded my trembling fingers to unfold my son's last letter which had come the day before when I was in no condition to read. I held it to my weary, tear-stained eyes.

"Dear Mom, I guess I'm kind of down today, and maybe I shouldn't tell you that because you've got enough to worry about. I don't want you to worry about me, too. (As though I wasn't anyway!) But, on the other hand, you may be the only person to help me figure things out. All my friends here are so carefree. I guess guys don't usually share their feelings. And things are pretty much going their way. But I keep thinking about you and Grandma.

"I remember when I was a little kid and got sick or hurt, you'd always pray for me. And I prayed, too. But then I grew up and wanted to be a man. I've got a great Dad. You know that, you picked him out! But he told me there isn't a God and I wanted to believe him and be independent like him. After all, he is my role model, you know. And the stuff he told me made sense. But then, so did the stuff you told me, about the Bible being God's Word and all.

"I guess the point I'm trying to make is that I want to pray for you and Grandma. And I can't. I feel like I'd be a fool to talk to someone who doesn't exist. But you're not a fool. And neither is Grandma!

"And your prayers seem to get answers. So, Mom, I'm starting to talk to God, just a little. I'm mostly asking Him to let me know if He's real. To somehow let me know. Is that okay? I mean, if He is real, if He actually is God, then I don't want to offend Him. Talk about getting started on the wrong foot!

"And maybe, when you're feeling better, if you could write me and tell me some more stuff about why you believe, and what I have to do if I decide He's real and I want to follow Him.

"That's all for now. I got to go to class. Love you much, Nate"

I finished the letter and held it to my heart. Tears were

again streaming down my face and I begged God for the strength and words to answer my son.

"Oh Father," I prayed earnestly, *"please help my son to find faith and peace in You. My pain and tears will be worth every second of it if Nathan comes to You because of this.*

"But, Lord, don't forget that the angel said your Spirit would work in my husband's life, too. I thought that Darren would be the one to lead Nate to You. It just shows you how little I understand. But You see the big picture, Father God. It looks to me like Darren is getting more angry at You because of my sickness. He told me yesterday that a loving God wouldn't treat His child like this. He closed the door on You many years ago. Now he's locked and dead-bolted it, and he's piling up stones of bitterness and resentfulness against it as a barricade. Soon he won't even be able to see the door or hear Your quiet knock. Oh, God please help ..."

"Cassie," Darren's sober voice interrupted my silent prayer. He'd poked his head in the doorway. "Are you doing any better? You've got a visitor. Gertrude is here again. She brought us some chicken soup and homemade bread for supper." My heart hit the floor. Darren had no idea of the emotional trauma my former landlady's visits gave me. I didn't dare complain to him, because Gertrude made sure everyone within yelling range knew of her claims to be a Christian. And I suppose she might actually be a child of God. I didn't know her heart. But, unfortunately, she was one of those representatives who frequently gave Him a bad name!

I forced a smile as I tucked the precious letter back into my box and brushed my hand through my unwieldy hair. I was sure she would be eager to spread rumors about my unpleasant appearance. According to my friend, Kathy, Gertrude was spreading the word that she, alone, seemed to be responsible for what little health I have left. I guess it must be the magical ingredients she put in the soup and bread we received regularly.

Kathy couldn't contain her laughter as she reported on the phone, "Gertrude is handing out copies of the chicken soup recipe she created especially for you. She insists that every time she brings you some, you improve. She wants to publish it, but can't decide whether to send it to *Happy Homemaking* or the *Minnesota Medical Digest.*"

"Please ask her to come in." I spoke through gritted teeth.

Darren replied with a smile, satisfied I supposed, that Gertrude's company was bound to cheer me up.

I stifled a groan as Gertrude made her grand entrance, bounding into my bedroom. She actually did bound. She wasn't the kind of person who just walked. Her intimidating presence was always felt immediately. She proceeded with a flourish to whip out a chair from the corner of the room, catching its leg on the foot of my bed post, giving me a jar that knocked my teeth together. Totally ignorant of the trauma she'd caused me and undaunted in her "do good" efforts, Gertrude steadied her chair, then yanked at my blanket. She gave it a violent shake over my head and stretched it out on top of my sweat-soaked body. Then, she tucked it firmly on both sides and up under my neck, pressing it under my shoulders with her rough, callused fingers.

I gritted my teeth and bit my tongue.

"That foolish man . . . " (presumably referring to Darren) " . . . that man has no idea of how to care for an invalid! He goes and sits by his computer, doing who knows what, while you lie here, helpless and catching your death of pneumonia. There! That's much better. Are you warm enough?"

"I . . ."

"Good." She arranged herself in the chair and bent over to retrieve her bright red Bible from her red plaid tote bag. Her tongue continued to flap, vocalizing mostly about the general incompetence and insensitivity of husbands in general, citing her late husband, Herbert, as a prime example. "Would you believe," she shook her head is dismay, "the day I came home from the hospital after my gall bladder surgery, he asked me to bake him a cake? Can you believe it?"

Ignoring my lack of response, she opened her Bible at the bookmark where she had evidently prepared a presentation for me, and laid it on her lap. Her ample breasts heaved as an audible sigh of pity escaped her lips. "Cassie, Cassie, how I suffer with you." A hand was laid dramatically on my arm. Gertrude planted a look

269

of feigned concern on her face. "The good Lord tells us to weep with those who weep. I have wept for you, Cassie. I also brought some of my original homemade soup and my four-grain bread that my grandmother used to make." She paused a moment, to let the importance of her gifts sink in and than looked at me expectantly.

I responded appropriately. "Thank you, Gertrude."

She nodded. "It's the least I can do." Her eyes turned to the window, and her mind seemed to wallow in contemplation. I attempted to sneak a bit of the heavy blanket away from my shoulders, knowing full well if I was caught, my fate would be direrer yet. I'd probably get two blankets thrown over me. Gertrude turned back and I froze, one shoulder exposed. She didn't seem to notice. I breathed a sigh of relief.

"Now, Cassie," her fingers ran over the pages of her Bible. "In the past months, I've tried to comfort you mostly with readings from the Psalms. But I believe today," she pursed her lips as she paused for effect. "the L-L-Lord (she stretched out the word as her hands lifted to Heaven) is telling me to take a drastic step of faith with you."

"Oh, dear Lord, what now?" I silently voiced my discomposure.

"I will read from the book of James, chapter 5, verses 14 through 16. 'Is anyone among you sick? Let him call for the elders of the church, and let them pray over him, anointing him with oil in the name of the Lord; and the prayer offered in faith will restore the one who is sick, and the Lord will raise him up, and if he has committed sins, they will be forgiven him. Therefore, confess your sins to one another, and pray for one another, so that you may be healed. The effective prayer of a righteous man can accomplish much."

She flashed me a triumphant look. I returned a questioning one.

"Don't you see, Cassandra? It is sin! Sin is the key! God has showed me it is your sin that is making you sick. Now you must confess it and then we will pray together and the prayer of faith will make you well. I have here a little bottle of olive oil, which I'm sure was used in Biblical times." She reached into her tote bag and pulled out the glass bottle. "When we pray, I will anoint your forehead." I stared, dumbfounded. She actually licked her lips, waiting, no doubt, in anticipation for the juicy piece of gossip with which to enthrall our neighbors.

When I failed to respond, she tried to coax me. "Cassandra, dear," once again her hand was laid on my arm. "God wants His children to be well. He says that Jesus' stripes healed us. The stripes refer to the scars from his beatings and sufferings on the cross, you know. But the devil," the hated word was expelled with viciousness, "wants to destroy us, and if we let him get his foot in the door . . . " she shook her finger at me " . . . by giving way to sin," another vibrant pause full of meaning, "he will reign in our lives!"

I felt weaker all over, if that were possible, and my body began to shake. The look of satisfaction in her eyes told me I was condemned as guilty in her mind. My efforts to stop shaking were useless. I was in no condition to deal with this super emotional woman. "Jesus, help me," I silently begged. The trembling continued, but words navigated through the foggy recesses of my brain and forced their way out.

"Gertrude," I spoke with a calmness I didn't feel. "Jesus healed my soul on the cross. My body won't be totally free from pain and disease until I get to heaven. Of course, I still sin. But I don't want to hurt my Savior by giving into it and living in sin. I ask for His forgiveness every day, and I try to please Him. This illness is not a punishment, Gertrude," I insisted. *Oh, little do you know!*

"Well!" she harumphed, and began to gather her belongings. She stood up and turned to me. "Cassie, I can see that I'm wasting my time and breath on you. When you see fit to repent and confess, you may give me a call, and I will be happy to pray with you. Until that time, I feel I must cut off my contact with you in the hope that you will face your rebellion and come back to the Lord!"

Gertrude stormed out of the room. I flung the rest of my blanket off and lay still, not knowing whether to laugh or cry. I was relieved that God took her out of my life, at least temporarily!

Yet in spite of my irritation, I felt sorry for Gertrude. She wasn't acquainted with the Lord of grace and mercy that I knew. The one who took my punishment upon Himself and gave strength to share in His sufferings in order that further good may be accomplished.

In the end, I cried. And that is how Darren found me.

He rushed to my bedside, gathered me into his arms and stroked my hair. Weary of all the pain, fatigue, and uncertainty, I let myself collapse against his shoulders and gave in to despair. Shadows of late afternoon began to creep through the windowpane and settle around us in the still, quiet air of the dark bedroom. "Cassie, Cassie," my husband gently rocked me back and forth like he would a little child. "I thought Gertrude would cheer you up. What happened? Did she say something to hurt you?"

My sobs increased. Frantic and miserable, I couldn't stop myself. I took a few deep breaths and great gulps of air, which helped. Finally, I managed to contain my emotions. I didn't want to complain about Gertrude to Darren. I didn't want to say what I feared I would say in a minute. Darren was treating me so well. He was the strong shoulder to lean on that I needed so desperately. I was so tired of trying to be a good Christian wife and witness. For many years, I'd longed for Darren to accept Jesus as his Savior and Lord. I wanted to share my faith with him and to serve the Lord with him. Always, I was conscious of how my words and actions would affect him. I prayed that God would use me to bring him to Jesus. That God would use my illness to touch the hidden places of his soul that were beyond the reach of words.

Now I feared that my weakness would overturn all the good intentions of the past years. Maybe my sinful attitudes would create a stumbling block for him to fall on. My next words could forever crush any hope for his salvation!

But I couldn't help myself. My unruly tongue let loose and spilled the harbored venom into his soul. "Darren, I can't take any more of that woman!" I blurted out. "She says God is keeping me sick because I sin and don't have enough faith. That if I was a stronger Christian, God would heal me." Infused with sudden energy, I sat up and gripped Darren's shoulders. "She doesn't know what she's talking about. It's not my sins and lack of faith that's making me sick!" Almost too late, I bit my tongue and shook my head, trying to shake her influence away from me as easily as a dog shakes the water from his furry body after he's had a bath. "It's not true, Darren," I pounded my fist against the bed. "But it hurts!"

"Hey, Little One," Darren grabbed my hand to restrain me and touched it briefly to his lips for a kiss. I lowered the liquid pools of my eyes in shame. Darren cupped his hands around my face and made me look at him. "I know, Cassie. I understand. I see your faith. I see how you've suffered in silence. I don't know how you manage as well as you do. I didn't used to think of you as a strong person. But you've pulled a strength from way inside that I never suspected was there. I admire you, Cass, and I'd like to give that woman a piece of my mind. If she ever comes around here again, I'll . . ."

"She won't." I pushed away from him and wiped the tears from my eyes with my hands. Darren whipped out a handkerchief from his pocket and handed it to me. "Thanks." Feeling suddenly calm and a trifle giddy, I blew my nose. "She's given up on me. I guess I'm not worth any more of her valuable time."

I paused, uncertain now of how to proceed. "But the strength you see isn't mine, Darren. God gives it to me. I don't have any of my own. I *am* a weak person."

Then with a sigh and a weak smile, I looked at him apologetically and started talking fast just to get it all out. "I'm so sorry. I know you think she's a Christian, and I don't want you to think badly of her, and I don't want to spoil your eternal future." My words heaped upon each other and tumbled out in a rush. "I mean, not all Christians are like her. But just because we're Christians doesn't mean we're perfect and . . ."

Darren held up his hand in mute protest and I halted in mid-mouth. "Calm down, Cassie." He placed his fingers briefly on my mouth. "You think I don't know a Christian when I see one?"

My mouth fell open in astonishment when he took his fingers away. I guess I'd never given him credit for observational powers where faith was concerned. I had thought he ignored the whole concept of religion.

"I don't know much about religion, Cassie, and I know it's not for me. But I also know that whatever you have is real. And I see the compassion of your friends from church, especially Kathy. I've seen it in my own home, as a kid. My mom and dad, my brothers." He hesitated, deep in thought. "I don't know what kind of religion that woman has, but it's not the same as yours."

Thank you, Jesus! My heart took a lilting leap. Then I quickly sobered. "But, Darren, why? How?" I stumbled over the question I'd wanted to ask him for years. "The rest of your family are Christians. Why aren't you?"

Darren's lips tightened and his jaw clenched. I wondered if I'd gone too far. He stood up and walked to the window where he stayed, his back towards me, shoulders hunched, and hands in his pockets. My eyes followed him, hungry for reassurance. A heavy sigh escaped his lips as he stared out into the gloomy, lengthening shadows of the setting sun. I waited in silent impatience.

"My dad wasn't a Christian when I was a boy. He was strong and healthy. He didn't need help like he does now."

"You mean his arm?"

He nodded and took a deep breath. Then he turned around and pulled a chair close to my bedside. I leaned my throbbing head on the pillow and fastened my eyes on his face.

My husband examined his hands as he spoke. "Mom became a Christian soon after Billy was born, so she says. It really hurt her, having a son who was blind. And I guess, at that time, the local preacher talked to her a lot. She started going to church and reading the Bible. Dad wouldn't have any of it. He said religion was for weak people."

"Just like Papa," I whispered.

Another nod. "I was only two when Billy was born. So I never thought much about his blindness until I got older. Billy was just . . ." he shrugged his shoulders. " . . . he was just Billy. I had to watch out for him and do stuff for him, but after all I was his big brother. I'd have done that anyway. My big brothers could see. My little brother couldn't. As I grew up, I realized how few blind people there were in the world. But I never did really feel sorry for him, because he was so much fun and we were close.

"Dad resented it when my brothers began to go to church with Mom. But they were just kids. I think he saw religion as something they'd grow out of," he chuckled. "I think it pleased him that I, alone, followed in his footsteps. Then the accident happened. I was just eight at the time and kind of a handful. I'd run off fishing that day at the little creek that runs alongside of the south pasture, you know?" He glanced at me, and I nodded in understanding. "I got back late and neglected my chores. My brothers were out in the field with Dad that day, so my jobs didn't get done. Dad had to spend extra time dealing with me and taking care of all the work. Then, after supper, he heard on the radio that it was expected to rain the next day. Well, it was harvest season and he was determined to go back out to the fields in the dark and keep at it.

"Mom told him not to go. I can still hear her, 'You're all tuckered out, Sven, and that's when accidents happen.' Well, he paid her no mind, yanked his jacket off the hook by the door, and stomped out into the night. Mom was nervous and worried all evening. Around midnight, she finally sent Seth to get Dad to come in. Well, you know the rest." His head bowed again. "Seth found him lying on the ground below the rise with the tractor tipped over, crushing his right arm. Seth ran back and told Mom. She sent me for the doctor while she and my older brothers went back out and managed to push the heavy tractor enough to pull Dad's arm out. The doctor said it was a miracle he didn't bleed to death. Of course Mom was praying all the time and I guess Dad credited her prayers with saving his life. So that's when he became a Christian." He looked at me and shrugged. "I guess our fathers were both right. People who are weak and needy turn to religion, and I suppose, if there is a God, He helps them, too. And maybe," a pause, "maybe what you say about God is true."

With eyes plastered on Darren's face, I held my breath. *Was this the moment I'd been waiting for?*

"But Cassie," the corners of his mouth tilted up slightly and I knew he was reading my mind. "I'm doing okay on my own, so don't get any ideas."

Ordinarily his self-assurance and attempt at humor would have caused me dire frustration at this point. But instead, my mind was focusing on the sensitive issue that must be tormenting his spirit. At least it must be influencing his sub-consciousness, even if he wasn't aware of it.

"Darren," I tip-toed his name.

"What?" His back-to-normal guard was up.

"Did you . . ." I hesitated, fearful to intrude, yet reluctant to let my newly found insight get away. "Did you feel responsible for your dad's accident?"

"Why? Why should I?" A brick wall was going up.

Again, I hesitated, wishing I'd kept my mouth shut. The certainty I had a moment ago left me. I didn't want to put the thought into his mind if it was not there all ready! But now Darren waited expectantly for an answer.

"Because you went fishing and Sven had to do your chores, so he didn't get done sooner in the fields?"

His mouth clamped shut and his jaw muscle worked. The dark silence in the room was permeable. Outside, a train rumbled by and a dog barked. Suddenly, Darren nodded once, a quick up and down head motion. Then back to ice.

"Oh, Darren," I reached out my hand to touch his knee. He stiffened. I saw visions of a scared little boy running along the road in the middle of the night. Hurrying to get the doctor. Hoping the doctor would be home. Afraid his father would die. Guilt, like an ominous figure, darting out from behind vague, ghost-like images along the road. Gripping his vulnerable young mind and stealthily maneuvering its venomous fingers until they were entrenched in his brain.

Darren seldom cried, but I was sure I saw a few drops sneaking out of his tightly squeezed eyelids. He was so proud of his independence that I hadn't had much experience at comforting him. But I knew he needed it now. I gingerly sat on the edge of the bed and ever so tenderly laid my hands along his neck, bending my head until my forehead touched his. He sniffed and I gave his handkerchief back to him. He took it and wiped the corners of his eyes.

"Come here, Cass," he motioned for me to sit on his lap. I obliged willingly. We sat that way for a long time, just holding each other and drawing strength from each other's warmth.

I broke the silence. "But you really know better, don't you, Darren?" I timidly inquired.

"Yeah, Cass. I know it's not my fault. I made it hard for him, but it was still his decision to work that night."

"And you were just a child."

"But you see, Cassie . . ." his voice trembled slightly. "Even when your head knows better, sometimes your feelings . . ." he thumped his chest and I heard an intake of breath. "Your feelings say different. It takes a long time for your head to convince your heart that your feelings are wrong."

I nodded my head in agreement.

"And," As he continued, I lifted my face to his and prayed that all the love I harbored for my husband would pour out of my eyes and funnel into his heart. I longed to sooth the empty spots of his soul and prepare them to make a dwelling place for his Savior. "Sometimes it takes a long time for your head to convince your heart that your head is right."

Darren left the room to heat up Gertrude's soup for supper. Alone again, I laid my head back on my pillow and thanked the Lord that most of my comforters were genuine. Kathy was a wonderful friend. In spite of the needs of her busy family, she often brought us a meal or sent a cheerful card. People from church offered to help, too. But Darren was too independent to receive help from anyone other than family or old friends. Pastor Gustafson came to visit several times and made sure I got the church bulletins when I wasn't able to attend worship services. I longed for Darren to talk to him. But, although my husband was polite, he avoided my pastor as much as possible, and never stayed long in the room when he came to visit.

I hated knowing that my family and friends worried about me. But I was forbidden to share the reason for my illness with any of them. Actually, I had no idea of the outcome of my trial. *Would God heal me? Or take me to heaven soon?* I waited with my loved ones to discover the result.

The frequency of my headaches didn't increase, but the severity did. My doctor suggested that we try a stronger medication. I wanted to refuse, but I couldn't see that I had much choice in the matter. The pain and nausea seemed unbearable. So, reluctantly, I tried the new drug. Almost immediately, I experienced a severe reaction. I began to hallucinate, so Darren asked the doctor to discontinue it. Doctor Johnston agreed, but it took several weeks for the medicine to completely leave my system.

That period of time brought new agonies. It's hard to describe the lingering hallucinations. I felt like I was trapped in a nightmare, not knowing if the things I saw, heard, and experienced were real or not. Reality had no foundation. It floated in and out of the shore of emotion, carried by waves of uncertainty and restlessness. I nurtured thoughts and ideas that seemed right at the time and later found them to be false. Poor Darren. He got his first gray hairs. He could no longer hide his anguish. I don't think he even tried anymore.

I doubted reality--my bed, my house, the sun, my husband, myself. *Did I doubt my God?* I don't remember. In lucid moments, He was there at my side. But much of the time I was awash in a sea of fantasy and instability. Even when I began to pull out of it and return to normal, the recent hallucinations haunted me. I was shaken by the experience and couldn't seem to sort out my real memories from the delusions that had been so vivid. Anxiety about the reality of my visit with the angel kept pricking my soul. *Maybe it was a dream or a hallucination.* I avoided facing the new doubts for weeks, but the pricks turned into jabs that I could no longer ignore.

One day, in the privacy of my bedroom, I cried out to God. The unending tumult and cares of the past weeks pressed into the depths of my soul. The monument of anxiety I had constructed in my mind caved in and all the pieces crashed around my heart. Everywhere I looked, I only saw chaos and catastrophe. My emotions exploded in fury and despair.

"Oh, Father," I begged for an answer. *"Was the angel real? Or was he just a hallucination? Did you truly ask me to take*

this disease? Or did I only imagine that I agreed to accept it?"

Silence. No answer. As the medication continued to wear off, reality once again molded itself to fit into the distinctive compartments of my mind. The security of truth was re-establishing a foothold in my life.

But there seemed to be no room for my angel.

Chapter 26

Each day passed into the next, merging into each other as smoothly as vehicles switch lanes on a freeway. An endless journey through highways of pain and struggles, intermittently diffused with side roads of tenuous tranquility. During those brief pain-free moments, the vise confining my back relaxed, allowing me to stretch my limbs and move freely.

How I reveled in these moments, hours, days, and weeks. I never knew how long it would last and wondered why I didn't fully appreciate my health when I had it, all those years when my spirit was unhampered by my body, aside from periods of fatigue or minor illnesses. Then my body was under the capable command of my brain. When my brain told my fingers to move, they instantly obeyed. When it ordered my legs to run, they willingly complied. But, now, under control of the lupus, my body often refused to co-operate. It balked. I was forced to fight my own bodily members to accomplish small, everyday tasks. It wasn't enough any more just to will. I had to struggle and push to overcome. The frustration was emotionally draining. Added to that was the fear, the tormented thoughts that frayed the edges of my mind. *Had I only imagined the angel's visit? Was the agony I experienced meaningless? Was I destined to suffer and die prematurely, leaving my husband and son to continue without me along the road to hell?*

The last few days had been surprisingly good. I had been given enough energy to accomplish some housekeeping. My closets were now organized and the windows washed. I'd started working on the kitchen cupboards. All the while wondering how long the reprieve would last. And why God was allowing it.

I wasn't left to wonder for long. Ingrid took a turn for the worst. Darren came home from the farm one day and told me that she'd been hospitalized again with congestive heart failure. We went to see her immediately. The next few days were a blur. Darren and I were in and out of the hospital, taking turns relieving other family members. Sven spent as much time as he could by her bedside. And Billy, dear Billy with his swollen unseeing eyes, sat and held her hand hour after hour.

Ingrid's doctor said it was only a matter of time. He had done all he could, and was only concerned now with making her final hours comfortable. We all knew we were losing her. Darren's brothers traveled home to be with their mother and help care for her. Since Ingrid also suffered a mild stroke, she continued to be hospitalized. At least one of the family was with her at all times.

At last, I was alone with her. We had finally convinced Sven and Billy to go home and get some sleep. At first, Darren stayed with me. We took turns sitting by her bedside and catching some rest on the couch in the solarium down the hall. But Darren woke early that day and went home to catch up on work he'd neglected since Ingrid's last heart attack. Seth and Luke would come around eight or nine o'clock. The shadowy hours of early morning emphasized the shadowy condition of my heart, which thudded in agony as I sat in the lonely hospital room.

Ingrid was failing quickly. Kind nurses had told us to watch for signs that meant the end was near. Her pulse continued to be irregular, along with her blood pressure. Her body temperature also wavered drastically. Intermittently, I wiped her perspiring brow and pulled the covers over her more tightly when she shivered and moaned. She wasn't given solid food or water any more because the stroke had caused her throat muscles to relax. Food could cause her throat to close and she would choke to death. So I fed her ice chips and tiny bits of sherbet when she was awake. I also rubbed Vaseline on her chapped lips and massaged her hands and feet with lotion.

The tips of her fingers and toes had turned blue, which signaled the decrease of oxygen in her system. A glassy liquid formed over her eyes, giving them a hazy, vacant appearance. She was too weak to talk most of the time, and it was hard to understand her when she made the effort.

It hurt to watch her. Yet on some disassociated level, I viewed with interest the physical deterioration of her body. The part of me that had once wanted to become a doctor was curious. Besides, I knew my own death could be very near, and I wondered if I would experience a similar process.

One lamp shone on the table near my comfortable green armchair. The room where Ingrid would die was sparsely furnished. Besides the chair, only a bed, a small table, and hospital equipment made up her surroundings. Splashes of color were the only cheerful note, flowers brought by loved ones. I longed to bring her home to a comforting, familiar setting, but the care she needed would have been impossible there.

I drew the armchair closer to her bed and, curling up in it, prayed that her transition to the next world would be smooth and painless. I looked at her thin, fragile hand, laying in mine. It was completely white, except for a bluish hue on her fingertips. Her face was a translucent shade of pale gray, similar to the way I remembered my own mother's face the night before she died.

My thoughts returned to those far away days. I recalled the precious gift of my mother's Bible that she had hidden in her drawer and the seed of spiritual life she had planted in my soul. My mother faced death without knowing if her only daughter would follow her to the gates of heaven. She must have been full of regrets, wishing she had come to know her Lord sooner and shared her faith with me earlier. I could empathize with her, as I faced death without knowing if my husband and son would come to the Lord. Yet, my mother's countenance had glowed with a picture of peace. And I saw the same peace on Ingrid's face during the past few days. I wanted that. When my time came to leave this earth, I wanted to be able to go with the same peace. *If only Ingrid could pass it on to me.*

As if Ingrid could read my mind, Her eyelids fluttered and opened. Instead of the vacant glassy stare I'd become familiar with in the past few days, her gaze now focused on me with a clarity of vision and purpose. Her mouth curved gently and she smiled. "Cassandra." It was a simple statement, acknowledging my presence. My heart thudded violently, in anticipation. I waited in silent expectation.

"How are you, my sweet child?" Her voice was soft and fragile, just a whisper, but the words formed clearly on her lips. She spoke with a calmness that emitted energy, so different from her recent feeble attempts at communication. This moment was a gift from my God. I trembled as questions raced through my mind.

"Oh, Mother Ingrid," I perched on the edge of my chair and pressed her hand to my lips. The words gushed out, questions I wasn't able to ask of my own mother. Tears blurred my eyes. "You are my spiritual mom." My voice cracked. "I'm going to miss you."

"I'm here now, Cassandra. How can I help you?"

Now the tears flowed. I could barely speak, but forced the words out. I had to make the most of the time I had left with this dear woman who had become like a mother to me. I felt so needy, and at the same time I wanted to comfort her. But she didn't seem to need comforting.

"Mom, I'm so tired of it all," I blurted out. "It's hard enough coping with my own illness. But I don't want to lose you. And I'm afraid for Darren and Nathan. I want to see them saved before I die. Sweet Annie will be with me one day in heaven, but I want to know my husband and son are coming, too!" I clasped her hand to my heart with both of mine. "But you're leaving first, and I. . . I. . . ." My words stumbled and crashed together like rocks tumbling over a waterfall. I took a deep breath and steadied myself. "I see peace in your face." I swallowed hard and pushed the question out in a whisper. "Will I have peace when I die? I'm so afraid."

Her gentle eyes pierced my soul and cradled it tenderly. I was tense, waiting.

"Cassandra, you can have it now."

"But . . ."

"What is peace?" Almost sharply, she demanded an answer.

"Well, I don't know. I guess it's sort of like a picture of a still, perfect lake, calmness, tranquility." Visions of Lake Clarity flashed into the screen of my mind's remembrance. On a clear day, the sun tossed sparkly diamonds on its clear, smooth surface.

"No, honey." Her words of rebuke pressed against my heart.

"Why? I mean . . ." I was at a loss to understand.

She smiled at me again. "Cassandra, do you remember that Christmas four or five years ago when you and your family spent a night at a hotel in Minneapolis with us? There was a pool and a hot tub?"

I nodded, dwelling briefly on the "safe" memories of contented family times. They were treasured moments.

Ingrid raised her feeble body up slowly, until she was on one elbow, watching me. I worried that she was over-straining herself, but she ignored the sudden panic in my eyes and continued. "Remember how much you enjoyed the hot tub?"

I nodded.

"You said it made you feel so peaceful. But, honey, a hot tub is not peaceful. It's not smooth. It's full of turbulence. The pressure of the water is never still. It hits you and pounds on your muscles 'til you feel like you're beaten to a pulp!" Her sudden energy amazed me, along with her wisdom. As I stared back at her, the door of my mind opened in wonder. Satisfied, she lay back down. "It's in the yielding you find peace. Let your soul go limp, let it lie loose." Her words came slower again, her eyes began to close. But her voice continued, soft and strong. "Let the trials of life mold you and shape you and make you strong.

"Trust, Cassandra." A clear emphasis on those two words, as if it was a phrase that should go together. *Trust and Cassandra.* "The secret is trust. God is in charge. He knows exactly how much pressure and pummeling we each need. So we can function the way He plans for us to do." Her breathing was growing deeper and slower, and there was a pause between each sentence. "You can trust the One who died for you. Your future is in His hands. And Darren and Nathan are in His hands. Lie back, Cassandra. Lie back in the water and float. Let the bubbles carry you."

Her eyes closed completely. I struggled with selfishness. She was leaving me again, but I still had one important question. I had to know about my angel. I had to know if he was real. God had told me not to explain about my illness, but He hadn't said that I couldn't mention the first visit of my angel, when I was a child.

"Ingrid, do you believe that angels can visit us on earth?" With a mounting sense of urgency, I rapidly voiced the story of my childhood, the day the angel rescued me from the oncoming train. I had never told anyone about this experience except my parents. Now I felt strongly compelled to share it with Ingrid. By the time I finished, I was afraid she'd fallen asleep again. But instead, her eyes opened wide and it was her turn to stare in wonder and awe. She spoke with an effort now as her breath was starting to come in gasps.

"Oh . . . yes . . .your angel is . . . real."

Her lids closed again and her hand relaxed in my trembling one. With my other hand, I wiped her perspiring forehead with a wet cloth. Then I leaned over and kissed her cheek. "Thank you. I love you so much."

A few minutes passed as she struggled to speak, making her nearly breathless. I reached to push the button for the nurse when her hand fluttered in a gesture motioning me to her. I leaned over and positioned my ear close to her mouth.

"What is it, Ingrid?"

"Rose . . .rose . . ."

Chills ran up my spine. I knew this had to be important for her to struggle so hard.

"Did you say rose? Rose what?"

She took a deep breath and coughed. "Rose journal. Read my rose journal."

"Yes, I will. I will read your rose journal. Now rest."

She sighed with relief. Then her chest heaved suddenly and she seemed to gag. I quickly reached out and pressed the button to call the nurse. I ran my hand gently over her brow, pushing back thin strands of hair. Then Darren was in the room with a nurse.

"I couldn't keep my mind on my work," he explained. "How is she doing?"

The nurse fiddled with some dials on the machine taped to her body, shook her head in pity, and stepped back to let Darren go to his mother's side. Time also stepped aside, temporarily. Time loosened it's grip on Darren's mother and drew the finite curtain aside to allow her to step into eternity. Darren and I both sat, transfixed, on either side of her bed, each of us holding a hand, our eyes glued on her face. Her breathing was slow and erratic. We could hear a rattling sound in her chest. But her countenance gave not the slightest sign of fear or torment. Her face displayed only peace. Perfect serenity and submission to her Father's will.

One last, long breath, and she left us.

Darren and I sat like statues.

The nurse's voice was quiet, as though she hesitated to interrupt, but needed to help us find closure. "You have my sympathy. Take your time. I'll go and call the doctor and the rest of your family."

When she left, Darren looked at me. I have never seen anyone look so lost. His eyes were wide circles of terror. The empty blank expression almost tore my heart out of my rib cage. Darren threw his arms around his mother and sobbed while I patted his back. My tears of loss mingled with tears of joy for Ingrid. I knew that for the first time she was face to face with the radiance of Jesus. My tears were for my husband's grief, and my own gratitude for the final gift God had allowed her to give me.

"Let me float, Father," I silently prayed. *"Help me trust You to carry me safely over life's trials. I'm in your hands,*

Father." I looked at Darren. For the first time, I was able to brush aside my own fears for his future and see him simply through eyes of pity and compassion. *"That's the way You must see him, Father,"* I whispered to myself. *"Help him. Oh, help him to find You."*

Sven and the rest of the family came to the hospital, and we comforted each other. The sun was rising by the time we left to go home. Darren and I slept for a few hours. Later, we would meet the others at the funeral home to plan the funeral service and make the appropriate decisions.

When I awoke, Darren was still sleeping deeply. I lay quietly, talking to my heavenly Father. The patterns of light the morning sun was painting on my bedroom walls caught my attention. I wondered what new formations of color and light Ingrid was seeing now. Having the heart of an artist, her eyes would eagerly absorb the glorious beauty of heaven. Her world had expanded in just a moment. I knew if she had a choice, she would never want to come back.

I pondered the events of the preceding day. In all the commotion, I had pushed aside Ingrid's last words to me. Suddenly, I remembered. *The rose journal.* I wondered what it was she wanted me to read. As soon as possible, I would go to the farm and sort through her journals to find the rose one. As I recalled, each journal was a different color. I smiled to myself. Ingrid was fascinated with the depths and hues of various colors. So it shouldn't be too hard to find the one she told me about. Maybe she wrote something about me. I would love to read her thoughts concerning me. It must be good, or she wouldn't have wanted me to read it! But what could be so important? With thoughts of anticipation and an unexpected sensation of peace, I fell asleep.

I spent the day after the funeral at the farm. Sven asked me to go through Ingrid's clothes and personal items, and decide what to do with them. My emotions were still somewhat numb, but I was not anticipating the job. I was eager, however, to read her journals and decided to do that first.

The men were busy with farm chores, so I was alone in the house for the first time. Everything looked amazingly normal. The furniture was in the same place, the smell of fried bacon lingered in the air from breakfast, and bright sunlight streamed through the windows by the dining room table, causing the crystal vase centerpiece to sparkle. Still, the room harbored a profound emptiness, a hollow void that claimed a presence as real as anything I could touch. I felt as if part of me had died too. If only the huge ache in my heart could fill the void in the room.

With a heavy heart and stooped shoulders, I climbed the stairs to Ingrid's bedroom. The room looked exactly the same as the first time I entered it on Christmas Eve long ago. I remembered the night Ingrid had sent me to her room to get a Bible, when I had peeked inside a journal that revealed her thoughts about me. The bed wasn't as neat as it used to be. Sven's efforts to straighten the bedspread were minimal. I smoothed out a few wrinkles and sat on the edge. Ingrid's largest assortment of journals was neatly stacked on the dresser next to the bed. I saw more in the bookshelves along the far wall.

They were many different colors and styles. Some had covers of tapestry; others were simple spiral bound notebooks. Most of them were in shades of greens, yellows, purples and golds. To my surprise, none of them came even close to the hue I associate with the color of rose. There was a beautiful red one, with a velvet cover that made me think of Christmas. However, I knew a woman with Ingrid's artistic eye would not have referred to that shade as rose. I knelt beside the shelves and hastily sorted through the pile placed there. No results. Two were peach and one had a multicolor design, but none were rose.

Where was the rose journal? Had she written something in it that was so secretive she felt a need to hide it? I examined the closet. Nothing there. I looked under the bed and in the drawers without results. In fact, an investigation of the whole house turned up nothing. In a couple of hours, I was back in the bedroom, discouraged and deflated. *If Ingrid had hidden it, why didn't she tell me where to find it?* Of course, she had a lot of trouble talking at the end, and maybe she forgot where she put it. I would have to ask the men if they had any idea where the precious journal could be.

I decided I may as well look through some of her other journals before I started lunch. The first one I picked up was labeled 1959. I smiled as I read some brief notes she had written about Darren at the age of four:

"My darling little son came up to me today with a big smile on his face and both hands hid behind his back. He said 'Guess what I have behind my back?' I said, "I give up. What?' He threw both arms around me and said, 'A big hug!'"

Other cute tidbits were interspersed with mundane records of daily duties performed, weather changes, and comments on incidents happening with the family.

I picked up another notebook labeled 1957, and flipped through the pages. One in particular caught my attention. Her handwriting was broken and irregular, as though she had written it in fatigue or despair.

"We know the truth now. I've thought it for some time. The doctor finally told us today. My precious little boy, Billy, is blind. He was born that way. He will always be blind. But for Heaven's sake, why? Why did this have to happen to my son? Oh, God, if you are there, why do you let things like this happen? If you can run the whole universe, can't you make one tiny baby see? I can't bear it. What will his future be like? Why did you even let him be born? Surely, Billy's whole life will be a failure! How do I raise a blind child? He'd be better off dead. And so would I."

Chills ran up my spine. I had no idea that Ingrid, my godly mother-in-law, had ever entertained such negative thoughts. I knew she hadn't always been a Christian. But we'd never talked about the past to the extent that I realized the depth of anguish she had experienced. Ingrid must have understood my feelings as a young woman more than I realized.

When had she accepted Christ? I searched further in that journal, but found no reference to any salvation experience. I picked up the one written in the following year and saw a brief note with a star next to it. This one she must have found important.

"Thank you so much, Father God. Billy made me laugh

today. Sven bought us a puppy. It's so cute, a darling, little brown and white collie, just a little pile of fluff. Sven put him down on the floor by Billy and that silly puppy licked him right on the nose and then on his ear. Billy didn't cry at all. He grabbed the puppy and rubbed his fur. He even giggled. I'd never seen him giggle before! The puppy jumped on his lap and the two of them rolled over and over on the floor. They were both so happy to have a playmate. They looked so funny and cute. I laughed until tears ran down my face. Sven grabbed me and hugged me. He said it was the first time he'd seen me laugh since we heard the news about Billy.

"Oh, God, you know I've been reading my Bible and look-ing for the truth about you. Only you could put joy into the heart of a blind child. I want that joy, God. Forgive me for not trusting you and wanting things my own way. The Bible says that Your ways are beyond our understanding. You are the wisest one. You are the boss. I guess if you loved me enough to let your only son be tortured and killed on the cross, I can trust You to do what's best for my little boy.

"So from now on, I will trust you. And I'll take all the joy you want to give me in this world. And glory be, I'll look forward to the day when I leave this earth and go to be in a better place with you, Father God."

"TRUST." This word she had capitalized and underlined three times for emphasis.

Tears streamed down my face and I struggled for control. Then I started to laugh out loud. I closed the journal and hugged it to my heart.

Trust. That's the secret. It's so simple and yet so compli-cated. Why am I always trying to figure out God? To understand how and when He is going to work? I've practically demanded that God save Darren before I die. It seems to make logical sense. After all, isn't that why I'm sick? But the truth is, I don't have to see results. I don't have to understand. My heavenly Father has us all in His hands. He will do what's right and what's best in His own good time. All I need to do is trust Him and do what He tells me to do. Isn't there a song like that? "Trust and obey. For there's no other way, to be happy in Jesus, than to trust and obey."

291

Of course. I knew now that those words had permeated Ingrid's soul, her whole being, becoming a way of life for her.

I bowed my head in prayer as the tears flowed.

"Oh, Lord, thank you for showing me the secret. Forgive me for my foolish anxiety and worrying. I don't know what pain or disappointment I'll face in the future, but I do know that You are all wise, all powerful, and mostly, all love. I am determined to trust You no matter what happens.

"Help me, please. I can't do it without Your help. Give me Your peace and joy that must be the reasonable outcome of trust in You. In Jesus' name, Amen."

I rose to my feet, feeling a great weight slip off my back. I lovingly set the journal back on the pile of books.

"Dear Ingrid," I smiled to myself, "If I never find your rose journal, I thank you for the rich legacy you left me today."

Chapter 27

I remember the Christmas of 1995 so well. It was wonderful to have both Nate and Annie home at the same time. Since August, the only time they'd been home together was for Ingrid's funeral. Usually, Nate and Annie took turns coming home so one of them would be with me as much as possible. I enjoyed having them each to myself, but I was most contented when, as Darren put it, "both of your chicks are tucked safely in the nest." I remembered Sven saying the same thing about Ingrid. Now I knew how she felt!

The lupus gave me a brief reprieve for the holiday. Annie took me to church on Christmas Eve for the traditional candlelight service. Afterwards, we went to the farm with Darren and Nathan. All of Sven's children and grandchildren were home this year. Seth, his oldest son, sat in Ingrid's chair at the table. Her absence cast a sobering pall over the family circle. But the joy of sharing Jesus' birth and the undiminished excitement of the children overflowed to fill the gap left by her parting. The Christmas story was read from the Bible as always, but no one played Santa this year.

None of the men were up to the "ho, ho" business. Candy and gifts were abundant, and the women made an effort to provide the traditional Norwegian specialties that Ingrid used to bake.

I was astonished to see how much Sven seemed to have aged in the few weeks since I'd last seen him. He walked slower and with more care. His pale, gaunt face testified to a loss of weight. But the light in his eyes was still there when he laughed at one of the children's cute remarks. It was obvious that the presence of his entire family was a comfort to him. He and Ingrid had been married over fifty years. Ingrid was such a big help to Sven after the injury to his arm. When she died, it was like he lost his arm all over again. They were truly dependent on each other in a unique way.

Christmas Day we spent at home, just the four of us. We all slept late. Annie made us a sausage and egg quiche, and we finished the lefse and cookies that Darren's sister-in-law sent home with us. After brunch, we played games. The mid-afternoon sun cast a bright glow of warmth and serenity on our cozy little group, gathered around the kitchen table. I was tired and worn out from the previous evening's activities, but my family was pleased to have me up and about. They had insisted that all the games today were Mom's choice. So we played my favorites, the word and letter games that nobody else wanted to play, since I usually won! Nate actually won the last game and gloated at his achievement. I decided he could use a little humbling. So when I got up to refill the glasses, I made a special point to "accidentally" deposit an ice cube down the neck of his shirt.

"Yeow, Mom!" Nate leaped to his feet, nearly knocking his chair over. Darren and Annie laughed as he shook and wiggled until the ice cube fell on the floor. However, Annie, who stepped behind her brother on her way to the sink with a nearly empty popcorn bowl, happened to put her foot down at precisely that moment, slipped on the ice, and promptly tipped over. She landed flat on her back with popcorn kernels imbedded in her hair. The astonished look on her face only caused more hilarity, once we were assured that she wasn't hurt.

Annie sat up, shook her hair violently, and sent the kernels flying. Leaning back on stiff arms, she looked up at the three of us. "Hmmm," she said, "Who do I blame for this? Mom or Nathan?"

Darren wiped his eyes and spoke with a grin, "I think Mom looks the most guilty."

I stood with both hands clasped to my red cheeks, struggling to contain my laughter as I observed my daughter's plight. "I'm sorry!"

"That's okay, Mom," Nate came and put his arm around me and winked, "It was worth it."

"You, you, horrible son of mine," I reached out to tickle his stomach like I'd done when he was a kid. He giggled and grabbed both my arms. In one smooth motion, he twisted me around so I ended up with my back plastered to his chest, confined as in a straight jacket.

"All right, all right! I surrender!" Tears of joy and delight streamed down my face as my son hugged me.

Darren helped Annie up, "Come on, honey. Let's go wash the dishes from lunch and leave these two to their escapades."

Nate released me as they left for the kitchen. Content, and filled to overflowing with the happiness of the moment, I sat down and took a great gulp of my icy cold lemonade. Nathan sprawled comfortably in the chair across the table from me and eyed me like he was examining an unusual specimen in a museum exhibit. "Mom," he inquired, now sobering, "how come you're more fun since you've been sick? It doesn't make sense."

I took a deep breath and sent up a quick prayer. "Do you really want to know?"

He nodded and spoke decisively. "Yes." He brought his own glass to his lips for a long drink. Then, refreshed, he set his glass down, straightened up, folded his hands on the table, and viewed me contemplatively. He meant business. So, I discovered, did I. Without hesitation, I proceeded to describe the precious last moments I'd spent with Ingrid in the hospital, including the encouragement she had given me to trust the Lord. I also told him the writings I had discovered in her journal. The ones referring to trust.

"So you see, Nathan," I concluded, "I've been God's child for many years, since you were a little boy. But it took your grandmother's death to pound into me the importance of just resting in God's hands. God is the creator and controller of the universe . . . and all that is beyond. He is certainly capable of handling the problems of my everyday life. Jesus proved His love for me by leaving heaven where He was adored and worshipped to come to this filthy, sinful world. He was ridiculed, rejected, tortured, and killed for me! That's love that can be trusted."

I fingered the silver cross that hung around my neck, and stared out the window. "The Bible says, 'underneath are the everlasting arms.' I picture in my mind the hand of God that is so big I can lay my whole body on it. I just curl up and rest there, knowing He's got me safe and protected. He holds me above all the suffering and heartache this world can throw at me. His fingers are open enough to let the trials of life sweep in and over me as much as is needed for my spiritual growth. But His fingers are curved so that I can never fall from His hand. One day, He'll close those fingers firmly around me and let all the contamination of the world fall away. And He'll shake the last, remaining drops off His hand and lift me up to heaven to be forever with Him."

My voice grew soft and distant. I could almost see myself there. "Then I'll see the face of Jesus, my Savior. And Mama, Grandma Lydia, and your grandma, Ingrid." I smiled as I looked at my son. His eyes were blurry. My heart sprang to life and began to thud. *Was it possible? Was this Nathan's moment in time? His time to touch eternity?*

Nate cleared his throat. "I read the books you sent me, Mom. The ones that gave evidence that the Bible is legitimate. I'm getting really close, Mom. I do . . ." he hesitated and looked me straight in the eye. "I do believe there is a God."

"Oh, Nathan," I reached out my hand to grasp his.

"I'm having some trouble with Jesus, though. I mean, I believe He was a good man and a teacher."

"But don't you see, Nathan?" My lips trembled as I spoke. "Jesus claimed to be God! What kind of a teacher would He be if

He lied to His followers? Certainly not a good one!"

Nathan shrugged. "Well, maybe He just thought He was God. Maybe He was delusional."

"But His life style showed that He was a man of wisdom, kindness and compassion. That doesn't fit the pattern of a crazy person."

Nate was nodding his head as Darren barged into the room. Well, maybe barge is too strong a word, but his entrance definitely had that effect. Nate quickly pulled his hand away. I gritted my teeth and I forced a smile at my husband.

"Hey, Cassie," his cheerful face showing complete ignorance of his untimely intrusion into our critical conversation. He plopped a dish of Christmas cookies on the table. "How about planning a spring garden? Dave, you know, the apartment owner, tells me that he'd like to set aside a small plot near the entrance of the building. If you will plan it, I can help you with the planting and weeding."

Annie followed him in, sat down and picked up a frosted star-shaped cookie. "I'll help, too, when I'm home. I know how you love flowers. You've always told me about your mother's flower garden and how much it meant to her." I took a peek at Nathan, who suddenly seemed quite interested in the possibility of my garden. He'd switched tracks quickly. I sighed.

Darren continued, "And my mom grew flowers. When I was a kid," he mused, "she even had a beautiful rose garden. I wish you could have seen it. You would have loved it. I thought it looked like a fairy tale garden out of Cinderella, or Sleeping Beauty. You know, like something you'd see growing next to a castle. Mom let me help her with it. But it took so much time and care. What with all the demands of farm life, it just got to be too much. It's a shame." He shook his head. "She was so proud of that garden. She even had a special journal, just to write details about her roses."

Roses? A journal? Something clicked in my brain. *Of course! It was a new twist on the rose journal. Ingrid wasn't referring to the color! She must have meant the journal that she'd written in about her rose garden. That's the one was I needed to find and read!*

Excitement rushed through me as I started to my feet. Then a torrent of darkness swirled around me, filling my head like a foggy stuffing. My muscles turned to mush as I staggered and fell into Darren's arms. The cave of my illness rapidly sucked me back inside as heaviness closed in all around me, suffocating and imprisoning my body and mind.

Far away, through the fog, I heard Darren speak, "Let's get her into bed. All the excitement and activity has been too much for her."

"No, Darren," with thick lips, I tried to protest. "The book. The rose one . . . " My eyelids flickered open long enough to see the concern on their faces and then closed again. I sank into unconsciousness.

Chapter 28

Fragments of images are all that remain from the weeks I spent in the hospital. They told me afterwards that my liver started to disintegrate. Evidently, the lupus chose that organ to attack. I remember starting that week with a blinding headache and my eyes not tolerating much light. I was hospitalized on Wednesday night. When my mind finally cleared about a week later, on Friday, I thought I'd only been in the hospital for a couple of days. The excruciating pain in my side and back had blocked most of that time period from my mind.

Darren told me that the doctor wouldn't give me pain medicine until he had made an accurate diagnosis. The pain meds might mask the true problem and make it impossible to treat. Various tests were run and the conclusion finally reached, so I was able to receive drugs for the pain. That, in itself, made me kind of woosy, but at least I was free of the physical agony. I was able to think more clearly and process information.

Through the dim haze of my memory, I recalled family members and my pastor and church friends filing in and out of the room, staring at me with grief-stricken faces. Someone, day or night, was always sitting at my bedside, holding my hand or rubbing my back. I vaguely remember Annie reading comforting words from the Bible, passages like the one in John 14, about mansions waiting for us in heaven, and Psalms 23, the comforting shepherd's Psalm. In her sweet voice, Annie also sang, "Jesus Loves Me," the song I used to sing to her when she was suffering from a childhood illness. I guess we never outgrow that song. Therein is the heart of theology, and the awesome comfort of knowing Jesus holds His children in His hands.

And He did hold me. If all the worries I'd clung to in my lifetime were stuffed into a box, the container would probably be as huge as the Eiffel Tower. But during my pain and illness, God gave me a wonderful sense of peace. His peace. Jesus was right by my side, His presence as real as Darren's. My mind was totally cleared of anxiety about my future. Whether I lived or died, I knew for certain that I would be with the Lord.

I do remember feeling concern for my family. They looked so pathetic. At one point, Darren sat in the chair next to me, reading the Bible. But he was reading from the Psalms, portions where David had cried out to God in despair and hopelessness. My heart nearly broke to see my husband's eyes filled with anguish. I wanted to reach out and touch his hand, to speak words of comfort and peace, to share the serenity God was giving to me. But I couldn't make my hand move or my lips open.

Annie, Nate, Billy, and Sven stood in line at the end of my bed, tense and stiff, looking like they were part of a military drill. Identical expressions of despondency were plastered on all their faces. It's been said that the eye is a window to the soul. My little girl's eyes were red-rimmed and swollen. Nathan's face was pale with worry lines etched at the corners of his eyes. Billy's vacant stare revealed a look of common misery, spanning the passages of time. Sven, dear Sven, who had just lost his wife, looked at me through empty pools of sorrow and grief.

I felt like shouting, "I'm all right. Jesus is here!" But the words of my heart wouldn't come out of my mouth. I lay in silence and prayed for all of them.

I didn't want to leave this world. My mother heart yearned to stay and meet my children's future spouses, and hold my grandchildren in my lap. I wanted to be with my daughter when she went through childbirth and to watch my son establish himself in the pathways of life. I wanted to see Jesus transform the despair on Darren's face into the glorious awe of a man who finally comprehends the hope of eternal life.

One gray morning my head finally cleared. I awoke to see Darren by my side in a familiar pose. His head rested on the back of his chair as he slumped with his feet stretched out in front of him. His eyelids were closed, but one large callused hand tenderly cupped my slender white one.

"Darren," I said.

His eyes popped open wide and he leaned towards me. "Cassie," he squinted to study my face. "You look better. Wow. We've been worried about you."

"Mom," Annie leaned over from the other side of my bed and began to stroke my forehead. I turned my head to discover that Nate held my other hand.

I smiled. *Could any woman feel so loved?*

"How can you all be here?" I asked, my words sounding a bit muffled to myself. I was still somewhat groggy. "Why aren't you at school . . . or at work?"

Annie explained, "It's a weekend, Mom. We've been taking turns sitting with you, but we all wanted to be together today."

I struggled to sit. Darren gently pushed me back. "Take it easy, Cass. You've been through a lot."

Nathan rubbed his eyes, which looked misty. "Hey, Mom, it's good to have you back. But you need your rest. We don't want you fainting again."

"Should we call a nurse?" Annie's hand rested lightly on the call button. We all gave her negative looks. None of us wanted an intruder to break up our treasured family moment. Annie removed her hand.

"Where's Doctor Johnston?" I asked. "What's wrong with me now?"

Worried glances were exchanged. Darren took a deep

breath. "Dr. Johnston says that your liver has been damaged by the lupus. But he's trying some new medicine. He and the specialists are doing everything that they can." His cheerful tone belied the concern etched on his face.

"I see." Something was pushing at the edge of my brain. A persistent thought, long buried and struggling to come out. I frowned and attempted to recall it.

"Roses," my eyes lit up. "Ingrid's rose journal. I want to see the one where she wrote about her roses."

Darren looked more worried, if that were possible. "I don't know if you should be thinking about planning a garden right now."

Nathan spoke up. "It'll be good for her, Dad. To get her mind on . . ."

"No, no," I shook my head and arched my back with discomfort. Annie adjusted a pillow behind me. "Here, Mom, drink some water." She held out a small glass with a straw in it and I took a small sip. Then I pushed the glass away with frustration. "I just want to read the journal. Ingrid told me to." I stubbornly insisted. "Darren, please."

"Okay, honey," he patted my hand. "I'll get it. Now get some rest."

It took him a whole week to get around to looking for it. In the meantime, the doctor said I could go home for a while since my body seemed stabilized, at least for a time. My family wanted me home as much as possible. Annie and Nate went back to school again. Annie offered to quit school and stay at home to care for me, but Darren insisted he could handle it as long as one of the kids came home on weekends. I was pleased to see how much Darren valued education for our daughter. Darren was a loving caretaker. I found myself falling in love with him all over again. I prayed that I could get back on my feet and serve him as the wife he needed. Then I remembered the reason I was sick, and realized I had to trust that God knew what He was doing.

Our affection reached a new level. It went beyond the passion of youth and desire for companionship of middle age to a true desire to merge our spirits and function as a unit. Darren almost seemed to share my pain, and his compassion was overwhelming. He often anticipated my needs and showed great satisfaction in caring for me. I marveled at his attitude and clung to him, longing for the day when Jesus would blend our souls in harmony with His own.

The sun shone brightly and reflected off the snow one late afternoon in January. Darren propped me up with pillows, set a steaming mug of tea next to my bed, and stood looking at me with both hands clasped behind his back. "Which hand do you want, my dear?" He looked like a cross between an eager-to-please little boy and a knight in shiny armor.

I giggled weakly with delight. "A present? For me?"

"Not exactly," he whipped out a book and presented it to me. "I finally remembered to look for the journal," he explained with a sheepish grin. "Actually, Annie reminded me, so I picked it up last night when I was at the farm."

I hoped the gratitude I felt showed on my face as I accepted the gift with an air of reverence. The urgent compulsion to devour it hadn't left me since I thought of it in the hospital. But I didn't want to nag Darren about it. He had so much on his mind and so much to do these days.

"May I . . ." I hesitated, not wanting to offend him. "May I please be alone to read it?"

"Of course, my dear queen. Your every wish is my command." He kissed me lightly on the forehead and left the room. "I'll go put some potatoes on for supper."

I smiled with contentment. Even though my husband wasn't saved, God had certainly blessed me with a man who could show me love. *"Hmm,"* I mused to myself, *"maybe that's something Darren is learning because of my sickness. He's always been gentle with me, but I hadn't seen such a giving nature in him before."*

My thoughts returned to the journal that I held in my hands as if it were made of gold. I wanted to savor the moment I had been anticipating. I was convinced there must be a special message in it for me. It had been Ingrid's dying gift. The book had a soft cover with a pattern in two shades of lavender that blended into a curving pattern, flowing in a flowery design. My heart thudded with excitement, and I felt more aware and alive than I had for months.

I opened it, to find the page edges somewhat frayed, as though it had been often used. Much of it appeared to be a reference book. Ingrid had sketched illustrations of the various plants in her garden, with diagrams of the planting layouts she tried. She had labeled each year's garden plan meticulously. The drawings were interspersed with notations of helpful hints she had discovered or comments regarding planting techniques that worked well. Here and there were paragraphs of daily events she'd evidently made note of to remember. And, of course, there were more cute sayings of her children, as in her other journals.

I paged through the book quickly, praying that God would lead me to the correct passage. *Would it be obvious? Or a hidden message that I would have to decipher?* Then, near the end of the book, my eyes landed on a few pages of writings, completely free of diagrams or notations. My thumping heart told me this was it. I put a hand over my heart. The miserable thing sounded so loud to my ears that I feared Darren would hear it and come in to spoil my time alone. But he didn't.

Eagerly, I began to read: *"What a beautiful morning, Father God. You've painted one more glorious sunrise for these eyes to behold. How perfect for this Mother's Day Sunday. I'm so glad I got to sneak away before breakfast today. Of course, most days, I cook for my men. But this morning Sven insisted on making the meal. He said since it was my special day, I should get myself outside and take a morning walk! So now I'm sitting here and trying to say 'good-bye' to the little town of New Bergen. Sven's giving up his welding job at the blacksmith shop here to go and take over his dad's farm, ten miles away. His dad died two weeks ago from heart failure. So now I will plant my rose garden all over again on the farm.*

"This is a beautiful park. I'm going to miss it here, so close to our house. The bench is kind of hard, but I'm all alone with the birds singing and the squirrels chasing each other up and

down the trees. It's like they're putting on a show for my own personal pleasure. Oh, and here comes an adorable little girl. What beautiful eyes she has, clear blue just like the ocean waters on sunny days. Oh my, the golden "princess" hair and cute white button shoes. They must be new. They're so shiny. I hope she's careful crossing the railroad tracks. Yes, she stopped and looked both ways before crossing. Good for her. Someone has taught her well."

Here the writing ended, and a long slash seemed to signify a break in the story. My eyes were now glued to the page and shivers ran up and down my spine and my arms and legs. My heart was in my throat. *Could it possibly be true?*

Farther down the page, Ingrid continued to write. *"I need to finish this story. It's been a couple of weeks. But I have to get this down on paper or I won't believe it myself in the years to come. Mercy me! If my own eyes could lie! But they don't, of course. My doctor says the broken bone in my leg will never heal completely. He says I'll always walk with a limp and have some pain and discomfort. If only I hadn't tripped over that branch and landed smack on a big rock when I was running to grab her! But I'm getting ahead of myself. I saw the train coming a second before the little girl did. She had come all the way to pick some yellow and purple flowers by the bench where I was sitting. I turned and opened my mouth to talk to her. But she gave me such a look of fright that I couldn't speak. Maybe she didn't notice me sitting there and I scared her. Or else she's just a very shy little thing. But she just turned and ran away from me, carrying the flowers, like she'd seen a ghost. I felt bad that I'd scared her. I looked up and saw this train coming on lickity split. The poor child was running so fast towards the tracks. I got to my feet and started running to yank her away. Then she stopped and turned and looked at the train. For a minute there, I thought she'd be all right. But when she saw the train she sort of froze, like she was stuck on the tracks.*

"Well, I speeded up and didn't see the thick branch lying right in front of me. Down I went, flat as a pancake. I hit my head on something hard so I was kind of dazed. I tried to get up, but it

hurt something awful and I couldn't move. That's when I just looked up at the sky and cried out to You, Lord, to save that precious little girl's life, her body and her soul.

"And just as that mean-looking engine came barreling down on her, I saw a man dressed all in white appear from nowhere. He picked her up in his strong arms as quick as a flash and lifted her right off the tracks. It seemed to take forever for that big train to rush on by. It made a horrible racket. I laid there with my heart in my throat, trying my best to catch a glimpse of her and that man between the cars. I never did see either one of them. When the train went on by, the little girl was not to be seen, or the strange man. I never did find out who she was. But I know for a fact, that was an angel the Good Lord sent in answer to my prayers, and I've prayed for that little girl ever since. God must sure love her a heap to go to all that trouble to save her from dying that day. He must have something special planned for her life. Maybe when I get to heaven I'll get to meet her. I hope so."

Tears clouded my eyes so I could barely make out the last paragraph. I blinked tightly a few times and forced them to focus.

"I don't know how long I lay there. Finally some nice people came along and took me home. Sven took me to the doctor's office right away and I've been down in bed ever since. I'm getting heaps better now, and Sven has been taking good care of me. Poor man, he's wearing himself out.

"But I got to see an angel!"

I closed the book and leaned back against the pillows, trying to take it all in.

Ingrid, my dear mother-in-law, was the woman in the park who prayed for me as a small child. She saw my angel, too. No longer would I wrestle with doubts about the reality of the messenger God sent to save me that day. The good, kind, strong one who held me in his arms and carried me to safety was truly sent by God.

How much God cared for me, even before I knew Him as my Savior and Lord! He had saved my body and soul, like Ingrid had asked Him to do. He'd given me His peace and taught me to trust Him.

I thanked God that my future was secure in Him.

When Darren came to bring my supper tray, he found me laying with closed eyelids and a smile of peace and contentment on my lips. I was hugging the journal.

*"Now I rejoice in my sufferings
for your sake..."*

Colossians 1:24a

Chapter 29

(The following two chapters were written by Nathan in a journal that his mother gave him.)

"January 3, 1996   It looked like a storm was approaching. Thick black clouds hovered so low they seemed to mix with the dirty white snow that rose in heaps upon the ice along the shore of Lake Clarity. A storm was brewing inside me as well. Waves of mixed-up emotions churned my insides. My heart pounded against my chest like a tiger rattling his cage. It had taken me the better part of the morning to find this place. My trusty old green Ford was my only companion on this pilgrimage. Now I was finally in sight of my goal. I gripped the wheel and twisted it sharply to the left. The tires dug into the grooves of the dirt road, now hardened and crested with chunks of ice, leading to the rock. Most of the roads around Lake Clarity had been paved since Mom lived here, but this old path was sorely neglected. I was glad. Some places shouldn't be allowed to change. This was one of them.

"I remembered this place from when I was a kid, maybe

seven or eight years old. Just before going here, Mom had taken Annie and me to show us the house she had grown up in. Even as a boy, I'd sensed the tension in her that day. She'd been almost free of emotion, cold to the point of numbness, so unlike her. I remember her words as we stood there looking at the house. It was impressive, especially to a kid, I suppose. The biggest house on the lake, rigid and imposing, even as it was elegant and luxurious. I wondered at the time how Mom could be happy in the small upstairs apartment that we lived in at the time.

"Annette, Nathan,' Mom pushed the words out like it was some sort of ceremony, a speech she'd rehearsed. 'You need to know where your heritage came from, where your roots are. This is where I grew up with my mother and father. When my . . .' here she hesitated, as though stuck. She almost choked as she said the next word, ' . . . father . . . moved away, and I went to live with Grandma Lydia, he sold it. I've never been inside the house again." She paused and stared out beyond the house to the lake. I clung to her hand and wished I could make her smile. I didn't understand what could be so sad about such a fancy house.

"She sighed, a long, heavy sigh. 'I don't expect I'll ever bring you here again. It was once part of my life, a house, but not a home. We have a home.' She knelt down and drew both Annie and me into her arms for a hug. She looked deep into our eyes and continued, 'Always remember, it is the love inside that makes a building a home. It's not the fancy or expensive outside, but the hearts that live in it and share their lives together.' Then, and only then, did tears form in her eyes.

"She stood up. 'I have one special place to show you, too,' she said. And she brought us here, to her thinking rock. Here she was able to relax. The tension fell away. She stood taller and I saw peace on her face.

"Mom helped us climb up on the rock, where we sat still and watched the waves beat against the shore, splashing us a little now and then with its wild spray. 'I used to come here as a child and teenager when I wanted to run away and be alone and think my own thoughts,' she said. 'I never felt like the house was mine. But this place belonged all to me.' She patted the rough rock and

smiled, 'Like it was carved just for me.' As a kid, I couldn't understand what she meant. But now, since I've met Grandpa and heard
her stories, I think I can.

"Then we were allowed to laugh and play. I was free
again.

"This morning, when I left her at the hospital, I knew I had
to come here. For Mom and for me. She looked like she was on
the doorstep of death. Her face was pasty white, and her eyes were
runny. She just lay there, silent and limp.

"The last few days with her opened up a new world for me.
Before she got real sick, she told me about the angel that saved her
from the train when she was a little girl. She explained how
Grandma wrote in her journal that she had seen the angel, too, and
prayed for my mom. I knew then that I had to go somewhere special and give prayer a serious try before Mom left us for good.

"I've always prided myself on my self-control and independent spirit, like Dad. But I couldn't keep the tears out of my
eyes as I stopped the car and slowly made my way along the rough
road to her rock. This time, getting up on it was easy. I barely had
to lift myself to sit on the top. I was quiet at first, just looking out
at the water, knowing it was the same scene that flashed through
my mother's mind a thousand times before. There is some comfort
in shared experiences and sights that don't change with the times,
but go on and on.

"Then I took a deep breath. It was time for me to do business with my Creator. Because of Mom's letters to me at school
and our conversations the past few days in the hospital, I'd come
to terms with my doubts and misgivings. Now I knew God existed
and I wanted to know Him. Simply put, I'd come to believe. I knew
I wasn't worthy of what Jesus did for me on the cross. I was dirty
with sin. The dirty, rough road I looked at couldn't change itself
into a super-highway. Likewise, I knew I couldn't change myself
into the man I wanted to be. For the first time in my life, I knew I
was helpless, totally incapable of saving myself. Only Jesus could
change me into something useful. Then and there, I told Him
exactly that, how guilty and full of sin I was, and how badly I need-

ed Him.   I asked Him to come into my life and fill all the empty places and make things right. I gave Him my allegiance. He would be my King.

"Then this tough guy started to cry.   I don't mean teardrops. I mean buckets. My shoulders shook and I thanked God for washing me clean. I begged Him to heal my mom and give her back to me so I could tell her what happened to me. And we could tell my dad together. I don't know how long I sat there. Time didn't matter. The storm clouds passed by and the sky began to clear. I saw the sun start to push its way out from behind a silver cloud. Gradually, I became aware of a presence.   I sensed a gentle strength.

"I looked up. In front of me stood a man. He was dressed in normal clothes, blue jeans and a white hooded jacket. But his face looked timeless and wise. Right away, I knew he was Mom's angel, the one who saved her from the train. My heart caught in my throat. I wanted to speak, but couldn't utter a sound. My whole body felt weak, like it was totally drained of energy. I wondered why I didn't fall backwards off the rock. But a stronger force held me still.

"The angel placed his hand on my shoulder. 'Son.' As he spoke a shiver ran up and down my spine and my hands turned to clammy rubber. 'God has heard your prayers. He sent me to tell you that your mother will live. I don't know how long. God has not seen fit to give me that information. But there will be a reprieve for her and time to enjoy her family as a healthy woman. Go in peace, my child. She waits for you.'

"Then, I must have blinked, and he was gone. I mean vanished, completely. There was not a sign of him anywhere, not even a footprint on the snow-covered path. My heart felt so light. If it had been a balloon, it would have lifted me off the ground.   I ran to the car and drove back to the hospital to tell Mom I had seen the angel, too."

Chapter 30

(Also written by Nathan, as part of his journal.)

"*January 10, 1996   This has been a great week! Mom is looking better and getting stronger all the time. She came home from the hospital Tuesday. Annie skipped school and stayed home to help Dad care for her. I had to take some tests at college, and put some work in at the restaurant, so I was gone all week. But I came home late last night, and now it is Sunday morning. Mom, Annie, and I are going to church.*

"*Our whole family celebrated Mom's fast recovery last week. Dad is taking it more soberly, but of course he doesn't have any faith to hold him up—yet. Now all three of us are praying for him, so he doesn't stand much of a chance! Dad worries that Mom is overdoing it and will get sick again. But he, too, can't help but be amazed at her quick recovery. The last tests they took at the hospital came back negative. The doctors are shaking their heads over it. They can't seem to figure out what went right this time. But Mom, Annie, and I know.*

"Mom gave me this journal to write down my thoughts. She says writing helped her get through the hard times in her life. She says she's so grateful for Grandma's journal, because she could find out about the angel and how Grandma prayed for her. I like to write too, so now I've started to make a record of my own life. Maybe some day, one of my grandchildren will find something fit to read in it that will help them too. I hope so.

"Naturally, this morning I got dressed faster than the women. Now they're ready, too. Annie looks so pretty. I guess my little sister is growing up. She's wearing a white dress. It looks good with her dark hair and brown eyes. She'll make a great catch for some lucky guy. Her heart is beautiful, too. Now that I know what it's like to have God living inside a person, I can see why she cares about people like she does.

"And Mom is beaming, positively glowing. That must be what happens when God heals a person. Her glow is coming from way down deep inside her. I bet if I could see her heart, it would shine like the sun, because all I'm seeing are the outside edges. But I'm glad I can see the rays of happiness escaping from her soul. Thank you, Father God, for giving me back my mom. Especially now that we can share Jesus with each other.

"Dad is sitting comfortably on the couch with his stocking feet on the antique coffee table that belonged to my Great-Grandma Lydia. He's got his favorite coffee mug in his hand and is reading the Sunday paper. He's happier than he was when Mom was sick, and he seems content again with his life. But he still looks lonely and sort of empty. He's heard all our stories, but he won't allow himself the freedom to believe and turn over the controls of his life to God. I can sense the gloom surrounding his soul as clearly as I can feel the light that is holding Mom, Annie, and me.

"Come on, Nate,' Annie walked towards me with her purse on a strap over her shoulder and her Bible tucked under her arm. 'Hurry up, or we'll be late. You can finish that later.'

"I gave her a look, silently reprimanding her. After all, I'd been ready for twenty minutes. But I kept my mouth shut. Today is not a day for harsh words. I suppose no day is, now that I think

314

about it."

(This next part was added on later, that night)

"After I shut my journal, I stood up and turned to Dad to say 'good-bye.' But that's not what came out of my mouth. Instead, I heard myself say, 'Hey Dad!'

"He lifted his head and looked at me with a sober expression. 'What do you want, Nate?'

"Surprise washed over his face at my next sentence, 'How about coming with us to church?'

"For a moment, I swear my heart stood still. Like the earth stopped rotating for five seconds. Mom and Annie froze in position. I can still see them as clearly as if I'd taken a photograph of that moment. Annie was holding her hand out to me and, with her big eyes, staring at Dad. Mom stood with one hand stopped in mid-air, reaching for the car keys on the hook by the door. It seemed as if time, itself, paused for a moment on the brink of eternity.

"Then Dad slowly folded the newspaper, carefully laid it on the coffee table, and stood up.

"All right.' he said.

"Wow!"

". . . Weeping may last for the night,
But a shout of joy comes in the morning."

Psalm 30:5b

EPILOGUE
The Resolution
1999

(Written by Nathan Christopher Larson)

Dad came with us to church for the first time that day. Since then, all of our lives have changed. Now we are a complete family, made whole in Christ.

But I wonder sometimes. *What if Mom had said "no" to the angel? What if God hadn't given her a chance? What if she had rejected God when she got sick?* I am so proud of my mom! She hung in there when things were tough because she loved Dad and me. Most of all, she loved and trusted her Lord. And I am so thankful to God. He didn't give up on us. Because of His faithfulness, my family will enjoy being with God in heaven for all eternity.

Because of my mother's story, I'll never again look at suffering the same way. We can only see this side of eternity. But God sees the other side, the side where all the agonies and heartaches of this life will be explained. Then we will know and understand His reasons for allowing our pain. I am convinced that we will even be grateful for our trials once we see how God works it all together for our good and His glory.

Mom was fortunate in a way, because she knew ahead of time that her suffering had a purpose. Most of us don't get to see the reasons for our circumstances while we're still living in this world. I expect there will be some suffering ahead in my life.

I choose to trust the one who suffered and died for me, and can see beyond my pain. I will trust God's wisdom, and someday, when I meet Him face to face, I will understand His purposes.

Author's Note

The cover painting of The Rose Journal contains symbolic messages. The red rose signifies the blood of Jesus Christ, poured out for us when He was crucified for our sins on the cross of Calvary. The rose petal that has fallen on the journal represents Cassandra's sacrifice for her beloved.

The crystal vase is a picture of the light of God's love that is reflected in His children, those who have given their lives to God in gratitude for the gift of His only Son.

The angel, a messenger of God, is watching from the archway of heaven. He is sent to our world to help the children of God and to carry messages of hope to God's people on earth.

The journals are the link to the past that binds one generation to another. Through the medium of words, the struggles, tears, and joys of the common human experience are used to pass on the truth of God's Word and give humankind hope for the future.

About the Author

Linda Ruth Stai has published several dramas and devotionals. She has also written and presented monologues of Biblical women for church services and events, and has experience as a public speaker. At present, she facilitates a women's Bible study group, leads a youth drama team, and is director of prayer at Edinbrook Church in Brooklyn Park, Minnesota.

Linda has experience as a newspaper reporter for the West Central Tribune and as a copywriter for the KWLM radio station in Willmar, Minnesota. She is a native of New London, Minnesota, and now lives with her husband, Gary, in Brooklyn Park, Minnesota. She has three adult children, Erika, Kaleb, and Joshua, who live nearby. Erika and her husband, Chay, are the parents of one son, Conner.

.

The author and publisher
would like to hear your comments.

For additional copies or information,
please contact us at:

Linda Ruth Stai
Dokka Publishing
7423 Abbott Avenue North
Brooklyn Park, Minnesota 55443
dokka_publishing@yahoo.com

Visit our web site at www.rosejournal.com